I0545759

Seven Years to Die
Betsy Michener-Lachino
Edited by
Christy Pingleton

Published by Betsy Michener-Lachino at KDP
Copyright 2018 Betsy Michener-Lachino

KDP Edition, License Notes

1

To Rolando, my husband. Thank you for your encouragement, and love.

To my sons, you are my heart and soul. Never quit dreaming.

To Liz, my best friend and sister by choice. I could never have _____ (fill in the blank) without you!

To Francis Ann, my big sister. You can keep the girls and the cats, I'll keep my boys and dogs. Thank you for your support and constant competition.

a

Prologue

I hate Nebraska in January. It's cold. Cold and dreary. None of the lush green of summer crops so green under a sky so blue you have to squint when you go outside. January though? Fucking ugly.

It didn't help that I was looking out the third-story window of a Holiday Inn that had a view of the highway. I would have rather looked at the barren cornfields. The view was shit, the room was shit, the place was shit. I was obviously in a shit mood. For what it's worth, I deserved the bad mood.

I was drinking the free coffee, feet propped on the heater, watching the sky turn from black to the dull orange of the winter morning and wasting time. I lacked motivation to move today. I had dreaded the date for years, and now it was here.

I closed my eyes and breathed deep the aroma of the coffee in my hand.

I wanted to be anywhere but here in the moment.

A stirring in the bed behind me got my attention, and I stood to make sure the occupant didn't wake up. I needed peace and quiet this morning. I needed to wrap my brain around what I was doing and why—I needed to settle my nerves and ready my soul.

He went back to sleep, his breathing evened, and his face relaxed back to the slackness of slumber.

Out in the hall a door slammed, and heavy footsteps trod past my door. I held my breath hoping that the steps would not awaken Joe, but in his typical fashion, he slept, oblivious to the outside world. I checked the clock. Six minutes past seven. Still early, still enough time to get ready.

But not yet.

Picking my coffee back up, I returned to my seat by the window and sat back down to try to find appreciation for the landscape. What I found was a renewed anger for the events that had led to this day, a renewed ache that I had suffered for years, and a terror that tomorrow wouldn't arrive.

3

Chapter 1

In the beginning, Davlin and I were like rats running the gutters of our hometown together. Like other white trash, latch-key kids growing up in Guernsey, Nebraska, we found ways to entertain ourselves, most of which resulted in me getting my ass beaten from one end of my living room to the other. More than one occasion ended in law enforcement being involved in my pranks and mischief, either by taking me home or by taking me away from a very vigorous punishment. Needless to say, entertainment in Guernsey was limited to vandalism, drugs, alcohol, and sex—none of which we were ready for when we first became friends.

No, the beginning of our relationship revolved around a simpler form of crime, my first petty theft.

I was starving to the point of insanity, at least that's what I told the cashier at the '79 gas station that caught me lifting a Snickers bar. I guess the rumbles from my stomach, holes in my pants and shoes, and my general lack of hygiene convinced him that I was in need of some form of sustenance. He let me go with a warning not to enter the parking lot again and shoved me out the door. I didn't mind the shove, and I certainly didn't mind him keeping the candy bar seeing as I had stuffed my overalls with chips and Little Debbie snacks.

Davlin found me pigging out on the porch of the vacant duplex two doors down the street.

"Girl, gimme those Doritos," he ordered. He was as dirty as I was, and his pants had the same grass-stained knees as mine, but Davlin was from a home with two parents. He lived in an actual house with a porch his mother called him from. Even though he was dirt-smeared and sweaty from the day spent running around town, the people of Guernsey looked at him differently than they looked at me.

"Give em here, or I'll go tell the owner you stoled from his store," he prompted again.

"Go on and be a little-bitch tattler!" I yelled at him, standing up on the top step of the porch I was on, making us a similar height. I wasn't much to look at. Skinny with knobby knees, dirty face and hair, but not from playing all day. I was left on my own on most days, and I certainly didn't have a mother who called to me from the porch and drew a bath for me each night. I was trash as far as the people of Guernsey were concerned. Trash with a whore for a mother.

My language stopped Davlin in his tracks.

He was the only kid I knew whose parents came home every night sober, the only kid in our grade who got new shoes to start the school year. Davlin had seen me at school but he had never spoken to me, so now when the boy who had the life I envied was asking me for something I had earned…I was livid.

He reached to take my ill-begotten chips out of my hand, I responded how I had survived—by fighting. My friendship with Davlin began with me giving him a bloody nose over a bag of Cool Ranch Doritos.

Thankfully, things improved after that. Davlin became my usual run-around buddy. He had ideas of ways to avoid trouble I had never considered. We were inseparable in the summer and damn near it during the school year. He didn't let people talk down to me, and I kept him from taking too much shit for it. We were a child form of Bonnie and Clyde without the felonies. It's probably a good thing that I discovered the joys of science and reading before we committed too great a crime for our age to get us off the hook.

By high school Davlin and I were both on our way to earning scholarships, mine in science and his in sports. I had fallen in love with science and reading, things that kept me out of trouble.

Davlin was the star. He could play any game that involved a ball or running. He could swim and dive, he had a rocket for an arm and the boy never seemed to get tired. Where Davlin had to work to get a C in Basic English, he excelled enough in sports that no one cared at all if he showed up for school on time or did his work.

5

Davlin played sports because without them he would be committing vandalism while hopped up on heroin, drunk out of his mind, fucking a honkey-tonk waitress. He knew that his life revolved around sports…but he always made time for me.

We had been friends for what seemed like forever and we knew all each other's secrets. Davlin cared for me and took care of me in a way my mother failed to, and it was with Davlin's kind nature in mind that I found my way to his house one exceedingly hot night.

There were any number of factors that added to the inevitable outcome of that night. Summer heat and a need to cool off, no parents to watch me or pay the electric bill, a friend with a window air-conditioning unit across town… I remember each step of how I ended up in Davlin's bedroom that summer.

Mom was out on one of her adventures when the power went out during a summer deluge, I was actually scared I would steam to death in our trailer. Guernsey isn't a big town, so getting to Davlin's house was no great hardship; getting into his attic bedroom in a rainstorm was a bit tricky though.

After trying my usual route to Davlin's room by climbing the maple tree outside his window and being successful only in bruising my ass, I was ready to try the back door. Davlin's mother was a housewife who did laundry every day; she would crack the window in the laundry room so she could smoke inside when it rained. On this day she must have been drinking too because she had forgotten to close the window.

I knocked over a stack of laundry and a jar of loose change climbing through the window, and I still hadn't figured out a good lie to tell if I got busted. By the time I had snuck past his parents dozing in the living room, ascended the loudest staircase in the history of the world, and tiptoed past his sister's closed door, I figured Davlin would have known I was in his house on my way up to his room…

Davlin hadn't heard me.

I walked in on him doing what boys do with dirty magazines. He was sprawled out on his bed with the latest Maxim propped on

6

his chest, his hand pumping away. I was mortified! ... Well, mortified and unsure what to do, because at that point he hadn't seen me standing at the top of the stairs that led to his attic bedroom.

I turned to leave, forgetting the trouble I'd had getting into his house, when Davlin called my name. "Becks!"

"Hhhhmmm?" barely a whisper escaped from my mouth as I turned to look over my shoulder, assuming my best friend had made himself decent and was struggling into his pants.

No, my response had simply made him aware of my presence and made me aware that my best friend, the boy I had shared every secret with, the boy I adored, was thinking of me while he jerked off.

I wasn't sure how to react to that.

What happened was that my friend bolted out of his bed, hitting his head on the low beam of the roof and knocking himself out. He was sprawled naked on the floor of his dusty attic retreat, and I didn't know what to do. I was kind enough to cover him with a sheet before rummaging through his dresser for a t-shirt that wasn't soaking wet to change into; after all, I had gone there for a reason.

Davlin came to pissed!

"What the hell are you doing here, Becks?" he demanded, jumping back to his feet, narrowly avoiding knocking himself out again.

Flustered by his anger, I tried desperately to explain myself.

"The electricity in the trailer got turned off, and I was sweltering in that tin can. I was sure you had heard me making so much noise coming through your house. I thought you knew I was here."

I couldn't explain myself fast enough to stop from blushing. I had turned away again to give him some time to make himself decent, to towel up or something, so I was surprised when he grabbed my shoulder to turn me back toward him.

He towered over me, angry and breathing hard. Inches separated us.

Davlin was my everything. I wanted him to kiss me, to strip me, beat me, use me! Hell, I didn't care; I just wanted him to know I needed him. I was a little seventeen-year-old girl with all the emotions and hormones that come with the age. Here in front of me was the one person I wanted to touch my body because he was the only person I had ever loved.

"What are you doing here, Becks?" he hissed.

Davlin was close enough that I could smell the fabric softener on the sheet hastily swathed around his hips; he was close enough that I could see the soft reflection of the bare light bulb that hung in the distant end of the attic in his eyes, and I could feel the energy, and frustration, and need roiling off his body.

"I love you," I whispered shyly, then finding confidence in my confession I looked directly at him and emptied my heart. "Since you came into my life, I have loved you. I see the way you look at other girls and I want to scream because I want you to look at me that way. I...I can't explain how much I want you to put your hands on me and love me, or just hold me. I can't explain how scared I am that you will tell me to go home, or that you will throw me on your bed and strip me out of my clothes. I want you to throw everything we are away and change it into something completely different."

"Stop!" he yelled, his anger shutting me up and making me flinch. He stood there panting, fighting himself. I was scared he would hit me for saying what I had.

Davlin turned away from me, picked up his discarded cargo shorts, slipped them on under his sheet, and then left. He just stomped out of his room, down the stairs and out into the storm to wash me away.

So, here's the part your panties are wet for.

I know you wanted to hear how Davlin came and ravaged me in the storm after I ran out of his house after him...but that's not what happened. More dramatic that way, but the reality was that my friend was embarrassed that I had seen him handling himself and that I knew he'd put my face on a supermodel's body.

8

Truth was, he was embarrassed that I had walked in on him, and I was embarrassed that I had bled my heart out to him. I did love Davlin, but he didn't love me the same way, and my pride was hurt as much as my heart when he failed to return my sentiment.

Mending my relationship with Davlin was taking time, and I was balancing between anger and sadness each day that passed without him. My unexpected arrival in his bedroom had occurred during the summer break between our junior and senior years in high school. By the time the football team started their two-a-days, I had only seen him twice, once to wish him happy eighteenth birthday and again for him to reciprocate.

I missed my best friend.

The fire that got lit under Davlin's ass came in the form of one of his teammates, Caleb McMahon. Caleb was big and fast; he was also handsome and knew it. Girls fell over him, did whatever he asked, and cried when he moved on to the next girl waiting in line. For some reason Caleb had his eye on me and made his opinion of me clear to his teammates—frequently.

Davlin had told me about Caleb in the past, but he never told me that Caleb talked about me in the locker room. Davlin had even guaranteed Caleb that I would never have sex with him, a statement I had made to Davlin often enough. Davlin had never told me that Caleb considered me his Mount Everest, a "goal to be achieved."

So, when Caleb arrived at football practice on a Monday morning and became prolific in recounting the many places and positions we had assumed during the weekend we had spent together, Davlin had reached his finite limit of forgiveness.

I got a call from Davlin's mother saying that he was in the Emergency Department and was being admitted for a collapsed lung that he had suffered at football practice, and that he was asking for me. When I got to the hospital, I was witness to the damage young men can inflict on each other.

Where Davlin had a punctured lung, Caleb's nose could barely be called a nose anymore. Davlin had smashed it flat. In the

9

Emergency Department, I saw Caleb getting rolled to surgery with his mother tearfully holding his hand as they were wheeled past. His eyes were swollen shut so I was saved from seeing his scorn.

Davlin had already been moved to another room for the night. I was given his room number and the directions to get me there. When I found it, I entered his room not sure what to say to my damaged best friend. His parents were just leaving when I walked in. They didn't seem happy that Davlin had wanted to speak to me alone or at all. Sharon glared at me and Allen looked through me as they passed; they had always hated me.

I sat in the corner of his room as the nurses and aides helped Davlin move slowly into his hospital bed with a tube taped to his chest. Once he was settled, he finally looked at me.

"This is your fault," he accused.

"What the hell are you talking about?" I stood up, ready to leave his room. "I didn't ask you to try to kill one of your teammates! You're crazy if you think you ..."

"I did this for you," he interrupted, a grimace of agony crossing his face as he tried to sit up when he spoke. He was bruised all over. He pressed his hand to the place where the tube went in and tried to stop the pain by putting pressure on it.

I shut my mouth and looked at him in disbelief. I wondered if he had a concussion from the fight.

The pain must have ebbed, because he found the strength to yell at me again. "I couldn't let that fuck sit there and tell everyone how he used you like a whore! Shit, Becks, I thought you would have better taste than to fuck Caleb! Every girl in town has fucked him!" As Davlin's voice grew louder, alarms started to go off on the monitors that surrounded him and in my head.

"Davlin," I tried to reach out to him and touch his hand. He pulled it away quickly and responded.

"No! Please just go."

My anger flared again. "What the hell did you ask me to come here for if you're not going to let me defend myself? Listen to me, you ass, you can't go anywhere, so you have to sit there and hear what I have to say!"

Davlin actually looked nervous at this point, like he was seeing the error in asking me to come to his room, but I was right; he would have to hear whatever dirty, detailed story I wanted to let come out of my mouth.

"I told you 'I love you' and you walked away! I am a stupid girl for loving you and letting you know it, but fuck you if you think you get to say who I do anything with!" As suddenly as it had flared up, my anger abated, and I felt ashamed seeing him lying on the bed in pain.

He seemed to sink into his pillow, as though trying to escape my words. I stepped back away from him to give him room. He just lay there in his bed, eyes closed, concentrating on his breathing.

"Please go," he requested. He was sweating, his heart-rate monitor was beeping fast, and I could see it hurt him to breathe deeply. He opened his eyes and looked directly into mine. "Please go. I almost killed someone because he could describe every inch of your body…and he did, to the whole fucking football team! Do you have any idea what all those guys are doing right now? Sitting down to a good stoke at your expense!"

Again, with the alarms; this time I knew the nurse was going to kick me out, so I opted to leave. I was embarrassed to tell him that everything Caleb had said had been true.

Yeah, I did it.

I had had sex with Caleb McMahon. I didn't care about him, certainly didn't love him, but Caleb had several things I had needed.

Caleb knew how to be careful with a new girl in bed. He had been gentle the first couple times we had sex. He was also adventurous; had been that every time we were together. Caleb had been willing, but other than Davlin, what teenaged boy isn't? Most important, Caleb was a jerk who would kiss and tell.

I chose to have dirty, naughty, wonderful sex with someone I didn't give a shit about, and this scene in the hospital was when I was going to find out if it was worth the pain and humiliation for both Davlin and I.

I walked around the hospital for a bit, returning when the halls were abandoned and the lights dimmed and the pace slowed.

"Are you in pain?" I asked having crept into the room.

"This is your fault." His voice cracked, and I saw a tear slip down his cheek. "I couldn't stop hitting him, and it is your fault, Becks! Damn it! I could have killed Caleb for the shit he said."

Davlin choked on his words and sobbed gently; he reached a hand to hold his aching chest. He looked wounded, not just physically, but as though his heart was beaten and bruised too.

"Do you hate me?" He didn't answer me, just sat there reliving the day.

I walked to the bed and touched his hand. He didn't pull away, letting me hold it and gently massage the pads of his palm. I could feel him relaxing, so I sat on the side of his bed.

I didn't know what to say, so I touched. I rubbed his arms and brushed the bruised parts with gentle fingers. At his cheek he rested his head on my hand; silent tears continued to roll down his cheeks. I brushed them away and leaned in to kiss each cheek where they would have dried.

He didn't pull away. I kissed his lips; dry and sunburned as they were, I kissed them gently. His mouth didn't open, but he didn't pull away. I was leaning on his bed, close to him but not touching so as not to hurt him or cause injury to his chest tube, but I felt his hand on my hip, resting gently; he didn't pull it away.

From his mouth I kissed his neck, breathing in the smell of his skin. I kissed his chest, careful not to touch his bandages or disturb the tube tethering him to his gently gurgling bottle sitting on the floor beside his bed. I kissed his body down the middle length of his solidness.

Davlin's breathing had increased, and I could hear the beeps of his heart-rate monitor increasing the further the length of his body I kissed, but he didn't pull away, he didn't say stop.

His hands were finding their own treasures and places to explore.

My perfect love came back to me on the worst day of his life, a day that changed both of our lives. He had to accept his part in hurting me, and I had to make amends. And we did.

Davlin told me he loved me that night, as I lay curled next to him in his hospital bed. I fell asleep to the stereo sound of my lover's heartbeat and the taste of him on my lips.

13

Chapter 2

"Pomp and Circumstance" is by far the most boring song in the world to play or listen to. The only people happy to hear its repetition are the parents watching their children graduate from high school. I would have been happy to have my diploma thrown at me!

Graduation day—hell, graduation week—was the most tedious and annoying time of my life, mostly because my mother realized I was receiving a full scholarship to the University of Nebraska. I think she assumed I would get a "sign-on bonus" or something and be able to support her.

What made graduation week drag for me was my lack of Davlin. With graduation comes celebration, and his parents had invited all of their family to come celebrate their son's greatness in sports. The invitation did not extend to my mother or me, so we celebrated simply, she by getting drunk on a box of wine, me by dismantling my childhood room.

On the Saturday of our graduation, Davlin came to pick me up to take me to the high school for the last time. He looked so handsome in his sport jacket and tie. He looked handsome and uncomfortable.

"What are you wearing?" I teased, pulling him through the door and down the hall to my room.

"My mom thinks this is what I'm supposed to wear under my grad gown." He leaned in to give me a kiss as we fell through the thin door of my bedroom.

"Well, take it off!" I ordered as I helped him out of the tweed jacket, freeing his arms to wrap around me.

We hadn't had any time together alone in weeks. His parents knew that we were no longer just odd friends. His parents also blamed me for Davlin being kicked off the football team and causing him to lose his ride to UN in football; not one to sulk over spilled milk, Davlin had accepted a scholarship in swimming instead.

Having freed him of his jacket, I had set to ridding him of his button-down shirt and tie. On his chest Davlin had had my name tattooed, 'Becks' in my handwriting rested right at my kissing height. Kiss it I did, in passing as I moved down his body to remind him that I had missed him, when a knock came at my door.

"Becks, aren't we going to be late?" my mother called through my door. I rolled my eyes at the interruption and continued unbuttoning Davlin's pants.

"No, we arrive after you, but you should go to get a good seat, Mom. Davlin will take me," I replied.

"Oh, okay baby, see you there. Becks, baby, I am so proud of you!" Her words immediately spoiled my mood for sex.

I hated my mother's rare glimpses of parental concern and compassion. They made me feel ungrateful, and I was. Here I was brooding over lost years with my mom, in the lap of my boyfriend, his gloriousness in hand, while my mom was on the other side of the door giving me maybe the third compliment of my life.

Giving up on oral gratification, I pushed Davlin back onto my bed and climbed on top of him. I was enjoying the comforting feel of him inside me when I realized he was distracted, and not by me.

"What's wrong?"

He stopped me and left me where I was but reached for his jacket, nearly toppling us off my bed as he stretched to where I had tossed it in my haste to see my boyfriend naked.

"I wore this ridiculous jacket so I would look proper when I did this," he proclaimed as he pulled a box out of his jacket pocket with a flourish. His eyes never left my face as he opened the little black velvet box to reveal a simple silver band with a chip of a diamond. It was beautiful.

"Marry me," he whispered.

I was speechless. I couldn't look away from his angelic eyes and honest face. I was captivated and stunned.

"When?" I asked. My response made him laugh.

"When you're ready. Marry me," he pressed.

"Okay. Now," I demanded.

15

Davlin was not usually a person of impulse, but for me he was.

His family was at the high school waiting to see him receive his high-school diploma, as was my mother who had never graduated. With our families trying to live vicariously through us, they sat wondering when "Pomp and Circumstance" would be played for their child. Davlin and I never showed up to receive our diplomas; our families sat amongst the masses on the crowded bleachers, fanning their faces with the program that listed our names and our achievements.

Sadly, they would never get to fulfill their desire to see their child walk across the stage to receive a rolled parchment, "Graduate" embossed on the top.

Davlin and I never crossed the stage because we had driven West to Las Vegas, stopped at the first chapel we could afford, and at the age of eighteen, Davlin and I were married.

Chapter 3

At college, we applied for couple's housing but were told we wouldn't qualify as undergraduates, so we found a cheap apartment off campus. It was our heaven. That apartment was the one place Davlin and I could just be Us. We didn't have to worry about what people thought of our relationship or that we were too young to be married. We knew Us, and we were fine with Us.

Davlin worked his schedule as much as possible to meet up with me after my classes. I had more class work for my degree in nursing, whereas Davlin studied history with a focus on military strategy and spent most of his time reading in the library. I asked him what he was going to do with a degree in military history one evening as we sat studying at the all-purpose table in our apartment.

"Teach. I'd be an awesome teacher. Not a lame ass like Mr. Mahome," he explained.

"Teach, huh? You hated school. You only showed up to play sports," I teased.

"No, I showed up to see you," he corrected, leaning over to kiss me and steal my remaining fries.

"Don't lie just because you chose a major you don't know what to do with," I teased more, taking my food back from him. He frowned and relented.

"Maybe I'll enlist in the army. I could be an officer." He smiled at me and winked.

I still remember that moment when the thought of military service came to his head. We were enjoying our dinner like we had done a million times before. Nothing was different except for that thought. I was studying some basic anatomy, and the man I married had just predicted his future...

For the four years of college we were able to spend together, we paid little attention to the world around us. We knew there was a war in Iraq, but it didn't affect us. We went to a memorial ceremony for September 11 and lay on a blanket watching fireworks each

Fourth of July, the sounds of a Sousa march blaring from car speakers. No matter what was going on in the world around us, we went to sleep at night knowing that all was right in the world because we were together.

For the most part people knew of our marriage and stopped overreacting to us by our third year at college. We were finally provided an apartment for couples, which we turned down. By that point we enjoyed living off campus, no need to move for the summer because we didn't go home and we had everything we needed.

The end of the third year of college was also the year I had a horrible urine infection and ended up on antibiotics. Little did we know that the medicine I was taking decreased the efficacy of my birth control pills... The third year at college was the year we got pregnant.

I tested positive on a random Tuesday morning. I hadn't been paying attention to my cycles since I did take "the pill" and had had no problems to that point. I woke up that morning feeling awful. Every movement I made would make my stomach lurch and the room spin. I wanted to throw up so bad but only had nausea. As I was lying on the floor in our bathroom with my cheek resting on the cool tiles, I remembered a gag wedding shower gift some friends had given me, having concluded that I needed a wedding shower and never having had one before. The bag contained two super-sized boxes of condoms (the irony) and a box of First Response pregnancy tests.

I can still feel that absolute dread that hit my stomach like a boulder as I was watching my urine saturate the litmus paper. I can only imagine what my face looked like when the two pink lines showed in the indicator window. Here I was weeks from my finals in my junior year of college, one year from having my Bachelor of Science degree in nursing, and I was pregnant.

Davlin found me on the toilet surrounded by wrappers and packaging for the six other tests I had run to the Quickie Mart to buy. I felt like I was having a "Juno-esque" moment when I realized

18

I was running out of pee and every one of those bastard tests was coming out with two lines. Davlin just looked at me crying on the toilet, my sweat pants and panties around my ankles.

Davlin came in and gathered me on his lap. He kissed my face and whispered reassuring things in my ear that I didn't believe. Things like, "It's going to be all right," or "We can make this work." I didn't want things to be all right, and I really didn't want to make things work—with a baby.

"I can't do nursing school with a baby! I can't even get our laundry or cooking done with everything that's on my plate! Davlin, you don't get to say everything will be all right! Your life and future didn't go to shit this morning!" I argued, realizing a bit late the absurdity of my statement.

He was smart enough to not point out the obvious fact that we did live our life together and that the baby would be both of ours. He just carried me to our bedroom and lay next to me. We silently envisioned our rapidly changing future.

I couldn't tell him that I didn't want to have this baby at this time. He couldn't tell me he wanted me to have it. So, we lay in bed, touching and remembering that we already knew what the other one wanted. The baby was a reality, and I couldn't change the truth that we were going to be parents. Ready or not.

"We can be parents, Becks. The baby doesn't have to be anything except the blessing it is."

"Davlin, how are we supposed to afford diapers, clothes, bottles, doctor's visits? We don't make money; we barely skim by on our scholarship funds."

"I can work. I can join the military. ROTC will take me now, and I can enlist as an officer. I was talking to a guy the other day," he confessed. But I was having a hard time hearing him. My ears had begun to ring and I felt sick again, this time not from morning sickness, but from fear.

I just stared at him. It had been a year since he had mentioned the military. I felt like he was hiding the secret of his desire to serve

19

from me. Like I would take the news of him joining the army better if it were for a good cause like supporting our family.

Without the baby we would have been fine. I was on track to receive a grant for the rest of my classes, and I qualified for multiple loans; I knew where I wanted my life to go. I knew that I wanted Davlin with me, but he still hadn't figured out what direction to take, or so I thought until he mentioned the army again. I guess he had decided, and this pregnancy simply put the nail in his coffin, so to speak.

"So...if we are going to be parents, maybe we should contact the housing office again and see if we can't get a place that doesn't leak like a sieve when it rains." My suggestion made a ridiculous grin spread on his face.

Davlin kissed me, thoroughly and passionately, but I felt a change in how he did it. Like he was pulling away from me to encircle the baby we now shared.

Midway through our senior year at college found Davlin and I living in couple's housing and me working as a nurse aide in the campus medical facility. Davlin had signed up for ROTC and had spent the majority of the summer at one type of training or another to catch him up on all the leadership courses he had missed out on through the previous years. He was now going to graduate a semester behind me, with the additional course load he had signed up for when he joined ROTC.

He would come home to the apartment, his face red from marching out in the sun or from performing physical training or other repetitive nonsense through the day. He would jump in the shower and then sit to polish his boots. Davlin hardly spoke to me; he certainly didn't joke like he did before signing up. He was focused inward, recalling information and procedure, whereas I was focused on the intruder in my womb.

Each night he would drop to the floor of our bedroom and perform one hundred pushups before climbing in bed to give me a quick peck on the cheek. I missed the long languid kisses he would give me; now I was lucky to entice him into having sex.

20

Each day my belly grew and bulged to the point of discomfort. By the time winter break rolled around our senior year, baby x was kicking with a force that made me drop items I had propped on my belly. At night when Davlin got home, I would be lazing on the couch with a bowl of applesauce propped on my belly to make the inhabitant inside stretch and kick so I knew it was alright.

I had to admit I had gotten more excited about meeting the person growing inside me. I had seen the ultrasound of the baby a couple weeks before and had opted not to find out the baby's sex. I thought that was something we should do together. Davlin had been on another "exercise" for field commanding. He had only made it to one appointment, so I didn't hold my breath waiting for him to show up to the ultrasound appointment.

As I looked at that monitor with the grainy picture of our baby, I was wondering if he was regretting any of his decisions that led him to where he was at that moment. I know I didn't. I was still in love with Davlin, I was successful in my classes, and if everything continued in my pregnancy undisturbed, I would have the baby the week of spring break. I would miss minimal class time, and all of my teachers were understanding of the situation. I was on track to be a nurse, Davlin was on track to be a successful officer in the army, and, with a little kick in the ass, he would become a functioning member of our family again.

The day that changed Davlin and me as a couple occurred on another random Tuesday in January. I was working at the hospital as an aide; I was seven months along in my pregnancy. I had a nice belly, small and round. The baby was active, kicking me and making me pay for the cheap cafeteria lunch I had just finished, when a trauma team came running through with a patient on their way to surgery. The pusher of the gurney didn't see me, and I wasn't looking at him but rather at Davlin, who had just walked into the lobby in full military dress uniform.

I walked right into the path of the gurney and took a blow to my abdomen that made me fall forward onto the patient. I apologized to the staff, who helped me to my feet. Someone asked me if I was alright, just as Davlin walked up and took me by my elbow.

"She's fine," he said, holding me steady. The team continued on their way, and Davlin and I stood in the lobby, he impeccably dressed and handsome in his uniform and me covered in blood and nastiness. I wrenched my arm free from his grip and stomped off toward the staff changing room where I could change out of my dirty scrubs.

Davlin followed me to the changing room and pushed in, following me.

"Why the hell do you do that?" I yelled at him the moment I was certain we were alone.

"Do what?" he countered, his voice calm to my near hysteria.

"Treat me like a fucking child! I'm not an invalid, and I'm not fucking helpless."

"I was just helping you up," he explained calmly, watching me take my scrub top off, trying to avoid painting my face in blood as I pulled it over my head.

"Help, my ass! You're treating me like a child. You have been since we found out I was pregnant and you decided to fucking join the goddamn military without even talking to me about it. Stop treating me like I'm a breakable idiot!"

All the months of his cold shoulders and lack of affection had had their effect. I was going to have it out with him, damn the place or possibility of someone walking in on us.

"You have been absent from our marriage since you joined. Are you not allowed to have a wife and family in ROTC since I wasn't issued to you? Asshole!" I had stepped up to him, my face red with rage, the tummy providing the only buffer between Davlin and myself. I continued venting, my anger and distress no longer able to be reined in. "You come home and ignore me, you miss out on our appointments and engagements, and you don't even speak to your parents so I have to! Where did you go?"

Unable to stop now that I was unleashing all my anger, I continued. "Why are you distancing yourself from this baby and me, because you are the one that wanted me to have it! And I gave into you like I always have, and right now, in this moment, I regret it."

The words were out, and just as they had left my mouth, my anger left me too. I was unable to feel anything else at that moment; I needed him to feel something for me, to give me back something. If it was anger in return for my lashing out, then I could have reveled in anger; what I truly wanted, what I needed was him to love me, and to say it.

I needed him to show it.

I turned away from Davlin and tossed my dirty scrub top into a hamper when he grabbed me, turning me toward him. He pulled me toward his body, crushing me in his embrace as his lips found mine. It had been forever since I felt any passion from his touches. This wasn't lust; it was his apology for months of ignoring me, for not helping or sharing in the pregnancy.

I was disgusting from my accident in the hall, and what had seeped through my uniform onto my skin was now soaking his dress shirt and tie. Not caring that I was getting him dirty, he lifted me so my legs could wrap around his waist, and we moved into the showers where we would be hidden from any staff that might come into the locker room.

His mouth met mine again as though he were overwhelmed by the immediate presence of our bodies together. This was the first time he had touched me since "the belly" had begun to show and become active. It was there now, sleepy and lazy; sluggish movements I ignored.

Davlin went to his knees, resting his head on the swelling growth that was his child. He untied the string that held my scrub pants in place, letting them fall around my feet. He helped me undress him of his now soiled shirt and pants.

He was as ready for me as I was for him. He lifted me effortlessly, and pinned me against the wall of the shower. Thrusting deep and making me gasp. I had missed him so much, and I showed him with my body. He held me, and loved me, letting me know he had missed me too. I came quickly, and Davlin followed. It had been

23

too long since our bodies had spoken, too long since we had had any enjoyment from each other's flesh.

He put me down, and I turned on the shower, letting the hot water wash us both clean of our sins. Davlin rubbed soap over the belly and across my back, turning me to face him.

"Becks, I'm sorry," he said, his voice a whisper, but we stood face to face, our noses nearly touching. "I'm scared, like I won't be able to do my job, I won't be able to leave when I have to go," he explained lamely, but continued. "I can't tell you how happy I am that you get to keep a piece of me when I do go, but I can't stop feeling like I'm not enough."

"Enough what?" I asked.

"Anything, everything. What kind of father am I going to be? Will I be good enough? What the hell kind of leader am I going to be? Am I going to get someone killed? Becks, I'm fucking terrified of every decision that I have to make."

I listened and loved him all the more for his confession. He rested his head on my shoulder and let me comfort him. I kissed his cheek and stroked his back, but I didn't know what to say to this man. He was someone different than the protector I had grown up with, he was a different man than the boy who had thrown caution to the wind the day we were married.

This Davlin was a different man than the one who had doubted himself and his decision to join the service. This Davlin was aware of what he had done and what was to come for us both. Where he had fear—perhaps all men in his position do—this man knew he would leave me, and he was trying to do that in the most generous manner, by leaving me with his child to love in his place. This Davlin knew he would have a mission to accomplish in a war somewhere far away and that I would not be a party to his success or failure in that place. I was responsible for making him successful at home, by keeping his child safe.

We stayed in the shower for a few more moments. I needed him. I needed him to love me, no matter how scared or unsure of the future he was. I knew what was in the near future, and that was

24

all I cared about in that moment. I kissed him again and leaned into his body.

Davlin and I joined again. This time as he held me against the back of the stall, thrusting hard, it was not passion or love; it was sex in the most basic form. It made us both feel good and let us know we were alive in that moment. It was what Davlin needed at that time and what I could give him as his wife, the love of his life, the mother of his child, as his best friend; I let him use me as he needed and took pleasure in his taking.

We went home after our encounter in the staff locker room. He held my hand, but again his mind was somewhere I couldn't gain access to. I wasn't feeling very well when we got home—the day had started out so well but then had put me through an emotional roller coaster—so I went to bed after kissing my husband good night.

"I'll be there in a bit; I just want to watch CNN for a while. See what's going on outside Nebraska." He said it jokingly but it was a knock on my complete lack of interest in politics or current events. I didn't have time with my class load and the pregnancy.

The last thing I remember was hearing him count out his push-ups. I woke up three days later in the hospital, unable to talk from the tube in my mouth, blood dripping into my arm, and no belly…no baby.

Chapter 4

When I had collided with the gurney in the lobby, the hit to my abdomen had been enough to cause an abruptio placentae. The placenta detached from my uterine wall, which caused the loss of blood flow to the baby, and I continued to bleed behind the placenta. I hadn't thought anything of the blood I had seen when I used the restroom, since we had had sex. A little bleeding after sex isn't cause for concern according to the maternity books I had read.

When Davlin had come to bed he didn't notice that I was bleeding. He never noticed anything when he was in his own world. He didn't notice I was pale and unresponsive in the morning when he came into the room to give me a kiss on his way out the door; he hadn't turned on the lights. I don't know how Davlin was so oblivious to my dying, but he was. He missed it.

Not that it would have mattered.

After Davlin returned from his morning workout for ROTC and his first history class, he noticed I hadn't moved and became concerned. It was hours after he had left, almost a full day since the trauma to my abdomen. Realizing something was wrong, he called 9-1-1.

I was rushed to the ER; the baby had no heartbeat and I was still bleeding into my uterus. I was taken to surgery for an emergency cesarean section that became a partial hysterectomy with the damage to my uterus. In that one clumsy action of colliding with a gurney, I had lost my ability to have children.

Davlin was beside himself when the doctor told him the baby had died.

His son had died.

He put a hole in the wall when the doctor said I might not make it through the surgery; my blood wasn't clotting.

My mother said that Davlin never got off his knees praying the whole time the surgeons worked on me. Not that Davlin and I were religious people. We weren't. But he had to bargain with someone in his grief and guilt.

As much as friends and my mother tried to tell him that he couldn't have known that something was wrong, he knew the truth. Davlin knew that had he bothered to talk to me in the morning, he would have known I was dying. What Davlin was unwilling to accept was that even if he had known I was bleeding earlier that morning, nothing would have changed our son's outcome.

Our baby had died within an hour of my accident.
Our son died while we were joined making love.

When I woke up, a nurse and a doctor were speaking to my mother. Davlin was holding my hand, tears dried on his cheeks. I could tell he had been crying; his eyes and nose were both red and irritated. I squeezed his hand to let him know I was awake.

"Oh, God! Becks! Doctor, she's awake. Take that shit out of her mouth so she can talk."

The doctor came and explained what he was about to do; the nurse assisted with barely enough room to move since Davlin wouldn't let go of my hand. The tube came out of my airway, and as I gasped for air trying to calm the nausea I was feeling, I pointed to my abdomen.

Davlin spoke first. "Babe, the baby was a boy." He barely got it out before the dam broke again. Shaking in his grief, he pulled me close to him and held me as the truth of our loss sunk into my brain.

When I started to cry, I couldn't stop. I cried for the obvious, my lost child, for the pain both physical and emotional I was feeling. I cried for my husband and the loss he must feel as both a father and a husband. I cried for my mother. My crazy mother who had come to sit in my room to make sure I would wake up. I cried because she would never be a grandmother. I cried for the loss of time Davlin and I had had during our pregnancy. I cried because he felt the need

27

to protect his now nonexistent family. I cried for my loss of future and the reality that I could never have a child, that I would never feel the press of a foot inside my womb again. I would never have the emotional pull inward that is a mother's right when she is with child. I cried for what seemed like forever.

Davlin sat up when I stopped shaking. When my tears finally stopped flowing and when I no longer needed to blow my nose repeatedly, we sat together, as man and wife, and listened to the doctor explain the damage and outcome of my injuries. He explained the reason for my hysterectomy and assured us that there were options for a young couple to have a family. That we could have a surrogate mother or adopt. I heard the doctor talking but didn't take his words to heart. I didn't care.

I was transferred to a regular medical floor and finished my recovery. By the following Tuesday, Davlin was taking me home. He had bought a new mattress and had paid a service to clean our room and house.

Walking into the apartment was a surreal experience; the random gifts friends and classmates had given us throughout the pregnancy were scattered about the apartment. In Davlin's absence I had taken up crochet and had made a layette for the baby in soft greens and yellows. I had made a hat, booties, and a blanket that now occupied a rocking chair Davlin had brought home one evening as an apology for missing one of our appointments. I saw each item as a sharp reminder of what I had lost, and I wanted nothing more than to break them all to pieces.

Just like I felt...Broken.

I didn't know what to say to my husband. Before the baby, Davlin and I had been able to find anything and everything to talk about. Before, we didn't worry about ROTC field training or the Middle East. Before, Davlin and I were comfortable walking around our apartment naked, joining when the mood struck.

Now, my husband couldn't look at me. I wasn't sure if he blamed me for the baby or if he just couldn't get the change in my appearance through his head, but we needed a miracle to save our marriage. We were two strangers who had grown in different directions, and I wasn't sure if we could search each other out to come together again.

Two weeks after the baby died I had to go back to class, if for no other reason than to finish what I had started four years before. Four years that seemed like an eternity, and I felt like a stranger in comparison to the girl who had started in my shoes.

The day I had to go back to class, Davlin was awake and dressed in his BDUs for ROTC. We had barely been able to touch each other or speak since I returned from the hospital. This morning wasn't any different. We didn't say anything beyond a functional good morning. I was watching his hands as he cut some old ham and cheese to add to an omelet he was cooking, when he broke the silence.

"I miss you."

I looked up from his hands to his face. It was so different. There was no longer the mischievousness of our youth, the sparkle that had been in his eyes when we snuck out of our houses to meet and make love on blankets on the soccer field at our high school.

The man in front of me had worry lines I hadn't seen before, sleepless eyes from trying to get comfortable enough to rest in uncomfortable places. There was a new pink mark, which would soon to be a scar, from a drunken fall he had taken over the weekend.

This face was a new one, but the soul that it belonged to was the same. I was searching for that soul, needed it as much as I needed air. If I wasn't willing to get to know this man who had changed his face and captured my own soul, I was doomed.

Us would be gone and dead.
I couldn't live without us.

29

"Would you change anything if you could turn back time?" I asked him my famous hypothetical question so he knew I wouldn't hold him accountable for his answer. It was our way of easing into an uncomfortable conversation.

He took a minute to answer and I was getting worried about what he might say when he looked up at me, with a small sparkle that resembled something I used to see.

With a grin on his face he said, "Maybe what I wore the day we got married. That stupid sport coat is something to regret." With a full smile that finally met his eyes, he came around the counter to me. He took my face in his hands; looking down at me he told me again, "I miss you. I love you and I need you back."

I had made a decision that morning to get out of our rut and mourn together the loss of our baby and the future we could no longer have or sever all ties and mourn all loss at once. He must have made the same decision, because from that point on, Davlin and I were a shadow of what we used to be. Together, we were going to face a new future, and as "Us," we would meet any challenge life threw in our direction.

Chapter 5

After Davlin and I graduated, me with my nursing degree and he with a bachelor's in history, we moved away from school and Nebraska altogether. His ROTC commitment meant that Davlin was a commissioned officer in the United States Army, and he still had more training to complete at Fort Bragg, North Carolina. We were provided a small house on base with other young officers and their families.

I was hired on base at the hospital to work in the Emergency Department. Because I wasn't military, I was considered a "civilian contractor." I wasn't addressed as ma'am, and I wasn't forced to drag my ass out of bed at five in the morning to run obscene distances in short shorts.

Davlin, on the other hand, did. Davlin was engrossed in his new job and wanted to share all his adventures with me. Being a nurse, I had to be rather vague about my day and the people I cared for, so I was happy to allow him to carry the conversation as we ate dinner.

He was animated when talking about what he had learned, but he was always mindful not to go too far and alienate me too much. He would eventually tire of reliving his day, and our conversation would turn to more family-oriented talk, even though our family was just the two of us.

We had a good routine in our life, well established and like clockwork. We would begin each day together in the shower. This time was not meant as time for sex, but more so to be close and reassure each other of our bodily changes. Afterward, we would have coffee as we shared the small bathroom primping for the day. In the afternoons when Davlin got off work, we would go to an officers' gym and work out. Davlin's body had gone from the bulky football player from high school who walked around with no neck, to a sleek, strong, and deceptively toned man.

I too had changed my physique. After the baby and my surgery, I decided to make myself like something about my body. I began to take pride in the way I looked just as Davlin did.

We would go on runs in the evenings after dinner, or I would swim at the indoor pool when the weather was too ugly for outdoor sports. I began taking spin and kickboxing classes. I did anything to shape up and keep my body moving since I couldn't always stop my brain from dwelling on the past or what had happened at work that day.

Davlin was my support for when the past weighed me down. There were days that often caught me off guard when depression would keep me in bed. Davlin was my ray of sunshine, cheering me up and keeping me motivated to move and not let the past ruin our future. Our routine was important to both of us, and it became something we both treasured.

On our weekends, Davlin and I would take day trips to get off base and away from the military life we were part of during the week. Sometimes we went to the coast, taking pictures of ourselves by the lighthouses that dappled the Eastern seaboard. But on longer weekends we would venture to Florida and Georgia to see historic battle sites, areas that held interest for Davlin. He would use his college education to tell me the interesting facts about the area we were visiting.

Our trips allowed us to be new people. We were in places where no one knew us. We could create a story about who we were and why we were visiting. On a trip to Louisiana, we were a newlywed couple, and as such we were expected to stay in our room making love. We did not disappoint.

On that trip, we made love on the balcony, my legs wrapped around his hips and my butt barely resting on the railing. It was deep night and there was little light passing down through the moss-covered canopy overhead. I could barely see Davlin's face with the combination of alcohol, lack of sleep, and simple night blindness. He appeared to me like a phantom forcing himself into me, pushing me to climax and then denying me, laughing as I cursed him for his taunt. Davlin enjoyed every minute of his control over my body as much as I enjoyed letting him have that control.

Not all of our trips were pleasant by any means. Davlin was a man, and trite like all men, he had an irrational fear of road maps and seeking assistance when lost. Many an argument arose in the front seat of our car as I pleaded with him to pull over and ask for directions and he acted as though he were temporarily deaf. The arguments were usually short lived and on more than one occasion led to make-up sex in a field or behind a decrepit house on a country road. I sometimes think he would get lost on purpose just for the make-up sex.

During his time in training, Davlin and I had a rather comfortable relationship. We were both home every evening to enjoy our time together, and we had weekends off to spend with each other. Up to this point, we had not experienced the hardship of the US Army.

Our happy little bubble burst on another random Tuesday when Davlin came home earlier than I had expected. It was two weeks after his pinning ceremony for his first lieutenant; I had come home after my shift at the hospital when Davlin pulled into the driveway of our house just before me.

I knew something was wrong, seeing the set in his jaw and the thought that kept him sitting in his Jeep, knuckles white as he gripped the steering wheel. I went over to the Jeep and opened the door, "Hey, Lieutenant. Everything okay?"

He finally looked at me, and for the first time I was truly frightened for him. His face was pale, and he looked as though he wanted to vomit.

"I got my orders today."

I took a pause, and seeing that he was waiting for me to ask about them, I attempted to lighten the mood. "Great, where are we going? Italy? Korea? New Jersey?" My bravado was wasted on him; Davlin knew I was terrified of the answer he was about to give.

"Afghanistan. I got orders to be S2 for an Airborne Infantry Company out of Fort Benning. I have to report for two weeks jump training starting Monday, then we move to Benning next month."

His news was something we had been waiting for. That didn't make it any less of a sucker punch.

I squared my shoulders and took a deep breath. "Okay, so first thing would be to arrange our move? Right? The hospital will be able to help me transfer to Benning's facility, and we have some time to get this all ready. Right?" My head was spinning, and my hands had begun to shake. I was feeling sick, and I had to grab the door of the Jeep to stay upright.

Davlin got out and pulled me to his chest. He rested his chin on my head and held me tight to stop my shaking.

"Yeah, we'll get it all taken care of. I have the rest of the week off to get over to JAG and get you set up as my power of attorney, so you can help arrange everything while I'm jumping."

I pulled back enough to look up at my husband. "So, this is it, huh?"

33

"Yeah, baby, it is. I'm sorry."

"Don't apologize to me for being who and what you are. We both understood what you were getting into when you signed up for ROTC and when you got commissioned."

I stood on tiptoe to kiss him, pulling his face to my level and holding his gaze with mine. We stood in our driveway holding each other until a car passed by and honked at us.

Hand-in-hand we went into our house, and for the first time since moving to Fort Bragg, North Carolina, we let life upset our routine.

Chapter 6

Our move to Fort Benning, Georgia, was chaotic, at best. With Davlin gone for his two weeks' jump training to become "Airborne," I was left with the responsibility of arranging our move.

I had little understanding of how to move in the army and didn't realize that we could have someone do the work for us, so when I went into the battalion offices to arrange payment and vouchers for our move, I was completely ignorant of what I was doing. The paperwork was endless with acronyms I didn't understand—I had no idea if Davlin's orders were for TDY, PDA, or FBI. I was lost and frustrated until a kindly elderly lady saw my confused glances and attempts at copying other soldier's answers.

"Honey, you need a little help?" she asked walking over to me.

"Oh mama, more than a little," I replied with eyes that showed my complete confusion.

"Well, darlin', come over to my desk and let's see if we can't figure out what it is you need done today," she said while pulling me to my feet, helping me gather my papers together.

An hour and three cups of coffee later, Davlin and I were set up to have our personal belongings packed and moved in one week's time, all items to arrive at Fort Benning the following Thursday. I was more than grateful for Mrs. Barker, and more than surprised to run into Heather Vaughn, another officer's wife from Davlin's company.

"Heather, hi! What are you doing here? Did Vaughn get orders too?" I asked as I gave her a quick hug. The poor girl looked miserable. Her normally impeccable makeup was smeared from tears; her nose was red and runny and her hair was falling from its French twist.

"Yes," she sniffled, "He's going to Fort Benning and then to Afghanistan."

"Oh, well, he and Davlin are going together then," I explained.

35

"Really? Eric didn't say anything about Davlin being transferred. Maybe he doesn't know. But I'm glad you are going to Benning too. Wait, you are going, right?" she questioned, each query asked before I was able to answer the last.

"Yeah, just arranged the move," I answered, tossing a glance toward the desk of Mrs. Barker, who was deep in conversation with a uniformed soldier.

Her eyes welled up with tears. "Oh my God, Becks! I don't know what I'm going to do! Eric is the one who does everything for me. He pays the bills, fixes the cars! He does everything in our house. He always jokes that I'm his trophy wife, and now here I am trying to figure out how to move us from one base to another just to have my husband leave me," she rambled and again, began to cry.

Completely sympathetic to her situation, I filled Heather in on the secret to moving in the military, and its name was Mrs. Barker.

I handed Heather a tissue and ushered her in the direction I had just come from, explaining, "Well, I do know where to start, because I am just as lost in this military move stuff." I led her toward Mrs. Barker and her endless pot of coffee.

An hour later we were walking out of the battalion offices, into a rainstorm that was predicted to cause blackouts along the seaboard.

"Do you want to come over for dinner, Heather?" I asked before stepping out into the downpour.

"I would love to, but Eric has been trying his hardest to branch his family tree before he leaves on deployment." She turned a pretty shade of pink at the mention of breeding.

"Well, maybe another time when the weather doesn't make you want to climb under the covers," I said, winking at her. She had a full blush and laughed.

"Maybe when we get to Georgia. I am totally going to need your phone number."

"Well, I'm not giving it to you until you come over for dinner. So, tell your man that Friday night he can keep it in his pants until after you guys get home from dinner. We are going out. We will meet at our house at six and go from there," I said, leaving no room for argument.

Smiling and looking much more in control of her emotions, she replied, "Well, if you're going to twist my arm, I'll have to fend my husband off until after dinner."

With dinner plans made for Friday, Heather and I dove into the rainstorm, running for our respective cars. Soaked to the bone from my rush to the car, I drove home thinking of how fun it would be to spend the night in bed with Davlin.

When I got home he was waiting for me in the kitchen. As I came in the door the power went out, leaving the house in eerie shades of gray. I put my purse and keys on the counter and walked in on my husband, who was leaning against the kitchen table, a beer in his hand, wearing nothing but his PT shorts. His hair was wet, dripping on his chest.

He said nothing as I came around the corner past the stove. I wasn't prepared to find him lurking in the dark kitchen and had to choke down a scream when I saw him. He looked at me with eyes that reminded me of a hungry animal; my natural instincts kicked in, making my rhetorical tail tuck under.

"Ever heard of 'lonely wives night,' " Davlin asked with obvious distain.

"Um, yeah, all the wives hitting the bars a couple weeks after their husbands leave on a deployment? Sure, urban legend, right?" I was trying to keep my tone light in response to his obvious anger.

"You're mine," he whispered. I almost wasn't sure if he had said it.

Then he moved. Slyly, he uncrossed his ankles and stood to his full height. His eyes remained intent on my movements, and again my instincts warned me to not move. I had never feared my husband, but tonight was something different.

Davlin took two steps toward me, closing the space quickly; I involuntarily stepped back until my back was pressed against the sink.

37

He moved toward me, away from the window. His face was cast into the shadows that filled our kitchen, and all I could see was a black silhouette of the man I had loved all my life. My body was at war with itself, unsure whether to be fearful or mad with lust. Davlin made my body respond in a fully lustful manner.

He closed the last bit of space not saying anything. He wasted no time being gentle. He reached for my shirt and pulled it over my head, immediately reaching for my bra hooks. He bent his mouth to meet mine. His kiss was a claim, an order that my body wanted to follow.

His tongue delved into my mouth, playing and teasing mine, as his hands moved toward the button on my jeans. I clumsily stepped on the back of my sneakers to pull them off my feet, helping him strip me.

Looking down at my face as he dropped his shorts on the linoleum floor, he said it again, "Becks, you're mine. I can't live if I think for a minute that you would forget me."

He didn't give me a chance to answer him, to reassure him that I would never be unfaithful, because once out of jeans and panties, Davlin picked me up, holding me by my hips, and immediately filled me. Continuing to kiss and suckle, Davlin held me immobile. He was claiming me, and I wanted to be claimed. With my hands braced on the counter and my legs wrapped around his waist, I rode my husband suspended in the air.

Trying to move so I could please myself, I leaned back and tried to increase our pace, pushing him faster. It worked. I felt a warm tingling starting in the pit of my stomach, heating the length of my spine. I cried out as I came; Davlin held me tight when my concentration went toward the ecstasy of my orgasm. He didn't care that I had climaxed; he was still in need, was still his.

I wrapped my arms around his neck and squeezed harder with my thighs. Davlin leaned me against the counter, his height a perfect match to set me down and simply fuck. Davlin quickened his pace and drove hard into me. I tried to hold him close to me, to stop his rapid and forceful pushing, but all I was successful at doing was sliding off the countertop. Davlin turned me around and took me from behind.

He thrust himself into me and pushed my body against the counter. The smacking of his flesh hitting mine was accented by the thunder outside. Davlin held my hips as he endured, speeding his pace a bit more. I heard his breath quicken and felt his grip tighten. He groaned moments later, climaxing.

Usually, Davlin made unintelligible noises during sex; this night, he said one word—"mine"—each time he had me.

Turning to face my husband, I kissed his neck, then up to his chin, moving over to his lips. There were thousands of times in our lives together that Davlin and I had made love, but this time he had had to prove his control of my body and his devotion to it. He had to prove to himself that I was his and remind me of that fact as well.

From the kitchen, Davlin and I went to the living room, where we made love sprawled on a rug. In a simple missionary position, my husband and I faced each other and moved together.

This time we were slower in our lovemaking. Davlin took the time to kiss and suckle as he moved himself inside me. The comforting warmth that numbed my body from womb to brain spread like oil as I orgasmed. Davlin held me to him, then forward as he, too, had release.

We listened to the world outside as the rain pattered against the windows. My head rested on his chest, and I listened to his heartbeat slow as we watched the storm worsen outside. We didn't care about anything beyond our walls; tonight was about us.

As the storm waned to a simple downpour, Davlin and I had moved into our bedroom. On my hands and knees, Davlin pulled my hips toward him as he had me from behind. Pounding with enough force to bruise, he made my body respond yet again. His deft fingers stroked me as he pulled me to his chest. With thighs spread, arms reaching over my head, and seeking his mouth, I opened my eyes to see Davlin watching our bodies in the mirror.

39

He was watching his affects, the movement of his fingers, the thrusting and pushing of me from behind. I held his gaze in the mirror and felt a voyeuristic thrill watching ourselves.

He knew me too well. Davlin had always been able to make my body respond to his. He was not a selfish lover. Davlin was ready to come, slowing himself, denying himself, as his fingers brought me to my peak again. My voice failed me, but my body did not. Shaking with pleasure, Davlin allowed himself his own pleasure release.

Exhausted from the frenzied lovemaking, we fell to the bed and quickly fell asleep. We woke hours later to silence outside; the storm had passed. Davlin kissed my lips, then my closed eyelids. He kissed my cheeks and returned to my lips, courting my tongue yet again.

"Promise me, Becks, that when I come home I'll find you here, lonely and pining for my body."

"Well, after a year with no company but Heather and my B.O.B., I'll be more than pining, honey; I'll be downright ravenous for you. I may have a hard time getting you home with your pants on."

He gave me a sideways look but quickly gave in to my jesting. "Davlin, I could never, would never, don't ever want to entertain the thought of another man. You've been my only forever, and you're going to be my only until we both die." I kissed him; with all of my being that I was able to give him, I kissed him and held him.

This time, our lovemaking was nothing but gentle. Davlin tenderly touched each breast as he bent his head to suckle each nipple, making them stand in the coldness his mouth left behind. I gently pulled and stroked his manhood, as I had once seen him do years before, in another dimly lit room.

Davlin came into me and rolled me on top. Leaning forward to kiss his lips, then back to take his length, I rode my husband. Pulling fast and hard, then slow, pausing and teasing him. Looking down at him as he lay under me, I realized he was getting frustrated with my playfulness.

"Davlin, I'm yours, but you're mine just as much. You can't forget what this is either," I instructed him. He had every reason to demand my fidelity, just as I had every right to remind him what he must come home to. We each had justified fears to face, and this night was about voicing those fears, giving us ample time to put them aside.

"Agreed," Davlin said. He knew that he was leaving me, and I had legitimate fear of losing him. It was the unspoken threat. Where I could give him my body, a pleasure to remember while he was away, and a promise that I would be here when he came home, Davlin could offer me no such guarantee.

We had gotten too deep. Needing to steer this night away from sadness, I leaned into Davlin and licked his cheek.

From that point on, the night became a mess of tickles and brief and vigorous encounters. We would fall asleep joined and wake to finish. Our bodies never stopped touching through the night, and in the morning when the house was eye-blinding with morning sunshine, we finally fell into a languorous stupor.

We slept the morning away, waking when our stomachs made us aware we had skipped meals and used up our energy.

Dragging myself out of bed, I went to the bathroom to take a shower; Davlin came and joined me shortly after. He washed my hair and my body, and I did the same for him. We stood in the warmth of the spray, arms wrapped around each other, my head resting on his chest at his heart. We stood there in silence until the warm water ran out. Then, wrapped in towels, we went to the kitchen to scrounge lunch.

"So, who found their wife cheating, or was the 'lonely wife night' thing just shop talk?" I asked as he made our brunch omelet.

"I love you," he answered simply, then continued his explanation. "I had had a dream while I was taking a nap waiting for you to come home." He looked over his shoulder at me, blushing slightly.

"Yeah, what kind of dream?" My interest was definitely piqued.

"Becks, let me just say that I woke up, chugged a beer, and when you came in I was feeling rather possessive of you, and apparently my brain and my cock were not thinking the same."

"What was this dream about?"

"I dreamed that I walked in on you and Eric Vaughn's wife in bed together." At that his ears turned red, his neck flushed, and he was no longer able to look at me. "Becks, I woke with a hard-on to end all. I feel like a damn pervert because of it."

Laughing until my sides hurt and tears came to my eyes, I told him how we were set to have dinner with Eric and his lovely wife Heather the following week. With the new plans set, Davlin turned a whole new shade of red.

"Aw, hell! How am I supposed to sit at a table with you two without blushing or disgracing myself?"

"I don't know, honey, but with enough alcohol maybe Heather and I can make that fantasy a reality," I teased. Kissing him on the cheek as he placed my plate in front of me, Davlin winked and sat across from me. We ate in a companionable silence, finishing and putting our dishes in the dishwasher. We got dressed and went for our run, which we had been forced to put off for the last several days thanks to Davlin's jump training.

A week and a day later, Davlin and I were living in a house that had no furniture, sleeping on an AeroBed, and living out of bags. We went on our dinner date with the Vaughns and had an enjoyable time. We all agreed to repeat the experience when we arrived at Fort Benning. Three days later Davlin signed out on travel leave from Fort Bragg, North Carolina, and we drove to Fort Benning, Georgia.

Chapter 7

Fort Benning was very much like Fort Bragg, at least for me it was. The military had kept my job as a civilian contractor in the hospital, and I was given my schedule upon arrival to the base. We were again assigned a home in junior officer housing. These houses were older, needing more upkeep, and none were private residences.

Our home was a duplex two-story split right down the middle. The house was shared with a captain and his wife and young son. We were introduced when we arrived, and the captain immediately took Davlin under his wing to explain the chore breakdown for the yard.

Our belongings arrived to our house the Thursday after our arrival. As Davlin became acquainted with his new position, company, and men, I unpacked our home and became acquainted with the roads and general layout of the base.

Davlin had orders to deploy to Afghanistan in January. It was now October, and as a result of his upcoming deployment, he had begun to, again, turn inside his head with worry. There was little I could do to pull him out of his brain when he became distracted with a problem at work. Distressingly, he would often bring his work home with him.

As the Battalion S-2, he was in charge of intelligence for the company. At home he was required to gather information provided in daily briefings, information that, when in Afghanistan, was supposed to help identify insurgents, determine safe troop movement, and determine the quality of current intel.

He spent his evenings in his study learning Persian Dari and Pashto, the official languages of Afghanistan. He was rarely found without a book on the history or population of the country. He had studied maps of the terrain and of the cities. Davlin was taking on the mission and leaving me behind. No longer did we have the quality communication or interaction we had enjoyed before he had orders to deploy.

43

One evening in late October, a couple weeks after we had arrived at Benning, I walked into his office where he was sitting at his computer with his headphones on, listening to his language learner CD, practicing his enunciation of common phrases in Pashto. "Davlin," I said to his back in a normal tone. He didn't respond, so I raised my voice. "Davlin!"

"What? Don't yell, Becks." He turned in his chair to look at me. Seeing the look of annoyance on my face, his softened. Davlin wasn't oblivious to the way I was feeling or to the way we had been strained. "Yeah, babe, what do you need?"

"You! For one damn evening, no fucking Pashto, no goddamn company, no fucking Afghanistan, no reports! No damn sharing with anyone or anything. I want my husband, because you are going to be neck deep in all this shit soon enough, and now is all I have before I have to give you up."

Having vented my selfish response, I suddenly felt very childish and I was unable to look him in the eyes. I knew that Davlin was trying to do his best by the men in his company. I knew that he felt a great deal of responsibility and fear for what was required of him, I also knew he didn't feel ready for the upcoming deployment. My rant didn't help my already-stressed husband.

Sighing, he stood up and pushed his chair away from his desk. "Becks," he said to my back as I leaned against the door jamb to his office, "I'm sorry."

I turned around and fell against him. Beginning to shake with premature loss and fear, Davlin put his arms around me and held me until the spell passed.

"Babe, let's go have dinner, and come home and get naked." He smiled down at me. "I can leave this alone for the rest of the night. Let's go do something together and leave all of this shit behind."

"I say skip dinner and get right to the naked part, " I suggested.

"Ah, no. We can't. I plan on keeping you in bed for awhile, so you are going to need a good meal." Jokingly he turned me around and manhandled me out of the room toward the front hall.

As we were putting our jackets on, the doorbell rang. Davlin opened it to the overly friendly and very excited faces of Eric and Heather Vaughn.

Heather burst into the hallway, hugging me tightly. "Oh wow, Becks, I have the best news, and I couldn't wait to tell you and I need you to help me, and maybe there's still time so we can totally do this together!" she rambled as she took off her jacket. Eric, having caught on to the fact that Davlin and I were heading out of our house, was trying to put Heather's jacket back on her.

"I'm pregnant! " she beamed.

"Oh sweetie, congrats," I said as I hugged her. Genuinely happy for her, I squeezed her and pressed her away. "Wow. You are going to be a fabulous mother." Again, completely genuine, I didn't have the heart to tell her we wouldn't be having dual baby showers. "Why don't you and Eric come join us for dinner? We can celebrate?" Davlin hid his smile in his jacket collar, seeing realization dawn on Heather's face.

"Oh, I'm sorry, just barging in like this! I was just so excited, and you're my closest friend. I really wanted to tell you." Heather had a habit of babbling; it was worse now that she was excited. She was also very infectious with her good moods and extremely difficult to say "no" to when in a happy state.

"It's no problem. We were getting ready to go have dinner. Why don't you two join us? We were just being boring; now we totally have something to celebrate."

"Well…Eric, what do you think? Can we?" she pleaded with her husband. Eric and Davlin had exchanged congratulatory back slaps and manly handshakes when the good news flew out of Heather's mouth, but this was about Heather, not Eric. He smiled at his wife and consented, so as a group, but in separate cars, we headed to dinner at a local restaurant.

Dinner was low-key but happy for all there. With her new knowledge of an inhabitant in her belly, Heather gave up on her strict diet. She devoured a chocolate mousse for desert after gorging on a full serving of fettuccini alfredo with two sides of breadsticks.

45

The poor girl could barely walk out of the restaurant. We said our good nights in the parking lot and then headed back home.

"You're amazing, baby," Davlin told me on the way home. "You really are a good friend to her. I can't imagine that it's easy for you to see her so happy. I thought you would have told her by now. You don't talk about him anymore, do you?" As Davlin spoke, his voice got softer and quieter. Whispering about our dead son.

"Nah, I don't like to think about it too much," I lied. Not a day went by that I didn't recall the feeling of his little feet kicking my abdomen or remember the anger I felt when I found out I was pregnant. I suffered an immense spectrum of emotions when I thought about the baby, and I went through it every single day. But Davlin didn't need to worry about it, so I lied. "I know I won't ever be 'over' the baby, but most days are at least tolerable."

The truth was, most days were at least tolerable. I could get out of bed, have a purpose, get to my job. I was able to function when Davlin was there to encourage me and make sure I was doing it. What the hell was I going to do when he was gone?

"How was tonight?" he asked, bringing me back to reality and the current moment.

"Doable," I begrudgingly admitted.

Pulling me close so I could rest my head on his shoulder, Davlin kissed my forehead. "I am proud of you. And sorry that I've been so deep in my mess that you're feeling left behind. Kick me in the ass when I get like this, okay?"

" How about you just leave work at work and when you're home you're mine."

"Want to learn how to communicate in Afghani with me?" he asked, giving me his cheesy grin.

"No, but for that I'll give you an hour per night while I go for my run."

"Fair enough. I'm all yours, except when you abandon me to go run," he agreed, smiling and kissing me again.

When we arrived home, he pulled the door to his office closed as we passed en route to our bedroom. After that night, Davlin and I were able to gain back some lost ground yet again. I was beginning to notice our pattern of falling away and returning in regard to his stress level. Each time he became focused on a task, he would put everything, including me, on the back burner, but then when he realized what happened, we were able to make our relationship stronger when we worked our way back together, like bones setting after a break. Each break makes the bone stronger and that much harder to break.

By Christmas, Davlin and I were back to sleeping in the nude, making love in sleepy movements as the notion struck any time of night. Over the holiday break, we chose to stay on base as opposed to going to Guernsey to see his family.

We spent Christmas with Eric and Heather, who also chose to stay in Georgia. The happy couple had purchased items for their unborn child, whom they assumed was a boy. As enjoyable as it was to see Heather's face light up with each gift she opened from Eric, the gaiety of the evening soon wore off and the effects of my bottle of wine began to weigh me down.

Davlin walked me home after I feigned sickness in the bathroom.

"Too much?" he asked as we left their house.

"Wine? Or unborn baby?" I asked, more belligerent that usual.

"Either? Or both?"

"I think too much unborn baby. And way too much wine. I shouldn't have drunk." I was a shitty drunk, not happy or overly lovey like some people. I had known better than to drink. But with all the sadness of the impending deployment, I thought I deserved a bit of liquid memory loss.

"Well, at least you didn't vomit on anyone, or burst into tears. And you can still stand! I'd say you're batting a thousand." He was enjoying teasing me as we walked toward our home surrounded by the silence of the wintery night.

Glaring at him through one eye, I fell backward into a snow-covered lawn and immediately began flapping my arms up and down

47

by my sides. Snow angel complete, I sought assistance from my entertained husband.

"Give me a hand, help me up," I requested.

"Nah, you're pretty like that. The snow all around you, your edges seem softer now."

"Lieutenant, I believe you may be drunk," I accused him.

Davlin gave me a hand and pulled me up. "Maybe, but nowhere near as drunk as you, love." Davlin pulled me close and kissed my lips so deeply I could taste the whiskey he had sipped all evening. We continued walking to our home a few streets away from the Vaughn's, his arm wrapped around my waist to help me past the icy parts.

When we arrived home, I slid out of my winter coat, dropping it on the floor. Feeling rather like I was floating as I moved through the house, I took off my dress with a tug of the ribbon that held the dress in place. In just panties and heels, I stumblingly made my way to the living room, aiming for the couch.

Davlin had sobered up with the cold air outside and was delayed outside bringing the garbage can to the curb. With the task complete, he entered the living room and saw me most unwomanly-like sprawled on the couch. In a vain attempt to keep the room from spinning, I had one foot on the floor, black heel still in place; the other leg was over the arm of the couch. Davlin came into the room, glaring down at me.

"Young lady, you're a terrible lush."

Lazily smiling up at him, I retorted, "Lieutenant, you are not drunk enough. Here I am all laid out for you with these panties stuck in place, and you won't even lend me a hand. What kind of gentleman are you?"

Leaning forward over the arm of the couch, he helpfully linked his fingers over the top of my panties. I wore nothing more than heels and a smile as my husband met me on the couch. He kissed my lips, then my breasts, and then proceeded to kiss me down the middle of my body.

With a drink-fuzzed brain, I was easily pleased by Davlin's actions. He nipped at the soft skin of my thighs and tasted my inner warmth before he suckled and teased me to an uninhibited orgasm that left me panting, warm, and exhausted.

After a few moments of incomprehension and total ecstasy, I opened one eye to look down the length of my torso to see my husband, his dark head resting on my stomach. I ran my hands through his hair, letting him know my brain had returned to my body.

"Thank you."

I felt him chuckle as he rested on my belly. "Um, what do I say to that? You're welcome?"

"Yes. Don't be rude."

He smiled up at me. Bringing himself to lay the full length of my body, he kept me warm. We turned in toward each other, and he pulled the couch throw over the both of us. I fell asleep in the arms of my love. As I did every night until he deployed to Afghanistan.

Chapter 8

Davlin arrived in Afghanistan on a Tuesday. He called me that evening to let me know he had arrived safely, that the flight was miserable, that he smelled horrible after so many hours on a plane, and that he was hungry. He had me laughing at his plight and crying in misery missing him.

"Babe, I miss you more than I can explain," Davlin told me as our allotted time for talking ran out. " I love you."

"I love you too. Davlin, please be careful. I can't live without you."

"You won't have to," he assured me as he was made to hang up.

A week later, seven short days, two very short phone conversations, two good-byes on the phone, and eighteen 'I love you's '—...not long enough for it to happen—...I was working in the emergency department and I had just started an IV on a woman who had come into the department with abdominal pain, when the battalion commander and the battalion chaplain walked up to me with a purpose...

In all honesty I don't remember much of what they said to me. Just seeing them walk toward me, I was praying they would pass me by. They didn't. I remember the polite greeting and the subtle movement from the busy department into a private office. I remember sitting in a chair I had sat distraught family members in, an ugly thing with easily cleaned fabric, rough under the hand and uncomfortable. I was seeing all the unimportant things surrounding me. I was unable to hear the words that came out of their mouths.

Davlin was missing in action, along with five other soldiers. I think I lost consciousness or simply phased out for a while, because when I became aware of my surroundings, I was hysterical. The chaplain had his arms around me, assuring me that Davlin and the other men would be found, that the army had no reason to believe that they were not alive.

I didn't understand. How could six grown men go missing? Through my tears, I asked just that.

"Well, ma'am, we cannot divulge the details of the troop movement or your husband's orders, but suffice it to say that he and the soldiers under his authority were in an area where it is very possible they became lost or turned around."

"So, they are in the mountains and just lost?" I asked, calmed a little by the thought. Being lost in the mountains was something I knew Davlin could find his way out of with all his soldiers safely beside him.

"Again, ma'am, I cannot give you details of where your husband and his men were, or their orders."

"Well, why do you think they are MIA? Did you lose them? Are you able to track their vehicle? Are they wearing some form of GPS? Do you have any reason to think they are hostages? What the hell can you tell me?" My anger and fear were beginning to get the better of me now that my tears had stopped. My husband wasn't dead, and I needed to know how to help find him. I needed to be able to do something other than sit in this ugly, dark, depressing room.

"We need you to understand that information is still being collected on the activities of last Friday," the commander said.

"He's been missing since Friday? He just got there! He talked to me Friday morning! Davlin couldn't have gone missing!"

"Look, Mrs. Robertson, right now we don't know what we don't know. We do know that we have been unable to communicate with Lieutenant Robertson and his team, and yes, they did have GPS on their gear. We found the GPS, but no soldiers where the monitor was."

"Okay, was there anything to make you think that the men encountered enemies or that any of them were injured?"

"No, ma'am. Like I said before, we have no reason to think any of the men were injured." The colonel sat, looking at me.

Frustrated and completely at a loss, I sat sniffling. The men rose as a soft tap at the door let them know my reinforcements had arrived. They left me to my misery and fears.

51

As the door closed behind the men, I fell to pieces. I cried until my head ached, my nose was raw from wiping it with the cheap hospital tissues, my eyes were swollen from crying, and my heart ached with loss and fear.

I wasn't sure what to think, where to start, what to do... I may have sat there through the entirety of my shift had Heather not come breezing into the room, tear tracks on her face, her makeup smeared.

"Oh my God! Becks!!! Baby, are you okay? I was at the battalion getting the address to the base in Afghanistan when the chaplain came in. He told me a friend would be needing my help, but he wouldn't tell me who, so I followed him here and had to wait for the commander to leave.... Becks, what did they say? Is Davlin okay? I haven't heard from Eric in two days, so I don't know what's happening.... Becks, what happened?"

Her babbling and noise did little to calm me, but the verbal vomit gave me a chance to gather my thoughts.

"The colonel and chaplain came and told me that Davlin is missing." Just that, that admission out of my own mouth that my husband had been listed by the US Army as missing in action...

...that broke me.

I cried on my friend's shoulder, leaving wet spots on her shirt.

"I...I don't know what to do.... Heather, I can't breathe!" At that point I lost control of my senses, hyperventilating. Heather called out the door for some help.

Captain Curtis and Captain Mirkes, two of my fellow co-nurses, arrived in the room with a paper bag and new shoulders to cry on. Both women had known me for very little time, but both also understood where I was coming from. They were career military as well as nurses. They had seen their share of families torn apart by loss and had felt the temporary loss themselves with their own hardship tours. They were my functioning support system while Heather was as distraught as I was.

When my panic attack abated, I was again able to recount what the colonel and chaplain had told me. Captain Mirkes let me know that she was married to the Battalion S2 officer for a company that had not been deployed. She said she would ask her husband to try to get what information he could.

With a plan in place, my friends had Heather take me home. Entering into the house, I felt cold and empty. The home we had shared for so short of a time was lacking Davlin. I passed his office on my way to the stairs to go to bed when I caught his lingering smell.

Davlin couldn't be dead.

He would find his way to where his company would be able to find him. There would be a search party or something military-like to find them. Davlin would bring his men home safely, just like he promised.

Heather helped me up to my bedroom, where I collapsed onto the pillow Davlin had used for years. The scent of his sleeping flesh permeated the pillow, conjuring images of his sleeping face. Fresh tears spilled over. I clung to his pillow and cried myself to sleep.

I awoke to the smell of coffee floating up the stairs. There were noises on the first floor of the house, and voices, quieted in secret conversation. At first, I didn't remember where I was or what was going on; then, like a knife to my soul, I remembered that Davlin was missing, and some secret surrounded the loss.

I got out of bed and moved toward the stairs, treading lightly to glean what I could from their conversation. I crouched on one of the upper stairs and stayed hidden in the shadows of the hall. I was able to see through to the kitchen where Heather and Captain Mirkes and another man I didn't know were standing in the kitchen talking, coffee cups forgotten as the man was telling the women something that had their total attention. Heather stood with a look of fear and horror on her face. I wasn't able to hear what the man said, but judging from Heather's face, it wasn't good.

I drew strength from the fact that Heather wasn't crying and decided it was time the people in my kitchen knew I was awake. I went back up the stairs to wash my face; the dried tears felt like crust on my skin. I turned on the light and saw myself in the mirror.

53

Appalled at my reflection, I let out a gasp. Splashing cold water on my face and running wet fingers through my hair did little to improve my appearance. With a last glance in the mirror, I turned out the lights and headed downstairs to hear what secrets had been uncovered.

At the base of the stairs I noticed the voices in the kitchen had changed; the quality of conversation had become friendlier. Everyone was looking in my direction when I came into the doorway of the kitchen. I gave them a weak smile and reached for a cup of coffee, with a silent prayer it would help warm the cold feeling that had settled in my stomach.

The pieced-together information that Captain Mirkes (a male captain) was able to gather along with Heather's information from Eric in Afghanistan was frightening and depressing. Davlin and five other soldiers had been sent on a search of a yet-unchecked area of mountains twenty miles from their base area. Davlin had been tasked to search the local mountains for caves and other strongholds available for the Taliban. Any resistance was to be reported, with orders to follow for possible engagement. Davlin had been sent with the squad of infantry men as their officer in charge.

The squad had driven into the area and then proceeded on foot into the mountain range. Their mission was expected to range from two to four days depending on the amount of terrain they covered each day. On the first evening, the squad had discovered a cave system that was unmarked on the area maps. Davlin had called back to Camp Houston to determine their course of action. Major Rawlings, Davlin's commander, had relayed orders to enter the cave system to chart it and to determine who, if anyone, resided within.

Captain Mirkes said that communication had obviously been limited with the men in the cave system. Davlin had requested more support prior to entering the caves but had been denied the extra man power. The second-to-last communication the command at Camp Houston had received was Davlin making command aware that the cave system itself was very extensive and the six men at the location would be unsuccessful searching the area without assistance.

Davlin was given a direct order to enter the system.

He acknowledged receipt of his orders, and with no further communication, Davlin and the five men under his command were lost.

A search-and-rescue group had been sent to the cave system after two days with no communication. When the S&R platoon arrived to the last known coordinates, they found a marker letting those who may follow them know which direction they had progressed. It was also their road map out of the caves. The team was able to follow the marks that Davlin and his squad had left. Their path was quite clear to all following.

The path taken by Davlin and his squad died in an anteroom at the end of a series of turns. Had he and his troops entered the room through the only entrance and had the room been as empty as it was when S&R arrived, then new direction markers should have been placed. There were no signs of combat or bloodshed. There were no signs that anyone or anything had been removed from the area. It was simply the end of Davlin's trail.

The other caves were searched, each ending in an anteroom with only one entrance. Each tunnel led to the adjacent one until there were no more adjacent tunnels. The entire system was like a building with halls that led to only one room, and side halls with no other purpose than to cause confusion. All the caves were searched, though it took a platoon five times the number Davlin had two days to complete.

Through the whole search, no sign of the missing men was found until the end of the second day. While the majority of the search-and-rescue platoon were in the cave system, there was a squad monitoring the exterior of the system to watch for any combatants fleeing from the area and to look for any signs of troop movement through the area, friendly or otherwise. What the exterior guard found was a pack from Sargent Pallen, the young squad leader, second in charge to Davlin. The pack showed no signs of damage or foul play. All his belongings were accounted for. The men were simply missing, Davlin included.

55

After two days of radio silence from the cave system number twenty-nine, communications were reestablished.

"Hate to be cliché, but Houston, we have a problem," reported Lieutenant Vaughn, the officer in charge of search and rescue of the missing squad of troops from Charlie Company, 2nd Battalion, 54th Infantry Regiment. "Request permission to expand search outside of immediate area to determine whereabouts of missing soldiers."

"Negative, Lieutenant, new imaging shows large combatant movement in your area. You do not have permission to engage at this time. Collect full man power and return to evacuation point. Copy all orders?" came the voice from the COMSEC-protected telephone line that had been passed from general, to Major, to remaining S2 lieutenant, to the lowly sergeant currently manning communications.

"Copy that." Breaking off communication with command, Vaughn ordered his troops into action. "Shit!" Taking note of the surrounding country, Vaughn realized that he would have to break protocol and let his wife know the news of Davlin's loss, so she could help Becks when she found out that her husband was probably dead.

Chapter 9

If Tuesday was a bad day, Wednesday was surreal. The wives and local families of the missing soldiers were asked to come to the battalion command for briefing and information collection. Davlin's mother and father had arrived early in the morning. Heather, bless her soul, had called after confirming with Chaplain Needs that they had been notified of Davlin's MIA status. She arranged their flight from Lincoln to Atlanta and had gone and picked them up, arriving at my house in time for me to have a very awkward breakfast with my in-laws.

We arrived at the company together. Heather, acting as my support person, never left me alone with Allen and Sharon. The other families looked very similar to us. Middle-class Americans, folks who had to travel all night to receive bad news. Sergeant Pallen was engaged to a tall dark woman with light brown eyes. She was beautiful in her misery, not a hair cut of place.

Specialist Felden was a single soldier with an aged father. The man looked like he had had a hard life and had been a hard worker. He told us how proud he was when his son had enlisted. Mr. Felden had hung a yellow ribbon around the trees in his front yard and had hung his single star in the window of his home, praying for the day his son would come home to him.

Specialist Allen had an odd showing at the meeting—Eileen, a local prostitute who was about seven months pregnant. She said that she and specialist Allen had been married in the court just three days before deployment, but she hadn't had any idea how to get her identification or how to let anyone know they were married.

Private First Class Dougard was a high-school waste of space. He had graduated as an underachiever, never planning on doing much with his life. Dougard had found his niche in the army; with firm command and a definite goal, life made sense to him and he became a decent soldier. There was no family present for Private Dougard. The local chaplain had gone to his father's house to inform him of his son's status, and the man who answered the door simply thanked him for coming and shut the door.

Private Francs had been a fresh face out of high school as well. Francs was a self-motivated boy and a devoted Christian, as his family told the rest of the people present. He was the oldest of five sons and a motivation to all his brothers, boys who now sat with their parents waiting to hear from the colonel and the chaplain.

With the families and close friends of the six missing men accounted for and together in one place, Colonel Barring stepped to the front of the room and introduced himself to the group. Expressing his condolences, the colonel made everyone aware of the same story he had told me the day before in the hospital. We were told how the men were sent on a reconnaissance mission and that they entered a cave with no further communication. Troops were sent to evaluate the situation and determine if the recon team had come in contact with hostiles, which was undetermined, but there was no reason to think that the men were injured in any manner.

He didn't mention that Davlin had requested more assistance to search the caves. Colonel Barring was making my husband look like an idiot who rushed into a situation he could not control. Heather held my hand and squeezed every time she saw my eyebrow lift or a look of homicidal rage come over my face.

The meeting was less than an hour. Everyone was invited to stay locally at the expense of the military and told that the search area was being expanded and there were constant flyovers with unmanned vehicles searching for GPS signals from the secured phone that Davlin was carrying or any other indication to point toward their location. The missing soldiers were the top priority for the battalion and the command. If anyone had questions or needed help finding a place to stay, they were asked to please see Sergeant Martin. The briefing was nice and neat and full of enough bullshit that I felt dirty leaving the room.

Everyone left their local contact information to ensure quick notifications. The families left tearful and heartbroken; everyone had hoped for more information than what they had been told the day before.

Heather and I went back to my house. Davlin's parents refused to stay with me, citing my need to mourn in private. Personally, I didn't feel a need to mourn; Davlin was lost, not dead. Allen seemed unwilling to accept any information, saying he knew this would happen, that his son would die in the military and it was all my fault." Sharon looked like she had been living in a bottle since hearing about Davlin the day before; she smelled like a still and seriously needed a good night's rest. Allen mentioned something about valium—I tried to warn him that alcohol and sedatives were a bad idea, but whatever I said fell on deaf ears.

All I wanted to do was lie in the bed my husband and I shared, smelling his pillow. Curled up and wearing his old pajama pants and a nearly see-through Roosevelt High Football tee shirt, I had just stopped crying when the phone rang. Heather answered before I had summoned the strength to move. I heard her side of the conversation and almost flew out of the bed when she mentioned the hospital. I was already on the stairs when she hung up the phone, heading up the stairs to my bedroom.

Nearly colliding at the base of the stairs, I asked her, "Did they find Davlin? Is he in the hospital?"

"No, sis, that wasn't Eric or anyone else from the command. It was Allen. He had to call 911. Sharon took the valium with a bottle of vodka and stopped breathing. They are at the emergency department right now. Allen was asking for you to come down."

Heartbroken, I let out my breath. I didn't realize I had been holding my breath until it left my body along with my strength. I fell to the floor like the flimsy balloon I seemed to be in that moment. Deflated and crushed, I wasn't able to tell Heather that I didn't care if Sharon lived or died. Horrible though it may sound, I had disliked her as much as she disliked me. I thought she was being selfish the way she had given up on her son.

59

"I can't, Heather." I tried to find the words that would explain to my best friend my total ambivalence toward my in-laws. "I can't help them right now......I—"

"It's okay, sweetie; I'm blonde but not stupid. I know you don't get along with them. Who the hell tries to overdose when their child is missing?... I mean he's not dead! Right?!"

I had never loved Heather more in all the time I had known her. Pregnancy had forced a growth in her, perhaps given her knowledge and understanding I hadn't seen in her up until that day.

"I'll go. I'm sure Curtis or Mirkes is working tonight. I'll explain what's going on. The girls will take care of everything." Heather was headed toward the front door ready to go outside when I grabbed her and hugged her.

"Heather, I don't know what I would do if you weren't here." I had begun to cry again, this time due to the compassion of my friend.

Hugging me back, she told me, "Becks, I know you would do the same for me. You've been my support through my pregnancy." She placed her hands over her growing abdomen and gently rubbed the smooth roundness. "Eric told me how you lost your baby..." She looked up shyly through her bangs, trying to judge my level of betrayal.

I didn't feel betrayed though, just relieved that she knew. "Yeah, I don't want to ruin your time. We can talk about that later." I couldn't think about my baby boy right now. My heart and brain had to focus on one tragedy at a time, and I didn't have time to move backward.

"I'm going to go to the hospital and do what I can there. Eric is supposed to call tonight at eight, so I'll be back before then. Do you want me to get something to eat?"

Heather was infinitely full of surprises. Her brain seemed to be able to process needs faster than my own body was aware of the necessity. "Ah, no. Eric is calling? What all has he told you? Does he have more information? When was the last time you talked to him?"

Word vomit flew from my mouth as my friend was backing toward the door.

Giving answers as quickly as I had asked, she replied, "Only the one time; I don't know if he found out any more; that's why he's calling; yesterday, when you were sleeping; and are you sure? I haven't seen you eat in the last two days. You're going to pass out. I'll get us both something, but I have to go. Go take a bath; you'll feel better." Without another word Heather flew out the door, letting it slam behind her.

I slowly gathered my senses and headed back up the stairs. A bath did sound good.

As I sat on the closed toilet, watching the hot water gain depth in the porcelain tub, I became transfixed by the steam, the swirling of the mist as it filled the small bathroom; I became aware again when the water began to make a new noise, that of water spilling over onto tile.

"Shit!" Grabbing a towel, I turned off the tap, pulled the plug, and allowed the water to reach a sensible level before re-stopping the flow. Removing Davlin's shirt and placing it safely on the vanity, I climbed into the bath, sliding into the water until my body was engulfed by its warmth up to my chin.

Thinking of everything that had happened in the past twenty-four hours, I was overwhelmed by my complete lack of action. What had I done in the time since I had heard that my husband was MIA? Really, was there anything I could do? I hadn't asked that question of anyone. Too focused on the fact that Davlin was missing, I hadn't had the presence of mind to ask my resources if they could help me get any information.

How far would I go to try to find my husband? Do I leave this in the hands of the military, depend on them to find him? How truthful would they be with me, or how much information would they be able to share with me?

A million questions and scenarios boggled my mind as I sat in the cooling water. Then, pushing it all aside, I conjured up Davlin's face. The face I had known since I was nine years old.

I pictured him at nine. The first day I had met him as he came upon me with my stolen loot. As a child Davlin had had light brown hair with streaks of blond from the hours he spent out in the sun. Like any kid who had two working parents, he didn't bathe as often or as well as a kid should, so he had dirt on his face from a playful afternoon at a pig sty. His nose was sunburned and peeling at the tip. He had a splash of freckles across his cheeks and the bridge of his nose, and the most beautiful brown eyes hidden behind a thick layer of lashes.

Davlin was scrawny in his childhood, yet he held the promise of becoming a breathtaking man. Even at nine he had broad shoulders and a slight waist. His arms were thin, but his legs were straight and strong.

By middle school, when he began to officially participate in team sports, his height had topped five and a half feet, his muscles were beginning to be more than just sinew on his bones, and his childhood freckles had faded to invisibility. By eighth grade Davlin was proving himself in both football and swimming, baseball was like breathing, and running was the only way he moved. Everyone in our town knew who Davlin was, either from his participation in sports or from the mischief he got into with me.

More times than I could recall, he had snuck over to my trailer in the middle of the night to lean against my bedroom door to provide resistance against any of my mother's suitors from coming to visit me. On countless occasions he had snuck food from his dinner table to his bedroom to feed me when my mom was on one of her benders, trading our food stamps for alcohol or drugs. All of our childhood was spent with each other from the time we met.

But although Davlin was amazing in sports, he was never much of a student. I helped him in school just as he helped me stay safe from my mother's boyfriends. During the winter when it was too cold to go outside for long periods of time, we would spend our time in his family's dining room under the watchful eye of one of his parents. Sharon would begrudgingly provide a snack, seeing as I was helping Davlin with his homework. Both his parents were very unwilling to accept that I had something to offer Davlin.

By time we had begun our sophomore year at Roosevelt High School, Davlin had a very steady following of beautiful young girls more than willing to provide him with oral stress relief. I had no claim to him, but the girls who tried to go steady with Davlin knew they were risking a broken nose if any whisper of rumor about Davlin reached my ears. Even when he was "dating" one of the blonde idiots, he would spend no less time with me. Our number in his dining room simply increased by one for a week or two; then as the girls realized that Davlin wasn't interested in their tits or ass, they left to roam the halls for someone else.

By the time I had told him my true feelings, before the whole fight with Caleb McMahon, Davlin had kissed his fair share of girls. He blushed when he told me about the first girl that jerked him off. We were best friends up until I heard him say my name in his attic room. That one night almost ruined my life.

When he came to my house in July to wish me happy birthday, just a week after I had gone to his house to do the same, I was so hopeful he had forgiven me for spilling my heart out to him. He was quiet and mechanical in the presence of my mother and her current boyfriend.

I had few true friends other than Davlin and had fallen into a funk after our fight. I was elated to see him walk up to the yard where we were having a barbecue to celebrate my eighteenth birthday. Mom had put forth an effort to make it a celebration by blowing up balloons and taping them to the carport and running a streamer roll through the metal uprights. Festive though it was, I wanted nothing more than to run away to Florida and become a drugged up go-go dancer. I missed my best friend.

When he walked up to the party, my mom jumped out of her seat and gave Davlin a hug. "Hey handsome, glad you could come to see my girl. Where have you been? She's been moping around; could have sworn you two couldn't be away from each other as long as you have."

With her natural lack to grasp the obvious, Mom rattled on to Davlin about my new anguish. According to her, I was being selfish with my time and should "snap out of whatever is wrong with me." 'Cause, hell, she had gone to all this trouble for me.

Davlin did stay, and I did "snap out of it" for a while. We laughed about a movie we had both been to see at the drive-in, though not together, like we used to. He told me about the old jeep his father had given him as a combination eighteenth birthday /congrats gift for receiving his scholarship to Nebraska. He ate charcoal-burned hot dogs and chips with baked beans as a side and sang a very out-of-tune "Happy Birthday" along with my mom and her beau. After the cake, Mom and her man left for the bar and Davlin became a little more like the friend I remembered.

We totally avoided the elephant in the room, talking about his football practice and what classes we had together our last year. He tried not to look at me, and I blushed each time we did make eye contact.

After several very long and uncomfortable silences, he announced that he had to go, that his mother expected him home.

"Becks," he explained, "I can't get it out of my head that you and I feel the same way, but we can't be what you want. I can't be your everything. You need to be with someone that can handle your shit."

"What the hell are you talking about? My shit?" Angry at his assessment of my life, I lashed at him. "Who the hell are you? You're the one beating off to a thought of your best friend, you fucking perv!" I knew I had taken a low blow, but fighting dirty seemed to be what he had wanted.

My life since puberty and my development of breasts had been a damn clown car of men trying to have some form of sex with me, and Davlin had always been there to make sure I wasn't taken advantage of, to make sure I didn't regret waking up in the morning. Many a night he had spent sober at a football victory party, while I was drunk off my ass, being a happy naked drunk.

"Becks, don't make me be mean…"

64

"Too late! Davlin, I don't understand your damn boy brain, but let me get one thing through that football helmet of a head of yours… I love you!!!! And I am not talking about some fucking puppy love; I have loved you forever, in every sense of the word. And I get it, you definitely do not feel the same for me. I only have to suffer one more year, seeing your face in class and in the halls. We don't have a reason to see each other outside of school, so…. Please go away."

Tears burned my cheeks, and I certainly felt like I couldn't breathe. All I wanted to do was to reach my hand out and place it on his chest to feel his heartbeat. How many times had I seen him sneak a kiss to a girl who wasn't me? When I did, I had gone home to wish that someday it would be me. I wanted so much to have him place his hand along the side of my cheek and guide my lips to his. I wanted to feel the softness that I knew his lips possessed, and to know the taste of his mouth… And wanting was what I was left with that day.

Davlin didn't say anything else to me, he simply walked across the street to a red jeep soft top, got in, and drove away without looking at me. I didn't see him again until the hospital.

I came out of my reverie chilled from the now cold water and cold room surrounding me. The daylight that had lighted the bathroom window when I climbed in the bath had faded to darkness, and I was in near blackness now in my befuddled state of mind. I had a difficult time making my chilled muscles work, but I finally pulled myself out of the tub and wrapped the bath towel around my torso. Even colder now that the air near the window kissed my wet skin, I stood and grabbed Davlin's house robe from the hook on the back of the bathroom door. Pulling the robe onto my chilled body, I trudged stiffly to our bedroom and burrowed into the cold sheets.

Heather arrived later than she had planned, carrying a cold lasagna. She rushed through the front door as I sat in the kitchen having decided that food would be necessary, and the kitchen

65

seemed to be the only room in the house that had a functioning heating vent.

"So, how's tricks?" I joked lamely.

As she placed the food in the microwave, Heather responded, "First of all, your mother-in-law is crazy. That bitch is certifiable, but she's going to live. Apparently, she 'just wanted to sleep,' at least that's what she told the psychiatrist, who didn't buy it and is placing her in observation for a couple days. Allen went back to the hotel after he knew Sharon wasn't going to die. They are just weird."

Snorting, I replied, "You're not telling me anything I haven't known for years, sister," I joked with her. The release of the tension she had tried for worked, and we were both more relaxed as she pulled our rewarmed lasagna out of the microwave.

Putting a plate in front of me, she continued, "Eric called me. No! Don't interrupt me," she warned. "They found Private Francs." She paused to judge how I would take the news. "They don't expect him to live, Becks. He wasn't able to give any details, but Eric said they were still piecing together what they think happened."

I sat stone faced, food forgotten. "Why do they think he won't live?" I inquired.

"He was shot in the head; the bullet is still there, and apparently he was shot a couple days ago. It's causing an infection. Eric really didn't give me too many details…. But he did say he was personally going to look for Davlin." Heather looked scared at the thought of her husband going into danger but was resolved to not mention it right now. She unconsciously rubbed her belly.

"Holy shit." I couldn't think of anything cleverer to say. But in my brain and in my heart, I was hopeful.

If Davlin was dead, I would know it. We were like twins that felt pinpricks across a hundred miles. How could true lovers not know if something bad happened to the other? As crazy a sense of humor as God seemed to have, I didn't think even He would entertain such a sick joke. No, I knew Davlin was alive. He would be found, he would be complete…he would come home to me.

Chapter 10

One month after Davlin was listed as missing in action, I was still making daily trips to the battalion headquarters to find out if there was any new information. Each day I received the same answer, and each night when Eric would call to speak to Heather, his answer was the same also, "Nothing new today, Becks. We'll keep looking for them. I promise.

Three days after the battalion meeting with the families, everyone was returned to their homes with the exception of Private Francs's family; they had been taken to Washington, DC, to see Francs when he arrived at Walter Reed Medical Center. Francs was doing surprisingly well for a person with a bullet in his brain. He was able to talk and see, but his memory was impaired and he was prone to fits of anger.

Davlin's parents continued to fare rather poorly. Allen returned to Guernsey without Sharon, who was undergoing evaluation for her suicide attempt. Her actions and Allen's inaction made me wonder how Davlin would feel when he found out about their childish behavior.

Back in Guernsey, families tied yellow ribbons around trees in their front yards, and the high school hung an MIA flag, as did the fire department and police department. The local newspaper ran articles about Davlin when he was in high school, and they called to get information on what happened between graduation and his commission.

Everyone took active parts in supporting the troops. Locally, the VFW was able to collect more donations to support families of wounded and killed soldiers than in the charter history. The support continued as long as there were articles in the newspaper reminding people that Davlin was missing, or other stories about local men and women in service. But people forgot, they moved on with the next season of football and baseball, kids had birthdays, the schools had their dances and homecomings. People moved on with their lives.

A month after he was listed as missing in action, during one of my weekly checks on the families of the missing men, I was told that Private Dougard's father had been found dead in his home. A suicide note was left behind. While speaking to Dougard's aunt, I was painted a picture of a very violent upbringing for the private. I hoped that he would be able to find some good in life when he returned home.

I was having weekly conversations with Eric Vaughn as well, trying to glean some information about what was being done to find Davlin and the others. To me it seemed that Eric was beginning to get tired of speaking to me about my husband, a theory that was confirmed three months after Davlin had gone missing…

"So, Eric, have there been any videos or any form of communication with the men who have Davlin or the other boys?" I asked eagerly into the phone Heather had just handed me.

"Ah, no. Becks, we never found anything to suggest that Davlin and the others were ever taken as prisoners. We are working pretty closely with the locals here, and they haven't heard anything about imprisoned American soldiers. We are doing the best we can, but we still have a mission to complete too. You may have to consider…"

"What? Eric? Consider what? That the US Army can't find their missing men? That they are not doing everything in their power to find him? That's what I think!" I was near tears. The thought that Davlin was being left behind, that no one was looking for him, was overwhelming.

I shoved the phone back at Heather and I stormed out of her house and toward mine. Walking the blocks back home, I was unable to appreciate the beautiful spring morning blooming around me; I was only focused on the rage at the people responsible for my husband being missing…but I had no face to focus on, no name to give them.

With tears streaming down my face, I slowed my pace and breathing, "Please God, let him be safe. I know he's alive, just let him be safe, let me know…." A horn honked behind me, pulling me back from my communication with a deity I had never believed in. I rushed across the street and up to the empty house I dreaded to drink myself to sleep.

By the time Heather had her baby son, five months had crept by. Five months of nothing, neither good nor bad news, about my husband. So, when baby Jobe was born I focused what joy I could muster on him. With his fat rosy cheeks and chunky thighs, everyone fell in love with the him immediately.

Eric had been given leave to come see his wife and son, so the day Jobe was born, Heather had the both of us present. Eric was ecstatic when his son arrived, holding the little boy so close he began to suckle his father's nose. Heather was glowing and beautiful, if not a little swollen from her pregnancy.

"Becks, thank you for being here for me," she said, her voice thick with affection. She reached for the baby, putting him to her breast. Eric sat at the side of her bed, leaning over to kiss the velvety soft head of his son, then his wife in turn. He turned to say something to me; then, seeing the look on my face, he got Heather's attention. "Becks, are you okay?"

My head snapped up; an unformed thought disappeared from my mind. I had been thinking about my baby, or the man who had fathered him, I wasn't sure; but the effect was a look of mixed hatred and loss, not an expression that belonged in the birthing room of your best friend.

"Sorry, Heather, I was...somewhere else."

There was an awkward silence, the only noise was the suckling of the baby at his mother's breast. Tears came to my eyes as I saw the concern on Heather's face and the anger on Eric's.

"So, do you need a ride home, Becks?" Eric asked suddenly, dismissing me from their happy presence.

"Eric, Becks is here for me. She's been my support person through all of the pregnancy; you can't kick her out," Heather pleaded.

"Heather, this is our time," Eric said with an air of authority. "Becks, you can come and visit after she comes home from DC. We are going to see her parents. I'm sure Heather will be happy to have

69

you come see her later." Eric was guiding me to the door. "Becks, this is my family." With steel in his voice, Eric gave an unnecessary warning glance and shut the door on my face.

I didn't get to see her or baby Jobe before they left or when they returned. Heather stayed in DC with her mother for an extended vacation after Eric returned to Afghanistan. She would call and email pictures of the baby, but I missed her dearly. I missed my giggly friend and the conversations we had that distracted me.

With Heather gone, I had nothing to fill my time. I had not been able to return to work since Davlin had gone missing, I didn't bother to exercise or maintain myself in any other way; hell, I hadn't shaved my legs in weeks. I hadn't done many things in weeks, including shopping for food. I mostly visited the Class Six for alcohol, preferring to drink my calories.

I spent the majority of my days in a state of drunken misery. The alcohol fueled my depression. I lay around in Davlin's clothes, clutching his pillow or wearing his robe. The bedside tables in our room were littered with empty liquor bottles and framed pictures of Davlin and me. I had no strength to fight my depression and no will to do anything about it. The highlight of each week was when I would go to the battalion to hear the latest report on whether my husband had been found.

Heather would be ashamed of me, and so would Davlin. I was feeling sorry for myself. Realizing it as I lay on the couch, eye to eye with a layer of dust so thick I could have balled it up in my hands and realizing that I needed to do something, I went upstairs, took a quick shower, and dressed in some jeans and a shirt that no longer fit with my steady weight loss.

I headed to the base exchange and gathered cleaning supplies, a new bucket and mop, and some light bulbs to replace the multitude of lights that had burned out in the house. After the exchange, I headed to the commissary to buy food. I hadn't shopped for food in so long, I had to restock on canned goods and meat. When I was done shopping, I headed home with a trunk full of bags and what-nots.

Once home, I put my fresh groceries away. The simple act of doing something so human was cathartic. I organized the cabinets. Feeling slightly compulsive, I ensured all the cans were facing forward. After the food was in place; a beautiful basket of fruit centered on the table; a steak marinating in the fridge; a potato washed, salted, and wrapped in foil; and a bottle of red wine chilling in the fridge; I grabbed the bag of light bulbs to replace the mass outage in my house.

The light in the hall was out, and having no ladder to change it, I was resolved to leave well enough alone. Moving on to the bedroom, I was met with a strobe of red light blinking from the answering machine that sat next to my bed. Pressing the play button, I was surprised to hear the voice of my sister-in-law Rachel. It was time for me to go home to Guernsey; my mother-in-law, Sharon, had killed herself.

Davlin's mother Sharon had not been able to cope with the loss of her son. Seemingly from the moment she was made aware that he was missing, she had become a drunk. Her misery deepened as time ticked past with no word of Davlin's fate and she became more depressed. Her first true attempt to kill herself had been the pills and alcohol she had mixed while she and Allen had been at Fort Benning for the family briefing on our missing soldiers. She had been hospitalized for two weeks then, detoxified of alcohol, and started on a regimen of medications and counseling. Better able to deal with her fears of losing her son, she had returned to Guernsey.

The return was the mistake that had begun her downward spiral. Never being much by way of support, Allen ignored all of her symptoms, playing them off as Sharon being a "woman." Being stuck in the home she had raised Davlin in, she was constantly reminded of the hole that now consumed her world. Whereas I had avoided speaking to my mother during our college days and since, Davlin had spoken with his mother on a weekly basis and had promised to do so while he was deployed.

71

Davlin's sister, Rachel, was no help. She had married out of high school, divorced within a year, and now had four children by three men. Rachel stayed away from her family when she could, coming around only when she needed someone to watch the kids or when she needed money.

Sharon was trapped in an old house with no hope, so she started drinking again and didn't stop taking her pills. Within a month of returning home, she had been found with her wrist slit as she lay in a bathtub. She had cut the wrong direction and fortunately had also cut a tendon, making it impossible for her to hold the knife in her other hand to cut the opposite wrist. She was hospitalized and committed to a psychiatric facility for another two-week period.

Established with a local grief counselor, Sharon was released on new medications and a new, dangerous education. She plotted her next attempt with precision. Stocking up on medications, she waited until Allen had gone to work; then, taking a month's supply of anti-anxiety pills, she lay in bed, a note seeking forgiveness pinned to her shirt.

This plan probably would have worked very well had Allen not spilled coffee down the front of his shirt when a dog ran out in front of his car. Returning home to change, he arrived just as Sharon had finished pinning the letter to her shirt. He walked into the bedroom to find his wife posed on their bed as though she were already in her coffin.

"What the fuck, Sharon? Again?" Allen yelled. He grabbed the phone, made the operator aware of what his wife had done, and then, having changed his shirt, left the house to go to work.

Her third stay at the psych facility was longer and more educational for her. Sharon was learning the ins and outs of manipulation. She was also made aware that she had type 2 diabetes that would require insulin for the rest of her life. Sharon was made aware of the disease process and the medications she would need to take; she was taught to take her own blood sugar and how to administer her own insulin injections.

After a month in the psychiatric facility, Sharon, Allen, and Rachel began family grief counseling, which Allen sat through, Rachel never showed up to, and Sharon cried through. The counselor had planned to see them once weekly as a family and three times weekly for Sharon.

For a month she had been attending her counseling, had weaned off of several medications, and was no longer requiring the assistance of medications to sleep at night, and she was losing weight. Her diabetes was under control with diet and exercise, so much so, that she needed very little insulin.

So, it was July, the month of Davlin's birthday, seven months after his being listed MIA, when Sharon was successful in her plan. It was a Saturday. Allen was downstairs in the living room watching television, and Sharon had made him lunch that they had eaten together. Their marriage had been better than it had in months, in full part to Sharon putting forth the effort. With no objection from Allen, she told him she was going to take a nap, feigning a headache.

Once up in her room, Sharon again pinned her good-bye letter to her shirt. Then, with three vials of Regular insulin, she began to inject herself with 100 units of insulin at a time. When she was found, two full bottles remained on the bedside table; the third bottle was nearly empty. The paramedic who responded to the call said she would have become unconscious once her sugar reached the twenties or teens. She had injected herself with enough insulin to drive all the sugar in her body into cells. With no sugar for use, she became comatose and then died quietly, with no one knowing what she had done.

I flew into Lincoln, rented a car, and drove the two and a half hours to Guernsey, arriving just as the sun was rising on the plains. I had traveled quickly, booking an emergency flight and leaving an open-ended ticket for my return. I had left no word with anyone back in Georgia, and I hadn't been able to reach Heather before leaving, so I had no one in Guernsey to lean on, no one except my mother.

73

Chapter 11

"You can never go home again." Thomas Wolfe was credited with saying that quote, and man, was he right. Not only had Guernsey grown, adding a Starbucks, McDonalds, a Travel Stop truck stop, and a Red Roof Inn all at the exit leading into town, the additions had caused closures on Main Street.

There were two new housing developments on the way into town and a new school as well. Trees had grown or been cut down, changing my memories of the streets I had roamed in my childhood. But it was more than the environmental changes of Guernsey that I was noting, it was also the people and myself. The Becks who now drove toward her childhood home was no longer the angry, defensive teen who had left years before; I too had changed and grown.

I opted to go see my mother at her trailer, to see if I could stay with her. Arriving at the trailer, I found more changes. She had planted a garden out front and had had the lattice that surrounded the trailer replaced as well. The trailer looked better cared for—I hoped my mother looked that way as well.

Parking across the street, I stepped out into the morning heat of a Nebraska summer. I went to the porch, contemplating waiting until seven to knock, when I heard coughing inside and someone shuffling around just beyond the door. I went ahead and knocked. The door was answered by my mother, a frail, aged, and obviously sick version of my mother.

"Becks, baby, I didn't know you were coming. Sweetie, come in." The slight woman in front of me moved aside, giving me access to the living room.

I stood staring at the woman who had taught me more by way of what not to do with my life than what to do. The woman who more times than not had missed my important days; the woman who sat by my side in the hospital, brushing my hair and washing my face when I had lost my baby; the woman who had never asked me for anything in my adult life. She had changed so much I didn't recognize this person who now stood in front of me.

"Mom?" Tears filled my eyes, and emotions made my voice thick. "Mom, what happened? Why didn't you call me and tell me you're sick? I would have been here a long time ago."

"Honey, I'm not sick really, I was diagnosed with lung cancer a couple months ago. I couldn't tell you then, Davlin had just…. We had just heard about Davlin. You need to focus on him, on praying for your husband so he can get back to you." She reached up and wiped away a tear that had fallen to my cheek.

I pulled her to my chest and cried into her thinning hair. Hair that had once been curly and thick was now gray and dull, dry and brittle. Her skin hung from her arms and face. I could feel the ribs of her chest and little else. The voluptuous woman who had once been the talk of the town was now wasting away, a victim of her vigorous youth.

"Don't cry, baby, I'm doing everything my doctor tells me to do. He says I'm doing well with my medicines and that I don't have any mega cysts."

"Any what?" I asked, confused.

"You know, you're a nurse. The cancer hasn't moved around anywhere. It's just in my lungs, and tits."

"Metastasis? What stage did the doctor say your cancer is?"

"Baby, you're not leaving right after the funeral, are you? You can stay for a while?" she asked, moving to the kitchen to put water into a dusty coffeepot. Continuing to try to distract my line of conversation away from her poor health, she requested, "Let's not talk about cancer right now. Let's talk about you. How are you doing? Have you heard anything about Davlin?"

Not distracted by her tact but agreeing that one bad item at a time was enough to keep me depressed, I answered, "No, Mom. Eric Vaughn was back on leave a while ago. He told me everything is being done to find Davlin. Mom, what doctor are you seeing?" Sitting across the counter from her, watching as she poured the coffee, I could see how my mother had all but disappeared.

75

The counter was lined with bottles of prescriptions, both liquids and pills. There were vitamins and herbals all neatly lined up according to the time of day she had to take them. I watched her fill her daily pill divider, each cubby filling with a rainbow of pills and capsules.

"With this much going in my stomach, I don't have much room left for food," she joked weakly. "Have you gone to see Allen and Rachel yet?"

Again, not falling for her ploy but accepting her desire to not talk about her diagnosis, I answered her truthfully. "Ah, no, I just got in town." I had a nearly crippling feeling of remorse and anger. I should have come home to see my mother, should have made the time to come visit, just as she had for me when I was in the hospital. I was a selfish person, and now the only person who I knew shared my blood was going to die.

I tried not to focus on her wasted appearance and shaking hands; instead, I changed the subject again.

"When did they build all that shit by the highway?"

"Oh hell, that whole mess of crap. Not a good thing to eat in all that mess. When that Starbucks opened, Craven's deli closed down. Craven's had some good food. The best homemade soup I ever tasted, and the whole place got closed by one expensive cafe."

"Wow, Craven's closed!" Nostalgia washed over me at the mention of the old downtown eatery. "Damn, Davlin and I had our prom dinner there."

That night, Davlin and I were just trying to make a memory, enjoy a good burger, and be together. The angry looks and whispers behind napkins were beginning to wear on my nerves, and I was warring inside over whether to cry or scream at the people of our town who disapproved of Davlin and I. Davlin was angry too; his neck had slowly been turning red.

We were going to leave without having our food when Mr. Gliddens and his wife came over and asked to join us at our table. Of all the people who were in Craven's Diner that night, the people who accepted us and looked at us now for the young lovers we were,

were the elderly couples. Men and women who had been married long enough to know that love is more than just a physical link. They were men and women who had survived separations due to war and famine, couples who had seen a life of change in the years of their marriages; changes in values and what made a family, changes in the balance of work and power in the family.

One such couple was Mr. and Mrs. Gliddens. Mr. Gliddens was a retired teacher, a man whom Davlin respected highly. In addition to being a teacher, Mr. Gliddens had been in the Army during WWII, he landed on Normandy on D-Day, and had served in active combat until three days before V-Day. Mr. Gliddens was injured by a fellow soldier when he tried to stop a fight. Mr. and Mrs. Gliddens met in a hospital where she was his nurse.

On the night of our prom, Mr. Gliddens saw some of the looks we were receiving; then, overhearing the whispered bits of disapproval, he came to our table and asked Davlin and me if he and his wife could join us. We gladly accepted their offer and made room for them at our table. They asked us about our plans after high school and where we were going to college; Mister Gliddens voiced his approval of Davlin's plans to pursue a history degree. They enquired about how we had met and told us stories of their youth as well.

By time we left the diner, the rude glances and sniggers behind our backs had stopped. That dinner on our prom night had given credit to our relationship and had formed new friendships for both Davlin and me. That night we had met the man and woman who had helped mentor us in our careers and counseled us in our marriage while we were in school.

In the tradition of prom, we had gone to the school and had our picture taken in front of the cardboard cutout that had been painted to look like a comet. The prom theme was "Under the Stars," so thousands of tiny white Christmas lights were strung in the rafters. There were super-sized balloons that made up the planets of the solar system, and more cardboard comets strewn around the gymnasium.

77

We danced to bad covers of popular songs. He held me close so my head rested at his heart while we danced. After the prom was over, Davlin and I went to the school-sponsored, drug- and alcohol-free after-prom party, themed to be a Vegas casino. We gambled our Monopoly money away, chatted with various groups of friends, and then, when we were sure enough people had seen us there, we slipped out the side door of the community center.

Davlin drove us out of town to a small lake, a little thing that was stocked with fish each year. It was off the beaten path and dark, with few passes made by law enforcement; it was an amazing place to make out. It being prom night, no one was there. Davlin was prepared for our personal after-prom party and had come equipped with sleeping bags and a cooler of iced Coca Cola.

Forgetting the earlier parts of the evening, Davlin was concerned with only one thing—me. He unzipped my dress to help me out of it and into the sleeping bags. Taking off his shirt and pants, he slid in beside me.

With my head resting on his arm, we looked up at the night sky, admiring the multitude of stars overhead. On the night of our senior prom, there was a meteor shower. I lay watching the falling stars as long as I could focus. Davlin wasted no time watching the stars and slid into the depths of the sleeping bag, his hands sliding the length of my torso, exploring as he went.

Up to this night he had never tried to satisfy me with his tongue, but that night he made me see stars in the most literal of all meanings. I had no idea what to expect, but when his tongue began to taste and lathe, he caused pulses of pleasure to move down my legs and up into my stomach. Within moments I was gasping for breath, begging him to stop; to my great pleasure, he did not.

We spent the night making love. Claiming each other and easing away from the missionary poses we had too often lain in. He would tower over me as he drove into me or grasp my hips as he took me from behind. I found the pleasure of control when I climbed on top of him, controlling the pace at which we moved. Up till that night, I had never climaxed with him, always after or not at all, but this night, Davlin seemed intent on our sharing the entire experience.

Davlin and I made love that night under the falling stars, content in our relationship and planning for our future. We dozed off and awoke just before dawn, dressing silently, gathering up our belongings, and ending the first night we had been able to sleep together as a couple. The first of many to come.

I was looking at the framed picture of our prom night, now hanging in the living room of my mother's trailer, next to the framed Polaroid of our wedding day.

"God, Becks. You and Davlin were an unconventional couple, but you sure were happy together." Mom had come to join me as I was looking at the cluster of photos on the wall.

"And we will be again when he comes home," I declared with a bit of venom in my voice.

"You don't believe that, do you? You don't believe that after all this time he is still alive and no one wants you to know? That the terrorists don't want to make everyone aware that they have some Americans in captivity? Becks, you are going to be heartbroken at some point."

I was resigned to not fight with my very ill and frail mother. I begged her, "Mom, please, don't. It is too much." I paused and softened my tone, asking, "Do you want to come with me to see Davlin's family?"

"Why don't you sleep for a while, honey? It's still early, and you look exhausted."

"I am. I can't sleep on planes. Is it alright then that I stay here?"

"Of course, baby, this is your home too. I just finished redecorating your room. It has been empty since you left after high school—what, six, no seven years ago!" She started walking me toward my room that was at the front of the trailer.

"Wow, it doesn't seem like it has been that long," I sighed, looking around the house and again taking in the changes, both in my mom and in the physical building. "I should have come home more often. Mom, I'm sorry. I do miss you."

79

"Honey, I know you miss me, and I know you have your life. You and Davlin did not belong here. People in this town never accepted you." She pulled me toward her, kissed my cheek, then released me. She had a look of pride on her face that brought new tears to my eyes. "I knew you would leave, and I'm happy for you, for the joy you found in each other. Go get some sleep now. I'll wake you up at noon; we can go pay our respects to Allen and Rachel."

I went out to my rental car to grab my bags, amazed by the competent woman my mother had become. I returned to the trailer and to my childhood bedroom. The room did not resemble the room I had spent my early life in. Mom had been busy painting and refinishing the headboard and bedside table. She had bought a new bedspread, white with violets. The overall effect was a feminine room with soft light. It was pleasant to be in, and with the new mattress Mom had purchased, the bed was comfortable to sleep in as well.

I slept until noon, when Mom woke me with a fresh cup of coffee. She had been getting ready to leave the house and had dressed in a flower print dress with a cream cardigan draped over her shoulders. She had applied makeup to make her sallow features brighter. The piece that made me choke back tears was the wig she was wearing to cover her head.

"You look beautiful, Mom." I felt ashamed of myself. I hadn't seen my mother in the time since I had lost the baby. Now, my mother was a wisp of the woman she had once been, and I feared my selfishness had stolen time away from us.

"You don't think the hair is too much? I haven't had the heart to wear it yet," she confessed.

"You look wonderful, Mom; the wig is good," I admitted.

"Well, get up, let's get this stuff done. Do you need me to iron your outfit?"

"Who are you and what have you done with my mother? My mom doesn't own an iron!" I was joking with her, and she was enjoying the banter. She sat on the bed while I got dressed, talking about nothing in particular. She sucked in her breath when she saw how skinny I had become.

"Becks, aren't you eating? You're skin and bones."

"Truthfully, no Mom, I don't eat that much, or at least, I haven't been. I've spent quite a bit of time drinking. Mom," I turned to look at her, seeking her assistance in zipping up my dress as well as getting her full attention. "Mom, I don't know how to live without Davlin. I feel like I just learned how to breathe again." With new tears in my eyes, I fell into her outstretched arms.

"Baby, we will get you through this." She kissed my head and set me straight. "Wherever Davlin is, he doesn't have to go to his mother's funeral; we do. Let's get ourselves together." She sat me on the bed and pulled my hair back in a French twist. Again, I was wondering where this woman had come from.

Once properly dressed and with a homemade meatloaf in her hands, Mom and I were on our way to Davlin's house. "You cooked? Since when do you cook?" I teased, passing the food to her after she slowly sat down in the car.

"Oh, baby. Once I got clean from all the drugs, and stopped saturating my liver in alcohol, and figured out that the clown car of men in my life had only been using me for sex…and it was not that good…well, after you went to college and were doing so well, I wanted to make you proud. I started to take classes at the community center in Allington. It fills my time. That's how I learned to cook and paint and sew."

I smiled at my mother, for as miserable as the situation was, she was being a very wonderful source of distraction. The woman who now sat next to me was not the woman she once was. I was rather enjoying the new mom.

We arrived at the Robertson's house, found a place to park, and went up the stairs to the front door. Before I had even lifted my arm to knock, the front door was opened by Rachel, Davlin's sister.

"Oh, Becks. I was so glad when you said you were coming. I can't do all this by myself. Dad has been drunk since Mom was

81

found, and she hadn't made any preparations." Rachel was obviously overwhelmed.

"Well, what needs to be done?" She opened the door to allow my mother and me in. With two trips to Miller's Funeral Home, one trip to the bank, and one trip to the cemetery, Sharon's funeral was arranged, her final resting place was arranged, and a headstone was to be made.

By six in the evening, friends of the family had begun to arrive. Allen was showered, in a clean shirt, and outfitted with a glass of whiskey. Rachel was functioning as a mother if nothing else, keeping her spawn from tearing the house down. My mother, as part of her new norm, had been cooking while I had been arranging Sharon's funeral. She had also bathed Rachel's kids, dressed them, fed them, and given them a dose of grandmotherly fear of God, to ensure their good behavior.

Once back at the house, I was greeted with various levels of compassion and friendship from my in-laws. Allen was too drunk to acknowledge my presence; Rachel and I had been talking through the day, so by this point, she and I were comfortable. Sharon had a sister who had arrived during our errands arranging the funeral.

Barbara was Sharon's oldest sister, the eldest of three children. She was never a person who had approved of Davlin and me. When Sharon had called her to tell her of our elopement, Barbara had come to Guernsey to yell at the both of us. She was sorely disappointed when Davlin merely took my hand and walked the both of us away from her barrage of profanity and anger, leaving his aunt to yell at his mother for her lack of action in stopping us from getting married.

On this day, Barbara was smaller. She didn't appear as the woman who had stoked fear in my soul. She was pale of face with eyes red-rimmed from crying and a nose red from wiping. When Rachel and I entered the living room with a plate of food for Allen, she stood, taking Rachel in her arms. The women cried on each other; then Barbara saw me standing beside Allen, encouraging him to eat.

"Becks," she sneered, "has the army heard any good news about my nephew? I always thought it a bad idea for him to enlist. You just had to force him into it, having that bastard baby! No wonder God took it from you!" She was yelling and crying, spittle flying from her mouth as she yelled.

Of the emotional trigger points I possess, she had pressed every one! I was getting ready to respond to the accusations she had thrown at me when I saw my mother standing in the doorway. She was looking at me to see how I would respond to the woman and her misunderstanding of the situation surrounding Davlin's commission, our child, our marriage. Now I bit my tongue; emotions were too high, and this was not the place to correct her.

I walked to Barbara, placing my arms around her stiff shoulders and held her. She didn't fight nor did she hold me or relent to my affection, "I am very sorry for your loss. Sharon was a wonderful mother and a pleasant woman to be around. I am sorry for your pain." I pulled back from the woman, held her at arm's length, and then, giving into the anger she had caused in my soul, I told her, "If you ever shit on my marriage, speak ill of me or my husband, curse my dead son, or decide to let your nonpatriotic ignorance show again, I will hurt you." I was shaking her, emphasizing each word with a little shake.

When I was done speaking, I pushed her away gently. She fell into an empty chair that was behind her. She sat with a "humph." I leaned in close to her and whispered, "Today didn't have to be like this, and tomorrow will not."

I walked out the door, past my mother, who followed me to the kitchen. I was standing at the sink, my back to her, when she came and put her hand on my back.

"Baby, they don't understand. They don't know what it was you and Davlin had…have. Baby, she just doesn't understand that you two couldn't be without each other. She never had that. She will never have a love like you do." My mom wiped more tears from my face. It had been an emotional roller coaster of a day, and my safety belt was the woman who had given birth to me.

83

Rachel joined us in the kitchen. She too wrapped her arms around me and hugged me, apologizing for her aunt. We stayed together until I stopped crying. Then, excusing myself, I went upstairs to use the restroom.

On my way back down the stairs, I was met by an old but familiar face. Standing in the hall was Caleb McMahon, dressed in somber black. He was talking to Rachel when I came into view. Rachel looked up at me, letting Caleb know I was there. He turned and looked at me with his blue eyes.

Caleb had been a handsome and confident teenager. Now, at twenty-six, he was lean and handsome in his business suit. His hair was cut close to his head. Not a blond hair lay out of place, and his skin was tan from working in San Diego. He took in my changes just as I had taken in his.

"Hey, Becks." His voice hadn't changed a bit. He walked to where I was, standing on the bottom step of the staircase. Taking me in his arms, he hugged me tight. Releasing the hug, he held me at arm's length, then leaned in and kissed my cheek.

"Hey, Caleb," I hugged him in return and suffered his kiss. "You are not helping me. No kisses, Caleb, his family is on a rampage," I whispered, putting him away. "Thanks for coming to the memorial for Sharon."

"Yeah, when I heard about her death, I had to come pay my respects. I know you haven't done anything for Davlin yet…"

"Why would I? My husband is missing. He has years of my devotion yet. You should be praying or at least hoping for his safe return," I scolded, walking out the front door and leaving the mourners and Caleb behind.

Chapter 12

I went for a short walk, taking in more of the changes on the street. I tried to breathe the stifling air, but the humidity and heat of the day were only making my mood worse. When I returned to the house, more people had arrived and I was in no better emotional state-of-mind than when I had left the house. The new arrivals gave their condolences to Allen and Rachel. Almost all, without fail, stated how sorry they were for Davlin's loss. I knew that explaining my position to everyone was pointless, so I just smiled and nodded my head.

By eight, my mom was shriveled and tired. I said goodnight and let Rachel know I would meet her the next morning at Miller's. Putting Mom in the car, I was once again confronted by Caleb, who had followed us out to our car.

"Becks, I wanted to apologize for what I said about Davlin. I understand you have to have faith that he's alright. Have you heard anything about him?" His understanding was throwing me off; Caleb was not known for his compassion.

"Um, no; Eric Vaughn, Lieutenant Vaughn, isn't being as helpful as he once was. I just keep in contact with the company and the battalion; I let the families know what I know." My failure to help find my husband seemed raw again as I was telling Caleb about it. I couldn't stand the look of apathy he was bestowing upon me.

"Look, Caleb, I appreciate your candor, but leave me alone. We aren't friends, and I don't like the way I feel around you." Closing my mother's door and heading around the front of the car, I looked back up at the boy who had taken my virginity and in doing so had won me the love of my life. "I'm sorry, Caleb. You don't deserve that, just please leave me alone."

Having run out of sympathy for others during the course of the day, I now needed to have a little pity party for myself. My mother was in no shape to listen to me whine; she could barely make it to the house under her own power. The day had been shit for everyone. The only speckle of good had come from the camaraderie Rachel and I had achieved.

With my mother safely tucked in bed and medicated as ordered by her doctors, I went to the kitchen to find something to calm my nerves and numb my soul. My mother's house had become a damn monk's cell, with not so much as cough syrup or mouthwash to grant me oblivion. I grabbed the keys to my rental and headed to the liquor store on Main Street.

Parking was easy—the liquor store was the only store open; all the others had been abandoned and boarded up. Seeing the failure of commerce in my hometown just drove another spike into my already depressed soul.

I had never been to Gordon's Liquor before. I had never been old enough nor had a reason, but the store rivaled the base Class 6 in not only quantity of liquor available, but also in quality. There were foreign brands and domestic, aged and triple malted liquors. My eyes went wide with anticipation of the damage I could do to my liver.

I grabbed a bottle of vodka—at least I think it was vodka, it was clear and the label was in Russian—paid, and headed out the door. On my way to my car I ran into Caleb again. He apparently had the same idea I did about starting tomorrow with a hangover.

Looking at my brown bottle-shaped bag, Caleb smiled and stepped aside, letting me through to my car. Sheepishly, I turned around. He was standing there looking at me.

"I really am sorry, Caleb. I'm a shit human, selfish, and honestly, I don't think I belong around other people. I'm not even good company for a dog right now."

"Stop feeling sorry for yourself, Becks. You're not any of that shit, and you know it. No one is punishing you except you." He walked over and took the bag from me. "It is a fucking shame that Davlin is missing, or dead or whatever. He…he was the man everyone knew he could be. The best kind of man."

I was surprised by the way Caleb was speaking about Davlin. I hadn't thought they had made amends before we graduated or any time after.

"Davlin is a hero. No matter how his story turns out. He was, is, a good man, and a hero." He cracked the bottle, took a sizable drink, and handed the bottle to me. Following suit, I took a drink in salute to my husband.

"I can't picture his face the way I used to be able to," I admitted. I hadn't told anyone, hadn't really admitted it to myself, but it was true. I had to glance at a photo to remember every detail now. "I dream about him, but it's always Davlin when we were kids or in high school. I don't see him the way he looked sitting at the kitchen table or at his desk working."

We started to walk down the street toward the elementary school playground, companionably sharing the bottle.

"You need a context," Caleb explained. He looked at me and saw my lack of understanding. "You can't just picture any day; you need to think about a day that was in some way memorable, like a day he broke something important or he surprised you with something. Try that."

I stopped walking and closed my eyes, thinking of a day that was memorable. I found a day, a summer day when we had lived in North Carolina…

It was summer, July, and we had both celebrated our twenty-third birthdays. We were on a day trip, driving backroads, looking at nothing in particular. We had found a yard sale that had a picnic basket and an itchy wool blanket. Davlin bought both and then stopped at a farmer's market a couple miles down the road.

As I was buying sun-warmed peaches and tomatoes, Davlin was across the street at a gas station buying sandwiches. He came out of the door of the building carrying a paper bag, grinning from ear to ear.

He hadn't cut his hair to military regulations in a couple weeks, so the hair on top of his head was floppy and unruly, showing highlights from his time spent in the sun. He was casual and comfortable that day, wearing a worn pair of jeans and a threadbare blue tee shirt. He crossed the street without a care in the world.

"Becks, you would be proud of me," he told me, smiling down at my face as I had to squint in the summer sun, seeing only his profile. His face came into full view as he leaned down and kissed me, a quick peck on the lips, then a longer languorous deal as he wrapped his arms around my waist, bending me backward to a low dip as he stopped kissing me and simply held me in his arms.

As he stood me upright I had to ask, "Why am I prouder of you now?" I took the bag of food he purchased and began to arrange it in the picnic basket.

"I asked for directions." He had the most comical and exaggerated "I'm a good boy" look on his face. I had to smile at him. He really was proud of himself and excited!

"Directions to where?"

"That is a surprise. Get your sexy ass in the car so we can get going." He opened my door and helped me into my seat in the Jeep. Then closing the door, he leaned in to give me another fast but thorough kiss. Coming around the front of the Jeep, he climbed in, putting his dirty white Cornhuskers hat backwards. Then, giving me a devilish grin, he started the engine and left the market before the memorized directions evaporated from his brain.

Davlin made several turns onto roads that were becoming less paved and more dirt with each twist. On a road that didn't even deserve that classification, more of a parallel deer path in the woods than a road of any kind, Davlin stopped, pulled the parking brake, and climbed out of the driver's-side door. "We're here," he called to me as he went around to the back of the Jeep to pull out the basket of food and the blanket. "Come on, babe, we have a little walk ahead."

I turned in my seat to look at my husband as he gathered our things. "Where are we, Davlin? We're lost again, and you decided this is the place to stop for a sexy lunch? This is the location of Deliverance!" In truth, the shade provided from the overhead canopy was refreshing, there were birds singing, and tree branches rustled as the squirrels ran to do what squirrels do. I could see up the path; we would be heading up the side of a hill, but then the view was lost in the leaves.

Davlin came to my door, his arms laden with a gallon of water, the basket, and the blanket we had purchased. Opening my door he smiled yet again, as though to mock my fear. "This is a beautiful place. It gets more beautiful up ahead, so come on." He stepped away from the door, allowing me space to get out. He shut the door, not bothering to lock the Jeep, and took off at a steady pace up the path.

I tried to take in the forest around me, hearing the animals around and now hearing a low thunder in the distance. I wasn't able to see through the thick green canopy overhead to determine if we were going to be drenched by a summer storm. I jogged to catch up to my husband who, with his rucksack hike–hardened legs, had gained fifty yards on me before stopping to give me time to catch him. He was excited, and I could see he was practically prancing where he stood.

"Davlin, I hear thunder, is it supposed to rain?" I was breathing hard, the changed incline that had brought us almost to the top of the hill had been a challenge for my treadmill-friendly legs. I stood trying to catch my breath in the humid air; then taking in my surroundings, I realized I could better hear the thundering. "What is that?"

Davlin took my hand, helping me to the top of the hill, actually a ridge, where we were just able to glimpse a waterfall halfway down the other side of the hill. "Barrnett's parents own this place. He was telling me about it the other day at lunch, said I should bring you up here. I guess it is where he proposed to his girl, but since you have been my old lady for a while now…" He nearly missed the cheap shot I took at his ear. Playfully we wrestled into each other's arms. "I needed to give you some time, something special. So here you go. I give you a beautiful day, just us and a basket of food. We don't have anywhere to go. No one but each other to talk to here."

"This is perfect." I stood on my tiptoes to kiss his mouth. "Let's go see it."

89

We made our way down carefully, the wet soil slipping out from underfoot causing an unexpected sit-down into the mud. But with several quick grabs of tree branches and trunks, and only the loss of our gallon of water—lost when I slid down the side of the hill rather unexpectedly—we reached the base of the valley with minimal damage. Looking back at the path of our descent, I had to laugh at the multiple areas of loosened soil made by my unsure footing.

Our feet eventually came to rest on the gravel of the stream bed, flowing quickly with clear fresh water from the falls and some unknown higher source. Davlin deposited our belongings. Then hand in hand we explored the waterfall valley.

We started on our side of the stream. Walking toward the falls, we were forced back up to the soil, the shore having disappeared into the depths of a pool of water from the falls. Cool from the spray, we continued on to a worn path that led behind the curtain of water.

The stone behind the falls was hollowed out from time. The ceiling was high enough that Davlin could stand with no worries of knocking himself out on the top of the cave. The walls were weeping from within, making the whole place seem like a bubble of water. Not watching where he was putting his feet, Davlin slipped on some green algae. Unable to catch himself on anything, he plunged through the wall of white rushing water, out of my view.

"Davlin!!!!" I screamed helplessly. I exited the cave the way we had entered, all the time straining my eyes to see through the water for him to come up to catch his breath. Out from behind the falls, I scanned the pool for him. Not seeing him immediately, I was beginning to have a sinking feeling in my gut and fear was taking over my brain. "Davlin!!!" I screamed again, running the side of the pool, searching for his body.

It was on my frantic return from a quick search further away from the falls that I saw his body, laying on the gravel shore, opposite from where I stood. I wasn't able to see whether he was breathing. Not thinking or caring about my clothes, I jumped from the soil embankment into the freezing pool, resurfacing after a slow trip to the gravel base of the pool. The water was muscle-numbing and the current from the falls was forceful, but nothing was going to keep me from Davlin. I still hadn't seen him move.

Keeping my eyes on him, I soon realized that I was getting nowhere but tired. The current was pushing me away from Davlin and toward a large rock that formed one whole side of the pool. Realizing there was a circular current, I relaxed, treading just enough to keep my head above water, and allowed the current to carry me away and then back toward Davlin. I was soon able to gain footing and walk the remainder of the way to him.

Kneeling next to him, I could see that he was breathing shallow breaths. I placed my hand on his back. "Davlin?" He did not respond to me. I put one hand under his hip and the other under his shoulder to roll him over so I could see if he was injured.

I used my legs to force his weight over. Just as his back was on the ground, Davlin threw his arms up and around my waist "AARRRGH!!!" he yelled, scaring me into screaming and trying to pull up and away from his joke. The result of Davlin returning from the dead and my trying to protect myself was my knee meeting his nose with a sickening crunch, then me losing my footing and hitting my head on the rocky shore, losing consciousness.

I awakened to a deep purple sky overhead. Itching from the wool blanket I was wrapped in, I looked around to see the naked backside of my husband as he fed wood to a fire. Just beyond the fire I could see the shapes of our clothes hanging from branches to dry, our shoes staked next to the fire just out of singeing range.

With a methodical check that all was right in his camp, Davlin turned back to me. Seeing my open eyes, he rushed forward to me. "Oh god, Becks, baby. Are you okay? Can you talk? Baby, I am so sorry! Can you move?" He was simultaneously lifting me to sitting, rechecking me for injuries, and reaching for a water bottle just out of his reach.

"D…" Scratchy voiced, I opted to wait for the proffered water bottle. Taking a generous gulp, I was again ready to try to talk. "Davlin, I'm fine, hungry, but fine. You knocked me out; you didn't

91

drown me." To prove my point, I stood a bit shakily and walked to the fire. Kneeling down next to it, I warmed my hands.

"You're mad at me?" Davlin was still where I had left him. He watched my movements, assuring himself I was alright and able to function.

"You played a shit practical joke on me! I thought you had drowned or been stuck in the undertow!" The fear I had felt prior to my being knocked out was retuning as anger. "Yes, Davlin, I am mad. I thought you were dead!" Standing, so I could look down at him, I walked over to him, better able to scold him. When I was close, I could see he was holding anger. His nose was swollen, and he had black marks under his eyes.

I was just getting ready to touch his face when he buried his face in my legs, wrapping his arms around my hips. I ran my hands through his hair and forgave him as best I could, all anger and fear forgotten with our touch.

Davlin's apology was forward coming, first he kissed my thighs, one, then the other. He put his hands on my hips, keeping me in place as his tongue began to taste and tease. My body responded to him. My pulse quickened, and my thighs spread ever so slightly to allow him access; my skin tingled as he worked me with his tongue.

Unable to stand any longer, my legs gave way and I fell into his lap, and in doing so, impaled myself on his ready member. Without waiting, I began to ride my husband, not losing the glorious build of my orgasm. I rode Davlin, leaning back to look up at the stars past the darkened canopy overhead. The night sky was our cathedral as we forgave each other without speaking. All of my fear and anger went into our actions.

Davlin was apologizing in the best manner he knew. He knew his joke had been in poor taste, and he needed me to forgive him. I did, but I still wanted him to know he hurt me, so I rode him, taking his length, almost pulling him out, then slowly gliding the length of him again. I enjoyed the teasing act that granted me the fantastic sensations that built in my belly. My breath was becoming short, and I no longer needed to look into the night sky to see stars. I was losing concentration and was unable to maintain my pace. Davlin took my hips and helped me reach my orgasm.

I cried out as shocks pulsed up my spine and down my thighs. I lost my breath and leaned against him, panting. I went to stand once my thoughts had cleared, but Davlin grabbed my hand and pulled me back to my knees in front of him.

With a hand behind my neck, he forced my face toward his. "Don't be cruel, Becks. You're better than me." He kissed my lips gently. "I am sorry for scaring you today." Another gentle kiss, then returning his hands to my hips, he pulled me back onto his lap.

I gasped as he drove into me, making our hips meet. He held my weight, lay me on the blanket, and drove into me, each thrust making my breath come short, each withdrawal a test of patience and will. He didn't endure long. Within moments, Davlin quickened his pace and thrust ever harder. The ferocity and force he gave was making my head spin and my body respond to his yet again.

I didn't consider the abuse he was issuing and the pain I would feel in the morning. I didn't care in that moment. I wanted him to bury himself inside me. I wanted him to beg for forgiveness of his stupid prank. And I dearly wanted to hurt him the way he was hurting me. I kissed his lips and bit into his bottom lip, drawing blood, and raked my nails across his back. He pulled back shortly, then leaned in and bit my neck. The sex had turned into a battle. We were going to leave marks on each other trying stupidly to win a pointless war.

I rolled us when Davlin was off guard. Taking the position of power, I pushed him into the ground and grasped his chest, my fingers digging into his flesh. I leaned over him, slowed our movements, and kissed him. He put his hands on my hips, holding us skin to skin, making it impossible to tell where we became two separate people. With the change of position, the senseless fight had ended, he had apologized, and I was accepting. I just needed love in that moment.

I kissed him again, put my hands on his, then our fingers intertwined. Once again, I paced our lovemaking. Gentler, kinder,

93

but no less fulfilling. I must have been concussed in some way from our collision earlier in the day. I had stopped listening to Davlin and had instead been listening to the stream behind me, absorbed in my own pleasure.

So absorbed in my own ecstasy, I hadn't paid attention to Davlin or what he was saying. When clarity returned to my brain, I was aware that he had been saying something for a while.

Confused, I asked, "What are you saying?"

"You haven't been listening?" Davlin looked genuinely hurt. "I was telling you how scared I was today when you were unconscious…I was baring my soul is all."

I looked at my husband, one side of his face lost in shadows, the other a mass of sharp angles and incorrect colors from the firelight. "No, you weren't. You were babbling about how you wanna wanna wanna something… Did you mention my butt?" His false seriousness evaporated in the air as I forced him to admit the truth of his confession.

We disentangled and sat close as we shared our food—the sandwiches, peaches, and tomatoes. Afterward, we lay nested together sharing the wool blanket, watching the fire. We spoke very little that night; we simply enjoyed knowing the other was there.

I woke the next day, cold and sore. Davlin was by the stream dressed in his damp clothes. Our fire had burned out during the night and the morning air was still cool, but the promise of a hot day was in the air overhead. I got up, wrapping the blanket to cover my nakedness as I gathered my shorts and shirt, pulling both on. I went to join Davlin to wash my hands and face.

He heard me coming, so I was unable to gauge his mood. His shoulders were stiff and his face was unreadable.

"Good morning," I tried cheerily, smiling at him as I hopped onto the gravel shore.

"You ready to go home? " His voice was cold and unloving. I looked back over my shoulder at him. He wasn't looking at me but instead at his hands.

"No."

My answer snapped him from his revelry. "What?" He was confused, as though he didn't realize I was in front of him.

"I said I'm not ready to go yet. I want to see the falls again, hopefully this time with a little less excitement, fewer falls, near drownings, broken noses, and fires." He gave a snort of amusement and then stood. Giving me a hand up the embankment, he stopped me at the top and kissed me.

"Okay, but can we make it fast? I'm starving."

We did see the falls without incidence again. The trip back up the hill was a bitch and a half. Davlin dropped the picnic basket with the blanket. We were about two thirds up the hill when this little sapling Davlin was holding onto completely uprooted and he went sliding back down the hill. He chucked the basket to get two hands out for grabbing tree trunks as he slid past.

It took us forever to get out of that valley. By the time we were at the top, my ass was black with mud, and Davlin had been coated from neck to ankles with fresh dirt. Both of us needed a hose-down before a shower. His shoes were caked with mud, and I had lost one of mine in a boggy spot on our way back to the Jeep.

We stopped at the first drive-through we came to marking civilization. Unable to get out of the car, we devoured lukewarm fries and Big Macs in the Jeep as Davlin drove us back to base.

Caleb laughed at me as I recounted an edited version of our adventure. He was right though; when I thought of Davlin in a context, like crossing the street in his faded shirt, or naked by the fire, I was better able to put his features in place.

My bottle of vodka was now empty, the hour was late, and I was barely able to stand; the effects of the day, the alcohol, and my lack of food were wreaking havoc on my system. Holding the bottle up to eye level, I decided now was an excellent time to begin my walk back to my mother's trailer.

"Caleb, I got to go home now." Swaying dangerously, Caleb grabbed my arm to steady me. "Thank you very mush. Imma go home." Taking three steps in the direction of my car, I promptly passed out and landed face-first on the grass of the baseball field.

95

I woke the next afternoon, sprawled on my bed, hair disheveled and strongly smelling of vomit. My head pounded with each beat of my heart, the sun was too damn bright, and my mother was cooking again, making my stomach turn. I pulled the pretty flowered comforter over my head and fell back asleep.

I was rudely awakened a short time later by my mother. "Becks! You need to get up and get moving, we have the viewing at five, it's already four. Dear god girl, you slept the day away."

With her excellent example of my poor time management pointed out, I decided that it was a good time to get out of bed. Grabbing my bag of toiletries, I went to take a shower and wash the vomit from my hair. Slightly renewed after the cleaning, I wrapped a towel around my torso and stepped out of the shower to find a fresh cup of coffee awaiting me on the counter.

Picking up the porcelain cup and breathing in the aroma, I was brought slightly closer to the world of the living. Grabbing the hair dryer and brush, I began the tedious task of hot air drying my thick head of hair. The heated air and the brush felt wonderful on my pounding head, but my coordination left something to be desired. Turning off the dryer, I called my mother for help.

"Hey Mom, can you come dry my hair? My arms are tired." She didn't answer, but I heard steps coming down the hall. Eagerly, I sat on the side of the tub, putting my feet back in the tub to give Mom access to the back of my head.

"What would you do without me, Becks?" came the familiar voice of my best friend Heather. She smiled at me as I turned to verify her presence.

I squealed and jumped up to give her a bone-crushing hug. "Ahhhhh! Heather, when did you get here? How did you know where I was? Why haven't you called me?" I spewed questions at her, as was our norm.

She turned me and sat me back on the tub to begin dividing my hair into manageable sections for drying and styling.

"I got here yesterday evening. You apparently had gone out for a drink, so I drove all over this town looking in bars for you. For such a small town, there are a lot of bars! I found you being carried by a very tall, very handsome, very drunk fellow. I promised to take you home, then kneed him when he wouldn't leave me alone after I had you in the car." I sniggered at the thought of Caleb laying on the ground grabbing his man parts after Heather assaulted him.

She continued to answer my questions in the order I had asked them. "Your answering machine. You never delete messages, so I heard the one from Rachel and I knew you would be here. I do try to call you, but apparently, I only get to talk to your answering machine, judging by the number of my own messages I had to delete to find where you went. Now look straight and let me fix you up pretty."

Smiling and feeling better knowing I had another person to lean on, I gave in to the ministrations of Heather's hands. Enjoying the pampering and the overall effect of her skills, I was surprised when I looked in the mirror to glance at my reflection. Heather had hot curled my hair and made me look like I had stepped out of a magazine. I actually felt pretty seeing what she had done.

I dressed in a simple black dress, cut just above the knees. A set of heels and a black purse completed my outfit. Coming down the hall, I heard Mom and Heather laughing; then the sound of Jobe's bell-tingling giggle joined the noise, and again my spirits rose.

I picked up the little baby, drool and stinkiness not enough to keep me from kissing his rosy cheeks or burying my face in his soft belly to kiss his skin. Jobe squealed in delight, grabbing handfuls of my hair in his pudgy fingers. The scene I was making made my mother smile; a tear grew in her eye, then receded before falling. Heather simply enjoyed the show.

We gathered as a group, armed with diaper bags, toys, stroller, car seat, and snacks, and headed to my rental car the same way I would expect Heather to leave for an extended vacation.

The day was somber with flashes of humor; Jobe was a constant distraction. His mobility around the funeral home was amazing. Unable to keep track of the baby and maintain a sensible

97

conversation with the people in front of me, I opted to catch the baby and enjoy his soft spots.

I was blowing onto the baby's belly when a shadow fell over Jobe and me. Looking up, I was surprised to see Mrs. Ballish, my freshman English teacher.

"Mrs. Ballish, how nice to see you, thank you for coming." Smiling, I gathered the baby in my arms and stood.

"You should be ashamed of yourself, Becks Robertson! Tramping around town drunk, with the boy everyone knows you slept with before Davlin! Lord, I hear he even carried you off the playground! Were you fornicating there? Whore!"

The verbal onslaught of hatred and misinformation battered me back onto the couch. With nothing more than Jobe to protect me from the woman, I held the little boy to my chest, trying to figure out a way to get away my enraged teacher. People near enough to hear the ugliness spewing from her mouth were beginning to stop and listen to her assault.

"You should be wearing black, mourning your lost husband, not hopping in bed with anything with a penis! You're just like your mother!" the old woman continued.

Seeing Heather and my mother breaking through the throng of interested mourners, I swiftly stood and thrust baby Jobe toward Heather.

"You listen here, you nosy old bat! I drink as a way of mourning! I mourn for my husband every damn night. If I want to drink myself stupid, who the hell are you to tell me anything? And as for Caleb, he is a friend and someone to cry to when I can't take people like you talking behind my back and staring like I'm the one who sent Davlin to war!"

With each word of my retaliation, my voice rose. I knew I was making a scene for the second day in a row, even as I realized, deep in my brain, that today was about Sharon and her life. I simply couldn't stop yelling at this woman who had always looked down on me. I turned to leave. Then as an afterthought, I turned back on the bowed old woman, "And if you ever speak ill of my mother again,

I'll be happy to kick your crotchety old ass, you bitch." The last was a whisper as I turned away from her wrinkled, shocked face.

Mrs. Ballish was a crone when I had sat in her class my freshman year. Always an ugly and hateful person, she had been worse since the death of her daughter Sophia. Sophia had been involved with a boy from Allington; their love affair caused quite a bit of gossip. It was rumored Sophia was pregnant when she ran away with her boyfriend. We never found out the truth; they were both killed in a car accident outside of Lincoln a few days after they left town. Mrs. Ballish had been awful to any young lovers ever since.

I took my mother by the arm, hooking my arm in the crook of hers. I guided her through the gathering people to the front of the gathering hall. I looked at Sharon lain in her blue church dress, her curled hair and her makeup giving her the appearance of a clown more than of the woman who had called me her 'daughter-in-law from hell.'

I had nothing.

I looked at the woman. I felt nothing. I felt no loss for a friend or companion. Sharon had certainly never been that. She had never embraced me, nor shown compassion or love. No, this woman lay in her maple casket, surrounded with white satin, roses, and carnations draped over the lid. This woman dressed in her Sunday's finest, hair styled in a manner she would never approve of; the body of a soulless, selfish, cruel, bitter, hating woman was all I saw. I felt nothing. I felt no sadness for Sharon or Allen, no pity for the family, no empathy for Rachel or her children. I felt nothing. Numbness settled into my core.

With my mother in tow I turned to Allen. The bloated, drunk man sat in a high-backed chair just beyond the foot of the casket. His eyes were bloodshot, his skin was taking on an unhealthy yellow tinge, and the fatness of his face was beginning to show the effects of gravity. Mom and I approached him.

"Allen," I startled him, "my mother and I are leaving. I am sorry for your loss and for Davlin's. I hate to think how he will feel when

99

he returns home to find a dead mother, a scheming sister, and a lush for a father. At least he will have me." I knew I was being petty and cruel; my mother stiffened at my words. "Stop drinking, or we will be burying you too, after a long and slow death. Get yourself together."

"Becks," my father-in-law said, his voice rough with disuse and his words slightly slurred, "I hate you. You're a terrible wife to my son. You killed his…."

My hand struck out at his face, stopping the words that were coming from his mouth. My mother wrapped her shriveled arms around mine. Heather grabbed my arm to stop me from hitting him again.

"Becks, let's go," Heather pleaded into my ear. "Let's go." I gave into her begging and turned to her, reaching for Jobe and supporting my mother at the same time. Heather wrapped her arms around my shoulders to guide our group to the door. Glances of varying ranges of hate, disgust, pity, and confusion were ignored as we made our way out of Miller's Funeral Home.

At the door, we ran into Caleb, signing in on the registry. He was handsome as ever, if not a little ragged around the edges as I was. He looked up to see the three women and the sleepy baby huddled together in support of each other. My mother wore a face of shock, realizing for the first time the hatred I had endured during my marriage. Heather's face showed surprise, amazed that a family suffering a loss could be so mean and hateful. My face, however, was blank, unreadable. I simply rested my cheek on Jobe's soft baby hair as he rested his head on my shoulder.

"Becks," Caleb called as we passed without acknowledging his presence. "Becks, what happened?"

"Stop!" Heather lashed at him. "You have no concept of propriety! You are the reason Becks has been beaten down all day! Stay the hell away from her!" Her face was red with fury and her hands were shaking as she turned to put them on my arms to guide me out once again.

Caleb stared, shocked at the sudden onslaught from this blonde stranger. Turning to assess the room behind him, he was met with looks of anger and distrust. Mrs. Ballish stood at the center of a group spreading her poison, glancing sideways at Caleb. Squaring his shoulders, he went to quietly pay his respects to the deceased, her husband, and her daughter, then quickly left the funeral home.

Back at Mom's trailer, the evening was heavy with humidity. The beautiful hairdo Heather had given me now hung limp as my hands as I sat in a chair, not having the energy or desire to keep myself from sliding out of it. A glass of lemonade appeared by my hand, then nudged it when I showed no intent of taking the glass.

Broken from my misery, I looked up at Heather. She gave a shrug and a smile, then joined me in one of the other metal lawn chairs. "So, how much longer do we plan on staying here in the heartland of hospitality?" Her sarcasm was not wasted on me.

Taking a sip of the tart drink, I smiled at her. Having had time to think about all that had happened since my return home, the conversations I had overheard and those I had been part of, and the changes in my hometown, I was suddenly overwhelmed. I wasn't sure if I should laugh, cry, or run down the street screaming!

Knowing that the latter would give fodder to the rumor mill, I ruled that option out quickly. I was tired of crying; slightly dehydrated from the night before, I didn't think it possible to produce tears in any case, so that option went to the wayside as well. I settled into laughing. A giggle that grew to a full laugh as the insanity of the situation dawned on me. Realizing the damage I had caused during this trip home, I quickly became hysterical. I laughed myself out of my chair, to the ground where I sat in a puddle of my spilled lemonade.

Heather and Mom looked at me with blank faces. My situation was well understood by both of them, the reality that had evaded my brain in my recent drunken state had always been known to them. My mother and my best friend had been trying to save me from my own actions and decisions. In my stubborn manner that had marked my character since childhood, I had crashed through Guernsey ruining my reputation once again.

When my hysterics ended, I again slipped into silence. I realized Davlin would be so disappointed in the way I had treated his father and sister during their time of distress. He would disapprove of my drinking, especially my drinking with Caleb. But more than anything, Davlin would never accept my self-defeating behavior. The way I had simply walked away without correcting the lies spread by the people of our lives.

Deciding I was hydrated enough, I started to cry. My hands shook in fury; my heart ached with loss for my husband; my soul feared his reaction when he returned home to this town, to these people. How would he react knowing what they had said to me or how they had treated me?

In my misery, my mom was my port of safety, a cove to protect me from the storm of my life, and Heather was my lighthouse, my guide to lead me to safety. Both women were constant providers of love, compassion, friendship, and worthy advice. Their combined efforts got me through the burial of my mother-in-law and the weeks that followed, when the attitude of the community worsened and became more hostile.

Chapter 13

After Sharon's funeral, I opted to stay in Guernsey to help my mom out. Her health was deteriorating, along with her waistline. I attended her doctor's appointments and sat alongside her while she had her chemotherapy. I held her shoulders as she suffered the post-treatment vomiting and chills, the aches and pains, and helped her when her weakness kept her in bed.

With each treatment, I saw my mother slip more into herself. I would sit with her for the first day after her chemo, watching her breathe as she slept. When she awoke the following day, she would be weak but willing to move. With assistance, I would take her outside under the carport, settle her in her lounge chair, and ply her with various forms of fortified smoothies and Ensure drinks.

I considered any intake a success and celebrated each day that Mom did not vomit. Little by little, visit by visit, we were able to find medication scheduling that didn't make her vomit.

On non-chemo days, Mom would lounge outside, in the shade and comfort of her carport. Rain or shine, she wanted to be outside. During storms, conversation was almost impossible; the constant thrum of rain on the aluminum sheeting of the roof was like sitting in a closet with a drum corp. Mom didn't mind the noise. She would watch the rain fall from the roof, sheets of water pummeling the soil underneath, forming puddles that eventually overflowed and flooded the carport. She would eventually consent to being moved back inside the house to the couch placed by the bay window so she could see the rain and feel the breeze with the window open.

We began to talk. Each day we would tell each other about past experiences. Mom had become a funny woman with age. She would tell me about things I had never known about in my youth. She told me about a summer that she spent on the back of a motorcycle, cruising around the US with a bike club. She told me about some of her lower times, like when she had traded sex for money; tears streamed down her cheeks as she explained how her drug habits led to her selling our food stamps for hits of coke.

Many days ended with me holding my mother's head on my chest as she cried into my shirt. She would apologize repeatedly for our past life. I tried reassuring her that our past had made our present so enjoyable. That the past was the past and nothing could be done about it. But the response that allowed her to sleep at night was when I reassured her that I wouldn't be the person I was had our life been any different when I was growing up.

With weeks spent in her trailer, Mom and I became friends. I had never thought it possible that I would enjoy her company, and I dreaded leaving her.

By the time Sharon had been in the ground two months, September heat was wilting my mother's flowers as well as her spirits. I decided it was time for her to leave Guernsey and come visit me in Georgia. She had completed her current course of chemo and was showing no signs of metastasis. With a pending lobectomy in three weeks' time, I wanted to take her on a vacation away from her reality.

It took some doing, but I was finally able to talk Mom into coming back to Georgia with me, coaxing her with the promise of a trip to Florida. We left Guernsey together in a used Corolla I had bought in lieu of continuing to rent a car at thirty-five dollars per day. The Corolla was old—the engine had turned more than one hundred thousand miles—but the owner who sold it to me had been the only owner, and he was a Toyota mechanic at the dealership in Allington. I was pretty sure it would make the trip.

We returned to Fort Benning, Georgia, after three days on the road and two nights in hotel rooms from hell. Our first hotel had no hot water for showers, the toilet overflowed, and one of the beds only had three feet. Mom and I shared a bed in a double room with squishy carpet from a flooded toilet.

My complaints about the room, our lack of service, and the general discomfort my mother had to endure were overlooked by the staff who rudely told me we could have gone to another hotel.

Murder on my mind, I had quickly helped Mom to the car and had driven as far as Tennessee when she began feeling sick. We stopped for the night in Nashville, staying in style at the Grand Ole Opryland Hotel. Mom and I dined on our balcony overlooking the indoor garden. She enjoyed a meal of Southern fried love, while I, recovering from the drive and the night before, fell asleep after a quick burger and fries.

We left Tennessee and made it back to Georgia by late evening the next day. August in Georgia is hot enough to cause you to strip out of your clothes down to your panties. The Corolla had no air conditioning, so as Mom and I encountered stop-and-go traffic, I was regretting the car and felt inhumane toward my mother.

It wasn't until we reached the base, as we were waiting at the gate to have my identification checked, that I remembered the condition of the house. All the groceries I had purchased in preparation to replace alcohol with food, the marinated steak that was probably no more than a red stain on my plate, the fruit that would now be a fruit fly colony, the vegetables that surely had taken root in my fridge. I blanched at the thought of the cleaning that would have to be done. More than anything, I feared the smell would make Mom sick. The thought was enough to make me wake Mom up and forewarn her as we drove the remainder of our journey.

I pulled into the driveway at the house. The yard was trimmed with military precision, and the shrubs that lined the front of the house were shaped to neat squares. I made a mental note to go thank the captain later for taking the burden of the yardwork.

I went around the car to help my mother out. She was wide-eyed, looking around at the lush trees thick with moss and the houses that made up the officer housing. They were nice, two-story duplexed buildings with porches and double doors, brick fronts with casement windows, and a covered porch on each side per family. The sounds of a party down the street drifted toward us, as did the smell of burgers and chicken thick with glazed brown sugar. My stomach grumbled in anticipation of food; it had been a very long hot drive from Nashville, and grilled chicken sounded wonderful.

Helping Mom to the front door, I was surprised when the door suddenly opened, a smiling Heather on the other side.

"Welcome home, Becks! Hi, Mrs. Frayer. How was the trip?" She reached for Mom, helping her through the door and steering her toward the living room. Mom gladly accepted the proffered arm, headed for the sounds of Jobe throwing his toys from his Pack 'n Play.

"What are you doing here?" I asked Heather as I was dumping our bags just inside the door. I glanced around the front hall of the house. The stairs in front of me were swept clean of dust; the kitchen appeared clean with the smell of homemade chili wafting through the door; and the table to my right where I dumped my purse, keys, and sunglasses was dusted, with a fresh bouquet of roses and black-eyed Susans adding a pleasant smell to the room. The living room to my left through an archway was brightly lit as the evening sun glazed every item in golden light.

My mom had been safely placed on the couch, out of throwing range of the baby. Everything was well in order in there too. The surfaces were cleaned of dust and dirt, special items were poised on tables adding accents to the furnishings, and the soft notes of an Irish CD came from the speakers in Davlin's office.

"I wanted to get everything ready for you two, so I came by yesterday to turn on the AC. Oh my god! Becks, the smell of your fridge almost knocked me out!" Heather explained, coming to the hall on her way to the kitchen. "I found a whole supply of cleaning stuff, so I put it to good use. There was a plate in your fridge that I just threw away, and your vegetable drawer was like a science experiment," she continued to recount as we both went to the kitchen.

Just off the kitchen was the laundry room with the door leading into the back yard. I dumped my bags of dirty clothes by the washer and popped my head out the back door. The cheery sounds of playing children reached my ears though I couldn't see them. I smiled, happy for my neurotic friend. Closing the door, I walked back into the kitchen where Heather was tasting the chili.

"Come taste this, let me know what you think. I don't think it's hot enough."

I walked to her, and ignoring the wooden spoon in her hand, I wrapped my arms around her and hugged her, attempting to infuse my gratitude into the embrace. Feeling insufficient, I held her and expressed my thanks.

"Heather, I wouldn't be able to do this without you. Thank you so much! For everything." Hugging her tighter as my emotions broke free of my reign, she let out a squeak and I let go.

Stepping back, I wiped a tear away from the corner of my eye. "I don't only mean this," I said, sweeping my arms around the kitchen, "I do. But not only this. You are just…amazing? The best? A godsend? I can't place you in any one box. You fit in so many of them!"

She blushed as I praised her thoughtful effort and blessed character. "I know you would do the same for me, Becks." She smiled at me as she stirred the pot of chili. "And you have. You've been a great friend to me, helping me through the pregnancy, listening to me whine about missing Eric. I love you. And you help the people you love." She gave me a quick hug, then turned to head for the living room where a steam-whistle screech from a dissatisfied Jobe was building to full volume.

We ate as a family that night in the freshly cleaned kitchen. The chili was amazing and perfectly spiced, accompanied by warm cornbread and honey. Jobe sat in his baby chair making a mess of his tray and his blond hair, while Heather looked like she was tired but rallied well, carrying the conversation when it otherwise died. Mom was able to tolerate the food but excused herself early to go up to her bed in the guest bedroom.

After dinner and Jobe's bath, Heather and I sat in the living room, watching the baby sleep. In whispered tones, she filled me in on the goings-on in Afghanistan as reported dutifully by Eric. She paled slightly when she told me the lack of news on Davlin but regained her animation when she filled me in on her plans for Mom's visit.

She was in the middle of telling me about one of her childhood trips to Key West when she finally fell asleep. I tucked a throw around her shoulders, checked the sleeping baby, and made my way up to the bed my husband and I had shared.

Mom did stay for two weeks on her visit, and we did attempt Heather's well-thought-out road trip. Just two days after returning to Fort Benning, we found ourselves back in a car, this time with a cranky infant and overly bubbly mommy, touring Colonial Georgia, finding our way through Louisiana, and then heading into Florida.

Mom walked the beaches of the Gulf in a state of nostalgia, becoming gregarious after a day spent in her head walking down memory lane. Over dinner she told us stories about her youth, about times when she had disappeared out of my life after I had become slightly self-sufficient. She told us about the time she had been drinking in Ohio and had woken up on the beach we were sitting on. She giggled to herself and blushed like a little girl when she told us about the dark Dominican man she had danced with, the first time she had run away from home.

Little by little, as the miles of greenness of the Everglades slipped past our windows, Mom unraveled more of her past. She painted a picture of a rebellious young girl, raised in the Bible belt, not sharing the beliefs of her family. She had been a young girl looking for adventure and finding it in the form of drugs, alcohol, sex, and the occasional unapproved leave from home. Starting in her early teens, Mom had begun to give her mother and father a hard time about their strict upbringing by becoming defiant.

She had received a punishment for using the Lord's name in vain the first time she had run away at the age of fifteen. Not having money or a plan on where to go, she had turned herself in a southern direction and started walking. It didn't take long for a man more than willing to overlook her age to pick her up. A construction worker on his way to a job in Orlando offered Mom a lift. She, not having any money or other way to provide a means of payment, had started her life as a prostitute.

She had the decency to cry when she told us bits and pieces of what she had to do to stay alive while in Florida after she had run away. She had sex with men, ran drugs, and worked at an ice cream stand until the boss's wife realized how the young girl had gotten her legitimate job rather illegitimately. She had danced at a strip club and had been filmed on more than one occasion performing sex acts on both men and women alike. She had gotten heavily into drugs by that point to numb herself from the pain of her existence.

It was after two years of self-abuse and abuse from others that Mom had sobered up on a beach on the coast of the Atlantic Ocean. She had been awakened by stinging rain hitting her face with such force it "knocked the sense back into me," she stated.

We were now at a hotel at Vero Beach on the east coast of Florida, having detoured off Heather's planned route to follow Mom's directions for her story.

"Becks, I tell you that rain was giving me a headache with each drop that pounded me," Mom assured me, grabbing my leg for emphasis. "And the sky! Girls! The sky was a maelstrom! I couldn't tell if it was one big cloud and one big storm or what! And the wind! I could barely stand in the wind!"

"How did you get there, Mama Frayer?" Heather asked, hanging onto every word my mother was saying. She was gracefully saved from the humiliation of learning so much detail about her mother's sexual exploits and other deviant behavior.

"I couldn't tell you, dear. But whoever had left me had been trying to hurt me. Not quite a hurricane, I was on the coast as Tropical Storm Dottie was about to make landfall." She was looking at me square in the face, and I knew the next words to come out of her mouth would be something I didn't really want to hear. "I didn't know it then, but I was pregnant too."

Whatever reaction she was going for, I guess she was slightly disappointed when all she got was a raised eyebrow from me. I had figured she didn't know who my father was; I had never bothered to

109

ask. I wasn't surprised to hear that someone had tried to kill her. Hell, they were probably done with her in whatever capacity they needed her for. She was lucky to have survived for as long as she did on her own with just her vagina to support her.

I had lost my sense of adventure. I wasn't as thrilled with Mom's story as Heather was, but a sick sense of humor prompted me to ask, "So, Mom, what did you do?" I had some steel in my voice, and I was glaring at her too.

"Don't look at me like that, young lady," she warned. "I am not proud of many things in my life. In fact, you are the only thing I am proud of. And it was sitting on that beach with sand and water stinging my skin, with the Heavens bearing down on my soul, with my body broken and humbled, it was out there," she pointed, "that I accepted that you would be born. I accepted my fate on that day and decided to live"—she held my gaze—"for you."

Unable to stand her gaze, I looked down at the grains in the wood of our table. I didn't know what to say to my mother who had obviously been scared and unsure about how to live her life. Thank you? Seems a funny thing to say when you're so angry about how you came into existence... But did it matter anymore?

Shaking my head to myself, I looked up and took my mom's hand.

"Thanks for not dying." I gave her a half-hearted smile and squeezed her hand. "I can't imagine how you felt. But thank you for what you did for me."

She smiled at me, squeezed my hand, and continued her story, telling us about her return home to her family. She had been accepted back at the house but had endured daily punishment to atone for her sins while away. She became a model daughter, hiding her pregnancy. It wasn't until her mother walked in on her during a bath one day that her parents knew about her advanced pregnancy.

Her father, hearing her mother scream, had run into the bathroom. Grabbing Mom by the hair, he proceeded to beat her, trying to make her lose her pregnancy. Throwing her from wall to wall, Mom had tried to take on the brunt of the abuse, trying to spare the bulging belly from his wrath. It was as she lay curled on the floor wrapped feebly around her abdomen, bleeding and dripping wet from her bath, that her oldest brother had come home.

Seeing the abuse ongoing, he had rushed into the bathroom to protect Mom from their father. He had physically placed himself over my prone mother, trying to check to see if she was still alive and fend off his enraged father at the same time, when he was struck in the head with the leg of a chair wielded by their dad.

Mom said that in his rage, her father had been blinded by fury and he was unable to stop until he registered the screams of his wife. Mom passed out on the bathroom floor in a puddle of blood mixed of her own from her hemorrhaging abdomen and that of her brother; who lay dead on the tile floor beside her, his head caved in and his eyes staring blankly at her.

She awoke in a hospital, confused and unsure of how she had gotten there. A doctor came to the room to tell her that her child, a girl, had been born early but was strong and going to survive.

Mom spent three weeks in the hospital. She had finally sought the assistance of the chaplain. She was able to leave the facility with me in her arms, gifted with a suitcase of donated clothes, a bus ticket to the Midwest where Mom had claimed to have a distant aunt who would help her, and fifty dollars of donations from the medical staff who had heard bits and pieces of her story.

"I didn't want to hear about my parents anymore. I saw my brother's grave just the once but didn't dare go home to see if my mother was there, living in her misery. I am sure Papa went to jail for killing Robert, but I never found out."

My mouth hung open as her story ended. I had an uncle, and a murderous grandfather? No wonder Mom hadn't talked about her youth before this. "God, Mom." I didn't have words... Thought escaped me completely.

"Stop, Becks. That loss, my brother, my family, that was a long time ago. I have been past it for a long time. I just wanted you to know that there is history in my life, things I am ashamed of... You, baby, you have always been the best thing I did. She paused for a

111

moment and stroked my cheek, taking in my features. It was something she had begun to do frequently.

She continued to speak, her voice softer and her heart achingly pained. "Seeing you as a woman, a wife, a friend. Seeing you grown up and not into drugs, or drinking yourself to death, or whoring to stay alive! I am so proud that even though I did those things—hell, did some of them in front of you—that you are you!" She was crying by the end of her speech. She had both of my hands in hers, gripping my bones as tightly as her weakened body could.

I looked at her, her thinning hair, her pale skin, pleading eyes, skeletal arms resting on the table... This was a woman I had never known growing up. This person, I would not have wanted to know or forgiven for her sins. If Mom had told me about all this when I was a teenager, I would not have had the ability to comprehend why she had told me about this...but now, I got it.

She had sacrificed then, went on with her life. She had steered me in the right direction, she returned home when I needed her, left me to find my way when I was able. This woman was exactly what I needed her to be when I needed her to be it, and right now she needed me to be something for her. She needed me to give her something, forgiveness.

"Thanks, Mom, I'm proud of you too. You did a..." I paused. What do I say? She was an unconventional mother? Lamely, I went on, "You did a good job; you're a good mom." I didn't really know what to say. I got up and went around to hug her. I could feel her shaking in my arms as she cried, her tears cleansing her soul.

We left the beach restaurant where my mother had taken sanctuary from a tropical storm, realizing that she was with child and needing to get her life under control. This was the place where my mother turned her life around, and the place she divulged her soul and cleansed herself of her past.

We got back in the car and drove home that night. We got to Fort Benning without incident beyond Jobe pooping up his back. Mom was up the stairs and in bed by the time I got home from dropping off Heather and the baby. Weightless from her confession, Mom slept peacefully.

Where she felt freed of her sins, I now felt burdened by my past, my guilt. I went to bed no longer able to smell the scent of my husband's hair on his pillow. I was wrapped in the comfort of his arms, wearing his old long-sleeved PT shirt, looking at a picture of us smiling together on our own trip to Florida.

We had been sophomores in college, on our spring break. Several classmates had arranged a trip to Daytona for spring break, and Davlin and I had hopped a ride. Not wanting to be a part of the drunken orgy that is college spring break, we had gone north to Saint Augustine and visited an alligator farm en route.

It was there, at the alligator farm, that this picture had been taken. Davlin had been amazed that such a thing as an alligator farm existed and had stopped at the gift shop as soon as we entered the grounds. He purchased a white t-shirt that had a grainy photo of a group of baby alligators all waiting with open jaws anticipating food and the question "Got food?" printed above the image.

We strolled across a bridge with coin-operated food dispensers at either end; several dozen baby alligators waited under the bridge for the morsels to be tossed into their waiting mouths. Davlin was intrigued and a bit disappointed that they didn't seem interested in eating each other.

We made our way to the main attraction at the farm: a mammoth beast too large to get out of his swimming area. We watched a handler feed the freakishly large alligator frozen monkeys. Davlin was selected out of the crowd to do the same. I snapped a photo of him reaching toward the gaping jaw of the reptile, his eyes full of joy at the insanity of his actions.

I was looking at the photo, reminiscing the day, trying to remember his face and the absolute joy he had worn feeding the alligator. I was trying my hardest to remember him in context, but I was failing. If I didn't look at the photo of his face, I would picture grown Davlin, the man I had sent to war, not the bright-eyed boy who had no idea what death was and had no fear of it.

113

I must have lain there for a while, until I heard Mom start to cough. The sound of it ricocheted through the house, making my chest hurt in empathy. I rose out of bed, taking one last look at my husband in his young adulthood, then went down the hall to help my mom who was too well aware of what death was.

We spent a few days at the house in Fort Benning. I tried unsuccessfully to tempt her into staying with me in Georgia. She adamantly refused, citing her comfort with her doctors as her reason not to move. We enjoyed our time together though, not arguing, just talking about unimportant things and a few important ones.

She began to tell me how she had planned her funeral already, a conversation I was not ready to have with her. She understood my reluctance to speak of her death. I was unwilling to accept that anyone I loved was dead or dying, but she knew I needed to know about her plans, and she said as much.

I drove her back to Nebraska, to Guernsey, in a better state of comfort. We took my Camry, fully equipped with air conditioning, and slept at Holiday Inn hotels with working toilets along the way.

I stayed on with Mom for a week, enduring the hateful glances of the townies while I was at the grocery store or paying her bills for her. I made two more doctor's visits and arranged to return in time for Mom's surgery scheduled in early November. It was on the way home from one of her doctor's appointments that Mom asked me to stop while we were still driving in Allington; she was feeling ill. We stopped at a coffee shop with glowing windows. I helped Mom to a spot on a couch that was just inside the door and then made my way through the dimly lit environment to the bar.

I paid the girl behind the bar for two "bottomless" coffee cups, filled our cups with dark aromatic blends from somewhere south of the border, and returned to find Mom in conversation with a dark-haired man. Placing her cup on the table in front of her, I had to smile at her as she was very animated in conversation with the man.

I sat in my chair and listened to them talk about cancer treatments and success stories. The man, a young guy around thirty or so with a shock of dark brown hair and brown eyes, had apparently survived testicular cancer and had recently opened the coffeehouse/bar/grill we now sat in. He and Mom had met in a support group of some kind.

Jarrod, the young entrepreneur, was an oddly handsome man. He had dark hair and dark eyes, long eyelashes, and a not-quite-straight nose. I realized I was staring at him when my mother had to tap my leg, making me blush in embarrassment.

"I'm sorry, I didn't mean to stare. You remind me of my husband," I explained, realizing too late the truth in my statement.

"Oh, you're married," he said with a slight note of disappointment. He stood to offer a chair, and I opted to sit next to Mom, slightly shocked by my directness with this stranger. Mom sat straighter, paying close attention to our byplay.

"Um, yeah. I don't know why I just mentioned him." I was flustered for no reason and becoming embarrassed by my reaction to this man.

"And will he be joining you ladies?" He began to search the filling room. "I don't want to cause problems. He's not the jealous type, is he? If he is, Magdalene, you're my lady for the night," he winked at Mom, making her blush.

"No, Jarrod, Davlin won't be joining us tonight." Mom reached out and held my hand. "Maybe you'll be able to meet him later." She looked at me with eyes that told me to accept my fate, but not rushing me to do so. I couldn't help but wonder again where this woman had been all my life.

The three of us had an unimportant conversation about nothing. Jarrod explained the how's and whys of opening his coffeehouse/bar, and about his plan to start providing a venue for local bands to play live on Friday nights. Mom told him of her pending surgery and my pending departure. Jarrod offered his assistance whenever she needed; Mom, of course, refused any offers of assistance. They seemed very familiar and comfortable with each other.

The evening was pleasant and unpressured. We left around nine to drive the twenty minutes to Guernsey. I left to return to Fort

115

Benning two days later with plans to return in six weeks to help my
mother after her surgery.

Chapter 14

The end of the year, the holidays, Mom's surgery…all blended from one day to another. I spent the holidays in Guernsey with Mom. Heather came over to help me in November and then left for DC in December. The end of the year went faster than I could have thought possible.

By the second week of the New Year, I had returned to Fort Benning to welcome Charlie Company home. Heather and I had planned a welcome home party for the troops and their families. We had arranged the counseling sessions required for returning families and the soldiers alike, and we ensured that the families were available to meet their troops coming off the planes.

On that day, Heather, Jobe, and I arrived on the tarmac of the airstrip where the troop plane was landing early. The weather was cold and miserable, the clouds were low in the sky, an icy drizzle was falling, and the surrounding landscape looked more like a gray wasteland. But nothing could dampen the liveliness of the families. Women had made welcome home signs, children carried balloons, parents wore "Proud Parent of a Soldier" pins. The whole group was festive with the exception of those of us who were waiting to see if the army had made a mistake, or forgotten to call, or played some kind of joke…

I didn't realize my own thoughts until I saw the people around me hugging their returned hero. The wives kissing their husbands, fiancés lifted off the ground, children crying and hugging their fathers' legs, tears, smiles, embraces…. I saw the celebrating families and realized, truly realized…

My hero hadn't returned.

With a numb soul, I welcomed Eric home.

"Becks, I have Davlin's things. His trunk and bags are on the plane. If you want, I'll help you load them in your car." He had his arm around Heather's shoulder. She was still sniffing from her emotional welcome home; Eric held a sleeping Jobe against his shoulder.

"No, Eric. Thanks, but I think I'll just come back for them later." I was stunned by my emptiness of arms, my unkissed lips, my breaking heart. I was fearful again… I was becoming rudely aware that Davlin was not home with me, that my husband was missing…missing from my life.

I drove back to our assigned house, went in the door and directly to the couch. I fell asleep crying into a pillow, the only thing my arms could wrap around.

I woke the next day stiff and empty. I dressed entirely in clothes that were my husband's, pajama pants and a long-sleeved t-shirt, clothes that no longer held his scent. I lay in our bed the entire day, staring at the framed pictures beside our bed. Through tear-blurred visions, I relived the days captured in the photos.

Our impromptu wedding at age eighteen when we were dressed for our high-school graduation. Davlin looked so uncomfortable in his sport jacket, but handsome with his normally unruly hair neatly combed. Another picture of our prom, the night we spent looking up at the stars, watching them fall from the sky. There was a picture of twenty-year-old Davlin holding a puppy he had found in the parking lot by our college apartment. The puppy was too small to be weaned, so Davlin woke up every two hours through the night to feed it. The dog had died the next year when it got hit by a car during a cat chase.

On the other side of the bed, another table held a picture of the two of us at Yosemite, in California, a trip we took after losing the baby, after recovery, after deciding to not lose "Us." In the photo, we stood in front of Yosemite Falls. I was still pale from the surgery and recovery, but happy to be with Davlin. He was protective and guarded, as though I might break.

It had taken us some time to relearn "Us" after the baby, but we did, and we had worked hard to stay "Us." That trip had been at the beginning of our quest. The picture framed behind Yosemite was one of us at Fort Bragg. Davlin had just finished his final jump at

118

jump school. His face was flushed with excitement, eyes bright. He was proud and very happy in this picture. He was grinning like a goon, having just grabbed me from a group and given me a kiss that left my head spinning, hence, my stupefied expression in the photo. I was falling over as my husband proudly displayed his manliness and ability to allow gravity to do its job. Normally when I looked at that picture I always smiled. This day, I just longed for my husband.

I spent the day sleeping between bouts of tears and depression. I moved only to use the restroom and drink from the faucet in the sink. I ignored my phone and general lack of comfort. I hadn't adjusted the thermostat for the winter storm that raged outside; I hadn't eaten in twenty-four hours either. I didn't care. I just pulled the blankets up to my ears and remembered the way my body felt when Davlin would pull me close to him so we lay like spoons.

I woke suddenly to a dark, cold house. I could hear the frozen rain pelting the windows, I could hear the television next door, as the noise seeped through the wall into my silent tomb. I woke with the feeling of having just been kissed.

I begrudgingly got out of the warmth of the bed to use the restroom. As my buttocks froze on the icy toilet seat, I contemplated going downstairs to adjust the thermostat, then decided against the effort in anticipation of getting back to the warmth of the bed.

Climbing back in bed, I lay my head on Davlin's pillow, catching a lingering wisp of his scent. I closed my eyes remembering the way it felt to run my hands through his hair, thick and soft. I loved to control him by holding two handfuls of hair as he performed between my legs. Keeping hold of him as I rocked to his rhythm, bringing him back to me as he made me come, so I could enjoy the feel of his hardness just after climax, making me go again shortly after.

I opened my eyes to a room bathed in bright morning sunlight. The pictures were missing from the side tables, but I had little time to worry about the whereabouts of the pictures because my husband was lying in bed with me. His eyes remained closed as he slept past my waking. I studied his face as he slept.

119

He had two days' worth of stubble on his cheeks and chin, the scar over his right eyebrow was pink as though new, his hair was longer than I remembered, and his lips were chapped. With those slight characteristics noted, I could also see he was breathing. Chest rising and falling, I put my hand over his heart to feel both his breathing and his heartbeat. The soft fabric of his Nebraska State long-sleeve t-shirt was as familiar to me as his face.

He opened his eyes when he felt me touch him. Deep brown and ringed in dark lashes, his eyes took in my face as I continued to marvel in his reality of being here in bed with me. He smiled at me and leaned in to give me a kiss. Our lips touched, and I could feel the slight catch as his parched lips parted from mine.

I didn't want to stop kissing him. I wanted to feel his lips on mine. I opened my mouth to tell him, but without a word spoken, he knew what I wanted of him. Davlin again leaned in to give me a kiss, this one deeper, longer, and more passionate.

His hands moved along my body, moving up into the shirt I wore, feeling my breasts as his mouth continued to pursue deeper pleasure. He took off my shirt, then moved his mouth from mine, to my breasts, then further down, kissing the length of my torso, past my navel. I grabbed two handfuls of his hair as he adjusted his weight to begin his oral homage to my womanhood. Just as I was anticipating the coolness of his breath and the warmth of his tongue on my heated cleft, I woke up, sitting straight up in bed.

I was back in my room, freezing. The temperature had dropped enough inside the house that I could now see my breath as I sat panting, intermittently shivering with cold and with lust.

Grabbing Davlin's waiting house coat, I wrapped myself hastily, slid out of bed into his slippers, and headed down the stairs to adjust the thermostat. While on the ground floor, I ventured into the kitchen, not bothering to turn on lights so as not to upset my dark and brooding mindset. I grabbed a box of crackers and a block of cheese, an apple, and a bottle of wine from the fridge; arms loaded, I trudged back upstairs to wait for the heater to warm up the house.

I lay in the bed, sipping wine, nibbling a cracker, watching the storm outside the window, and began to wonder what Davlin was doing that moment. I tried to cast my soul to him, pray for him, psychically send thoughts to him… I tried to have a conversation in my mind, tried to plan with my husband who wasn't here to make plans with me.

After finishing off the bottle, my thoughts clouded and broke to pieces as my head reached Davlin's pillow once again. The next bout of my dreams was cloudy, soft-edged pictures floating through my head. Our wedding picture, as I dreamed it, where we were once again at the altar saying our vows. As we kissed our kiss as man and wife, my dream picture morphed into the picture I saved but never framed, the ultrasound of our baby. In my mind's eye I could again see us at the doctor's office, hand in hand as the doctor pointed out the legs and arms, the heartbeat of our baby.

Tears began to slide down my cheeks as I fuzzily began to awaken from my drunken dreamscape, and I realized I was crying in reality. Trying to pull myself out of my alcohol-fueled dreams, my body and brain required more time. Again, I fell asleep, feeling the arms of my love draped across my body as we lay nestled again, close. Sharing our body heat, I finally fell asleep believing he was in bed with me.

I awoke the next day empty of tears, empty of desire to move or function. I stopped taking phone calls, I ate only nibbles of food, I was drinking heavily in my bed, and I had quit bathing. For two weeks I survived on dry cereal and vodka. My personal hygiene had failed, and I had absolutely no desire to react to my surroundings. I spent my wakeful hours studying the pictures in our home—framed pictures on the walls, photo albums, those I felt necessary to carry in my wallet—the pictures allowed me to picture Davlin in context in the fullness of his life. Without the pictures, he was a faceless shape, like a person looked at with the sun behind his head.

I was losing my husband.

Three weeks after the return of Charlie Company, I had finally run out of food in my house. I had even eaten the jar of dill pickles

121

topped with mustard. I had long since exhausted my supply of alcohol, and in my sober brain I realized I needed to go shopping.

I showered quickly, washing off three weeks of sleep, sweat, tears, and self-pleasure, as my dreams of Davlin had lately become quite erotic. Many times, I had awakened in the peak of a dream-fueled orgasm. I dressed in a pair of jeans that hung off my body and Davlin's blue t-shirt. I pulled my hair back in a ponytail, still dripping wet down my back. I failed to grab a jacket, simply taking my purse and keys. I ran to my car and drove to the commissary.

When I got to the base grocery store, I realized the depth of the anxiety that was overwhelming me. I sat in the driver's seat of my car contemplating nothing, simply scared to open the door and move. Anything that meant "I am alive, I need this to survive." I could barely do it, but open the door I did. The coldness of the air registered and prompted me to move quickly into the store.

As I was pushing my cart through the produce area of the grocery store, I was overwhelmed and panicked. I grabbed fruits and vegetables alien to me, things I wouldn't know how to use. It didn't matter—I couldn't focus on what I was placing in my cart; I was just grabbing things so I could leave sooner.

The further into the store I ventured, the tighter the vise that gripped my heart felt. Grabbing items as I sped down the aisles, I failed at being able to focus on what I was putting in my cart. I simply wanted to leave and knew I couldn't do it without food.

The dairy aisle was wider with no overhead items to make me feel as though I was being crushed, so I slowed my frenzied shopping and lay my head on my arms, breathing deeply. Rationally, I knew I looked like a crazy person. I was standing next to the milk crying, having burned through the store in a blind terror. I was entirely unable to rein in my anxiety as I went through the store.

"Becks?" I heard behind me just as a hand fell on my shoulder. I raised my head to find Eric Vaughn looking at me with genuine concern on his face. "Becks, I've been calling you for the last three aisles. Heather can't get you on the phone. She thought you went back to Guernsey since you haven't opened your door. Are you alright? You look like you're going to pass out."

I couldn't answer and was only half able to follow the path of his words. As I stood there, I felt the rotation of the Earth; overwhelmed by stress and my emotional instability, I passed out in front of the yogurt at the commissary.

I was awake within seconds of passing out. Luckily Eric had quick reflexes; he saved my head from hitting the floor. My eyes opened to the sight of several faces within inches of my own and a crowd of interested housewives beyond them.

"Ma'am, please don't move. We called an ambulance and it's on the way," a pudgy white man was saying to me as he held me in place with his hand on my shoulder, ensuring I didn't try to get up off the cold floor. "Oh please, I can't see what you slipped on, please just let us know so no one else falls. What did you slip on?"

"Man, she didn't slip," Eric told the man, obviously annoyed. "She passed out. Can't you see she's sick?" Eric then proceeded to pick me up from the floor, cradling me in his arms. We reached the front of the store as the EMTs were wheeling a gurney into the store. Eric placed me on the narrow bed and called Heather as the paramedic began his head to toe check for bumps and bruises.

By the time Eric had ended his call with Heather, the medic had checked my eyes, shining a light to make my pupils react, and checked my blood sugar and other vital signs. He became concerned when he looked at his handheld monitor for my sugar and found that I was registering in the thirties. My blood pressure had also caused some concern, and the man was starting an IV in my arm.

"Eric, can you call Davlin?" I asked.

"Becks, what's wrong with you? He's gone. Davlin is gone. Remember?" Eric was holding my hand, trying to comfort and correct my mistake; he was being quite unsuccessful at both tasks.

The paramedic who was working with me began asking Eric questions, gathering more information. I was no longer concerned with either of them. My head was floating and I felt sick. I tried to vomit but was only able to retch. The medic was ready to go, and out to the ambulance I was wheeled. I lost consciousness on the way to the hospital, just to be awakened by the odor of ammonia and rough voices and movements.

"Ma'am, can you hear me? Are you taking any drugs? Sir, what can you tell us about her…." "Oh, Becks! Wake up! Hey, is she going…." " Ma'am, we need you to lift…." "Oh, shit, her sugar is…." "Bolus! Get her pressure…."

I couldn't follow any conversation, line of thought, action, or direction given to me. I knew some of the voices around me and had no idea who most of them were. I didn't care. I just wanted to sleep. I found my oblivion and slipped into it. There, I had no realization that Davlin was still missing; I didn't know that my mother had cancer and was dying. I didn't feel loss of the child I was never able to hold in my arms. No, oblivion was peaceful and perfect. I had no dreams that made me cry. I was able to see clearly, and I knew that Davlin would come home to me. I wanted so dearly to stay there -- forever.

I woke up in a hospital bed confused and hungry. There was an IV dripping fluid into my arm, a cuff to measure my blood pressure on the opposite arm, an uncomfortable pressure in my bladder like I had to pee, and no way to reach my nurse; my button was on the table just out of reach.

I lay in the bed taking in my surroundings. The room was dark, and there was no light seeping around the blinds—nighttime. The hall was quiet, no early shift chatter—late night. The dry erase board on the wall told me my nurse was Lt. Jackie Hunt, RN, and the date was three days past when I last remembered seeing a calendar.

After watching the minute hand of the clock make a full rotation, I started to yell for help. My voice was hoarse and not to full volume, but my annoyance and persistence paid off when an equally annoyed nurse came into my room.

"Nice to see you're awake, Mrs. Robertson. How are you feeling?"

124

"Like I have to pee, and I would like to have some water too, please."

"Well, you have a catheter in, which is why you feel like you have to urinate. I can get you some water though." The lieutenant was either exceedingly busy late in the evening, or I had interrupted some activity. She was definitely not happy to see me awake and yelling for help.

As she walked back in, I saw her smiling at a young man in the hall. He was openly watching her movements, and she was accenting her steps and swinging her hips slightly more than was necessary. Aware of why she was annoyed with me and internally feeling slightly remorseful of interrupting her tryst, I was still her charge and needed her help.

"Look, obviously you have somewhere else you would rather be, with someone else; can't say I blame you, but for now I need your attention. Take the cath out, help me up to the bathroom, and let me see my chart. Then I will leave you alone for the rest of the shift. Oh yeah, food, please, something to eat."

Lieutenant Hunt looked at me for a rather long time, looked out to the hall at the man waiting for her. "I don't have orders to take your Foley out, you can only have clear liquids like water to drink, and patients aren't allowed to see their charts. Go back to sleep and the doctor will be in to see you in the morning." She made her declaration and began to walk out of my room when I interrupted her quest for sex.

"Can I have my call light and phone? I'm sure there are no restrictions for those." I had become just as annoyed with her as she was with me.

The lieutenant was an attractive woman who was obviously used to the attention of men. Her suitor was watching her from the hall, waiting to see the end of our clash of wills.

The lieutenant, taking the high road, placed my call light on the bed by my hand and moved the phone to the bedside table, now within my reach. After complying with my demands, she left the

125

room, smiling at the man who, on second glance, I decided wasn't that handsome.

I pulled a name from memory, a friend I hadn't spoken to in a year, Captain Julianne Mirkes. I used the phone to call down to the emergency department. Luck was with me that night, as Captain Mirkes happened to be working and was available to come visit an old friend.

It took her less than five minutes in my room to hear the abridged version of what had brought me into the hospital, and even less time to hear of my mistreatment from my nurse. Julianne was not a person to butt in where she was not welcome, but patient treatment and satisfaction was very high on her priority lists, and she knew damn well what the lieutenant and the young man were doing, and it wasn't working.

She contacted the officer in charge of the hospital, a colonel doctor who had spent his career in the service, caring for soldiers and their families. He was very much a no-nonsense man, military to the core, and very annoyed at being awakened at 3 a.m.

In rather short order, a mini-drama played out in the hall as Lieutenant Hunt and her boy-toy were discovered in the room of an intubated elderly man, fornicating to the rhythm of the man's breathing.

The boy, a civilian, was immediately fired and escorted by MPs off post. The lieutenant was considered to have abandoned her post and arrested under both military and civilian laws on abandonment. I truly didn't mean for the night to end in a career-ending arrest, but the woman was cruel and most un-nurse like; Florence Nightingale would not have approved.

The drama ended just as the shift was coming to an end. My new nurse was more compliant with my requests for food and taking the tube out of my bladder. My doctor arrived to explain my anxiety attack at the commissary, fueled by my electrolyte imbalance from poor nutrition over the month. I had caused my own problems, and my depression had finally landed me in a position where I had to take action or risk more serious problems.

126

I stayed on in the hospital for one week, receiving IV fluids with electrolytes, getting dietary counseling, and speaking with a grief counselor and a psychiatrist who prescribed antidepressants. I was warned to refrain from alcohol, information I knew already, but appreciated the reinforcement.

While in the hospital, I had daily visits from Captain Mirkes and from another friend I had depended on after Davlin went missing, Captain Curtis. Both women were friendly faces, determined to keep my spirits up. I would walk around the hospital with them, pushing my IV pole as we went past the nursery to look at the new faces in the world, or down to the Cancer Treatment Center to speak with patients fighting for their lives. Julianne knew how to put life back in perspective for me. She also got me thinking of going back to work and getting my head out of my ass.

With Davlin officially listed as MIA for sixteen months, my life had fallen into ruins. I had stopped working, eating, and bathing; I had been hospitalized for malnutrition; I was trying to pickle my liver in alcohol; and my mother had cancer. His family had also gone to shit, in that his mother had committed suicide, his father was drinking himself to death, and his sister had disappeared off the radar since Sharon's funeral almost a year before.

My house hadn't been cleaned in I couldn't remember how long, my clothes hung off my body from my extreme weight loss, my hair was stringy and ugly, and my skin was blotchy and oily. My life was in need of some upkeep and cleaning. I needed Heather!

My best friend had brought me home from the hospital and said she would be back as soon as possible after making sure Jobe was alright with Eric. I took this time to stroll around the first floor of the house, taking in the dust-covered tables, the musty smell of the couch, the grimy windows. I passed Davlin's office and pushed the door open. The desk was just as he had left it. I wasn't ready to go in, so I pulled the door shut, leaving the military part of Davlin in the office. I went to the kitchen and peered into the open cabinets. No food, no clean dishes, no clean linens. What the hell had I been doing?

I ascended the stairs noting the dust that had collected in the corners and along the walls. The banister had a feeling of built-up muck. I was beginning to have a defeated attitude about my home, when I remembered that I had to do something to get my life together. I squared my shoulders and continued up the stairs to the second floor. I went into the bathroom to turn on the water for a bath, when I saw the dirt that rimmed the tub.

"What the hell?!!!" I cried to no one but myself. "Becks, you're a damn mess. Get your shit together." I turned from the tub, the bathroom, the pile of laundry in the hall, the dust bunnies collecting on the stairs. For a moment, I wanted to run away from the whole damn mess, running away from my life and the past. Instead, I ran out of the house with my purse, avoiding the vanity mirror on the visor as I drove to the commissary and the base exchange to restock cleaning supplies, food, and even pick up some clothes that wouldn't require my constant readjustment to avoid mooning the people behind me.

I returned home and had a sense of dèjá vu, then went to work cleaning the mess that was my life. No marinated steak this time, just down to the business of cleaning. I had been out shopping for two hours, so Heather was worried when she had arrived at my empty house thirty minutes before me. She too had had a plan to help me get my life literally cleaned up; she had brought items to do a home facial and some spa soaps, oils, lotions, creams, and scents, all of which filled a bag that now sat by the front door when I arrived home loaded with bags of food.

Together, Heather and I made short work of the unpacking and organizing. She offered to help me with the house, but I refused her aid tonight.

"This is going to sound totally stupid, Heather, but I kind of feel like I have to clean the house, like it is helping me 'clean up' everything else in my life." I looked at my friend, smiled at her, and then continued, "I can't believe I let myself get this bad. With Mom being sick and her surgery, then the holidays without Davlin, and

128

seeing all the other guys come home, I…I lost what hold on my emotions I had."

"Becks," she came and hugged me, "no matter what we find out about Davlin, be it tomorrow or years from now, you need to know that you have done everything right. I couldn't hold myself together like you do."

Her comment made me laugh hysterically! "I just got hospitalized, Heather!" I wheezed, still laughing. "Look at the mess my house is. I don't even have any clean panties right now!"

Laughing stopped, I was now kind of angry, but not with Heather, with myself. "I have completely fallen apart! Davlin would never accept this… Hell, if it were reversed, he would have been a fucking pillar of strength."

"No, he wouldn't. Davlin would have been hospitalized long before you were." Her seriousness soothed me. I needed serious right now. "He wouldn't have been able to function without you, Becks. You are at least strong enough to get out of bed each morning. I would never have that strength." Her last sentence silenced her.

We stood awkwardly in the hall looking at our feet. "Want to split a pizza with me? " I asked Heather. My peace offering out in the open, she grasped the olive branch with a nod.

Two hours later, we were in the freshly cleaned bathroom, white tiles once again white, floor swept and mopped; smelling of pine needles. The mirror was a clear surface no longer boasting white spots of toothpaste. The toilet was blue-watered and sterile. The room was completed with towels fabric-softened and folded uniformly, filling the shelf.

I had showered in the freshly cleaned stall. My skin was pink from scrubbing with Heather's spa scrub, and cleanly shaven. I finally felt human, more so than in the past six months of heavy stress. Heather, totally in her element, shaped my eyebrows, exfoliated and moisturized my face, and colored my otherwise dull hair, giving shimmer to my locks.

129

We were sitting in the only clean room of the house, eating our pizza, keeping the rest of reality at bay. We had agreed that one room was enough for the night. I did feel better after the shower and grooming. I looked better after both as well.

Heather was skilled in her own way; she was a crafty woman, always full of ideas and the ability to make her ideas reality. For Halloween, she had made Jobe a lion by crocheting a hat and diaper cover complete with tail. She had sat on the porch of her house with Jobe, handing out candies to the children, as the parents commented on the adorable baby.

"I feel like I should have done this when I was younger, like during a sleepover at a girlfriend's house in junior high," I revealed as a pore-reducing mask dried on my face.

"You never did?" Heather asked, surprise evident in her voice.

"Never had a sleepover. Didn't have a lot of friends. My mom was not the type of mother to ensure I had quality girls to spend time with, and her reputation usually got doors slammed in my face. Davlin was my only real friend until high school."

"Well, you should have slept over at his house," Heather joked after a long pause following my childhood memory.

I smiled, cracking the mask. "I did."

"What! You whore!" she joked. "Tell me about it."

"Ah, well, it's one of the reasons Sharon and Allen hated me," I confided. "We were thirteen or so, innocent and just friends at the time. Davlin was getting in weekly fights over me with one idiot boy or another. He had come home with a black eye on a Friday after school, having been in a fight with Caleb who had called me trash, yet again. The black eye and the fight were nothing new, but Davlin and his family were supposed to get their family portrait done at Sears on Sunday, so the eye was an issue." Heather hummed in understanding but didn't interrupt the story.

"Well, Sharon saw her son come in the house with me trailing right after him, trying to help by offering an ice pack. She arrived in the kitchen in time to see Davlin give me this totally random look of complete forgiveness and...I don't know, love. He was fighting for my honor, and to his parents that was more than a friend should do, at least more than Davlin should have done for me.

"She screamed at me to get out of her house, to stay away from Davlin, that we weren't allowed to play together. I was already out of her house, running toward the field I would cut across to get home, when I heard her call me a slut. She said, 'You little slut, stay away from my good boy!' " Heather stopped working on my hair and was looking at my face in the mirror to see my eyes.

"What a bitch."

"Yeah, but I didn't let her get away with calling me anything. Davlin would stick up for me at school, when it came to the boys calling me names or talking about me, but I could hold my own with the girls. I may have been short and scrawny, but I had been fighting off my mom's drunk boyfriends for a while. I could throw a decent punch. I walked right back to his house, never taking my eyes off hers. I went up the four steps onto their porch and punched her right in the gut." Heather let out a whoop of surprise. "The punch shut her up 'cause she couldn't breathe, so I grabbed a handful of her hair and told her, 'Don't you ever call me a slut! I'm a child!' I was crying by that point, and she saw it. I pushed her onto her butt and pointed my finger at her. I asked her, 'What kind of mother calls a child a slut?' "

Davlin came to my rescue then. I was crying, tears streaming down my cheeks for fear of what my punishment would be for hitting Sharon and fear that Davlin would hate me for doing it. He didn't. He grabbed my hand, and we ran off together to the field and then past my trailer park. We ran through a couple more fields, completely out in the open 'cause all the corn had been harvested. Here and there were patches of trees. Places where farmers would rest under the shade. We went into one of those and sat to catch our breath. We just leaned against each other for support. I fell asleep leaning on his shoulder. We both woke up after dark and were scared as shit.

"We walked back to Guernsey. I must have fallen five times 'cause the moonlight made the ground look distorted. Davlin took me straight to the door of my trailer, but it was dark inside. My mom hadn't made it home that night, and I was scared to be there alone. Davlin took my hand and we went across the last field and both climbed the tree in his front yard, into his bedroom window. His mother found us in the morning spooning in his bed. Davlin had his arm over my body, shielding me from her." I smiled remembering the rather unladylike things she had to say about me then, but she never called me a slut again.

Heather laughed, "Was that the only time you two spent the night together before you were dating?"

"No, it pretty much became my norm to sleep at Davlin's on Friday and Saturday nights. I just got smart and was awake by six or seven to be out of the house before Sharon and Allen woke up. I've been sleeping with Davlin more than half my life." I smiled at the realization.

I took a deep breath, said a prayer for my heart, and opened my eyes. "Ready for the rinse cycle?" I asked my best friend.

Chapter 15

I went back to work at the hospital in June, eighteen months after Davlin's deployment. Captain Mirkes was happy to have me back on staff, and I was overjoyed to be useful again. With slightly rusty skills, I reoriented to the hospital and was eventually released on my own to care for the patients who entered the base Emergency Department.

July came and went, and I allowed Davlin and my own birthdays to pass without incidence. I didn't want to bring attention to a day that had always meant so much to the both of us, so I offered to work. I kept myself busy at work and at the gym. By the time the one-year anniversary of Sharon's suicide rolled around, I was back to my ideal weight and back into a routine of running and classes at the gym.

I was as happy as I had been since Davlin went missing. I could joke and laugh with the other staff in the hospital, sometimes even accepting their invitations to meals and parties to celebrate their children and holidays.

I still went home at night to an empty house and talked to my memory of a husband. I had not gone into his office since he had deployed and had no intention of doing so, until a storm broke a branch off a tree and sent it crashing through the window during an early fall storm.

The storm had knocked out power, sending me to bed early; the shattering of glass got me out of bed and down the stairs, ready for a confrontation with a thief. I only found the broken window with an enormous branch too big for me to move on my own resting across Davlin's desk, his computer monitor the only true casualty of the accident.

I called the base housing management department's twenty-four-hour hotline and reported my broken window. Within two hours maintenance men appeared with boards for a quick fix for the night and promises to return in the morning with a new casement window. They were able to muscle the branch back outside where it belonged, put up the plywood, and left for another emergency.

I stood in the door of the office wearing his robe. I took in the carnage left by the leafy assault. There were stray twigs and leaves scattered around the room, files and papers had blown to the corners, pieces of the monitor were splayed across the floor, and Davlin's lovely leather chair was dripping wet, a puddle of rain ruining the waxed wood floor beneath.

I picked up the papers and files, wiped up the wet floor, swept up the monitor pieces and leaves, and then turned off the lights and shut the door again. I was more willing to go in after that night, sifting through the desk for envelopes instead of buying a new box as the need arose. I organized the monthly expenses from his desk and even set the computer up for internet after acquiring a new monitor. I had let myself into the part of the house I had always associated with Davlin's deployment and his being lost, and I found that my feelings for the room were ridiculous. The study no longer felt off limits. In fact, it was almost comforting to sit in the chair that hugged me slightly the way Davlin had.

The holidays came with bad weather, making travel hazardous, but travel I did. Not having to request leave from the post, I simply requested a vacation to be with my mother for Christmas and New Year's, due to return in early January.

My trip to Nebraska was bittersweet. Seeing Mom was always a blessing, but this year she had news of cancer once again. She had avoided telling me about her new diagnosis, worried that I would become overly upset and end up back in the hospital. I tried to reassure her that I was functioning much better than the last time she had seen me. I made a poor attempt at a joke reassuring her I was taking showers again. She didn't find my joke funny but did lighten up as over the visit I showed no signs of driving into oncoming traffic or drinking away reality.

I supported her during her doctor's appointments, just as I had the previous year. Each time we were going home from the Allington hospital, Mom would request we stop at Metro, the coffeehouse owned and run by her support-group buddy Jarrod, the guy I had said reminded me of Davlin. Mom was aware of the similarities in the men, and I think she enjoyed seeing me squirm when engaged in conversation with him.

On one visit Mom had insisted that we stop at Metro. I didn't want to, but being her chauffeur, I had to go where she wanted me to go. Her usual spot on her couch was taken by a group of local college students. Books and papers were strewn across the battered coffee table in front of them, endless coffee cups were balanced on top of the piles, and coffee rings decorated the pages beneath.

Mom had to venture ever so slightly further into the restaurant, where she decided to sit at the bar where she could talk to Jarrod while he worked. I got her situated and then sat next to her on the bar stool. Jarrod was just setting a beer in front of a couple loud young men.

"Enjoy!" he told the guys as they challenged each other to drink the light contents as fast as possible. He was laughing and smiling as he turned toward us. Shooting his eyebrows up in a "What-are-you-going to-do?" gesture, he came over to take our orders, or at least pretend to.

Jarrod was a handsome man; his smile was contagious, and I found myself laughing with him as he explained who the men were and what they were doing. Mom was quiet as she watched us interact. We were laughing and sharing embarrassing stories of our earlier drinking days, most of mine starting with, "When Davlin and I were…" I knew it was annoying that I was always mentioning him, but he had been such a huge part of my life, none of my memories started with anything else.

In time, Mom was ready to leave. She had just received her last course of radiation and had a CAT scan scheduled for later in the week. She invited Jarrod to join us. He accepted, promising his friend to be there in her time of need.

He had walked us out to the car, leaving the bar in an employee's hands. He opened the door for Mom, helping her steady herself as she lowered into the car. He hugged her awkwardly in the seat and then shut the door, turning to me.

"It's nice that you agreed to be with Mom at the study. You don't have to go, you know; she knows you have a business to run."

"Magdalene is my friend, and so are you. I want to be there for both of you." He smiled at me, and I felt a flutter in my chest.

I was embarrassed by my reaction to his smile. Attempting to flee both Jarrod and the way I felt around him, I said, "I have to get Mom home. Thanks again, Jarrod. See you Thursday then?" I blushed furiously and prayed the night was dark enough to hide it. He embraced me in a friendly hug, then opened my car door for me, shutting it after I was settled, and waving as we drove away.

"What are you doing, Becks?"

"I don't know, Mom. Davlin… I don't know," I said, flustered that I couldn't answer her.

"Don't hurt the people helping you. If you feel something for Jarrod, maybe you should act on it. Davlin has been missing for a long time, and you do need to move forward."

"Stop it!" I snapped, slamming the brakes too hard at the light. "You don't get to dictate my grief or my 'lack of movement.' You never held on to a man long enough to love him or be hurt when he left." Tears were streaming down my face as I threw her past at her. "I don't know how I'm supposed to feel! And it doesn't help that you throw Jarrod in my face all the time!"

The car rang with echoed words as our argument died out. I had a point, Mom had a point; neither of us were right or wrong. I really didn't know how I was supposed to be living my life. I was trying to do as many "normal" things as I could, but unfortunately, most twenty-something activities involve couples, which I was a broken half of.

A car behind us honked as the light had been green for a while. I began driving again toward Guernsey, feeling ashamed of my feelings and what I had said to my sick mother.

"I'm sorry…"

I returned to Fort Benning, Georgia, as anticipated in early January. A year after Davlin was supposed to, two years missing in action, with no word of efforts being made to find him or his missing men, no information of a backpack or rifle found. Nothing. My monthly visits to the battalion headquarters resulted in nothing more than the feeling of failure renewed.

As weeks missing became easier counted in months missing, I realized that I could do nothing here in Georgia. I was far away from the people who loved me and were my support, other than Heather, who had her hands full with Jobe and Eric. I could work anywhere, and I had to get away from this monthly obsession to learn the bad news that my husband was still missing and that nothing had been found of the missing soldiers. I could realize that anywhere. It was time to go home to Nebraska.

Mom had been excited to hear of my impending return. She was understanding when I told her I would probably be renting an apartment in Allington; the hospital was there, and I certainly didn't want to live the next several years with blades in my back from the inhabitants of Guernsey.

By March I had made arrangements with the base and the hospital for moving back to Nebraska. I had applied for a job at the hospital in Allington and been offered a job in the Emergency Department almost immediately. I had asked Mom to help me find some apartments. She was doing walk-throughs and describing them to me over the phone at night, a process that was doing little to help me find a place until she suggested she email me listings.

Surprisingly, as I packed up my belongings in Georgia, I was receiving daily listings and pictures of apartments in Allington. Knowing full well that my mom could neither email nor figure out a digital camera, I was forced to ask who her accomplice was.

She became shy and refused to answer me.

"Mom, who is the agent I should call to arrange to see one of these apartments? I found a cute loft I want to get some more pictures of."

137

"Oh, no agent, honey, just call the numbers that are along with the pictures. If you want more, just let me know which one it is. I can call easier than you can. Is it the third-story loft above the downtown business in Allington?"

"Yeah, how did you know?" She had become psychic with her chemotherapy!

"I know the owner. Good friend, actually."

"Who, Mom? " I was tired of her cat and mouse act.

"Jarrod. The loft is the third floor of his building where he has The Metro. He lives on the second floor, owns the whole building." She sounded skeptical of my liking the loft, but somehow happy to hear that I did.

"Oh, well, can I have his number to ask the monthly price, and let him know I'm interested?" The thought of speaking with Jarrod again almost made me blush, thinking back to our last encounter.

She quickly spouted out a number from memory and got off the phone to call him herself. I wasn't sure if she thought of my living in the loft as a good or bad thing, but it seemed ideal to me. The location was within a mile of my work, not in Guernsey, close to stores and the therapist I had arranged for, and, best yet, only twenty minutes from Mom. I thought it seemed perfect, and being a loft, I wasn't ending up with a typical home, something I had always despised.

Apparently, Mom had given Jarrod more than a heads-up for my impending call; just as I was finishing packing the box of dishes, ready to take a break and make the call to Nebraska, the phone rang. I answered on the third ring, happy to hear the voice on the other end.

"Becks?" he enquired with his slight accent. "Your mom told me you were interested in the loft."

"Yeah. Hi Jarrod," I felt stupidly giddy that he had called and was ashamed of my reaction. Maybe the loft wasn't a good idea. If I was reacting like this to a practical stranger… I didn't understand where my happiness of his attention had come from. Breathing deep, keeping my schoolgirl in check, I found my voice again.

138

"Yeah, of all the listings Mom sent me, the loft was definitely most of what I need. I love the windows and hardwood floors."

"Yeah, the loft is huge, but it is cheap to heat and cool. The biggest problem I can think someone would have with it is finding enough furniture to fill it." He laughed as he began to tell me more about the building and the loft he was willing to rent to me.

Thirty minutes later, I had a verbal contract to rent the loft from him. We didn't stop talking on the phone for another hour. He inquired about how I was feeling. He asked about my job search and was happy to hear I would be working locally. The man was pleasant to speak to. I could understand why my mom enjoyed his company so much. He was a rare, genuine person with a quick laugh.

After hanging up the phone, I resolved not to be around Jarrod too much; that could cause problems as my body had begun to mutiny. Many a night I woke panting from a vivid dream of bodies and touches. Most times I knew Davlin had been the male partner in my dreamy exploits, but there were times that was not the case. I could never be sure who the person was, but I knew it wasn't Davlin; the touch was different, and the way I felt in the morning was different.

I called Mom back to let her know of my arrangement to rent the loft. Again, she acted oddly, as though she didn't want me around her friend. Perhaps that was it, that she was being possessive about Jarrod. Or she was doubting my restraint and devotion to my missing husband.

I knew I would be fine living in the loft. I had every intention of working and continuing to function as an adult. Allington wasn't the largest city in Nebraska, but it was indeed a city. There were small art studios and live music on Fridays at clubs and bars… I would be able to make friends and fill my time. That was my goal, to fill my time with more than just Davlin and our past.

Heather was angry that I was leaving. She and Eric had been having a hard time since his return, and she found my house a safe haven. I felt bad for leaving her, but there was mutual understanding of why I had to go.

"Becks," she confided one evening as we were finishing packing the living room, "Eric hates me now. He honestly doesn't look at me the same. Like Jobe has changed me or something! He doesn't ever want to have sex anymore or fool around in the shower. He won't touch me!"

I listened to my friend vent, wondering if she really didn't see the changes that had occurred since having Jobe almost two years before. Her hair no longer took an hour to manage, she simply pulled it back into a ponytail or braid; her wardrobe had changed from stylish fitted jeans and sleeveless shirts, heels, and makeup to sweats and t-shirts, sports bras, and tennis shoes.

"Heather, when was the last time you dressed up for him? Or put on a sexy bra and panties and sat on his lap at the table? Sweetie, Eric came home to a family when he left a sexy wife. You had your schedule and your routine without him, but it's been a year. You have to be willing to bend that routine a little to let him back into your life. Bedtime for Jobe doesn't always have to be eight o'clock, and you don't always have to wear a nursing gown to sleep. Get him interested again, girl! Go jump his bones!!!"

She blushed at my advice; then, looking at her reflection in the mirror leaning against the wall, she agreed that perhaps some new clothes might improve some things. She hadn't shopped since losing her baby weight, but she now had curves she had lacked before Jobe. Heather looked at me in my old cutoff jeans and t-shirt.

"I'll go get sexy panties if you do too. Even if you don't show your pretty panties off to anyone, you'll feel better too." She pleaded with her puppy eyes, grabbing my arm and pulling me toward the door. The thought of the mall was daunting, but I too caught a glimpse of myself in the mirror.

My hair was slack and boring, brown again, Heather's earlier makeover having worn off months ago. My clothes hung off my frame. I'd never been the most stylish person, but now my clothes were disreputable. My skin needed a little pampering, and I could use a new supply of makeup myself.

"Tell you what, Heather, I have to finish packing today; the movers come tomorrow morning. After they leave we can go to the day spa on Halliday Street. I won some passes and need to use them. We can make it an afternoon of pampering. Sound good?"

"Yes, but what about sexy panties?"

"Help me finish packing that bookshelf and labeling the boxes, and we are done, girl. We can go buy sexy panties as soon as this is done."

We finished packing the living room in record time and headed for the mall downtown. There, we went on a mini shopping spree. We went to Victoria's Secret, had measurements and fittings for bras, selected a mound of cute panties, and a few nighties each. With our pink-striped bags in hand, we then visited several other stores, buying jeans that didn't hang off my hips or hug Heather's in the wrong places, blouses and shirts for everyday, and for semi-dressy occasions, I bought a dress to wear to an interview and a couple skirts that just made me feel pretty. Heather went wild buying some low-cut shirts that accented her new cleavage.

During the time we spent shopping, we were both happy, laughing, and talking about nothing important. We had more fun than I had had since before Davlin had left, and I was grateful again for this woman God had placed in my life. While shoe shopping, I got misty-eyed over leaving her.

"Ahh sweetie, don't worry about me. Becks, I promise to come be an inconvenience all the time." She laughed and smiled through her tears.

We both left the mall with armloads of bags from various stores. I was happy to have gone shopping, having thrown out most my old clothes while packing them since none of them fit me anymore. Heather was plotting her attack on her husband.

"Do you want me to watch Jobe tonight?" I offered.

"No, he is up in DC with my mom. I told her about our trouble, and she suggested the same as you. She said we need to get to know each other again. You old married women sure are smart."

141

She winked at me and smiled. "Do you want to come for dinner? Your house is all packed and everything."

"No! Lord, you and those new panties need your privacy. I still have to pack Davlin's office. Finish, I mean. That room has been a pain in my ass! I keep stopping every time I come across a piece of paper and read it!"

"Do you need help?" Her voice softened, understanding how hard packing Davlin's office was for me. "I can finish it for you."

"No, it's cathartic, in a way. I am finding pieces of papers that trigger conversations we had, things he bitched about before leaving. I found his Rosetta Stone CDs and began learning Pashtu, not that it's going to do me much good in Nebraska!" I smiled and laughed. I was trying to be strong for my friend and myself. "I can get it done; I just have the desk to finish and I'm not going to spend all night on it. I just can't dump the drawers in case there is something from the company I find and have to return."

She nodded her head in understanding. "Call me if you want any help. What do you think I should cook for Eric?"

Subject changed, I was again happy as we headed back onto base, the setting sun shining into the car, making us squint to see." I don't know, what is his favorite thing to eat?" I winked at her as I said the last word, making her blush furiously and smack at me.

"You're a nasty bitch!" she declared, laughing.

That night as Heather and Eric enjoyed, hopefully, a private dinner and entertainment at home, I ordered a pizza and set to the task of finishing packing my husband's desk. There were files of papers that were legitimate enough and not anything that needed to go to the company. He had a drawer of regular business stuff: stapler and staples, paper clips, and letter opener. He had a set of pens I had given him when he graduated from college. They were beautiful silver things with weight, engraved with his monogram. I had pictured him grading papers with one of them.

He had a folding framed picture in the back of the drawer; the frame was unfamiliar to me but had been handled frequently based on the wearing of the spine and the button to hold it closed.

I opened the frame to reveal two pictures. The first was of me. It had been taken in the kitchen of our first apartment back at college. I was young, twenty or so, young and stupidly happy to be cooking on our single-top range, in our roach-infested apartment. I smiled looking at it, remembering how happy we had been there. Long before we got pregnant or lost the baby.

The other picture was of our son. I realized, looking at the picture, that Davlin had been holding his tiny body in his hands. The baby rested perfectly in his daddy's palms with his legs curled up toward his chest just as he rested in my belly. I sat staring at the picture, tears falling freely from my eyes, rolling down my cheeks, finding no resistance to gravity. My nose ran and I shook with emotion. Having never seen Davlin with the baby and having only a few ultrasound photos and those the nurses took for me of the baby swaddled. I had never seen this picture before.

I cried out loud, not holding my emotions back. I felt all my grief laid raw again, as though the loss of Davlin and our baby had just occurred. I cried until my head ached and my nose was stuffy. I got up to go find tissues and get a drink of water.

Coming out of the kitchen, my phone rang. Checking the caller ID, it was a number I didn't know, but the area code was for Guernsey. Fearing it was my mother, I answered.

"Hello?" My voice sounded agitated to me. It must have frightened the person on the other end.

"Hey, Becks," a familiar and sexy voice sounded. "It's Jarrod. I was calling to find out if there is anything you need me to get for the loft before you move. I know it can be daunting when you have to get moved and settled. I can't imagine you doing it by yourself."

Surprised in every way by receiving this phone call, I smiled to myself, temporarily forgetting the photo laying on Davlin's desk just feet away.

"Ah, no, Jarrod, thanks. I have everything in order, I think. I already called the electric and gas companies to put my name on the bill, I don't watch TV so I don't need cable…" I was interrupted by the man on the end of the line.

143

"Wait a minute, you don't watch TV? You're not into The Amazing Race or American Idol? You're not a diehard, can't miss an episode of Survivor? What kind of American are you?" He was taunting me, and it was working to raise my spirits. I carried the phone back to Davlin's office, maintaining the conversation. The distraction was helpful.

"Nope, I hate reality shows. I like the goofy, balls to the wall, Japanese game show where people slide down hills in mushroom tops and crazy things like that."

Laughing, he replied, "Yeah, I know that show, MXC...." And so went our conversation. I put him on speaker so I had both hands available to pack, and he got to enjoy the noise of me dumping drawers and books into boxes. Jarrod proved to be an excellent distraction from Davlin and my past.

I stayed on the phone with Jarrod talking about his business. He had to kick out his first belligerent drunk guy that night. He had even paid for the cab to his house. We talked about my mom and how they had met. She had cried on his shoulder during a group meeting after she started talking about me. He told me about why and how he ended up in Nebraska—a girl (of course) who broke his heart.

The general feel of the conversation was that of pen pals, only over the phone. I sat on the couch after finishing Davlin's study, sipping a bottle of beer while I told him about Heather and our shopping spree. All the time I was speaking to Jarrod, I held the folded frame, stroking the soft leather.

I told Jarrod about our plans for the next day, our pending trip to the spa..."In fact, I think I'm going to get good use out of the facial and cucumbers on my eyes. It's late!"

"Oh, shit, I keep forgetting the time difference. I'll let you go. Call me if you think of anything you need before you get here, okay?"

"Jarrod, I'll be there in four days. I'm sure any necessities are going to be en route with the movers or packed in my car. Besides, I'm a big girl. I know where the twenty-four-hour Walmart is if I lose my toothbrush." He laughed at my joke, a sound that was genuine and deep. It made my body react as though anticipating sex, which confused me…. Lord I should stay away from him, I thought to myself. In my reverie, I missed what he had just said. "What? I'm sorry; I missed that."

"I said have fun with Heather today and call me tomorrow before you leave base. Your mother is frantic about you driving by yourself. I'm sure it will make her feel better if I can keep her up-to-date on where you are."

"Doubt it, she hates that I am moving into your loft. She won't tell me why though."

"Yeah, I know. She thinks I'm going to make a pass. Really, Becks, I want you to know, I am really just a friend. I can respect that you are married. I can't imagine what it is like for you to not have him home or to not know where he is, but I would never…"

"Of course not. I know. She knows how I feel about my Davlin. She knows I would never cheat on him, and that is what it would be, cheating. I…I love my husband." Jarrod was silent on his end of the line. "Hello?"

"Yeah, I'm here. Good night, Becks. Just call me if you want to tomorrow. Have fun with Heather." Then he hung up.

I stood looking at the phone, then hung up my end. There was no way he was falling for me. He knew I was unavailable. We had only really talked on the phone. He didn't know anything about me, not really anyway. He's a handsome man with probably a dozen women hunting him. I was sure I could just be the friend who gives girlfriend advice or warns him when a broad is a complete bitch. That was all I had to offer anyone right now. My heart was still devoted to my husband.

I turned off the lights, filling the rooms with darkness and boxes that made darker shades of shapeless masses in the spaces once filled with collections of items Davlin and I had kept for one reason or another. Tomorrow, our life would be packed into a truck to be driven two thousand miles to a home we had never shared together. That thought stopped me at the foot of the stairs.

145

I took a big breath and turned around, opting to go for a walk instead of going up to the bedroom. Outside, the air was crisp and cool. Spring had taken hold of Georgia days, but the winter still had hold of night, frosting the grass during the early hours of morning. I walked through the front yard marring the perfect whiteness of the frost, my feet crunching with each step. My shoes were wet when I reached the sidewalk, but I didn't care. I wanted to move and use my lungs. I headed down the tree-lined street toward Heather's house. At this time of night no one was up moving around, so I had the night to my own thoughts. I barely paid attention to where I was going until I ended up at a playground Davlin and I had gone to one day.

He had sat on the swing, holding his legs in the air so I could push him. He wasn't really having fun, but he was being a good sport coming out with me. After a few minutes of silence on his part as I talked to his back about a patient that had come in with a broken arm from falling off a playground toy, he finally put his feet down to stop his momentum. He stood, pulled me to his chest, and held me with his arms wrapped tight.

I didn't try to pull away. I could hear his heart beating rapidly and I could feel the tension that ran through his shoulders. Finally, I felt his lips on the crown of my head. I turned my face up and his lips met mine. He kissed me long and full, a passionate kiss, a leaving kiss.

With the end of the kiss, I looked at him, trying to judge his mood and manner. He wasn't normally tense or unwilling to tell me his thoughts. He took my hand and we left the playground walking, but not toward our house.

It was fall, October, three months before his deployment.

"I made my will today, baby." Ahh, that explained it. He was thinking about death. I stopped walking and looked at him. He gave a sideways smile and nodded his head in a "come-on" movement. I started walking again, and he started talking again. "I made it, and I want you to follow it if anything ever happens to me. I'm leaving all the money to you, obviously. There will be my life insurance from the service, but also the policy my parents bought me when I was a baby and the one we took out on each other when you became a nurse. That alone is enough money for you to live comfortably for a while.

"If I die overseas though, you also get a portion of my pay until you remarry. I don't want you to get that for too long, okay?" He tried to smile at his own poor humor. We had stopped walking and he had turned to look at me, holding both my hands now. "You're not a person to be alone, Becks. I've always been around to help you, and I know you don't need help, but you do better with it. Baby, don't shake your head at me. I know you better than you do, just like you know me better than anyone in the world.

"I don't want you to pine over me like I'm the only man who could ever love you. I'm just the first. I won't be the last."

Appalled, I asked him, "Why are you talking like you're dying? You're not allowed to leave me, Davlin! I'm only loaning you out for a year, and you better come home to me." I had started my rhetoric with every intention of joking with him to try to lighten his mood but was unable to maintain the joke. "You can't leave me. If you think for a second that you're not going to come home, then we need to go! Let's go. We can go to Canada, or to Switzerland, someplace where you can't be forced to go to Afghanistan!" I was losing my control and had become panicked.

"Baby, calm down." He pulled me back to his chest. Kissing my head as he rubbed my back, calming me with his closeness, he said, "I am only telling you my wishes. I'm not predicting my demise. I will come home to you, and this whole conversation will be something we can joke about later in life." He had to hold me for a few more minutes until I was ready to make our return walk home. It was a silent affair.

When we reached the house, Davlin opened the front door for me. Once inside the front hallway, I turned and threw myself at him. He barely got his hands up to catch my weight, my force knocking both of us into the front door. I crushed my lips to his, seeking proof he was alive and real. I tore at his clothes; his jacket and

147

sweater fell to the floor. He tried to slow my mania with caresses and slow long kisses, but I had a need to feel him, and he soon responded the way I needed him to.

With our clothes spread in all directions, I wrapped my legs around his waist as Davlin used the front hall table, a sturdy antique piece, to support my weight as he plunged into my depths. Hard and fast, he forced my thighs open wide as his body crushed into mine. His breathing had sped up, and I could feel his heart race as I held his face to mine, controlling him with my grip in his hair. God, he filled me! With each stroke, I moved back to achieve my selfish pleasure; his body had always seemed made for mine.

I didn't last long; within minutes, my legs were shaking, my stomach melting, and my brain emptied of all but bubbles as my orgasm filled my body. I lost tension and Davlin held on. His rhythm and speed maintained as I came back from oblivion to take my pleasure again.

We came together later and joined again almost immediately. That night was one of proving to each other and to ourselves that we were alive. Late that night, as the moon cast shadows through the bare tree limbs on the floor in our bedroom, I lay nested with my husband, stroking his arm as it lay across my body. I knew he wasn't asleep, but I didn't know what to say to him beyond come home to me...

Now as I returned to our house, I realized I had asked something of my husband that he could not promise. He hadn't come home to me, not yet. But I would wait. I would bide my time waiting for someone to find the man I had loved all my life. I knew in my heart he wouldn't break his promise to me, and I wouldn't break my vow to him.

Chapter 16

After turning in my keys to the housing inspector, having lunch with Heather, and stopping by the company and battalion to give my forwarding address and other information, I was in my Jeep Cherokee, pulling a small trailer of immediate necessities, driving west toward Nebraska. Already at two in the afternoon, I was emotionally drained and unsure how far I would make it before having to pull over.

I had monitored the loading of our belongings by the military movers, leaving an air mattress, my bags of clothes, several boxes of belongings I considered my worldly treasures, a case of framed pictures I was unwilling to leave in the movers' hands, and the two computers Davlin had had in his office. The Jeep and trailer were full to bursting with just those things.

Lunch with Heather had been an entirely emotional event. She didn't touch her salad; she just sat sniffling. I was carrying the conversation, trying to keep it light, joking about her reaction to her first Brazilian wax. She cringed at my mentioning it, but finally gave into my teasing and opened up.

"Come on, Heather, you know I need you to come out and see me in a month anyway; I'm allowed to paint the loft." I waggled my eyebrows at her, knowingly tempting her with her passion for decorating. A stark white and empty loft was too much for her to ignore.

"Okay, but you have to promise to call me every day." I raised my eyebrows at that suggestion. "Alright, every week, twice a week." That was a slightly more reasonable suggestion.

"Alright, twice a week. I promise."

The rest of the meal we sat talking about nothing in particular. At the end of the meal, I paid the bill and walked out to my waiting, loaded Jeep.

"Call me tonight wherever you stop, so I know you're alright. Just call me while you're driving, alright? That way if anything happens, I can get you roadside assistance." Neurotic Heather was coming out of her cage.

"Heather, I will call you tonight when I stop. I don't want Eric pissed off though, so warn him that I might call late. I think I'll stop in Memphis tonight, or just past, then finish my long haul in the morning."

"Sounds good." She teared up again, then wrapped her little arms around me, squeezing the air out of my lungs. For as small as she was, Heather was strong, more so when emotionally charged.

"I'll call you, and you're going to come help me unpack in a couple weeks, so stop crying. This is the same time span as when you went to DC to visit your parents and abandoned me," I joked with her, and she knew it was true. We would see each other. She was my best friend, and I depended on her too much to let a few miles get in the way of our friendship.

I squeezed her tight and kissed her cheek. "I'll call you when I get on the road. I have to stop by the battalion; then I'm officially no longer a resident of Georgia."

"Don't forget to call."

"I can't. I don't want you worrying, and I know you're going to be calling me anyways. You and my mom."

"See you soon, Becks." She came and gave me another rib-crushing hug and a peck on the cheek, then climbed in the driver's seat of her BMW. She drove out of the parking lot of the Olive Garden we had just eaten at, waving out her window as she drove past out on the road.

I climbed back in my Jeep and drove back to Benning, arriving to the battalion headquarters just as Colonel Barring was arriving from his lunch.

"Colonel!"

He turned and smiled, recognizing me immediately. "Hello, Mrs. Robertson. How have you been? I haven't seen you in a while." He shaded his eyes; the early summer sun was blindingly bright this time of day. "Is there anything you need?"

"Well, I was coming to let you know I'm going back to Nebraska. The housing officer was pretty relentlessly calling to see if I was going to keep the house or if he would be able to assign it to an actual officer who was at the base."

"Son of a bitch! Give me his name and I'll have his balls." The Colonel turned red with fury before my eyes.

"Oh, no sir. I was more than willing to move after I ended up in the hospital. Thank you for the flowers, by the way. I can't stay here anymore." I took a deep breath, then continued my explanation. "I miss Davlin so much, and I know I am making a nuisance of myself, being down at Charlie Company every month. I am a crazy person right now." As I stood before this man, proud and distinguished in his uniform, a true officer, a leader, I missed my husband more. Colonel Barring was what I thought Davlin would have eventually become.

"Becks, you have every right to ask what is being done to find your husband. Not knowing is probably worse than just knowing if he were dead. God forbid. You are the only family member of the missing men who is still in contact with the company. I know you are having a hard time, and I have to say, I'm sorry to see you leave."

The colonel's words brought tears to my eyes. With Davlin and the other men missing over two years, but not yet seven, I felt like a coward or quitter, going home. I had lost contact with many of the families of the other men missing with my Davlin.

The colonel had ensured that Chaplain Needs had, at the very least, spoken to the families of the missing men monthly. The chaplain had come to the hospital to visit me during my recovery from my self-inflicted malnutrition. He had come to the house monthly; whether I would see him or not, he came.

I was walking away from a strange support system, but one that could change any day. I was grateful for the support I had received, but I needed to become more independent and reacquaint myself with my family, my mother, and Rachel, Davlin's sister, maybe even Allen.

"Sir, I came to say thank you, and good bye. Good luck too." I had tears in my eyes as I said the words. The colonel pulled me into his arms and held me like a father figure. I wrapped my arms around the uniformed officer and cried onto his lapel.

"You're going to be fine, Becks. You're going to find some way to be happy, with or without Davlin. I promise that you will be made aware of any changes. I will let you know when we find anything."

I pulled back from his grasp. Taking a deep breath and looking around at the buildings I had visited almost weekly since my husband deployed to Afghanistan, I asked, "Am I giving up?" I felt pitiful and defeated. I was running away from ghosts! I was leaving everything I knew to move toward a life that I didn't know how to live by myself.

"Of all the couples I have ever met, of all the women who have looked after their men, and of all the men who gave their hearts to a woman, I have never before seen a couple like you two. He told me one night how you two ran away and eloped instead of walking for your graduation." He smiled, obviously remembering something about Davlin's story. "He said he had never been more sure of anything in his life than when he jumped in the car with you and left for Vegas."

I smiled remembering our wedding. I had to laugh remembering how his hands had shook as he placed his gumball-machine ring on my finger. It was ugly, cheap, and stained my finger green for months, but he had put it there with the promise to love me and honor me until death parted us… I had it still, around my neck on a chain that never left my body.

"Thank you, sir. I have to go, but I left my new address, my number is the same, and, of course, you have Davlin's family information." Drawing another deep breath to give me the strength to move, I said, "Goodbye, Colonel Barring."

"Zander, Becks, it's Zander. Good luck to you." We shook hands and I turned to leave when he called me again. "Becks, wait!" Pulling his wallet out of his pocket, he handed me a business card. It had the battalion insignia and his name in Copperplate Gothic.

Below his name were several numbers. He circled the middle number and handed me the card. "This is my cell phone number. I may or may not be here; you know we move around where we are needed. But if you ever hear something that sounds more like bullshit than the truth, call me. I will find out for you. And I promise, Becks, I'll be there to let you know in the end, good or bad. I'll let you know." We shook hands again; then both having places to be, we went our separate ways.

I entered Colonel Zander Barren's numbers into my cell as soon as I got to my Jeep, then called Mom. I got her answering machine, which I made aware that I was officially leaving Fort Benning. I called Heather to let her know also. She and I talked as I drove off post; then afternoon traffic became heavy enough to require my attention, and I ended our conversation promising to pick up when I reached Memphis.

The number of entrances and exits while maneuvering away from Fort Bragg was a maze that eventually would get me going toward Birmingham, but once on 85 South headed into Montgomery, I had time to think. I was painfully aware of having left Heather. I missed my friend and confidant already. But as the miles ticked away, I realized that for the last year and a half I hadn't been living. I had not been a functioning person.

I would spend entire days doing nothing. I had nothing to show for almost two years of my life. I had simply wasted my time moping around the house in anticipation of bad news that I was sure I wasn't going to receive. As I merged onto 65 North, toward Birmingham, I had decided to live again.

My thoughts and fears about moving home were unfounded. I wouldn't have to tolerate the ignorance of my hometown. I wouldn't be living there. I could make friends and have hobbies to fill my time. I would work again at a job that I had learned to love again.

I was feeling lighter, having made a conscious decision to try to live happy again, when my phone rang on the seat next to me, pulling me out of my reverie.

"Hello?"

153

"Hey, Becks, it's Jarrod. I was calling to make sure your move and drive were going alright." His voice made a warm spot in my stomach, a spot that concerned me. I did want to talk to him though. I enjoyed hearing him talk about his adventures, and he reciprocated. Jarrod had become a friend, albeit a dangerous one.

"Yeah, the leaving was kind of hard, but Heather did well," I joked. "Seriously, I wanted to cry all day. I went to the battalion to let the colonel in charge of Davlin's unit know that I was leaving. He made me cry."

"Ah, shit. You alright?" His voice was genuinely concerned.

"Yeah, it's been better the farther away I get from the base. Besides, I made a decision to be a happy person. Jarrod, do you know I have literally wasted over two years of my life sitting around reliving my past? I have cried myself to sleep almost every night." I wasn't shy telling him these things; I had told him before during our other phone conversations. "I have to try to live a life independent of Davlin, and it is hard so far."

"Well, I can't say I know how you feel, 'cause I haven't ever been there and I don't know anyone else who has been in a position as hard as yours. I respect that you have your vows, Becks, but how long can a person go without love and that bond of marriage?"

"Jarrod, people live without a marriage and feel unloved all the time. My mom was never really married and hardly ever felt loved."

"That's not true. She had you, and she knows you loved her." I felt abashed hearing him say that. Jarrod knew my mother in ways I didn't think I ever would.

"Yes, I do love her, and I did as a child too. You're right, when there is a child in the picture, there is unconditional love. I don't have that, but I have her. And she loves me." My comment was met with silence, so I continued. "I am married, and I will consider myself as such until Davlin is found or until he is declared dead. I will not break my vow to him. I have to have something to hold on to."

I was being honest with myself and with Jarrod. I didn't want him thinking anything other than friendship could come from our relationship, and I needed to voice my stance out loud. "Jarrod, you can respect that, right? You and I can be friends, and I can depend on you and you can depend on me… But that has to be the extent of our relationship." Again, silence. Ominous silence on the other end of the phone.

"Well, I guess I can be your friend, but I am something else to you too."

"What? Don't say family, I have a strict belief about that shit."

"What? No, I'm your landlord too. So you better be nice or I'll charge you double for rent!" And with that comment, the tension bubble that had built burst. We continued to talk about bad drivers and fancy cars I was encountering. With Jarrod as a navigator, I was able to miss evening rush hour at Memphis and, making great time, I continued north once again toward Saint Louis.

As more headlights turned on, I realized how badly I needed to stop for the night. My back ached from the long drive, and my head ached from straining my eyes in the dark. I was halfway to Saint Louis. I had made it further than I had originally planned for this first leg of my trip. Finding a Holiday Inn just off the highway, I pulled in for the night. Grabbing my clothes bag and purse, I alarmed the Jeep and went to check in.

The room was a typical ordeal with a single bed, TV sitting on the dresser, a table, a couple nightstands, and a functional bathroom. Grabbing my toiletries and my bathrobe, I went to the bathroom, not bothering to close the door. I ran a bath of barely tolerable hot water and sank in up to my neck. Enjoying the heat seeping into my muscles, I began to relax. Not willing to let my thoughts wander backward to the many nights Davlin and I had spent in hotels like this, I began to think of the future.

I had a job waiting for me in Allington. I had done a phone interview with the director of emergency services for Allington Trauma Center and had been hired on, many thanks to the glistening letters of recommendation that had accompanied my resume. My prolonged absence from nursing was forgiven, considering the circumstances, and I had completed a Trauma Nursing Core

155

Competency in Atlanta before restarting work at Fort Benning. I really had been ready to go back to work.

I had never really made great friends with the other single nurses, mostly because I had never been able to go to bars or out on girls' nights to male strip clubs. I had always had the responsibility to go home and cook and clean for my husband. I never felt as though I was missing out on anything, even the next day as everyone was standing around the nurses' station gossiping about who took who home. I was ready now to have some form of adult friendships with other women of my profession. I was almost twenty-seven, and I had had little adult contact other than Heather for a very long time.

I was ready to live by myself. The loft would be the first place I would live alone, able to choose what goes where. I was excited about reinventing my surroundings to fit my tastes as an individual Me, not as Us.

I stayed in the bath, letting the water cool as my thoughts flitted from Davlin and the items on and in his desk, to the bar I was going to live above. The building and the area of Allington were old and becoming quite rundown until young business owners like Jarrod stepped in. The last time I was there, not only was Jarrod's building renovated, but also the two across the street and the old corn-canning factory. Long since closed, it had become a haven of activity as it was being converted to an indoor farmers' market on the ground floor with the upper-level stalls being rented out to various shop owners and vendors to sell their goods all year long out of the weather.

I was excited to be a part of a renewed town, a new life, and purpose for everyone! I thought of my mom, sitting on her couch with the throw that Jarrod had just given her. What a gentleman! I pictured how happy Mom had been as he draped the blanket over her lap. I thought of how my mom had changed—not just her physical change, which was overwhelming, but also her personality. She had become so supportive and compassionate. She was most unlike the woman I thought had raised me.

My thoughts shifted to Jarrod. What a strange man he was; immediately openly friendly, offering to help a stranger, continuing to help my mom. He called and laid his life open, shameful acts and acts of kindness alike. He would faithfully call to ensure my safety and had remained friendly even with my rude declaration of single-purposed friendship. He was handsome and kind. He probably fed orphans and adopted lost puppies.

I splashed myself out of thinking about Jarrod. I couldn't afford to allow the man to be placed on a pedestal in my mind. Davlin had the only place in my heart that was worthy of a pedestal. My husband.

As my muscles relaxed and the heat of the water made sweat bead on my brow, I drifted back to a hot summer day of our youth. I was thinking of Davlin dripping wet without his shirt on as he stubbornly pushed a friend's tractor out of a mud pit during a summer storm. He and a couple friends had played chicken with tractors—Footloose, anyone?—and both tractors had wound up stuck in the mud pit.

Teenage boys are impulsive; teenage boys in trouble are frantic. These boys were bound to have their asses handed to them for stealing tractors and for getting them stuck, where one would have been used to pull the other out.

At the time Davlin was eighteen and in prime shape from football training and swimming and diving. His back muscles strained, glistening wet as he and the other boys tried to push the steel mass out of mud two feet deep. The rain ran down his spine, trailing past the waist of his pants that were falling off his hips. I could see the whiter skin of his butt beginning to show. Davlin hated wearing boxers, and he was in serious danger of showing all in attendance what God had graced him with. The girls standing around were laughing at the hilarity of the situation, but I could see that their eyes were trained on Davlin, not their own boyfriends.

Just thinking of his back straining and his hair dripping wet down his back, his triceps and biceps bulging as he worked in the mud and rain… My hand slid down my stomach to my wet

157

slipperiness. I closed my eyes and remembered his wholeness, how overwhelmingly large and perfect he was. Up close, during his teenage years, Davlin had been massive and unstoppable. A selfish lover, but a willing participant for repeat acts of depravity.

Thinking of his power, my stroking increased and I began to tense my muscles in anticipation. His intense eyes staring at me through his dark lashes, his cocky mouth smirking at me as he drove himself into me that night. My body was a ball of tension as I pulled my legs up toward my belly, thighs tightening on my forearm, but my fingers kept reminding me of how good Davlin had felt. He had come out of the mud pit, glorious and invigorated from releasing the tractor, but obviously wanton. His look had been intense, and he paid no attention to anyone else. He just walked up to me, wrapped his arms around me, and crushed his lips to mine. We stood there oblivious to the stares of our classmates and friends, careless of the downpour of rain that was washing away the mud that clung to his pants, heedless of our responsibilities; he had need of only one thing, and I was more than willing to oblige.

Flashes of light and a feeling of intense warmth filled my body as I reveled in my orgasm. Bodiless, boneless, senseless; I stayed in the tub until all senses returned and I was back in the bathroom of a Holiday Inn, somewhere outside of St. Louis. Reality having returned, I pulled the plug to release the water in the tub, stood, pulled the shower curtain closed, and cleansed myself of the day, as what remained of the hot water rained down on me from the showerhead.

In bed that night I opted for oblivion over nostalgia and took a sleeping pill. I turned on the television to a mind-numbing rerun of a sitcom and fell asleep to the sound of a laugh track.

The next day I awoke to cloudy skies, wet roads, and a forecast for rain all the way into Nebraska. I left my room and went to enjoy my complimentary continental breakfast. I called Mom to check in. Again I got her answering machine. Worried, I called Jarrod to see if he had seen her.

"Hello?" A sleep-thickened voice answered on the fourth ring.

"Jarrod? It's Becks. Have you seen my mom lately? I've been trying to keep her up-to-date with my move, and I can't get her on the phone."

"Ummm." I could hear the mattress springs of his bed creak as he moved. "Umm, yeah, I saw her here last night. She was with Donald, another guy from our support group. I think they are sweet on each other."

"Oh. Well, I guess that's…something." The announcement that my cancer-ridden, reborn mother was dating sounded more like old times to me. "Well, I guess I'll just call her later. I'm headed out of the hotel, and I have a good ten hours of driving today."

"Yeah, be careful, weather said rain all day. You alright pulling the trailer in the rain?" He had fully awakened by this point in the conversation. I couldn't help but picture him laying in bed sans shirt, leaning up against the headboard of his bed talking to me with his hair disheveled and his face creased from hours of sleep.

Shaking off the image, I challenged him, "What happens if I say 'No, I don't feel comfortable towing a trailer in the rain?' "

"I'd tell you to detach it from your car and we can go get it with my truck when there is better weather."

His bluntly honest, caring, compassionate, and smart answer silenced me. He really was a good guy, too good. I cleared my throat and chugged the last of my coffee before talking again.

"Thank you, Jarrod." I had to pause. Never before had anyone made me feel so ashamed for my behavior and attitude. I knew I was being unfair to him. He had only been thoughtful and friendly. He had never actually made a pass or said anything along the lines that we were anything more than just friends. "I'm sorry that I'm such a shit to you."

"Well, you should be sorry. I'm awesome!"

"Yeah, modest too." We both laughed. "Seriously, thank you."

"You're welcome. Now, I'll call you later. I run a night business, remember! I'm sleeping, damn it." His tone was playful and light.

159

"You own a coffeehouse, you lazy ass! Get out of bed and go open your bar." I laughed at his grumbling that responded to my demand and hung up. It was long since time to be on my way home.

My arrival home was met by no parade or party. I had arrived just in time for dinner rush at the restaurant. Jarrod had little time to spare beyond showing me where to park my Jeep and where the old freight elevator was to get my belongings up to the third-floor loft.

He wasn't able to accompany me up, merely handing me a set of keys on a chain with a four-leaf clover set in glass on it. I grabbed the bags from my front seat, then opted to unload the backseat into the freight elevator too. I took the rumbly and slow ride to the third floor, able to see the inner workings of the old shaft through the wood siding. Each floor had a drop and rise door to gain entrance to the foyer by the doors leading to the inner lofts.

At the third floor the elevator stopped, swaying slightly. I opened the doors to both elevator and foyer, shoving my bags and boxes out onto the landing, worried that someone might call the elevator to the ground floor at any moment.

With all bags unloaded, I opened the door of my rented third-floor loft and took in my new blank canvas. The space was immense!

Along the east wall, opposite the door, was a wall of windows that looked out to the street below. The front of the loft faced south; the soft red and blue neon of the restaurant sign shone through the three windows along the front. Just to the left of the door was the kitchen space. The refrigerator next to the counter made an L-shape to share the only interior wall of the loft, which separated the bathroom from the rest of the space. The bathroom was at the northernmost end of the apartment, with three windows that were overlooking the side street and the alley where my Jeep was parked.

All the walls were white, and the floor was hardwood. I could see in my mind's eye what I wanted the apartment to look like. I was excited to get started. I shoved my bags and boxes in the door, grabbed my keys, and headed down the elevator that sat waiting for me. I unloaded the contents of my Jeep and the trailer into the elevator, then repeated emptying the elevator into the hall, then into the apartment.

When I was done "moving in" what I had brought, I had a small pile of boxes, two CPUs, an inflatable mattress in its storage bag, an overstuffed extra-large leather chair, four bags of clothes, and a small fireproof safe and three crates of framed pictures. I moved the chair toward the windows overlooking the street. I took the inflatable mattress to the front of the loft and plugged it in to inflate. I tossed my bags of clothes toward the inflating mattress and pushed the other boxes and crates to the interior wall, clearing the entire center of the loft again.

I switched off the light, closed and locked the door, and took the stairs down to the ground floor where I came to another locked door. Using another key on the chain, I gained entrance to the restaurant. The door was at the end of the hall where the restrooms were located. I stepped out to the main room and went to take a seat at the bar.

I asked the perky blonde tending for the night if she had seen Jarrod.

"Oh yeah. I've seen all of Jarrod," the busty thing taunted, giving me a devilish look.

"Well, can you tell me where he is? I need to talk to him," I asked in a bit of a bitchy tone. The blonde behind the bar seemed like a bitch, so I should have been speaking her language.

"I don't know," she shot back. I had obviously stepped on her toes. "I have to work, and if you're not going to order a drink, you have to leave the bar."

"Casey, Becks is my new renter for the upstairs loft," Jarrod proclaimed as he walked into hearing distance. He put a friendly arm around the pretty girl's shoulders. "Becks, this is Casey, my girlfriend." He wasn't able to look me in the eyes when he said it. When he did look at me, he gave me a shrug.

"Nice to meet you, Casey." I immediately dismissed her and changed the subject back to what I had come down to speak with

161

Jarrod about anyway. "Do you have any restrictions on what I can do with the loft? Do I need to have approval for any project?"

"Ahh, no. You're going to start a project now? It's seven at night!" He laughed at my impatience.

"I have so many ideas going through my head, I'm not going to be able to sleep with them pulsing through my brain!"

"Alright, get started," he laughed again. "Do you know where the hardware store is?"

"Yeah, I'm from here, remember?"

"Yeah, not Allington, I was just asking!" Casey watched us banter back and forth with a look of pure hatred for me.

Her silence wasn't lost on Jarrod either. "Um, yeah, so let me know if you need anything in regard to the loft. Rent is due the first." He winked and turned back to his angry girlfriend.

Ignoring Casey, I left the restaurant that was loud with weekday dinner conversations through the back door. Hopping into my Jeep, I drove across town to a family-owned hardware store that I knew had some amazing products available. The owner had a side hobby of glass blowing, and he had begun to turn his creations into functional art. As I walked the aisles looking up at the beautiful blown-glass light fixtures, I wasn't paying attention to anyone else in the aisle.

I rudely bumped into an oncoming shopper, in the form of a couple also looking up, the same as me. Laughing and apologizing, I stopped talking when I recognized the face of the man who recognized me as well.

I stood staring at Caleb McMahon. Catching myself, I apologized to the woman pushing a cart loaded with paint cans and tools.

"Hey, Caleb. Please excuse me," I addressed the woman.

"Yeah, no problem, Becks. Ah, this is Tara, my girlfriend."

I extended my hand to the woman—a tall, beautiful woman— who kindly smiled and dismissed our accident.

"Nice to meet you," she assured me in a thick Euro accent. An awkward silence followed the apologies, as we looked at each other.

Breaking the silence, I asked, "Renovating?"

"Yeah. We bought a house on Mission Avenue. One of those old numbers that is going to cost me more to fix than it is worth." He smiled his million-dollar smile, then asked, "Did you move home or are you visiting your mom?"

"Just moved back. I needed to be around for Mom. She's getting worse. I wanted to be around some familiar faces too; makes it easier not having Davlin."

"Yeah, I can imagine," he responded.

Tara didn't know who we were talking about and asked, "Who's Davlin?"

"Her husband," Caleb answered. "We all went to school together."

"Where is he?" she continued to pry.

"He's missing in action from Afghanistan," I explained. The confession ended our conversation. But in saying it, I hadn't had the heart-wrenching pain I had suffered the first time I had had to admit it out loud.

"Well, we have to go," Caleb stated. "It's nice to see you. Welcome home." He reached for their cart and walked Tara toward the front of the store.

I finished my shopping at the hardware store without running into anymore old friends. On exiting I had a trunk full of paint, rollers, pans, wood, lacquer, brushes, mineral oils, and any mixture of other tools needed to create the home I was envisioning. The two items I was most excited about were two of the blown-glass light fixtures for the kitchen space and the bedroom space.

The first, for the kitchen space, was blue and green fingers of glass, each with an LED light at the collective base. With over fifty fingers of different lengths, the blue and green glass mixed with clear glass bulbs that extended out all hodge-podge. The overall effect was that of being underwater at sunrise. The blue and green hues cast over the walls and floor, intermixed with dashes of sunlight and the light provided by the clear bulbs.

163

The fixture for my sleeping area was made in tones of pink and yellow. The hundreds of balls, again each housing an LED, were strung together like a bunch of grapes. The pink and yellow made me feel as though I were looking at the world from inside my own body. I felt safe as the light cast upon me, like I were in a womb.

After the hardware store, I proceeded to a group of stores clumped together. I stopped at Bed Bath and Beyond for curtain rods and drapes to provide my needed privacy, and I got a new bath mat. From there I went to an import store where I found three hand-crafted room dividers. Purchasing all three, I had reached the maximum capacity of my Jeep.

Back at the loft, I was able to fit all the purchases on the elevator, then force them into the hall. As I opened the door to the loft, I had a strange sense of déjà vu. I hated that feeling! It usually made me feel sick to my stomach. I had never been in a situation like this before, so I was unsure where the sensation came from.

Brushing it off, I took my purchases inside, excited to get started.

The next morning dawned through the windows on a room that the night before had been white. Now happy yellows and bright blues spanned the space. The kitchen had no natural separation from other parts of the house, so I created one by hanging large framed pictures from chains with a picture frame on one side and a mirror opposite. The hanging art broke the long room on one end. At the front of the loft, the room dividers became an obvious break, separating the "living room" and the bedroom. The painting had taken the majority of the night, but now with the task complete, I felt relieved that I wasn't surrounded by so much emptiness.

Exhaustion had finally set in, and around four in the morning I had fallen onto the inflatable mattress that temporarily served as my bed. I was so exhausted I never heard my phone ringing.

I awoke in the late afternoon hungry, thirsty, stinky, and sore. Finding water easiest, I drank from the faucet, not bothering to find a cup. Thirst quenched, I went to the bathroom to run a tub of hot water. Killing two birds with one stone, I soaked away my soreness and rid myself of paint splatters and the smell of mineral oil.

Emerging from the bathroom pink, clean, and still hungry, I threw on one of my new outfits I had bought with Heather. In a pair of gray pants and a soft pink top that hung off one shoulder, paired with a strapless bra and a pair of heels that happened to be on top of my clothes, I looked pretty when I saw myself in the mirror. Quickly mousse-scrunching my hair, applying the slightest hint of lip gloss and a spritz of body spray, I grabbed my purse and headed down to the restaurant.

Down in the main room I was happy to see my mom at her designated spot on her couch. Seeing me walk out of the dark hallway, she waved me over. Her eyes took in my outfit. One eyebrow rose in question as I walked over to her.

I was laughing at her expression by the time I reached her seat. "Hi, Mom." I hugged her tight, then sat next to her on the couch. I could see why she liked the spot; from here she could see the whole restaurant and the comings and goings of everyone.

It was easy to find Jarrod. He was manning the bar with Casey. He glanced up, having seen me pass by en route to Mom, smiling and waving. I waved back and sat to have a chat with Mom, scolding her for her lack of concern for me over my move.

That evening and many more over the next week were pleasant. I found myself slipping into a nocturnal schedule, which was fine, seeing as my job at the hospital was going to be at nights. I had the painting complete in one night, light fixtures hung the next night, pictures framed in old six-paned windows and hung by chains creating additional separation of kitchen and living room.

The bathroom had been spruced with colorful towels and a bath mat. I had spent a small fortune at Pier One, purchasing colorful stemware for the kitchen. I had constructed a large island in the middle of the cooking space, topped with bowls, a fruit basket, canisters, and an oriental cat cookie jar.

By time the moving truck had arrived, the apartment was partially furnished yet still requiring couches and a bed. With our life

165

neatly packed in boxes, I debated how much I wanted to unload in my Davlin-free environment. He had always turned toward modern metals and wood, whereas I had secretly loved the bright tones of Indian silk and mosaic tile.

I was still debating how to incorporate the leather-bound books and sleek CPU when I opened a box of framed photos. I smiled at the picture of Davlin in uniform; his hair had been cut way too short, but he was grinning at me. The picture had been one I had snapped just a week before he deployed. It had been winter, so his ears were red with cold and the tip of his nose was scarlet from his near-constant wiping. Someone had grabbed his well-insulated GorTex jacket earlier that day, and he hadn't yet recovered it. Still in good spirits even if just for show, he had smiled for me. My hero.

I took the picture to the bedroom space of the loft. I had already moved my bed frame and mattresses to the area, made easier by my retractable wall. I had also brought in my bedside tables, now piled with pictures of Davlin and me. Looking at the growing mound, I realized I needed more space or less sentiment.

I contemplated the issue as I screwed together the bed frame. With headboard and footboard upright, I maneuvered the box spring over to the frame and let it drop freely, remembering belatedly that I had downstairs neighbors.

Cringing at the racket, I fixed the box spring and then mattress in place before pounding started at my door. I went to open it, expecting an agitated Jarrod; instead, Casey was at the door. Even having (obviously) been awakened by a manic upstairs neighbor, she was gorgeous. She was clad in a t-shirt and men's boxers, her hair was loosely braided, and last night's eye makeup was smeared under her lashes.

"What the hell are you doing? Knocking down walls!?" She suddenly wasn't pretty anymore.

"I just got my things delivered. I'm sorry, I'll try to be quieter," I placated.

"You better." She turned with a whip of her hair. As she stomped away I heard her say, "bitch."

What the hell? I had never had anyone act like that, especially an adult! Waiting until I heard the door downstairs shut, I purposefully stomped back into my bedroom area.

Later in the evening, I went down to the restaurant before the dinner rush. Jarrod and Casey were at the bar talking. I walked over and sat. Jarrod turned and grimaced. Casey hit him in the back of his head and stormed out of the bar.

"What the hell?" I asked.

Jarrod sighed, "She'll be back later, maybe. What do you want to drink?" Our conversation became laid back as though we were old friends, not people who had known each other only a few months.

Casey didn't come back. Jarrod told me about her very strong jealous side. He called it her "Hyde-side."

"She is beautiful and can be incredibly nice, but Becks, you seem to have brought out the worst in her."

I felt bad for Casey's response but had to tell my friend the truth. "Jarrod, I think you dodged a fucking bullet with that one."

He didn't comment.

Chapter 17

I started work, full-time at the local hospital. I was working nights in the Emergency Department. My orientation to the facility and to the unit were uneventful. As was my usual practice, I kept my mouth shut, allowing people to show their colors. There were the typical mixes of people working in and around the ED: loud and bossy nurses, overworked doctors, whorish paramedics, haunted cops, and any degree of wanton patients.

I was busy enough to keep my mind off of my reality, but not quite busy enough to avoid the drama that was my place of work. I was able to get a good grip on the soap opera by the time I was off my orientation. I knew who was sleeping with who, I knew who hated who because of who they were sleeping with, I knew who was having an affair with one of the doctors, and which local police officer was the biggest dog. I couldn't care less who was schtooping who. Frankly, I found it entertaining. It made me miss Davlin. Luckily, I was too exhausted to cry when I got home each morning. I would fall into my bed just as the morning sun was daring to press over the buildings across the street.

I had been at work just three months when a traveling nurse from Florida came to fill an open position in the unit. His name was Stosh, an experienced trauma nurse who seemed to have nothing but disdain for our small rural Emergency Department. He was arrogant and bossy. He had little respect for our doctors and alienated all the ancillary staff by treating them like surfs on his royal land. He was a tall and handsome man, who seemed amazed when women had the audacity to speak to him or attempt to tell him what to do. He was a jackass.

On a particularly busy Friday night, one with several motor vehicle accident victims, two football injuries, a suicide attempt, and a woman who had delivered a baby in her car, Stosh took it upon himself to usurp the chain of command in the department and disregard the charge nurse.

Having an assignment that meant he had to care for the two teenagers who had long bone fractures and were at high risk for bleeding, received during a football game, Stosh refused. "A monkey can take care of them. I'll get the MVA patients. I'm more experienced to care for them."

"Just work your assignment!" Clara, our charge nurse was telling him, looking past him as yet another ambulance rolled into the bay without having called in on the radio to warn us what was coming. "Quit arguing and take care of the patients you were assigned."

"I won't! You're not using me to the best of my abilities. You shouldn't even be able to give me an assignment," he sneered.

I was at the nursing station gathering supplies to care for one of the multiple MVA patients when I overheard his rudeness.

I dropped my supplies and walked to where he and Clara were speaking. I placed myself between the two of them and interjected, "Stosh, if a damn monkey can care for the boys with fractures, then I don't see anyone more qualified than you! You haven't mastered the social skills of a kindergartner. Quit pretending you're God's gift to the Emergency Department. Shut your mouth, get your charts, and take care of your patients. If you don't like being bossed around by women, you should have chosen a job that isn't a female majority profession."

To date it was the most I had spoken since I had been hired. Taken aback by my outburst, Stosh stood there staring at me, as though he wasn't aware that I had the ability to talk. Having overheard my diatribe, Dr. Tummens, one of our female doctors, stood up and started to clap and cheer. Encouraged by the doctor, the other staff began to cheer as well.

"I don't think anyone would miss you if you left, Stosh, and seeing as you hardly work, it wouldn't be a big deal for us to carry your patient load." I turned to go to my patients, wading through the staff, still cheering the defeat of the Great Ass, their congratulations and thanks following me into my patient's room.

Friendships were much easier to form after that night. In fact, that night, at the end of the shift, several nurses invited me to "a totally cool coffeehouse with a knockout bartender." I declined, knowing that they were headed to the same place I was, only I would be on the third floor sleeping as they oogled Jarrod or one of his staff.

Stosh did stay for the length of his contract. He was much more amicable and became a much better team member after that night. At times we were forced to work in close proximity, during codes and such. When passing each other in the hall or while in the break room, he always seemed as though he had something to say, but never did.

The other staff nurses became friendly, chatting about their children and families. Some asked about my husband, having seen my wedding band; I would always answer that he was deployed overseas in the army. As far as I was concerned, it was the truth. None of them associated Davlin or me with the local soldier who was missing in Afghanistan.

Day by day, I would work my twelve-hour shift, drive home, shower, and fall into bed exhausted. I worked five days a week, covering shifts that were short, making my days melt together. I often lost track of what day of the week I was on. If I wasn't sleeping, I was washing laundry or lying on the couch too tired to move. I hadn't been down to the restaurant in weeks, hadn't seen Mom since the first day in my loft, and hadn't grocery shopped in almost as long, having survived off of hospital food and patient trays.

By July I had worked myself to skin and bones again, eating only when I remembered due to my dizziness or the shakiness of my hands. Really looking at myself in the mirror of my bathroom, I realized how thin I had become. Pulling on one of my shirts and a pair of jeans I had bought with Heather earlier in the year, I was appalled when the jeans slipped past my hips.

"Shit, Becks, get yourself together," I told my reflection. There were deep bags under my eyes; my hair was stringy and dry; my cheeks were hollowed out. I couldn't remember the last time I had eaten a full two thousand calories in a day. I looked worse now than

I had when I was drinking every day. "You are certainly not the girl Davlin married," I told my reflection.

Belting my pants tight, I grabbed my purse and went to the store to buy provisions. I spent the latter part of the day prepping lunches and dinners for the next week. By the time evening had rolled around, I was tired of preparing food and gave up and ordered Chinese takeout.

I spent my next three days off work in the loft. I watched the sun rise and set from my bed on the first day. As the bright orb slowly traversed the sky, I lay in bed daydreaming about sharing the bed with Davlin. This time I had to look at the framed pictures almost constantly to see his face. The second day, I wrapped myself in a blanket and curled up on the couch. I sat watching romantic comedies and dramas, crying at the happy and sad endings. I fell asleep watching lovers kiss after seemingly endless separation. I wasn't surprised when I fell off the couch, waking after a rather erotic dream involving Davlin and me. At least I think it was Davlin since he had no face, but I felt him.

I pulled myself off the floor and made my way to bed. Sleeping the remainder of the day, I woke late in the evening, the neon glow of the business signs below illuminating my sleeping space. Realizing my dangerous mood and my descent into depression were in full effect, I forced myself out of my bed. Pulling on a loose-fitting dress, I descended the stairs to the restaurant below. I took up Mom's regular place on the couch in the front of the bar area, wrapping myself up in a provided throw.

Jarrod had seen me come down. He walked over carrying a large cup of coffee. He placed it in front of me, then taking a seat next to me, he pulled me onto his shoulder. "Anything I can help with?"

I shook my head in denial, a random tear slipping out of my closed eyes.

A familiar voice chimed in, "It's Davlin's birthday. Only a celebration of his life can get my daughter to take a day off of work."

171

I opened my eyes to see my mother glaring at me. Her face softened as she saw the extent of my self- imposed damage.

"Awwah, Becks. Baby, aren't you eating?" She scooted me to the side and wrapped her arms around me. I gratefully went to her soft shoulder and buried my head in her hair.

I must have looked like a crazy person, sitting in the middle of a busy restaurant crying onto the owner and a customer. I must have looked like an emaciated, poorly groomed maniac pulling people to me to cry upon.

"Becks, why do you keep doing this to yourself?" Mom asked me, as she petted my head. "Baby, you need to mourn and let the pain end."

I pulled away from her embrace. "Davlin is not dead! Mom, I need someone else to believe that with me." I stood, swaying slightly from dizziness and lack of food. Another hand grabbed my waist and another was on my shoulder supporting me. I turned to look into the face of Eric Vaughn, Heather standing just behind him holding Jobe.

"Hey, sister," she said, controlling her face, "let's sit and have a birthday lunch for you and Davlin."

Seeing that I was steadier now, Eric released his hold and I went to my best friend, hugging her tightly and making Jobe squirm in his mother's arms.

"I missed you."

Jarrod quickly arranged for our party to have the private dining room usually reserved for wedding parties and business luncheons. We sat around a large table, still being set by the hurried waitstaff. Heather sat to my right with Jobe gleefully banging his spoon against the plate from his high chair.

Seeing the baby, so full of life and mischief, I smiled at him and then at Heather.

"It's been so long since I smiled at a baby." I was tired, and it was audible in my voice. I wasn't physically tired—I had slept away almost three days—I was emotionally spent. I didn't know how to feel at any given time. I felt guilty when I was happy. I was tired of

172

crying and being sad all the time. I was confused about what I was supposed to be doing with my life and time until Davlin came home. I admitted as much to the friends and family who surrounded me at the table.

"Look, I know you all want me to accept that Davlin is dead. I do realize that that is the most likely situation. I am not oblivious to the fact that nothing was ever found of him or his men. I have to have faith. I have to believe and keep some part of my heart faithful to my husband." I looked around the table at the various faces that now gazed at me. Heather with tears in her eyes, my mom with fear, Jarrod with kindness, Eric would not meet my gaze. "I have nothing but hope to cling to. If I lose my hope, then everything about Davlin is gone…" I had done a pitiful job of explaining myself to them. I was sure they would continue to encourage me to give up and bury the past….

"Becks, no one has ever given you any reason to think anything other than what you do now, " Eric said. His voice was rough with emotion and now as he looked at me, I could see the pain that marred his face. "No one ever told you about his mission or the recovery efforts."

Chapter 18

Camp Houston, Afghanistan.
As S-2, Davlin was responsible for determining the reliability of the intelligence coming in to the camp, aiding in troop movement, and determining the best route to achieve whatever mission was given. He had immense responsibility and had prepared as best he could before deploying to Afghanistan.

On arrival overseas, the officers were assigned trailers, much like the enlisted men, though slightly less crowded. There were only two officers to one trailer where enlisted had four to a trailer. Eric and Davlin had been assigned a trailer together. As friends they were happy with the arrangement.

"I put up posters from Maxim magazine as soon as we arrived at the camp," Eric laughed sheepishly, avoiding Heather's gaze as he confessed his lack of husbandly conduct. "Davlin had three framed pictures of you—two that he put by his bunk—and a ton of loose pictures he taped on the wall. He was pretty sad when we got to country. He said he felt guilty leaving you with nothing to keep you busy, like Heather being pregnant. He hadn't told me you guys weren't able to have kids, so when I joked that he should have left you fat and pregnant to make sure you would be where he left you, he got pretty pissed off and left the trailer."

Eric was speaking directly to me now, though everyone was listening to him retell the how's and whys of their deployment and Davlin's eventual loss. "He came back after dark. We were under blackout orders due to sniper fire we had been receiving, and I had been pretty worried because he had left without his protective gear. Shit, he didn't even have his coat and it was fucking cold after the sun went down. He came back though, late, and went straight to his bed. He had shut the curtain that was our door between the two sides of the trailer, so I knew to leave him alone. The next morning, he was up and gone before me, so I didn't get a chance to talk to him until lunch."

I was no longer eating. I sat captivated by what he was saying, my meal forgotten in front of me. The few bites I had taken sat heavy in my stomach as I heard of Davlin and Eric's disagreement. Davlin was hard to anger, but when it did occur, there was hell to pay.

"I went to his desk area in the command building and sat right on his desk, making him pay attention to me. I knew he was pissed off at me and I could see him trying to control himself. He could, you know, keep himself calm no matter what. Anyways, I was kind of worried that he would blow in a minute, but even that would be better than a year of silence from him.

"Dude, I'm sorry I insulted you and your wife. I know you're worried about Becks. She is a beautiful woman…but she is also the most devoted woman I have ever seen. I didn't mean to make you question whether your wife will be faithful to you while you're gone."

"I don't worry about Becks." He looked up at me then, and I finally figured out that he was in pain. Like he physically hurt being away from you. "She is strong, and yeah, I know she won't cheat." He kind of pulled into himself. I got off his desk and sat in the chair at the end, just kind of looking around the command area. I wasn't supposed to be there. It was none of my business, but then suddenly he confided in me. "We lost a baby when we were in college. Our senior year, she was seven months pregnant and a freak accident killed the baby and almost killed her too."

"I didn't know what to say, I mean, what do you say to someone? Fuck, Becks. I'm sorry…" Eric trailed off and took another drink of his whiskey, then continued.

"Davlin looked totally haunted when he was telling me about your son. He said they took you to surgery, but the baby was already gone, had been for awhile. The nurses brought him out to Davlin. They took him to a room and let him hold the baby. He told me about how his little head fit in his hand, the whole baby, he could cup in his palms."

175

Eric had a tear in his eye. He was drunk, and the alcohol was making him weepy as well as loose tongued. He didn't care what effect he was having on my emotions; he needed to confess what transgressed between he and Davlin, no matter the cost to the witnesses.

Unable to stop, Eric continued. "He said he was in denial, that he just looked asleep, but he was cold and didn't move." Eric looked at Jobe, asleep in Heather's arms, his face flushed with life, a soft snore escaping his body with each breath. "Davlin couldn't stop talking about how small the baby was, and how perfect he was. He had fingernails and toenails, his hands were the size of his pinky. Davlin was describing the child you two had made, a baby he said he gave you a real hard time about when you found out you were pregnant. He said he felt like he didn't deserve to be happy." Eric was looking straight into my eyes, repeating my husband's confession.

I sat in my chair with tears spilling down my cheeks.

Many nights Davlin had drawn him for me, our son. He described the soft roundness of his head and how it fit in his hand; he would show me how he held his miniature feet to his finger to remember their size; he would break down when he got to how difficult it was to lay the baby down, to hand him over to the coroner. I was surprised he had shared our loss with Eric.

"I went back to work, and Davlin had his job to do too, but that night back in our trailer, we played a couple games of Gin and talked again, like friends, totally ignoring the conversation from earlier that day; he had accepted my apology and I had been given his trust.

"Two days later, Davlin was given a report about insurgent movement that seemed really shady. He didn't agree with the intel and he was telling me how he thought it was a setup for an ambush. Becks, I was at the meeting when Davlin voiced his concern and said he didn't think it wise to go into the caves or anywhere near the mountain area he went missing from."

I was numb. Hearing that Davlin had tried to stop his or anyone else's going into the caves, the place where he went missing. He had known! He knew that something was going to happen there and had tried to tell the commanders.

"Why didn't they listen when he said it wasn't safe?" I asked, my voice rough and hard with anger.

"They did." Eric was again looking directly into my eyes, as though we were the only two people in the room. "He volunteered to go with a small group of soldiers to do recon, more to collect info from a distance to determine if obvious movement of insurgents was noted. They weren't supposed to go in the caves, just see if it was possible that the intel was true. Davlin knew what he was doing. He wanted as small a number of soldiers put in danger as possible to gather the information about the area. His plan would have worked pretty well, too, if he hadn't had the two dumbest privates in the history of the US Army under his command."

As it was, Private Francs and Private First Class Dougard were, unfortunately, assigned to the same trailer for lodging. PFC Dougard, a white-trash boy with few prospects in his hometown, had joined the army to earn a paycheck and get out of his father's house. He was dirty, his uniform was never regulation, and he was constantly being reprimanded for his behavior or appearance. Private First Class Dougard had already been demoted twice in his four years of service. He had been facing dishonorable discharge when the company came up with orders immediately stopping his discharge.

Private Francs was the polar opposite of Dougard. He came from a Christian family with red, white, and blue blood. Patriotic to the core, Francs had enlisted straight out of high school, been awarded the APFT award for physical fitness in Basic Training, and was in general an excellent soldier. His appearance was regulation and better, his salute was brisk, and his understanding of his mission complete.

The two boys, so very different in personality and values, were assigned one side of a trailer. Two specialists from a sister company were assigned the other half. Dougard had been rooting through the other soldier's personal belongings when Francs had returned to the

177

trailer after dinner, the second day in camp. Francs, being honorable and not a thief, had reported Dougard to his chain of command. Davlin was the officer in charge of the platoon that contained both soldiers. Punishment was left to him.

Davlin had argued that Dougard be released prior to their deployment. He had been the person who had initiated Dougard's dishonorable discharge. He had set paperwork in motion to have the boy court martialed, all of which had been stopped with the battalion-wide deployment. Davlin felt nothing for Dougard. He knew he was the type of idiot to get people hurt or kill out of spite and stupidity.

Davlin had put in another set of papers to have the PFC dishonorably discharged. Major Walters, the second in command of Camp Houston, had refused and recommended Davlin do "everything to maintain troop strength."

"Honestly, I don't see how one man can affect troop strength so much, or at least I didn't until a couple days later. Dougard is the reason Davlin is missing."

Eric was absolutely serious in his statement. He was telling me information that had never been shared with me during the two and a half years since Davlin and the other men went missing.

"The men who went on that mission were selected by the higher-ups, except for Dougard. He was a tagalong, having been given direct orders to be no more than ten feet from Lieutenant Robertson at all times." Eric snickered at the memory of the idiot PFC trying to out wit Davlin. "Davlin almost put his boot up his ass the first hour. Davlin had Dougard performing the most asinine duties.

"The guy would be whistling "Taps" to a crushed weed, and then have to bury it in an appropriate grave. He made him sweep the floor of the command center with a toothbrush. He had to move boxes from one end of a room to the other and back again. Davlin wasn't being mean to the guy, he was just annoyed, and if Dougard was busy, Davlin could sit with his laptop and maps and consult with the other intelligence officers as long as Dougard was within ten feet.

"If Davlin had to use the latrine, he would make Dougard keep his chair warm… Holy shit, that guy hated Davlin by the end of the first day! The second day, Davlin went to Major Winters and had the leash let out to twenty feet, giving Davlin the ability to shut a door between him and Dougard.

"Davlin was working at his desk when I brought his shadow in to the command area. Dougard had been lounging out in the shade, watching the rest of the men check vehicles and practice setting up communication towers. The ass was chilling out, smoking a cigarette. Davlin was livid.

"By the time they left a week later on the recon mission, Davlin had Dougard exhausted and begging for court martial. He had busted his ass at least three times a day, dropping him to do hundreds of pushups or sit ups or making him sprint from place to place. Dougard was not allowed to simply walk anywhere. The guy was demoralized and in pain.

"I warned Davlin to be careful of the lunatic; angry and stupid are a bad combination. Davlin listened and always carried his sidearm. He also grew eyes in the back of his head." Eric paused here. He poured himself another drink from a bottle of whiskey that had been brought for toasts. He swallowed the contents of the glass in one pull, then poured another. Looking up into my eyes, he confessed, "I think Dougard killed Davlin while they were on their mission."

I was stunned, speechless. I simply sat staring at Eric, unable to move or speak.

"Why's that?" Caleb asked. I hadn't seen him come into the room, but apparently hearing about our impromptu party to celebrate mine and Davlin's birthdays, Caleb had shown himself in, sans Tara, I noted vaguely. "Why do you think that Dougard killed Davlin, and if he did, where the fuck is he?"

We all turned our gaze back to Eric as Caleb came to sit beside Mom and me, pouring us both a drink as we continued to listen to Eric.

"Dougard tried before they left on the mission," Eric stated simply.

"Whoa! Tried what, Eric? To kill Davlin?" I stuttered. My brain was having a hard time processing the information that was being given to me, and in truth, I wasn't sure if I wanted to hear the rest of the story, now that death and Davlin were being stated together.

"Yeah. We—me and Davlin—we were walking back to our trailer one night, two nights before the mission. Dougard had been released from his leash for the night. We were between some of the troop trailers when I got hit in the back of the head. I blacked out. When I woke up, Davlin and Dougard were on the ground fighting. Davlin was obviously winning. Dougard was a big boy but undisciplined and trying to muscle Davlin, who was not only strong but well controlled. Davlin had his knee in Dougard's chest and was whispering something to his face. Davlin saw me moving, and he came to help me up.

"Dougard, the piece of shit, had gotten up when Davlin got off him, and came charging at us with a knife. Davlin moved away from the idiot, who fell into the trailer next to us. Davlin grabbed Dougard's neck and smacked his head into the building. He was out cold.

"We got up and went to our trailer. Davlin said if he was stupid enough to admit to assaulting an officer, he deserved what he got. Davlin thought Dougard was going to whine to the chain of command about the fight. He didn't.

"Two days later, Francs, Dougard, Allen, Felden, Sargent Pallen, and Davlin were rolling out for two days of recon in the mountains. I don't know what happened when they reached the mountain range and settled into their mission, but I do know Davlin had been relaying information on insurgent movement. He had just sent pictures of the caves and had been given orders to go in to clear the caves. Davlin had requested larger troop numbers to clear the caves.

He kept reemphasizing his mission was for recon. The next message we received was that Private Francs had been shot; then we lost communication."

I had goose flesh on my arms. I was gripping the whiskey glass in my hands so tightly my fingertips were white.

"Why do you think Dougard killed Davlin? If Francs had been shot, and Davlin was already reporting that insurgents were in the area, maybe Francs was shot by them and the others taken prisoner," I asked when my voice returned.

"Maybe that is what happened," Eric admitted, "but when we found Francs, he said Dougard had shot him." That stopped the conversation completely.

I sat silent, in shock, unable to move or realize what had just come out. I had a thousand questions swirling in my brain and no ability to grasp one to steer the conversation or uncover more information. Eric was better able to move us forward.

"We were tracking Davlin and his group. Everyone had GPS. Satellite images of the area at the time we lost communications showed muzzle flashes. They were firing their weapons, but not across the valley they were monitoring. The flashes were all on one side of the range. Whoever was firing at them was on the same side of the valley as Davlin." Eric was trying to make me see reason.

"That could be anyone, Eric! What if the insurgents had seen Davlin and the others and come to where they were to fire on them? Nothing is being proven here! If Dougard killed Davlin, where is his body? Or Sergeant Pallen? Or Felden or Allen? Where are their bodies? It's not like Dougard could wrangle them and herd them to their slaughter and hide the bodies, and what? Where the hell is he?" I was beginning to feel the familiar anxiety that tightened my chest. I had to get away, back up to my apartment where I could feel safe.

Eric had no more answers for me. He had been drinking more whiskey and was becoming blurry-eyed.

"I think it's time to wrap up the birthday party," Heather said, taking control of the situation. She had been silent through the revelations and now seemed to be in thought, the same as the rest of us.

"Becks, baby, why don't you come home with me?" Mom invited.

"Oh, no Mom, I'm just upstairs. I am exhausted and I just want to lay in my bed. I...fuck!" I screamed, startling the others around the table. I was going to break apart again. I could feel insanity and fear taking hold of my brain, and I declared as much. "I don't know anything right now!" I wrapped my arms around my mother and hugged her tight. She held me away and kissed my cheek, rocking me gently from side to side.

"Come by tomorrow? We can talk; you can think." She held my face and made me look at her. "Becks, this didn't help. Eric didn't help." She looked at him, his head resting on the table, drunk. "I'm sure he feels better for unburdening his soul, but we are still in the same place we were this morning. Don't let Eric's words burden your soul. Go sleep."

"Becks, I have to take Eric to the hotel and Jobe needs a bath," Heather informed. "I'll come over later? Is that okay?"

"Yes," I responded, then changed my mind. "No, just go to Mom's in the morning. I'll meet you there." I was drunk from my one whiskey. In the excitement of the day, I still hadn't eaten. I hugged Heather again, holding my friend for support. "I am so confused. What just happened? I don't understand what Eric just told me..." I was lost and floundering in my lack of understanding. I needed to have comprehension of what had been said, but all I had were more questions and an even foggier grasp of what had occurred the day my husband had gone missing.

"You and me both, sister." She stood back, taking in my appearance. She sighed and shook her head. "Tomorrow?"

"Yes, absolutely." I hugged her again, then Eric in turn. He stumbled slightly but recovered, putting his arm around Heather's shoulder.

Jarrod, ever aware of my well-being, had a meal made and packed for me to take up to my apartment. He handed me the

Styrofoam container and hugged me. "I'll come up later to check on you."

"No, it's okay. I'm okay, Jarrod. Really, my plan was to go upstairs, take a hot bath, and pass out on the couch. Now I've revised my plan to include eating some food between going upstairs and passing out." I tried to smile at him, but my face and brain were not functioning to decrease my friend's anxiety. I had lost my ability to lie.

"Well, pass out on the couch or not, I'm still coming up to make sure you're alright. I have a key, remember?"

"You're not allowed to use that," I feebly protested. In truth, it felt nice to know that so many people cared enough to worry and to want to check up on me. "I'll be fine, but if you insist on coming up, I'll leave the door unlocked."

"I'll lock it on my way out." He smiled at me, hugged me, and gave me a quick peck on the cheek.

I turned to leave the room, Styrofoam dinner box and bottle of whiskey in hand, and remembered Caleb. He stood by the door of the private dining room waiting patiently for me to remember his presence.

"I'll help you up to your apartment." I smiled at my old friend and nodded.

Together we walked down the dark back hall of the restaurant. I unlocked the door leading to the elevator, giving passage to Caleb, and then locked it behind him. We were silent as we went to the loft. I fumbled with my keys, which he took from my hand and opened the door without difficulty.

He followed me into the loft, taking in the bright colors, the pictures, the beautiful light fixtures, and the mild state of disorganization that had begun to take hold in my apartment.

"Nice place," Caleb said as he walked around the room looking at the pictures displayed. "I remember this one!" He smiled, looking at a picture of he and Davlin, age sixteen, shirtless at the city pool among a group of other, brainless boys. The herd of boys had decided to descend on the city pool in white shorts while a group of

183

older women in the community were having their water aerobics class.

The fifteen boys involved charged into the pool area clad only in white boxers, surprising the women engaged in their morning class. The boys jumped in the pool among the women, resurfacing into their bosoms, then fleeing the pool, the white of the boxers doing nothing to conceal their freshly shaven "man areas."

The women had stared and screamed at the sight. Taking less than a minute, the boys' stunt was missed by no one in town. Word quickly spread to the police station that there was a band of rapists out in town having just attacked the elderly women at the pool. It was chaos in town that day! The local teen boys were gathered together by the police and individually questioned on their personal grooming habits.

Eventually, all the boys who had participated in the prank were found out and made to apologize to the ladies individually, and to the town publicly. The boys were mortified when several of the ladies commented on their parts, blushing furiously as the widows made their own naughty comments at the boys' expense.

The picture Caleb was looking at was of the boys as they exited the pool, many of them showing moon as their boxers fell off their hips. They were a vibrant group of boys, their smiles and laughs captured in black and white as they rushed past me—I hid just inside the doorway to the locker room at the pool, snapping photos of them in action.

"You realize you have a full-frontal picture of me in your living room. You have my first and only porn photo in your living room." His tone was joking as he shook his head, laughing.

"Well, I don't consider that porn. It's blackmail evidence if any of you delinquents ever run for public office," I teased him. "Want some of this food? Turkey and Swiss croissant?"

"No, eat your food; you look like shit," he teased back. I knew my friends were worried about my weight loss and my overworking. I took a bite of the sandwich; my body suddenly remembered the joy of food, and I was ravenous. I finished the sandwich in a couple minutes as Caleb continued his photo trip down memory lane. He would laugh at some of them or comment on others.

Finished with my sandwich, I brought the whiskey and two glasses to the living room. I grabbed a photo album full of pictures from our youth. Caleb was in many pictures with Davlin. They had been such close friends until "the fight."

Sifting through the pictures, we were both becoming quite nostalgic the drunker we got. By the end of the album, I was swaying as I sat on the couch. I had forgotten that I was down quite a bit from my normal weight; Caleb was simply glossy-eyed. He turned to me and stared.

"Wha shoo lookin at, Caleb?" I slurred.

"I was thinkin. Thinkin, member when we were together? You were so sexy. I knew you were…were juss usin me…Becks, I didn't care. I…hell." He leaned over. Unable to find words or make coherent thoughts, he showed me how he felt.

He pulled me close and kissed me, full and long, first with closed lips; then, as the kiss deepened, our tongues touched. Lost in a fog of emotion and alcohol, I responded to the kiss. The last several days had been so miserable, I had cried so much…. The afternoon had done nothing to answer my questions in regard to what had led up to Davlin's going missing. I was just as crazy in that moment as I had been when I was told that Davlin had gone missing.

I missed him! I missed Davlin in so many ways. I missed talking to him late at night as headlights passed over our bedroom ceiling. I missed the small touches he bestowed throughout the day and the kisses on the back of my neck. I missed the companionable silence we could share snuggling close reading on a rainy Sunday. I missed having him guide me into a room with his hand on the small of my back, not as my owner or master, but as my protector. I missed his lips and his kisses, his hands on my body, and the way we felt joined together. I was losing him, and here I was, replaying the past using Caleb to replace my need for Davlin.

185

As that thought passed into my brain, I pushed away from Caleb. His eyes fluttered open and he took me in.

"I can't have you, can I?" he asked, suddenly soberer.

"I don't know that Davlin is gone." I shook my head in denial. "Caleb…" What? What could I say to make our infidelity and recurrent trysts all right? Nothing! It wasn't all right, and he needed to leave and stay away, or I did. "Caleb, I can't have you around. I get confused when you're around. I love my husband, and until I am told otherwise, he is alive." I was ashamed of myself. I stood shakily and walked to the door. Caleb followed me with his head down, hands in his pockets.

Just outside the door, he stopped and turned. "Becks, Allington is a small town. We are going to run into each other, and I am still going to want you." His eyes had cleared, and his words rang with truth. "You can't live in denial forever. You have to move on eventually."

Honestly, it felt good knowing that someone could still want me. I felt more beautiful having heard the words cross his lips. I felt something for Caleb, but the sparks of fire his kiss had started in my stomach had to be extinguished.

I couldn't burn for him.

"Go home to Tara, make babies, renovate your house…live. I'm stuck, Caleb, and I can't move forward," I feebly explained.

"How long, Becks? How long are you going to wait for a man who is dead in the ground?" His words became angry at the end. He was hovering close to me, threatening and challenging me.

"It takes seven years, Caleb. I have seven years until Davlin is considered dead if there is no body found." Tears had begun to slide down my cheeks as I began to realize how lonely I would be by the time those years had passed. I was barely functioning now! "I have to wait, seven years to die…"

I shut the door on his pained face and went to my bed.

Chapter 19

The day after shutting Caleb out of my life, I arrived early at Mom's house. She was up, pattering around her kitchen getting the meat ready for the grill. I went to my old bedroom and lay on the bed. Heather and Eric arrived two hours later, Jobe's squeals of happiness waking me from my nap.

Rubbing my eyes, I entered the living room smiling at my friends. Eric gave me a hug and a friendly kiss on the cheek. Heather came and hugged me; full of need for affection, I held on to her as long as possible.

"You need to talk?" she asked into my ear as we hugged.

I nodded ascent and we went back to my room.

"What's wrong, Becks?" she asked as she shut the door. "You look like you had a bad night."

"I did. I kissed Caleb last night."

"Damn it! Again?! You really need to stay away from that guy!"

"No shit." I was so ashamed. I would never cheat on Davlin, but I was so hungry for affection, and I told Heather as much.

"I know, sweetie. People are not meant to be alone. You do have needs, seriously. Sex is actually an important part of adult functioning. Or something like that."

"I miss sex. I miss having my lips kissed, hand holding, touching, fighting over blankets or pillows, waking up to a beautiful face. But mostly I miss sex, Heather!"

My friend looked me over with a critical eye. "Aren't you clicking your button?"

"No. Well, not consciously. I think I must be in my sleep 'cause I wake up in orgasms pretty damn frequently!"

"We need to go get you a vibrator. Mine saved my marriage." She winked at me conspiratorially. "As far as missing human contact, you need to be around people more. You spent the first year that Davlin was deployed locked away in your house, and the second year, locked inside your house, hidden in a bottle. You need to get

187

out and have some fun. Live! I'm not going to say it is what Davlin would want, but it is what you need. You need to be around people, drink, have fun, have girls' nights, go bowling, join a damn club! Do something, because you are close to death right now."

Her rant spent, Heather sat on the bed next to me and pulled me close so my head could rest on her shoulder. "I miss sex. If I didn't think it was cheating, I'd get a girlfriend as wanton as I am."

She laughed at my poor excuse of a joke. "Well, if my husband deploys one more time, I'll be your girlfriend and we can just keep it our secret."

We both laughed and went out to join the party

Over burgers and dogs, Heather updated me on her comings and goings. She was going to start working again as a CPA at her family's firm in Washington. Eric was resigning his commission and retiring to go work as an electrician, a job that didn't require he know how to fire a weapon. They were both excited about the next step of their life after the military.

Eric didn't mention Afghanistan or Davlin again that day. Mom had invited her boyfriend and Jarrod. Both men arrived with happily wrapped gifts. Mom's boyfriend even brought a bouquet of flowers to brighten the mood. All in all, the party was a success. There was no drama, and no unexpected guests.

I got home that evening around nine to a note taped on the door of my loft:

Becks,

I know that when we were together in high school, you were using me to achieve a goal, to get Davlin to realize how he felt about you. I gave you what you wanted, but I fell in love with you, and I almost died at his hands because of you. Yes, I know it was my own fault for running off at the mouth about how great you were in bed or how good your mouth felt. In all honesty, I was a dumb shit teenager, but my feelings for you have never changed. Each time I see you, I want to hold you and love you. Each time we talk, it's easy and I know we would be a beautiful couple, if you would just stop

188

fighting. I could love you the way you deserve, and I would wait for you if you asked.

Yours,
Caleb

I took the note inside, sat at the bar in the kitchen, and stared at the piece of paper, repeatedly reading his words.

"FUCK!!!!!!" I screamed! Grabbing the cookie jar, I threw it across the room. The porcelain crashed into the wall and shattered across the floor. I grabbed the nearest item at hand and threw it. I kept throwing plates and cups until my cabinet was empty, which is about the time that I finally realized that someone was pounding on my door.

I threw the door open ready for war. I was looking at Jarrod, a sincere look of concern on his face.

"Are you alright? I heard you screaming and breaking glass." As he was saying it, he scanned the wreckage that was my living room.

"No!" I threw myself into his arms and cried. He wrapped his arms around me and held me as I cried out my anger and frustration and fear. I was babbling about how I couldn't live alone, and how I didn't know what to do with myself.... Jarrod took my chin in his fingers to make me look at him.

"Becks. What can I do?" A simple question. What could he do? What did I need? At that moment I needed a man to love me.

With overflowing eyes and a breaking heart, I answered him in the most honest way, "Love me."

I woke the next day in the strong arms of a man who only months ago I had promised strict friendship. He smiled at me and kissed me, a soft but complete kiss, one of many over the last several hours, one of many I was having a very difficult time remembering.

"I have to go open the shop. I'm late getting it unlocked." He apologized. "Sleep some more, but come talk to me when you get up."

I nodded my consent as Jarrod stood up. "Jarrod," he stopped and turned to me, his smile quickly turning to a look of understanding. "We didn't…" I trailed off.

"Ah, no, we didn't." He looked angrily at me now. "Not from lack of your trying. You kept begging me last night, but I had a feeling that the morning would play out like it is." He pulled his shirt on. I noticed he had slept in his jeans. "I didn't want you to break your promise to Davlin." He had finished putting his shoes on by that point, and he finally stopped long enough to really look at me. "You didn't break your vow to your husband, just your promise to me."

Jarrod left the loft, letting the door slam as he left. I could hear his descent to the restaurant below. I lay in my bed trying to remember the night before, but had only vague glimpses of hands touching, lips caressing, bodies meeting… I had the feeling that the night was intimate, and I knew the shame I felt now was earned, just as Jarrod's anger at me was well deserved.

I closed my eyes from reality, trying to fall asleep, trying to remember the night before, trying to forget. But the lingering warmth of Jarrod's body and my complete sense of loneliness made sleep impossible.

I got up and got dressed. Leaving the safe haven I had created and ruined in a night of weakness. I wanted to go see my mom, seeking reaffirmation that I am, in fact, a bad person. I needed to be far away from Jarrod; I really needed to put distance between his kisses and my lips.

When I got to the garage, I noticed Jarrod was sitting in the alley behind the building, staring at nothing. I was very unclear about the activities of the night before, and I wasn't ready to ask him what, if not sex, had occurred. He looked angry in his thoughts, and I didn't want to bring his anger down on me, yet. I wanted nothing more than to get in my car and feel the miles begin to separate us.

As quietly as possible, I shut the door to the building and began to creep to my Jeep just feet away. Failing in my attempt to be quiet, I tripped over a concrete parking block and fell.

Jarrod approached. Seeing me lying on the ground, he offered his hand and asked what I had been dreading.

"Regrets?" he asked me. He had obviously caught on to my attempt to avoid him. Jarrod was not going to make this easy on me.

"Of course," I answered, still looking at his face to judge his response. "How could I not feel guilty for putting you in the position I did last night? I wouldn't blame you for hating me for using you."

"I've never been used before. I have got to say it does suck. Shit, Becks, you said you loved me last night. I guess I knew you weren't seeing me." He stood up and began walking back into the building. Turning around quickly, his anger came to a head. He raised his voice, causing me to pull my shoulders up around my ears. "What the hell was last night, Becks?"

Indeed! What was last night? Had it been a night of sexless love? Passion without ultimate joining? What was it when a couple can fall on a bed in an embrace, joined in a kiss that makes your heart flutter and your breath come short? When hands caressing breasts and kisses across the slope of them bring sensations to the whole of both involved? It was fucking cheating!

The night before had been the most intimate nights of foreplay! Jarrod had touched, caressed, kissed, and handled parts of my body I had forgotten about…and I had learned the layout of a whole new man. His hair was soft and smelled of a different shampoo. His beard was two days of growth, both soft and raspy against my skin. His stubble had brought new sensation to my skin as he had kissed my neck down to my breasts.

Jarrod had callused hands, work hardened from his manual labor applied to his business. His hands had touched and held, gripped and caressed. Each touch experienced with this new sensation, with this stranger's hands, had rippled need through my body. I wanted nothing in life in that moment than to feel his strength as he held my wrists, keeping me from moving as he kissed me hard enough to make my lips ache.

191

Jarrod had kissed and touched nothing more than what I had offered to him. His actions were experienced, but with the restraint of a teenage boy on his first date. We did not have sex, but our desire had been gratified by the mutual caresses and strokes, freely opened legs, and slightly lowered jeans.

I had forgotten the pleasure that could arise in the body simply by having talented fingers caressing panty-clad parts. By the time Jarrod had moved the white cotton of my panties aside to provide release from my building need, I was beside myself. Where his fingers were skillfully teasing, building my climax, I plunged his fingers into my depths, something I know he would not have done. I rode his hand as I would have ridden his cock. A long-forgotten sensation of satisfied desire, made new by a new partner, was gratified with mutual masturbation.

Jarrod is a working man, but not a man who works out. His muscles were different than Davlin's. Davlin was a combat-ready soldier, able to run distances with a heavy rucksack on his back. Jarrod was a cancer survivor who had renovated a building with his own two hands to create something where there had been nothing. With the muscles of a carpenter, his arms and back were strong, though not rippling with muscular strength. I wanted to experience every difference in their bodies, to know Jarrod like I knew Davlin.

I allowed Jarrod freedom to explore my body with his hands and mouth, something I reciprocated gladly. His beard-stubbled chin and muscled back were not the only differences between the two men. Jarrod had pierced ears, entertainment for chewing. He also wore a chain around his neck, a Celtic symbol of healing, that rested at the base of his neck. He had a scar on his chest from his days receiving chemotherapy, the area where he had had a Port-A-Cath placed for easy delivery of medication. The port had been removed, but a scar remained; this I kissed, but I did not linger, as he had many more places to explore with both hands and lips.

While Jarrod satisfied my needs with his hands, I had repaid the favor in kind. As I kissed the length of his torso, I unbuttoned his jeans, enjoying the unintelligible noises he was making. Pants loosened, I allowed my hands to explore his body hidden by his boxers, firm already as I caressed and played, and large as I gripped him, freed from the confines of his clothing.

My hand wrapped around him, I had stoked him fast and slow, long and firm, and playfully running a finger over the tip of his head. Jarrod was losing his ability to kiss, the more I teased him, pulled him, until he placed his hand over mine and kissed me firmly as, together, we finished him off. His kisses stopped as he came, his breathing heavy. He was beautiful in his climax, peaceful in his recovery.

As the night deepened outside, we lay in my bed looking at each other; gentle touches and whispered words passed infrequently. It was as I was beginning to doze off more content and relaxed than I had been in years that I heard him say "I love you." The most perfect end to an otherwise horrible day. My love had come back to me.

"Nothing," I answered him. I felt sick, because I had told him he was what I needed. I probably told him all kinds of things. He had to have known none of them were aimed at him, but his misinterpretation of the night before was ruining what it had been. I wasn't even entirely sure of what it had been! He had been there to fill a role, to help fix a break... Job complete, he had fixed the damage Eric and Caleb had done yesterday. Now I had all new kinds of damage, self-inflicted.

"You need to go, Becks." Jarrod turned on his heel and left me alone, headed toward the kitchen entrance. I wasn't sure what he had meant by leave. I wasn't sure if he just meant the garage, the building, or Nebraska altogether. As it was, I was out of glasses, having shattered all of mine the night before, so I did leave. I went shopping. I returned to the loft, entering the building by the back door to avoid Jarrod. On the door of the loft was an eviction notice; Jarrod had signed the paper with so much force that he had ripped the paper. I took the notice and my cups into the loft.

I looked around the room, reality drawing sharply to light at what I had broken. I was a fucking idiot. Taking in the wreckage that was my life, I sank to the floor, rested my head on my folded arms, and cried for my lost friendships and for my own weakness. I had cheated on the love of my life and ruined a wonderful friendship in the process.

"What the hell is wrong with me?" I asked myself. "I break everything I touch."

With eviction pending and my fragile sense of reality ebbing away, I took a number out of my wallet. The only thing Stosh and I had talked about, after I embarrassed him in front of the nurses' station, was travel nursing. I had asked him how he had gotten established with a company and about some of the places he had gone. When he wasn't being an arrogant, sexist ass, Stosh was a funny guy. He tended to pigeonhole people into categories, a practice that had gotten him in trouble pretty often.

He was, however, a wealth of information in regard to travel nursing, and he gave me a number for a nurse recruiter. It was this number I called. I had an over-the-phone interview and an email waiting within moments to create my resume for the company.

After calling the recruiter, I went down to the dumpster out back of the restaurant where I had spotted several boxes earlier. The boxes were still there; so was Jarrod.

He was smoking a cigarette, leaning against the back door of the restaurant. He saw me coming and squared his shoulders for battle. I didn't say anything, hurt and hurting in turn. I felt horrible for changing our relationship, but I also was hurt that he was kicking me out instead of talking to me.

I got the boxes, not looking at him. I certainly wasn't going to say anything to him if he wasn't going to say anything to me. I was acting like a spoiled baby, and I knew it, but so was he.

"You don't have to move," he said to my back as I walked away, boxes in hand. "I was hurt, and I thought if I kicked you out, I wouldn't hurt so much."

I stopped and turned to look at him. "And now that I'm willing to pack up, you think you won't hurt when you see me? Jarrod, I'm toxic right now, and very unavailable! I never should have asked you to sleep with me last night. We both knew it would change things between us. You know I'm married and not willing to accept that Davlin is dead. What I am now is a damn hypocrite! A hypocrite who ran off a great friend because she wanted a night of physical contact, to feel a warm body next to her again, and lips that weren't in a dream…" My voice cracked as my dam broke again. I really did need counseling, but not here in Allington. I had messed it up already, and now was the time to run away.

Jarrod came toward me, to comfort me or beat me down some more, I wasn't sure until he put his arms around me and held me until I stopped crying. He kissed the top of my head, and when I looked up at his face to thank him for his kindness, I couldn't say the words. All I wanted to do was kiss him again…

And that want hurt.

I pushed away from Jarrod, breaking the embrace that filled my body with warmth. I was responding to Jarrod the way I would respond to Davlin. My thoughts drifted again to the foggy images of passion the night before.

"Jarrod, I think it's best if I do go. I have a strong tendency to fuck people up, and I can't be responsible for hurting you."

"Shit, Becks, only you can make a man feel one inch tall each time you open your fucking mouth."

"Jarrod, I am being serious. What? Do you want to put your life on hold for the next four and a half years until I can legally be considered a widow? What if they find Davlin? What if my husband is in some cockroach-infested jail in Afghanistan and he's liberated? What should I do then? Break your heart and his? Tell him I didn't wait, that I started to love someone else and that he needs to make a new life like I did?"

"He's gone, Becks. You have that option too. To accept the facts that are in front of you. Davlin is dead."

My hand struck out so fast to stop the words from spilling out of his mouth, I hit him with a force that spun him. I immediately regretted hitting him. Jarrod turned back to me fast, grabbing both

195

my arms to pin them to my sides. His face was inches away from mine. "You will never hit me again." He hissed the words through a clenched jaw.

I understood his anger, but I was scared. Anyone would fight if they were being restrained. I tried to get my arms free, squirming, but Jarrod just applied more pressure to my bones.

"Stop, Becks." His voice was authoritative, and I did stop fighting him. He was looking directly into my eyes, holding my vision, and I nodded. Jarrod released my arms. Not knowing what to do, I simply pushed past him, back out to the alley; gathered the boxes; and went to the elevator.

The next several days were a series of scheduled work shifts interspersed with phone interviews with hospitals in various locales, and packing. Heather had stayed back when Eric and Jobe went back to DC. She helped me pack and helped me load my rental truck. We made a good work team and were able to clear the loft in a day.

I stood in the door, taking in the view much as I had the first day I had moved in. For as much as I had changed, the loft still looked the same. Colorful instead of white, the open floor plan was bare and minimal. The beautiful light fixtures, which I had opted to leave behind, were now lacking the vibrant-colored glassware that reflected their hue, casting a rainbow of softness across the loft.

I shut the door, took the keys off my keychain, and placed them in an envelope. With the elevator holding the last of my things, those belongings not going into storage, we descended one floor and paused just long enough to push the envelope under Jarrod's door, and then proceeded to the ground floor.

Heather helped me load my air mattress, my bags of clothes, my sleeping bag, a couple boxes of important pictures, and another of Davlin's important documents. We were both struck with a sense of déjà vu. I mentioned the sensation, and Heather laughed as she admitted to the same. We climbed into my Jeep and left Allington to go to Guernsey for a night before starting our journey to Boston the next day.

Chapter 20

October wind chilled my face as I walked back to my apartment at the end of my shift at my current travel assignment, Boston General. A level- one trauma center, Boston General was a hotbed of activity all day every day. There was no such thing as a slow day in their Emergency Department.

That was a positive point to the job as far as I was concerned. I was too tired to think about my messy life each day. I would leave the hospital and walk the three blocks to my apartment, shower, and fall into a coma for eight hours before restarting my routine again.

I had started to see a therapist when I arrived in Boston. My guilt over the night with Jarrod was too much to overcome alone. I drank myself into the hospital at one point, and Heather was dealing with Jobe and Eric being an ass. I probably should have found an indifferent third party to cry to as soon as Davlin went missing, but being stubborn had gotten me so far in life I apparently thought I could muscle my way through his loss. I was wrong about not needing someone to talk to. Just like I was wrong about moving back to Nebraska, and many other decisions I had made since Davlin deployed.

My therapist, Laura Hillen, was a nice woman. She was a grief counselor with a specialty in helping soldiers and their families cope with the loss of their pre-deployment lives. She also, of course, saw the spouses and children of soldiers killed, and me. I had the distinction of being neither here nor there.

Laura had been a godsend. I was able to tell her the darkest thoughts I had about Davlin and our pre-deployment life. I revisited the loss of our son and admitted I had felt jealous that he had seen the baby when I had never been able to. She listened when I explained how hard we had worked to come back to each other and how I thought we were only stronger from the loss. Laura listened to me recap the first year of Davlin's deployment. Then I fumbled through explaining my year of waiting around the base for someone to tell me good news about him. Realizing I was either going to die in the hospital or work in it, I had opted to go back into nursing, something that saved my life. Laura was quiet and reserved as I told her about my move home to Nebraska, and she helped me clarify my actions that led up to my night in bed with Jarrod.

The act of voicing my near infidelity out loud and how I feared Davlin's reaction were two emotions that contradicted each other. I did feel guilty, for so many reasons, about the night I had spent with Jarrod. I had guilt so heavy I thought it would smother me, and I had such little hope that Davlin would be found. I had reached a point of despair. I had not yet reached acceptance of his loss. I still fought saying that he was dead.

As far as I was concerned, Davlin had a little over four years to come home. Those four years I was going to give him to come back to me. I was trying to find a way to balance the different parts of my confusing life—my lack of support, my sick mother, my fear of what people think of me—I was a mess, but I felt better voicing it to Laura.

I was getting ready to go back to Guernsey to be with Mom as she prepared for her final colon resection; her last two had not gotten all of her cancer. She had wasted away to almost nothing. Her ability to absorb nutrients was almost completely gone. She vowed that this surgery was going to be her last. With the surgery scheduled to happen in less than a week, I was trying to prepare to go home to be with her, knowing I would run into both Caleb and Jarrod.

During my last session Laura had suggested different methods to communicate with Jarrod. She recommended that I apologize, something I agreed with completely. I had been home in August when Mom had a surgery. Things had been very uncomfortable between Jarrod and me then. Mom caught on and had figured out bits of what we had done. She assumed we had had sex. As ashamed as I was, we might as well have fucked on the bar of The Metro in public.

She had said she knew it would happen, that our chemistry was too strong and my need too great for us to avoid it too long. I told

199

her that she was being ridiculous. I tried to explain that we didn't have sex, that it was just "intimate." She, being ever aware of my actions and feelings, pointed out that I still felt guilty about whatever I did do.

I missed my friend; if nothing else, Jarrod was that. Unfortunately he wasn't only my friend. He was amazing and the only person who had succeeded in making me feel whole since Davlin had been listed as missing. My problem was that I was stuck between choosing between a very real, very alive man who may or may not love me, or waiting…simply being patient to see if the man I did know, with every inch of my being, came home to me.

I wanted to wait, to give him the four years, a period of time everyone else disagreed with, but time I needed as well. I had been living a life of sorts here in Boston. I had been going out at night with some of the other nurses. There were things to do here that I enjoyed.

Recently I had taken a cooking class, learning how to cook gourmet food in my own kitchen. I had also started to crochet again, a hobby that had provided me with a rainbow of colorful scarfs, hats, and a lopsided sweater, but my own creation nonetheless. I had taken a swing-dance class with one of my coworkers. We were getting ready to start ballroom dance when Mom gave me the date for her surgery and I had to back out of the current class, promising to take up the next.

I was living, a life of sorts. I was trying. Laura was happy with my improvement but voiced her concern over my seeing Jarrod during Mom's surgery. Due to the stress of the situation, she warned me to not be overly friendly and to not put stress on him. I was not allowed to depend on Jarrod for emotional support. He was there for Mom. I had her phone number on my cell and was given the freedom to call her at any time necessary.

I was readying my apartment to leave for my two-week return to Guernsey when my cell rang. Jarrod and a picture of his face showed on the alert screen of my phone as I picked it up.

"Hello?"

"Becks, it's Jarrod." His voice hadn't changed, still deep with an odd not-Nebraskan sound to it. "You need to come home now."

"Yeah, I'm getting ready. I should be getting there tomorrow night; it's a long drive."

"Fly. Your mom is in intensive care. She's trying to wait for you to get here, but she isn't going to make it long."

Unable to speak, I let out my breath in response to his words. Fear gripped my heart and squeezed my throat, making it hard to breathe.

"Let me know which flight you're on. I'll pick you up in Lincoln."

I did fly into Lincoln, and Jarrod picked me up at the airport. The three-hour trip to Allington was uncomfortable and excruciatingly quiet. He didn't say anything to me until I asked about my mom.

"She had been at the hospital getting some blood work done when she passed out in the lab. They took her to the Emergency Department, and she coded. The doctors intubated her because she wasn't wearing her medical alert necklace. When I told them who she was and who you were, the doctor said to call you. Even intubated, they don't think she will last long." He got choked up as he was telling me what had happened to her.

I was already crying, had been since he called me. I feared losing my mother. "You were with her when she coded?" I asked.

"Yeah. I tried to tell them not to do it, that she had a DNR; it just wasn't on her file, so they had to do everything… You know."

"Yeah. I know." We both fell silent again. I was thinking of the odd couple that was my mother and me. There were so many hurtful words that had spilled out of my mouth. We were a difficult couple, but we did depend on each other for many years.

How do you prepare to say goodbye to your mother? I was scared of what I would see when we got to Allington, afraid she wouldn't be the person I remembered from just months before. More than anything, I was afraid that we would be too late. I had so

201

many scenarios going through my head, I began to suffer from a migraine.

I closed my eyes and tried to let the rocking of the car lull me to sleep. It must have done the job because I woke as Jarrod pulled his car into a parking space at the Allington hospital.

On the intensive care unit, I was shown to my mother's room. She was frail and diminished by the medications that had tried to stop the growth of her cancerous tumors. She was on a ventilator, and there were IV lines supplying her nutrients and fluids she was otherwise unable to take in. She was not the person I had seen only months ago. Her last round of medications had been the worst, costing her the most.

I sat in a chair, gently lifting her hand and kissing it. I saw no medication hung to keep her asleep, no sedative, no muscle relaxer to keep her from pulling out her lines and tubes. Whatever had caused her collapse had all but emptied the shell of the person who was in this bed. The thing that made my mom my mom, be it her soul or whatever, was gone.

I sat remembering recent and long-past conversations with my mother. I was grateful for the time since Davlin's loss that we had had. Since he had gone missing, I had found more time for my mother, time I would not have otherwise given her. I had learned about what had made her the person she was, and in that education, realized the extent of my life she had had a hand in.

I stayed with her, holding the limp hand, knowing she was gone. I shed some tears in my nostalgia, but didn't allow regrets of time lost or things unsaid.

After an hour, Jarrod and Mom's physician, Doctor Michael Bazen, arrived to discuss some testing performed early in the day that did show Mom was brain-dead. While her heart could still beat, there was no higher functioning, and her body would eventually stop functioning.

I understood, had seen it and anticipated what he had told me. I was presented with a clipboard of papers to sign, "Cessation of Life"

202

forms necessary to discontinue Mom's life support. I signed the forms and went back into her room.

I took a last look at the form that had been my mother. The body in the bed held no pull on my heart; I knew I had to let the vessel go. I leaned down, kissed her forehead, and sat to hold her hand.

Doctor Bazen turned off the ventilator, disconnected the tube from her body, and had a nurse stop her IVs. It took only minutes for her body to give up, the monitor mounted on the wall showing an end to the electrical activity of her heart. As an alarm on the monitor began to emit a screeching noise to alert staff Mom's heart had stopped, I leaned my head forward onto the bed and cried.

Still holding the hand of my dead mother, my body convulsed with grief. I was alone! I had no other siblings. My mother and Davlin had always been my only family, the only people who knew my past—Davlin from childhood, Mom from birth. I had no one left to tie me to reality, no one left to live for!

As I cried, I felt a hand on my shoulder. Thinking Jarrod had decided to show some empathy, I went to reach for it and my hand was caught in a warm, soft embrace. I looked up to see the bright blue eyes of my best friend, and the only face I needed to see to know I did still have someone—Heather, bless her soul.

Having spent time in Mom's room with Heather and later Jarrod, Eric, and several other people Jarrod said were in the support group with Mom, I was ready to go. But go where? I didn't really want to go back to the trailer. I knew I would have to, but I wasn't ready. I no longer had an apartment. Heather and Eric were not yet booked in a hotel. I had an odd sense of floating.

Heather, grasping my impending anxiety attack, suggested we go to Metro and have a mini-celebration in Mom's honor. Jarrod was happy to provide the locale and left to make quick arrangements for the unscheduled Celebration of Life.

Heather never left me. She stayed near enough for me to rest my head on her shoulder or to wrap her arm around me for strength. Always within touching distance, my best friend was my anchor, ending my sense of floating.

At Metro, we were again provided a room to have our meal and remembrance, but it soon became evident that the small dining room would be insufficient for our needs. Jarrod closed the restaurant to the public. Word of my mom's passing had spread quickly amongst her friends. People I never knew existed arrived at Metro, their faces streaked with tears.

I had parked myself in Mom's customary spot on the couch at the front of the restaurant. Heather had taken up a post to my right and Jarrod, my ambassador to Mom's many support groups, on my left.

I had no idea she had been in so many groups! Not only her cancer support group where she had met Jarrod, but an Al-Anon, and Narconon group as well. She had joined a group for soldiers and their families dealing with deployments and the returns of their soldiers. The myriad of different people coming to pay their respects was mind boggling! She had never mentioned any of the groups or her people, but as surprised as I was to have ex drug and alcohol abusers or cancer survivors or broken soldiers or their families come up to me, no group of people affected me more than the people of her first support group, a group for families that had lost a child or baby.

"Magdalene has been in our group for several years now. She joined shortly after you lost your son. She was distraught and so worried about how you would cope with the loss. She would often joke that you handled the death of the baby much better than she could have," explained Joanne, a member of Family Loss support group. "She was amazed by your strength. So proud of you."

I was speechless. So many new revelations about my mother, so many secrets I had never been told. In a way I felt guilty for not knowing that my mother had all these people to depend on, that she needed them. And yet I felt jealous that they had so much time with her!

"Thank you, Joanne. I…" I didn't know what to say to this woman who knew so much about me, but whom I hadn't known existed. "I am grateful that Mom had so many friends to depend on. I had no idea." Again, overwhelmed by my mother's social group, I looked around the room at the small clusters of people talking and laughing, some crying or simply watching.

"Of course not, dear. Your mother always said you took the strength and guts out of her when you were born, leaving the sensitive and soft parts behind." Joanne winked at me and smiled at her joke.

My mom had been a drug-abusing, alcoholic, whoring, biker bitch who left me for any length of time after the age of eight. She had numbed herself and her past transgressions with bottles of cheap vodka and whiskey, sought oblivion in pills and blow. She had had any number of men in and out of her life, a few who were less interested in her and more in me… But for all the drugs and alcohol, bikers and truckers, lonely nights and empty bellies, Mom had protected me the best she could.

"Becks, maybe you should say something to everyone," Jarrod suggested.

I nodded and stood, walking to the bar area where everyone could see me.

"Excuse me," I called, my voice sounding hollow and odd in my ears. All faces turned toward me, Jarrod turned the music down to a soft drone. The floor was mine.

I looked around the room, taking in the clothing and hair of the various people: bikers in leather with various patches sewn on their vests, church-going folk with sweaters and handkerchiefs in hand, cancer patients with fuzzy heads and eyes that were all too knowing of my loss. So many people of different creed, races, class, and profession; how rich her life was.

"I am amazed!" I said, barely a whisper. I looked down at the floor in front of me, taking in the scuffs of the wood. I looked up again at the faces. "I am amazed," louder now, "by the wealth of my mother's life." A collective sigh was released by the people of the

205

room. Apparently, Mom had made them aware of my ability to overreact, and they may have thought I would take the knowledge of their existence as a betrayal on her part. I didn't.

"I am amazed by the faces and voices I have experienced today. Just hours ago, I thought I had lost the only true link I had to my life. I thought that my memories were all I would have of my mother..." I looked around the room again, seeing what my mother had seen—kinship. "I am so grateful to you. To each and every one of you in this room and even to those who could not be here, thank you. I cannot explain enough to you how much it means to me knowing that my mother not only had you to turn to, but that she chose to turn to you.

"I can't say that I knew my mother in a very intimate way, not for all the different parts of her life. She would share with me what she thought she could, and likewise, she would share with you what you had in common. I guess if I had the time to speak with each of you, I would be able to make a very accurate accounting of her life." To this I received a generalized laugh as the mood continued to lighten.

"I can't say that I am not sad that Mom died; I am, but I am truly grateful that her pain and fighting are over. I am amazed... Amazed by the life she has had, the love she has received, the friends she made. I am proud of the woman she was, the mother she was, and the inspiration she will continue to be."

To this I received a general applause that quickly swelled to cheers, hugs, and general handling that landed me with a hundred tear-shared kisses from all present. The evening continued as I made my way around the room, hearing anecdotes about Mom's past, stories of meetings and thoughts she shared.

To each of the people in the room, my mom had been a different person. To the alcoholics, she was a sinner and repentant. To the drug users, she was recovered but not cured. The military families knew who I was and about Davlin; Mom's loss of him had prompted her joining the group. To them Mom was familiar, a source of pride and encouragement, continuing to be strong through

Davlin's continued state of missing in action. The cancer support group was a mixed bag of people currently undergoing chemo and those in remission. Mom's loss was a vivid reminder of their continued fight with their disease, but a blessing that her fight had ended.

The saddest of the people I spoke with were Joanne and Mark, the couple from her child-loss support group. They had known Mom not only in the group itself, but also outside of the group on a personal basis. They shed tears for a friend, not only a fellow supporter.

We hugged each other, tears spilling down our faces. "I have to make arrangements for Mom's funeral, but can I get your number if I have any questions?" I asked her, sniffing profusely.

"Oh honey, you don't have to do anything. Your mom arranged the funeral a year ago. Everything including the cost is taken care of," Joanne explained. "I have a number for you to call. It's her lawyer who has all the arrangements prepared."

Again, my mother's preparation surprised me. I took the proffered card and thanked her with a nod. Having received enough support from my mom's people and in dire need of a drink, I returned to the bar and grabbed a shot glass of brown liquid, not caring what I drank.

The whiskey burned from mouth to stomach, heating my bloodstream and giving me the warmth I had been seeking. Jarrod was behind the bar, doling out drinks free of charge. Eric was two stools down from me, obviously drunk. I was going to avoid his company as long as possible. I turned back to the room that was beginning to empty slowly, searching for Heather, who I found in conversation with one of the women I vaguely recognized as one of the military support group folks.

Heather embraced the woman and brushed a tear from her cheek. Looking up and seeing me free of company and resorting to drinking, she waded through the crowd back to my side.

"Hey, babe!" she joked cheerfully, smiling halfheartedly. "How you holding up?"

207

I considered before answering. "Well, I flew here through the night, with only horrible visions of what I would find and experience. I arrived to a shell of my mother, which means the last thing I said to her was 'I love you.' " I smiled at her, then continued. "I did have to watch a doctor turn off her vent, but I was so numb I almost felt nothing! But this! Wow! I have had such an array of emotions assault me tonight. It is seriously difficult to feel sad right now." I looked to my friend, pleading with my eyes that she might understand my confused emotions.

"I totally understand, Becks," she assured me. "How can you not feel good seeing all these people who turned out today to honor your mother? This isn't even her funeral! Magdalene touched all these people enough for them to drop what they were doing just to come together to celebrate her."

We took in the picture before us. The groups had begun to melt together, soldiers with bikers and truckers, grieving families with drug abusers, all joined by the commonality that was my mother. We both sat back listening to the babble of stories that flowed from the groups. But with the babble added to my general lack of sleep and assisted by alcohol, my body was being lulled to sleep, and I had yet to find a place to sleep.

"Where are you and Eric staying?" I asked Heather, snapping out of my stupor long enough to inquire.

"I don't know where he is staying, but I'm staying wherever you are. You need me right now. Eric can fend for himself." There was an obvious bite to her tone. This wasn't the time or place to bring it up, but I touched her arm in understanding of her marital difficulties. She gave me a weak smile and then glared at her husband now passed out at the bar, his head resting on his arms.

"Why don't we load him in the car and we can get him a separate room at the Holiday Inn?" I suggested.

She looked at him with a look of disgust on her beautiful face. Sighing, coming to an internal decision, she shrugged her shoulders. "I guess that would be the sensible thing to do."

Jarrod had been cleaning the bar around Eric. He looked up to see the look of complete disdain on Heather's face. He recoiled slightly, then offered, "Do you need help getting him upstairs?" We both looked at Jarrod, not understanding what he had said. "I didn't tell you, I fixed up the loft for you. Eric can sleep on the couch in my apartment."

The offer was more than I had expected from Jarrod after our last encounter. Heather was relieved of the responsibility of Eric, and in that state of relief, she grabbed a tumbler and started to imbibe with me.

Jarrod and one of his cooks got Eric up the elevator and planted on his stomach on his couch. When he returned he locked the front door of the restaurant. The number of guests had dwindled down to a dozen or so. Everyone was at the bar making toasts to Mom for her various talents and good deeds. With each toast reality slipped slightly further away.

The last thing I remember from the night was a toast made by Jarrod. "To Magdelene, the woman brave enough to fight cancer, strong enough to quit drinking, smart enough to quit using, faithful enough to believe in hope, and blessed enough to have passed it on to all who know and love her. Salude!"

Chapter 21

After the funeral, the packing up of the trailer, and arranging for the estate auction, I returned to Boston. The week spent in Guernsey and Allington had been peaceful. Jarrod had been friendly and helpful but showed none of his previous compassion.

Heather and Eric had had daily fights—yelling at each other, name calling, and a couple slaps across the face administered by Heather. She confessed to me that Eric had cheated on her. He admitted to his infidelity, then refused to end the affair but not grant her a divorce. Heather had been making his life hell. Her lawyer had filed all the papers for the end of their marriage. She need only wait the allotted time until the marriage was deemed null and void, time she intended to make miserable for Eric.

Caleb had come to the funeral, handsome as ever with his girlfriend in tow. He had been friendly and truly compassionate and concerned. During our conversation his mouth was moving but his eyes continued to look at me lovingly. I couldn't fight off his advances and deny my feelings for Jarrod. I was hopelessly confused as far as these men were concerned.

My best and only defense was to steer clear as much as possible of both men. In Jarrod's case, he avoided me beyond simple civility. Caleb was no more difficult to avoid, as his girlfriend was nearly always within kissing distance.

By the end of the week, I had successfully managed to avoid both outside the funeral and official wake. The funeral itself was quite an affair. I had never thought so many people would celebrate her life, but I was immensely proud of my mother as the two hundred guests, the people who had known her as a friend, the people she grieved and shared with, prayed for her eternal rest and gave her the most beautiful farewell.

I had expected all to leave after the graveside service, yet all guests stayed as her coffin was lowered into the ground, then each took a handful of dirt to toss into the hole that housed her coffin.

Along with the dirt, each gave a black-eyed Susan as well (Mom's favorite flower). By the time the line of guests had filed past, there was nearly a foot of dirt and flowers covering the lid of her casket.

I found my mother had indeed planned each detail of her funeral. The flowers and dirt had not been in her planning, at least not that I had known about. I was touched by the acts of remembrance displayed by the people in attendance. Her sign-in book at the viewing was full, people left photos and notes of kindness within, and flowers overflowed from the parlor down the hall of the funeral home. Heather and I were hard-pressed to collect the cards, let alone pick some plants to keep.

Joanne had made a beautiful quilt; Martie, a woman from her soldiers support group, had made a crochet throw as well. The Al-Anon and Narconon groups had gone together to buy a gilded Bible with her name embossed on the front. If I had ever had a concern when I had left my mother to go off with Davlin, my heart was relieved of the guilt in seeing how much love and support she had sought out.

Back in Boston, I continued to see Laura weekly, talking about my fears that had been resolved by Mom's passing. By the time my first contract had ended in January, I had reached the time for my annual trip to Fort Benning, Georgia, to assure the US Army I was still interested in finding my husband.

This year the trip that usually wore my soul down was comical in that Heather and Jobe accompanied me. Heather, freshly devoid of a husband, was radiant. She had begun to polish her look, not as a single mother, but as a haute mama! She was once again in pre-pregnancy shape, fitting into her slim jeans, wearing heels, and keeping her already blonde hair highlighted with even blonder streaks.

Heather had always turned heads without much effort; now she stopped traffic. Jobe had become a burly three-year-old. Where his mama was light and fair, Jobe's blond baby curls had darkened to brown just as his eye color had changed. The bulky boy still tried to have his mother carry him, an act that looked as though it should be

211

reversed with him carrying her, but Heather obliged her baby, hefting him up when he asked.

The trip was made in stormy weather when we left DC. As we drove 95 South toward Georgia, Jobe decided to play a new game insuring the most reaction from his two mommy-figures. Jobe had been subject to any number of colorful phrases during Heather and Eric's divorce. Now he took advantage of his captive audience by repeating some of his father's choice words.

"Das a shit truck, Mama!" Jobe exclaimed to Heather as a dump truck entered into traffic near us.

"Jobe! " Heather exclaimed. "That is a bad word. Don't say it!" She glared at her son in the vanity mirror. Jobe simply smiled at her.

"You shut your mout wo man!" her offspring imitated Eric.

"Pull the car over, Becks." Heather said through clutched teeth. She had turned in her seat, glaring into the face of the little boy.

"Heather, he's just repeating what you and Eric taught him."

"Damn right wo man!" the little monster testified. His outbursts of manly verbalization ended after that. No longer willing to accept his baby abuse and no longer caring if I was pulling off to the side of a major highway, Heather busted his little butt for speaking to her that way!

That night in Charlotte we decided to stop. Jobe was still pouting when I mentioned the pool the hotel had. With spirits lightened, the little boy began jumping on the bed, demanding to go to the pool.

Heather had been tired when I picked her up from her apartment. The trip and her son's abuse had done nothing to elevate her mood. With Jobe screaming and bouncing, Heather did something so out of character for her sweet and loving personality— she grabbed Jobe by the arm, pulled him to her, and yelled at him to stop his noise and jumping.

Stunned by her vehemence, Jobe began to cry. His high-pitched steam-whistle cry brought me to their room where Heather sat on her bed staring at nothing. Jobe, seeing me come in the room, ran to me, hugging my legs and nearly causing me to fall over.

212

I got the little boy settled in my adjacent room watching SpongeBob SquarePants and eating pizza, then returned to my friend who remained catatonic.

I sat next to her on the bed but moved to the other side when she refused to look at me.

"I said I would never hit my child," she said, her voice flat and distant.

"It builds character," I assured her. "Besides, he needs to know he can't say what he said or bully you around. Who's the adult?"

Heather looked up at me, as though she just realized I was there. "I promised."

"You can't make that promise," I argued. "Sometimes kids need to be punished. How else do you expect him to learn?" We talked parenting for awhile. Heather asked my opinion on how I would have handled the divorce, and I had to reiterate that I couldn't say due to lack of imagination. I was eventually able to get to the root of her problem and her sudden mood change.

Eric, in true asshole method, had sent her a picture of an ultrasound: his adulterous love child, far advanced in development. Eric and his girlfriend were preparing to welcome another son into the world, and Eric no longer needed reminders of his past.

In a text, Eric had turned over his parental rights to Heather. She had only just received the message when Jobe began acting like the man she now openly despised.

"Do you need to talk?" I asked her. Heather's face, so animated and happy earlier in the day, had become stone.

"No."

"Alright. I'm going to keep the door open and keep Jobe with me. Come over when you're ready, okay?" I received no flicker of recognition. I rose from the bed, taking one of the plastic card keys, and went through the door into my own room.

Jobe had fallen asleep amongst a mess of pizza, stuffed animals, and my clothes he had apparently decided to sift through. Trying to remember he was a child and not a demon, I took a deep breath and began to pick up my belongings.

213

Repacked, I cleaned off the bed. Apparently, I was going to have to sneak Jobe back in his mother's room after she fell asleep. I could still hear Heather crying softly into her pillow, so Jobe still had some bunk time with me.

I changed into pajamas, finished dusting pizza crumbs off my bedspread, and climbed into the bed. Jobe, being less than three feet tall, took up an amazing amount of space! Even in the king-sized bed we now shared, I found myself on the edge of the bed.

After an hour of being chased around the bed by a sleeping Jobe, I finally grabbed the little boy, tucked him close to my body, and brushed his hair until he settled back into a deep sleep. His limp form made me hot, too damn hot to have him right next to my body, but with movement came more chasing. Steeling myself for a hot night, I cuddled the flaccid child into my body and fell asleep with the scent of pepperoni wafting up from his open mouth.

I awoke confused and disoriented, a common feeling I suffered when spending the night in a hotel. Jobe was sprawled to my right; Heather was curled into a ball on my left. Her arrival to the bed must have been what awakened me. I pulled the comforter over her curled form. I turned toward Jobe, pulled his body toward mine, and fell back to sleep.

Later that day when the sun finally awakened us, Heather and I avoided speaking about the night before. She had collected herself nobly, refrained from cursing Eric's name, and focused on being a mother. The remainder of the trip to Fort Benning was uneventful. Jobe managed to avoid angering the women in his life, and I was again informed that no new word in regard to Davlin's whereabouts was available.

I was no longer deeply disappointed in hearing the same news. I no longer felt as though the world was collapsing on my body or that my soul was being wrenched from me. I was sad and disappointed and annoyed. I was becoming angry at my husband for his part in being missing and at the army for not finding anything or to being able to provide closure. I was no longer sure of my ability to withstand seven years of uncertainty, seven years of waiting, seven years of pausing my life.

"What the hell are you talking about?" Heather demanded of me later that day as we sat watching Jobe play at a McDonald's playground. "You haven't put your life on hold, nor should you. You can't be a skeleton of a person for seven years. No one begrudges you working, having friends, taking classes, or generally living! You can't stay in an apartment all the time."

"Yeah, I guess. I just feel stuck!" My impatience and aggravation were beginning to show.

"Then do something! Where is your next assignment?"

"I haven't picked one yet. Stosh asked if I wanted to take his spot on a 'Mission to Mexico'; I guess he decided Central America wasn't really his thing."

"Whoa, what's a 'Mission to Mexico?' " Her interest peaked, Heather grabbed at a point in the conversation and ran with it.

"It's kind of like Doctors Without Borders, but these are mostly new doctors practicing skills but donating their time. Stosh did it a couple years ago. He said he spent most of his time walking new orthos through fixing clubbed feet or ENTs and plastic surgeons who were correcting cleft pallets."

Heather sat staring at me. "Why aren't you going?"

"What? Because I have to leave the country! What if they find Davlin and I have to get home, or if something happens..."

"To who? Me, I'm a big girl. Your mom is gone, Davlin isn't going to miraculously show up next week, and you—" She sighed, realizing what she had just said, but moved on anyway. "You need something, Becks. With your mom gone, you have kind of disappeared, and I'm scared for you again."

I had been thinking of Mexico since Stosh had mentioned it. I spoke minimal Spanish; I had a passport that had never had a speck of ink stamped in it. In reality there was nothing keeping me here. I had no pending assignment. I had been considering staying at Boston General, but now with more options open, I had some choices to make.

215

Two weeks later I was walking down the hall to my first shift back at Boston General. I had been rehired on a three-month contract to work in the trauma unit, and I was happy to be back to being useful. Nursing is a job that you can give only so much of yourself to—your physical presence and knowledge—but you must refrain from giving the parts of you that go beyond compassion for your patients. I had no capacity for anything beyond minimal compassion. I cared for my patients in the physical sense of the word, but when I left from my day at work, I had no problem leaving them behind. I did my job and did it well. Beyond that I ate, slept, and worked.

Heather had encouraged me, by phone, to start taking my classes again, or volunteer or something. She kept telling me I was burying myself in my apartment, and I knew she really was concerned. I did want to go out, live life, and enjoy being around other people. Yet I still felt obligated to be the faithful wife awaiting her hero's return. I was slipping back into my bad habits of self-pity.

I had just hung up the phone with Heather when I looked around my apartment. She hadn't been lying when she said I was burying myself in my surroundings. I had a week's worth of laundry to take care of, dishes and take-out containers needing my attention, a pile of unopened mail, and a new stack of books silently begging to be opened and read.

As I sat on my overcrowded couch, piled high with blankets and jackets, I looked around the room, slightly overwhelmed by the mess I needed to take care of. I was contemplating the pile of books, deciding if it was worth my time to delve into a fantasy or romance. Indecisive, I threw myself back against the couch, knocking the blankets to the floor, which toppled the books, which spread across the floor, spreading mail and tipping forgotten cups of water and coffee. The impromptu domino effect had left me trapped on the couch with a puddle of day-old coffee at my feet.

As was my usual wake-up call, I took in the mess I had made and equated it to my life. "Okay, Mom," I said to no one, "I am going to get off my ass and clean my apartment. I can already hear you bitching at me to clean this mess up. I can hear you scolding me for letting my house get this bad and for falling back into my depressed ways...." Great! Now I'm crazy, speaking to my dead mother, but in truth I could imagine too clearly what she would be saying about the garbage dump I had been living in.

I jumped over the back of the couch, landing on some old bread. "Uggh!" Encouraged, I dived into my cleaning efforts. Within a couple hours I had sifted through the mail, cleaned the fridge of moldy cheese and leftovers, rid the apartment of garbage, shelved the books, divided the laundry, and swept the floor. I had three full bags of clothes sitting by the door with a box of detergent resting upon them, waiting to be taken to the 24-hour laundromat. These were my next task to undertake. I grabbed a romance novel from the shelf, shoved it in with the whites, grabbed my quarter rolls, and headed out the door.

At the laundromat I had started my loads, taking six washers and one double loader for my comforter. I had started to read the sappy beginning of my book when a tall man with black curly hair walked in the door. I paid him little attention but did notice he didn't divide his clothes correctly. Minding my own business, I returned to my book.

As the washers moved from wash to rinse cycle, I noticed a growing commotion from one end of the room where a young woman and her little boy were getting bothered by a couple of teenagers. The general gist was that the teens were keeping the little boy cornered, not allowing him to return to his mother. The woman was crying to the boys, pleading that they let her child go, when the dark-haired man walked over, his interest having been peaked long before mine was.

The man placed a comforting hand on the woman's elbow, offering his assistance.

"You boys having fun?" he questioned, glaring down at them. The man was easily six-foot-three with broad shoulders and an annoyed voice. His face was that of a young man who had seen hard times. I guessed his age to be thirty at the most.

217

"Fucker, mind your own business. Dick!" one of the brazen boys, an acne-faced white boy with droopy pants and a greasy Red Sox hat, spat. The teen stepped forward as though challenging the man, adding another person between the now hysterical little boy and his mother.

The second teen seemed to be enjoying the game less now that the man had come to save the day. He cowered behind his friend but kept hold of the little boy's jacket.

The man stepped toward the pimple-faced boy, directly into his face, and made him aware. "Boston Police," he said as he pulled out a wallet with a silver badge now displayed. "This is my business. Fucker." He smoothly reached past both boys, took the little boy's shoulder, and guided him past his captors to the open arms of the young mother.

With the little boy out of the way, the now identified officer took both boys by the upper arms and turned them toward the door where a marked police car had just arrived. The officer took the boys to the waiting police car and stayed outside to speak with the newly arrived reinforcements.

I was impressed with the smoothness of the little boy's rescue; truly that situation could have gone much worse. The officer was still outside when his washer had finished. Looking to see if maybe he was coming back in, I was sure he would be awhile outside. I opened his washer and took his clothes to an available dryer, feeding it my own quarters.

The woman and her child had long since finished their laundering and had loaded her car. She had spoken with the uniformed officer outside and had repeatedly thanked the man who had offered his help. She had just driven off into the evening when the cruiser with the teens had left the parking lot and the off-duty officer returned to the laundromat. He glanced at his open washing machine and was just beginning to turn red in the face with fury when he saw me looking at him, pointing to the dryer that held his tumbling clothes.

"I moved them for you. Hope you don't mind."

218

The man walked to the bay of dryers, glanced at the timer, added another quarter, then turned to me. "Thanks." He stood a couple feet from me looking awkward and uncomfortable.

"You did a nice job with those boys. Are they going to jail?" He remained standing, his hands jammed into the pockets of his jeans and his shoulders curling around himself.

"Ah no, the lady didn't want to press charges. I guess I scared them enough. They were pretty apologetic. How much do I owe you for the dryer?"

I laughed, something I hadn't done in awhile! "Yeah, I'm going to say nothing. You're the savior of the Soap-n-Suds!" Still laughing, I jumped down from the folding table and went to my first dryer that had stopped. "So, are you off duty or undercover patrolling laundromats for deviant behavior while fabric softening?" My joking tone was not lost on him, and he smiled slightly. He pulled himself up on the table across from mine and joined me in conversation.

He was quiet, mostly allowing me to carry the conversation, and I was talking about nothing, really. I mentioned some of the news I had read about involving the police. I mentioned where I worked and that I had frequently seen officers in passing during my daily duties. He was polite and interjected when something piqued his attention. In general, he simply listened. When laundry was folded and neatly packed away in the bags, he helped me carry them across the street to my apartment building. It was that night that a friendship was formed, which revolved around the Soap-N-Suds.

Chapter 22

Ryan and I ran into each other periodically at work, responding to domestic violence reports made by staff nurses or other violent crimes that required police intervention. I had probably seen him many times before in the Emergency Department, but as often happens when you are introduced to something new, you tend to notice it more. I was taking more notice of my new friend and he me. We made a loose arrangement to do laundry around the same time each week so we could share each other's company.

After the initial excitement the first week of time-share laundry service, Ryan and I had easier times talking and joking together. We stayed away from personal subjects for the most part, instead talking in general terms about things we had seen or done in the past. He saw my wedding ring and didn't comment. I saw the lack of a band on his finger and likewise did not comment.

We had companionably been fluffing and folding our laundry about a month when I mentioned that some of the nurses were going to Danny Boy's Bar down the street later that evening. It was meant to be an impromptu bachelorette party for one of the girls who finally nagged her boyfriend into proposing. Not wanting him to change his mind, she had rushed him to the courthouse to apply for their marriage license and was fulfilling the marriage contract the next day. With such short notice, Danny Boy's was the best we could do to make a party official.

I mentioned the pending get-together and asked Ryan if he would like to come. My normal activities after washing laundry usually involved cleaning my apartment or ironing my bedsheets. Anything that changed my boring routine was welcome. So I had jumped on the opportunity to go to the bar this evening. I thought I would share the invitation with my companion.

"I'm not picking you up!" I had to explain, in response to the raise of his eyebrows as I mentioned Danny Boy's Bar just down the street . "I'm married, but my husband is deployed in Afghanistan. I seriously have been sitting in my apartment for weeks if I haven't been at work. My best friend said I have to get out, and I was getting ready to go to this bachelorette party my coworkers are throwing."

He smiled, a real smile that reached his eyes. "So you're not trying to pick me up?" He was joking and having some fun with me. "Tell you what, I'll go to Danny Boy's in an hour. I have to go home first. I can't let my clothes get wrinkled, and I think I should call for backup."

We agreed to meet up at the bar in an hour. I took my bags of laundry up to my apartment, put my clothes away, changed into jeans and a dress shirt, and donned a pair of heels. I walked down to Danny Boy's Bar, just a block away from my apartment, and met up with several of the nurses from the Emergency Department.

We had been indulging in several pitchers of beer. The group was boisterous and high spirited. Apparently, it had been a good day at the hospital ,and Erica, the newly engaged nurse, was trying to make it through a list of bachelorette "must do's" in a single bar. I was engaged in animated conversation with Claudia, one of the other traveling nurses, who was describing a sexual encounter she had had with one of the doctors at her previous place of employment. I was encouraged by one of the check-offs Erica had just completed, when her gaze shifted from my face to somewhere beyond me, and her eyes grew large.

I turned to see what she was looking at and saw Ryan and three other young, tall, and quite handsome men. I waved and smiled at him and received a smile in return as he approached our end of the bar.

I made poor introductions on both parties' parts, then moved to a table just beyond the bar, sitting just on the edge of the conversations and challenges ongoing between the nurses and the newly arrived officers. Perhaps it is a natural thing for police officers and nurses to bond, just as firefighters and medics are able to befriend the nurses. All joined by the tragedy and chaos of our lives, we all seem to make quick friends with mutual respect. Often there are people who react to the chemistry they feel toward each other

221

and a brief but intense affair occurs. I had seen the aftereffects of such trysts and secretly enjoyed the voyeuristic nature of them.

Quite unknowingly, I had made a friend who would be adding quite a bit of drama to my life and those of my coworkers, who were now adding the officers into their groups and starting conversations with them.

I took the opportunity tonight to find out a little more about my washing buddy. Ryan was a five-year officer of the Boston Police force, having transferred in after completing a tour as an MP in Iraq. He had grown up in rural Massachusetts, enlisted out of high school, and been deployed right out of basic to Korea. After his year of hardship, he returned home on leave and met up with his high-school sweetheart. They had gotten married during a holiday leave and been stationed at Fort Sill, Oklahoma, until his deployment to Iraq.

I had glanced at his hands as he folded laundry and saw no ring, nor a telltale white band of sunless skin. Having never seen either wife or wedding band, I ventured to ask where his bride was.

"No bride anymore." His face clouded slightly, then he continued. "When I got home, my house was as empty as my bank account, and she had me served with papers the day I got back stateside."

"What a bitch!" I exclaimed. It wasn't the only time I had heard about a woman leaving her soldier and taking him for what she thought was rightfully hers. Still, every time I heard about it, I felt sick to my stomach remembering Davlin's order to wait for him and then flashing back to my night with Jarrod. Even though we had not engaged in sex, the time together had been intimate, and I still felt guilty as though I had cheated on Davlin. I must have been blushing, something that Ryan misinterpreted as my own infidelity in a similar fashion.

"What the hell is that look for? Where is your husband?" he asked in a hard and hateful tone.

"I don't know. Davlin has been missing in action for over three years now."

Over a shared pitcher of beer and a basket of stale pretzels, I shared the abridged story of our life. Just as Ryan told me his history in short, I was open to his questions. He seemed like an old friend, though we had only known each other a month. His time in service made him a "brother-in-arms" to Davlin, and after seeing him save the little boy in the laundromat, I had to admit he impressed me.

Ryan asked questions to get some clarification of my tale, but otherwise simply sat across from me taking in beer and words.

"So now, I am in year three of his time missing, my mom is gone, and I pretty much have no family. Well, except for Heather and Jobe."

"She's your hot-mess best friend, right?"

"Yeah. That's an accurate description of both of us. I guess that's why I like her so much. She's as fucked as I am. Well, slightly less. She can have dirty divorcée sex." He was laughing at me and my faked jealousy.

"So, what's it like? Knowing you have a husband, but not knowing where he is or when he is coming back?" Ryan was serious again, his look intense.

I looked down at my hands, at my wedding ring. I was feeling the effects of the numerous beers and other drinks consumed in toast to my soon-to-be-married coworker.

"I'm jealous." My answer surprised him. His eyebrows rose again, and his eyes widened. My eyes were moist with my honesty and weakness laid out, but it was true! Why not be jealous of the people who get to live, who get to love and flirt and touch and make babies and go on vacations and make new memories! Why not hate a little? My thoughts must have shown slightly. I was looking at Erica, who was slow dancing with one of the other men who had come with Ryan.

I wanted to have such indiscretion. To not have to care what other people thought of me or my actions, but those thoughts were those of a high-school girl, not a married woman.

"Yeah," he looked around the room of laughing people, smiling and animated in their conversations, "I get it." He looked across the

223

table at me and raised his glass in toast. "To hating the happy bastards!"

"Fuckers!" I agreed, drinking from my glass deeply. I lowered the glass and l laughed at him and his feigned anger.

We spent the remainder of the night talking like we were back in the laundromat. Our conversation had gotten way too heavy, and the alcohol consumption was doing little to improve our moods, so we nonverbally agreed to turn to more placid and unemotional topics like sports and weather.

The night ended with me being walked home in the company of four Boston police officers, the majority of us legally drunk. After depositing me safely on my stoop, key in lock, the officers, Ryan included, caught a cab to their various homes.

I woke the next day with a well-earned hangover. I was shuffling my way around my apartment when a knock on the door made me spill my coffee on my hand. I opened the door expecting the landlord or another tenant complaining about my late and loud return to the building the night before. Instead of an angry face, I opened the door to the blindingly radiant smile of Heather.

She and Jobe had been in DC visiting her parents, who had insisted on keeping their grandson so Heather could come and visit me in Boston. She looked wonderful. Her smile reached her eyes, and she was obviously happy with whatever she had been doing with herself.

"Oh my god!!!! Becks!" She screeched in my ear as she hugged me tightly. Finally having realized I looked like hell rolled over twice, she held me at arm's length, taking in my entire appearance. I hadn't washed my face the night before nor bathed after coming home, instead opting to aim directly for my bed to make the spinning stop. My hair was sticking up in various directions, and my breath smelled. "You are not allowed to get depressed again. Aren't you seeing that shrink still?" Her tone was exasperated.

"No. No, it's not what you think. I was out late drinking with some friends last night. You would be proud of me. I even got walked home by four hot guys," I teased her.

"Hot guys, huh? You have one hiding in your panty drawer?" she teased back.

Our conversation became quite disgusting and crude for being between two women. Heather told me about the trip to the Bahamas she had recently undertaken. She had left Jobe with her parents then too, opting instead to take an old friend from college, an old sweetheart. The fun of the week-long vacation over, she had again returned home to her son and her real world, where she was working in her father's office, learning the ins and outs of the office. Heather was a CPA. She simply hadn't worked since marrying Eric and was now having a difficult time adjusting to the thought of working daily.

She talked to me while I showered, dried my hair, and made myself look like a living person as opposed to the half-dead fish with hair I had resembled on her arrival. Once she was done telling me the latest about her father's lawyer's personal assault on Eric and his finances, she began to ask me about my new friends.

"So, who are your hot cop friends and when do I get to meet them?" The interest was nearly killing her. Her eyes glistened with anticipation of steamy details I could not provide about the men and Ryan.

"Only one is really my friend. Ryan, he's the cop in the laundromat I told you about. He brought some 'backup' last night," I explained. "He is single, very good looking. You should meet him. You two would make a disgustingly beautiful couple. People would hate you." I winked at her and grabbed my phone, sending a text inviting him to lunch.

It was while I was packing up my purse that I received the reply in declination. He was already at work and found my slothfulness distasteful. I stared at the screen on my cell phone, weighing his humor, when I received the ;P after.

"2-night, have 2 work now ," he explained in text.

"OK, have friend for u 2 meet," I warned him. "Look good, she's hot-mess ;p," I returned and warned.

225

We sent a few more short messages determining where and when to meet for the night and ended the messaging.

Heather and I spent the day in an area of Boston known for its antique stores. Heather was seeking out an authentic roll-top desk for her office in DC. She was currently looking at a beautiful mahogany number that must weigh a half ton, when my phone began to vibrate.

I answered quickly after seeing Colonel Barring's name flash as the phone rang a Sousa march. "Hello! Colonel Barring, how are you?" I asked, suddenly breathless.

"Hello, Becks." He sounded far away on the phone. I could hear helicopters in the background and wondered where he was. "I wanted to be the one to tell you…" My stomach dropped, and I suddenly had the absolute need for support or I would fall over. "We found the remains of Sergeant Pallen." Silence.

Relief flushed over me and filled my soul with hope once again. What a shit I was to be grateful that it was Sergeant Pallen and not Davlin who was found. I could go on hoping and praying that he would be found, and Vanessa…what a lucky bitch. She would truly get to go on with her life.

She already had, of course. She had moved home and married some random man who was sure to be home every night. She would now have the ability to sleep soundly knowing he was not locked in some hell. She would have a place to go cry and tell him how she missed him and his touch.

I was standing with my phone in hand, tears silently sliding down my face, unable to move when Heather came to my rescue. She took the phone from my hand and spoke with the colonel. She was made aware of the information I had been unable to obtain in my sudden state of disbelief and envy. She ended the call, pulled me close, and held me for awhile.

After a bit of time, she pushed me from her, took my shoulders, and asked, "Would you rather have heard that it was Davlin?"

The question was frank and to the point, but the truth of it made me consider…Would I rather have that knowledge and proof that my husband was dead? Would I rather be released from the remainder of my self- and societal-imposed time of waiting? I shook my head in response.

"Does it sound demented that I'm happy for her, for Vanessa? I'm seriously jealous of her." I was leaning on an antique table. We had been able to ignore everyone and everything around us; our ability to cut off reality had been perfected as our personal conversations deepened over time. We were paying little attention to the salesman across the table from us until he pounded on the table, startling us back into reality.

Heather whipped her blonder-than-blonde head around at him.

"What is your problem? I was truly considering purchasing the mahogany roll-top and have now reconsidered." She whipped her head back around after her verbal lashing of the salesman, wrapped her arm around my waist, and we left the store in a friendly embrace, leaving the man in the dark aisle unsure what had just happened to his commission.

Chapter 23

An hour later we sat on a park bench engaged in conversation about the pros and cons of ignorance when Heather's phone rang. She took a look at the number and smiled. She winked at me and answered.

"Hey, sexy thing. When are you coming to see me?" She listened to the response on the other end, then interjected a few "Nope" or "Um humm" into the conversation.

I had no idea who she was talking to or when she might be meeting her new somebody, but with her plans completed, she ended the conversation and hung up.

"Let's walk some more. You can't waste good weather moping." We walked toward my building, admiring the trees and the neighborhood. Kids were just getting out of school for the day. Uniformed yet individualized, they walked past us in groups of threes and fours. Loud and rowdy, I was pulled into a memory of my youth....

Davlin and I had known each other for very little time when we had started the school year. He had recovered from his bloody nose, nobly for a ten-year-old boy. He hadn't even pulled my hair or hit me back. We were wary of each other after the interaction on the porch after my theft at the gas station. I knew he wanted to turn me in, but he had wanted the chips more, and his parents weren't going to give him money to waste on junk food.

We had companionably sat eating junk food the first day we talked and then each day after that for the remainder of the week. Davlin would provide a distraction, falling into a shopping cart saying he got hit, slipping and falling on spilled soda, crying for his lost mother—anything and everything. He was a beloved child in town. While Davlin distracted, I lifted. I stole anything and everything I could get my hands on while people were coddling him. On one occasion, I was able to take three whole bags of groceries from a check stand while everyone was hovering over Davlin, who had just slipped on a bag of ice he was helping a woman to place in her cart.

We were smart enough to not try the same place twice, and after ten days of successful gorging on sweets and other stolen groceries, we had run out of options for free meals. Davlin took me back to his house the Monday before fifth grade was supposed to start. His mother ran me off the porch before I could even set foot in her house. She explained to Davlin that I was trash, just like my mother, and she would not have him hanging around with the town's next tramp.

He didn't understand what she was talking about but got the gist of her disgust and hatred of me and my mother. Unperturbed by his mother's prejudice, Davlin began stealing from his own kitchen to provide me with at least one meal a day.

It was the second day after his mother had run me off, just days until school started, that Davlin showed up at my trailer just as dusk had arrived. I was outside trying to make myself invisible. Mom had some "friends" over—bikers with a taste for cheap vodka and blow. Mom and her group had been inside for only thirty minutes or so, but I could hear glass breaking as they became rowdier. I figured I would be spending the night outside under the trailer or in the next-door neighbor's tool shed—better to stay out of the way just in case.

I was trying to see into the living-room window, not yet ready to go to sleep with an empty belly. I was trying to judge how long the group inside could hold up and whether I might be able to sneak in and hide in the kitchen pantry. Even dry oatmeal is better than having an empty stomach.

Standing on tiptoe, I was still unable to see into the living room. I could only make out the shadows and occasional silhouette of a body passing the window when a hand fell on my shoulder. I let out an involuntary shriek, then gulped it back in as I turned and saw Davlin standing behind me.

Even at ten, he was taller than most of our classmates. He still had baby soft blond hair that fell into his eyes frequently, freckles

229

across his nose, and the soft cheeks of a child, but the promise of a man was just beneath the surface of his skin, etching out his bones.

Seeing my new friend relieved me. I fell into his arms and hugged him dramatically.

"Holy shit! I'm so glad it's you and not one of my mom's friends arriving late." In fact, our driveway and front lawn looked like a Headbangers Ball with all the Harley's parked askew. I would have heard a new arrival, but I was relieved just the same.

Mom had always tried to keep her friends' sweaty mitts off of me and on her, but after she was taken with drink, she often ceased all form of parental activity and it was a free-for-all for her friends. Many a night I had been sleeping in my bedroom when an amorous couple would fall on my bed, pushing me to the floor as they coupled in front of me.

There were worse nights than those when I was in the same room as drunken lovers. There were nights when I was able to sneak out my window and nights when I wasn't…. I always knew virginity was a state of mind, and even if I was never raped in the most traditional sense, no man had ever had me before I gave myself to Caleb. I was still made to do and watch sexual acts no one of my age should have been involved in.

People talked about me and my mother, but so few people cared enough to try to help me. Davlin was the first to save me on a weekly basis. It started that night outside my trailer as Mom and the local bike club partied the night away. Davlin had brought me a plate of roast beef and vegetables, mashed potatoes and gravy, and some rolls. I began to devour the food before his hands left the rim of the plate.

The meal was amazing in more ways than just taste. I had often looked at pictures of dinners laid out by housewives and wondered how people could have so much and not offer any to those without. Naive and ignorant of my mother's status in life, mine too, I couldn't figure out the reasons for the bad looks, the purses held tighter, and the looks of disdain. I also couldn't figure out why Davlin had run

230

around with me for almost two weeks, stealing food when he had so much available at home.

I asked him, as we lay hidden under the trailer. Footsteps frequently passed just above our heads; crashes and doors slamming added to the noise.

"You needed some help or you were going to get caught," he replied smugly.

"Oh, so it wasn't for the junk food?" I smiled at him, the marks of our first meeting and subsequent battle still healing on his face.

"Nah"—he looked me straight in the eyes—"I did it for you."

We were silent after that. Mom's party spilled outside onto the carport and I shied away from the noise, trying to disappear into the darkness. Davlin followed me deeper into the shadows.

We were essentially stuck under the trailer, trapped by the lattice that was tacked in place to hide the wheels and chassis of the mobile home. I had found ways under the house often enough but had always been able to get out undetected. Now all my exits, loosened pieces of lattice, were in the direct line of sight of drunken bikers.

We looked around, testing lattice opposite the party, but were forced to stop when a couple, otherwise unable to find an appropriate place to engage in intercourse, proceeded to have sex at the rear of the trailer. We were stuck, so with nothing else to do, we curled together for warmth as much as for comfort and fell asleep together.

We woke several times in the night. Crashes and loud conversations kept us from sleeping too soundly. After several hours the party began to ebb and bodies began to decrease, though the parking lot of Harleys remained.

I woke during the night, feeling Davlin start beside me. We remained quiet, though the darkness outside let us know the lateness of the hour. I had been wondering what Davlin was going to tell his parents. How he was going to get out of trouble for his being stranded here. Certainly, the truth would cause more problems than help.

Putting my finger to my lips, I began to crawl to the loosened piece of lattice at the front of the trailer. Able to escape our sanctuary, we stood together, stretched, and smiled at each other. In unsaid agreement, we began to walk away from my trailer toward the field we traversed to get to each other's homes.

Well down the street, away from my home, I finally spoke to him. "Aren't your parents going to beat the shit out of you for being out all night?"

"No, I told them I was spending the night at Brandon's house," he explained, an odd smile at the corner of his mouth.

"Who's Brandon?" I didn't know any Brandons in town. Maybe he was someone new, someone worthy of Davlin's friendship.

"You are genius," he explained calmly.

I stopped in my tracks, again amazed at the skill of deception he was able to achieve. He had been playing people in this town for a long time, and they all assumed he was an innocent goody-boy.

I shook my head and continued to walk with him to the edge of the field. Once there, I stopped. "Aren't you coming?" he asked me.

"Where?"

"To my house. I have a tree house out back. There's all kinds of stuff in there for us to eat, and a couple sleeping bags so we don't have to sleep in the mud under your trailer with the daddy long-legs."

I went that night and many nights after. By the time we were freshmen in high school, the tree house had rotted and was torn down. By then I was able to climb the trees in his back yard, gaining entrance to his room that way. I slept with Davlin a hundred times before I ever loved him or confessed my love for him. He truly was my best friend and my savior.

Seeing the kids now running down the street, headed for their afternoon activities, I had to take a minute to thank God, again, for giving me Davlin. I smiled at Heather and we went on walking toward my building.

Heather decided to set up shop in Boston, a move I was ecstatic about. Her peppy bubbliness kept me semi-peppy and semi-bubbly. What I was thrilled about was Jobe! The little monster was my biggest distraction. Because he wasn't mine, I got to spoil him like an honorary auntie and then send him home sugared-up.

Between her job and her "sexy" mystery man, Jobe had a lot of time with me. I stopped picking up overtime to fill my hours. Instead I took over watching Jobe in the afternoons after he was out of preschool.

The babysitting worked out so well that Heather and I agreed to rent a townhouse together to provide Jobe with continuity. I also think it was to get me to stop taking him to the candy store right before dropping him off back at home. We found a nice three-story brownstone within walking distance of his school and the hospital. Heather was the only one inconvenienced by a daily cab commute.

We had moved into the townhouse by the time my birthday rolled around. Twenty-nine gave me a bit of an anxiety attack as I lay in bed that morning. I was staring at the ceiling fan, picturing helicopters and desert camps and daydreaming about where Davlin had spent his birthday, maybe in a hole, or a dark cave filled with bugs or vermin. I was making myself sick and depressed, until I noticed a giggle coming from the end of my bed.

I found the energy to raise my head off my pillow, no longer focusing on an old water stain on the ceiling of the room, and saw Jobe's head peeking up from the foot of my bed.

"Are you crying 'cause you're getting old, Auntie?" he queried in his sweet baby boy voice, his big eyes holding no hint of mischief.

"No. Not crying, just got a bug in my eye, buddy." I had to lie to Jobe. Since his father had abandoned him and his mother, Jobe had become a sensitive little boy. He would cry each time he saw a baby bird dead on the ground, pushed from its nest too early, or during a movie where a parent was lost. Bambi was on a permanent "No Viewing" list in our house. Jobe didn't know about Davlin, and he was not going to learn about him today. "Come here and look. I think it's still there," I chided the little boy.

233

Jobe gladly climbed up on my bed, crawling over my legs and jamming his knee into my stomach in his passing.

"Ooff! Oh buddy, you are getting too big for me!" I rumpled his hair as he tried to pry my eye open, searching for the errant bug within.

"I don't see a bug, Auntie." Taking his job seriously, he continued to move from side to side, demanding I move my eyes around for him. Finally he declared my eyes bug free and lay with his head on my chest, listening to my heart. "Can I use your ears, Auntie?" He loved listening through my stethoscope—lungs, hearts, bowels—didn't matter to Jobe, all body parts were worth a listen to as far as he was concerned.

I grabbed my nursing bag that lay just beside my bed and was pulling the tubing out of the mess within, when my door burst open with a loud, "HAPPY BIRTHDAY!!!!" They scared the shit out of me and embarrassed me to boot. Heather stood holding a tray of breakfast breads and coffee. Ryan was next through the door carrying flowers and a bouquet of balloons. Jarrod came through the door last, smiling at the scene they had all interrupted.

Surprise is an understatement when it comes to describing how I felt at that moment. I had no time to speak to or inquire about the guest list of my impromptu birthday party before being serenaded with an out-of-tune version of the birthday song, followed by hugs from friends and child alike.

"What the hell?" I asked Heather as she handed out rolls and cups of coffee from her tray of goodies now perched on my desk. I had sat up and was still taking in the attendees in my room.

"Well, I have to confess, Ryan and I have been dating for awhile now, and I ran into Jarrod the other day downtown." She wouldn't look at me, so I knew she was lying about part of what she said.

"Ryan." He turned toward me, sitting on the end of my bed. He didn't seem perturbed by the fact that I was still in bed and in my pajamas. "How long have you and Heather been dating?" I was avoiding the elephant in the room.

"Umm, since I gave her a parking ticket a couple months ago," he grinned sheepishly. My eyebrows raised at the breach of protocol he was involved with. Officers weren't allowed to date people they had met while on the job, people they had reprimanded. But apparently Heather had paid the ticket and then actively sought out Ryan.

"Wanton, isn't she?" I joked with them both.

"What's that?" Jobe chimed in, his doughnut eaten and the remains spread on his face.

Grimacing at both his face and my slip of tongue, I grabbed a napkin and proceeded to clean the little boy's face, answering his question.

"Just means that she is needy." I lied again, hoping he would soon forget the word and my false definition.

"Becks," Jarrod spoke to me, still standing by the door, "can we talk?" Everyone in the room looked at him with mingled expressions—Heather with wariness, Jobe with blankness, Ryan with disdain, and me with sadness.

"Yeah, but can we do this, all of this, downstairs? Can I please get out of bed and dressed?" The mob left my room, and the silence that followed made me feel overwhelmingly lonely. I would not dwell on or return to previous avenues of thought or the confusion that always assaulted me when it came to Jarrod.

I had spoken with Jarrod a couple of times since he had arrived in Boston. In retrospect, I guess I wasn't surprised that he had shown up today. He had been witness to my birthday depression before, and he had rekindled our friendship when he had arrived the month before to begin his newest business venture.

I hoisted myself out of bed, stood looking out my window at the sunny sky outside, and came to the decision to be happy today. I dressed in a yellow summer dress, one that made my hair look shinier than it really was and complimented my brown eyes. I brushed my hair into a pretty ponytail and quickly applied eyeshadow and blush, finishing with some lip gloss. I was prepared to go to my birthday breakfast and any other activities my loony

235

friends had planned. Today was not going to be about missing Davlin.

I missed Davlin all day. From breakfast, triggering memories of the meals he would prepare for me to celebrate; to the round of putt-putt golf, another memory of a date we had gone on with Allen and Sharon to prove we were not always having sex every minute of every day; to the dinner and dancing; Jarrod's hands reminded me too much of how Davlin would hold me.

There were new memories formed, of course. Jobe was a constant source of comedic relief, his childlike manners and lack of verbal editing meant no one had a secret that day. Heather and Ryan were still trying to figure out when and how to make Jobe aware of their relationship. Their delusions of his ignorance were quickly evaporated when Jobe rather loudly declared, "Mom and Ryan were back by the restrooms kissing, Auntie Becks. I saw them."

Heather turned red in the face and tried to quiet her offspring. His public table manners were lacking, and his declaration had made people at the surrounding tables of our restaurant look at both of them. They made a beautiful couple, and people were prone to telling not only the two of them, but also Jarrod and me, who were often walking arm in arm.

Jobe had asked Jarrod if he was my boyfriend. Jarrod smiled and winked at him.

"Jobe, I keep asking her, but she says she isn't allowed to have a boyfriend yet." This revelation made Jobe look at me with true confusion on his face.

"How old are you, Auntie? My mom says I can't have a girlfriend until I'm sixteen. She said I can't kiss a girl either!" He scanned my looks, glanced at his mother, and confirmed, "You do look younger than Mom."

To gales of laughter, I answered the precious child, "No, I am just not ready for a boyfriend yet. But Jarrod knows the deal." I glanced over Jobe's head at Jarrod, winked at him, and smiled.

I could never, would never ask him to wait for me. He knew where I stood, that I was waiting, and I was filling the time I needed in any way I could without guilt being attached. We had spoken rather earnestly the first time we were able to sit down when he first came to Boston.

We had gone to a small coffeehouse to talk, sitting across from each other. I was filled with confusing emotions. He had sat there, his hands wrapped around a porcelain cup with the name of the coffeehouse on it. He stared into the blackness in his cup. I sat looking at him, refusing to start the conversation.

"I'm sorry, Becks," he had begun, not looking up at me. Finally, he lifted his gaze to meet my face. "I have so much to apologize for." I shook my head at his confession, but he raised his hand to stop me from speaking. I realized he had a point to make and had been building up to the moment.

"When we… That night…" He broke off, looked at me again, took a deep breath, and continued. "I do care for you." He stared intently into my eyes, not allowing me to look away.

"When you asked me to… When you asked me to come into your apartment, I knew I shouldn't have. Everything with Eric, the revelation of how Davlin went missing and everything that Caleb caused you to think about… I don't know what all passed between you two before that night and in your apartment, but I did know you were in pain from whatever he had said or done, and I let you use your pain against me."

I was shaking my head again, bits of the night flashing through my memory. I had had too much to drink and too little to eat leading up to it all. I did, however, remember asking Jarrod into my apartment, and my bed. To his credit, we had not had sex.

It had been a night of intimacy. Much like teenagers too scared to actually have sex. Lips flowed across expanses of skin. Nibbling and teasing occurred. His hands had explored my body, and at his touch I had responded.

I had felt like I was in a fog the entire time as I lay in my bed, the light of the restaurant sign casting a red neon tone to the contents of my room, including the man who rested above me. Jarrod's face had been a mix of shadow and light. My reality was distorted both by the environment and my massive alcohol consumption. My memory made me painfully aware that my hands and mouth had enjoyed his body as much as his had enjoyed mine.

All in all, I was content through the night. My body curved into Jarrod's, I slept peacefully without fear or pain. When I woke in the morning, realizing I was scantily clad and in bed with someone, I had assumed the worst of the night before. Jarrod had been too angry with my reaction to fully disclose everything to me. As the truth came out, our friendship eased back to a ghost of what it had been before.

When he had come to Boston, I had thought it was for me. In our first meeting after his arrival, I had made the mistake of saying so. He had quickly corrected my misconception and made me aware of his expansion of his restaurant.

I didn't question Jarrod regarding his business. He was a success in his own right and was continuing to be so in Boston. He was a good friend and had agreed to maintain our boundaries, something that often made us blush when we caught each other watching too long or sliding from distant, neutral conversation into intimate, secret conversation. The general arrangement was challenging for both of us, because neither of us could deny our feelings.

So here we were, a group of friends—a couple, early in their relationship, learning about each other; and another odd couple, not able to call it what other people saw it as... I wasn't sure if having Jarrod around was doing harm, but it certainly sparked my return to my therapist.

Chapter 24

July birthdays and anniversaries passed without too much drama.
August came, and Jobe started preschool. He arrived at his school
with an entourage of moms and men in different styles of dress. His
teacher was entirely unsure who to address. She had a difficult time
following our quick layout of our family group. She ushered Jobe
into his room, shaking her head to clear the confusion.

Jobe was a sponge, absorbing the information given, coloring
inside the lines, reciting his letters and numbers, singing rhyming
songs each day as we walked home. By the time the leaves were
changing color, Jobe could write his common words and knew
Danny the Dinosaur by heart.

Heather and I were so proud of him. We looked like a hot
lesbian couple when we showed up for meetings and conferences
together. Our ability to finish each other's sentences didn't help put
the teacher at ease. Her confusion simply grew when Jarrod or Ryan
followed along to hear about the child who had captured their hearts
as well.

On weekends or my evenings off, Jobe and I would venture
into the building Jarrod was converting into his new restaurant/bar.
It had once been a fire station, one of the oldest in Boston, but
Jarrod had funds to upgrade the building. He wanted to make this
venture as successful as the one in Nebraska.

Jobe loved to visit. The fire pole was still serviceable and safe,
so the little boy could and would spend hours running up the stairs
to slide down the pole and then run back up again. He wore me out
watching him run!

As it was, Halloween was coming up, and Jobe was unsure of
what he wanted to portray this year. He loved me and loved to come
see me at work. Heather and Jobe were my saviors when my brain
wasn't functioning and I had forgotten something. Jobe would gladly
run into the Emergency Department, gaily carrying whatever I

couldn't live without, his eyes growing large seeing the mayhem that usually was my time at work. He liked the medics and the doctors.

Jobe had secretly confided in Jarrod one night that "Nurses are pretty to look at, but the doctors and paramedics are the ones who get to play with the blood and guts."

His other option was to be a police officer, a prospect that made Ryan puff up like a damn peacock. When Heather had asked why Jobe didn't want to be an accountant, the child started at his mother in disbelief.

"What would I go as, Mom? A calculator?" To this response he received gales of laughter from the other adults in the room, and an indignant look from his mother.

"Ungrateful little…" she trailed off as she pulled the little boy to her chest, squeezing him and making him squeal with laughter.

In the end Jobe decided to be a paramedic. He wore a purchased costume embellished with my old stethoscope and completed with a "real" badge, Ryan's probational officer badge. He was being taken around by Heather and Jarrod, she not wanting to go alone in the city. Ryan had to work, as did I. Halloween was a big night for tummy aches.

I had been at work for a few hours, flowing from area to area. No bad traumas had come in yet. No one mentioned it; the superstitious nature of nurses and doctors had long warded off bad juju. When patients had the nads to mention how quickly they were able to get a bed, their temperature was quickly taken and knowledge imparted while their mouths were busy not talking. If they said any word in regard to the current number of patients in the department, the next temperature was going to be taken rectally.

I had just finished administering medications to stop a woman from vomiting when our trauma radio blared to life. Everyone turned to listen, silently praying for a heart attack or low-speed MVA. No one likes sick and injured, but some things are much easier to fix than others.

The call was from Paramedic Barker, a veteran with a cool head and great assessment skills. "… En route with a twenty-eight-year old female versus motor vehicle, patient was thrown twenty yards after being struck by vehicle. GCS of ten at this time, massive trauma to bilateral lower extremities, open abdominal wound with significant blood loss…. " The injuries were endless. This lady was fucked up and coming to one of the few places where she had a chance to survive the encounter. Our teams were well trained, our doctors top notch, and our crews in the field bringing them in were the best responders.

Barker continued, "I have established two large-bore IVs, vital signs are 88 over palp, patient is intubated, unable to gain a sat on my monitor, heart rate 150, weak and thready. Patient is in full C-spine precautions. We will be at your back door in thirty seconds…" It was like a bomb went off!

Everyone had a job, and everyone knew his or her part. In seconds, nurses, doctors, techs, and security were all moving with a common goal! Dr. Martin and I went directly to the room to prep it for the patient's arrival. We heard the sirens down the street, the ambulance bay doors being held open by Dr. Dewri, our trauma surgeon.

I was just finished priming some IV lines into a rapid infuser, when the gurney holding a lump of bloody blankets rolled through the door. Brought to the room, the patient was moved as a unit by the staff onto the gurney, and then hell broke loose.

With no wallet on her person, the victim had been identified by a child on the scene, a boy from the neighborhood who knew and played with her son. She had blonde hair and was petite, her nails were taken care of, and her designer clothes were lovely. I was only partially focused on the patient in front of me as I began to wonder if the information we were receiving was wrong. Was it Heather laying in front of me? Was Jobe the little boy and Jarrod the assumed spouse?

I was snapped back into reality when Dr. Dewri mentioned the officer in the doorway. I looked up to see Ryan, white-faced, holding the hand of a little boy. The child's dark hair and tear-streaked face were not those of Jobe.

241

Knowing that the woman was not Heather made it possible for me to focus and do my job. At length, the woman was taken to surgery, and the aftermath of the trauma set in for all of the staff who had worked so hard to save her life.

It was well past my shift when we, the trauma team, were able to leave the room. Bloody gauze, used tubing, disposable gowns, masks and gloves, wrappers, and boxes littered the room. There were sprays of blood on the tile and walls, and our goggles were all going to need to be sent for sterilization. But the woman left our care alive and was doing well in the hands of the surgical teams.

It would be a long night for Dr. Dewri and his team, but my part of the day was over. I signed off on the notes transcribed by the scribe in the trauma, washed my hands and changed into "normal people" clothes, and headed out into the cold early morning that marked November's beginning.

When I got home, Heather was in the kitchen. She was wrapped in a robe, her hair not yet perfect, her makeup not yet complete; she was simply there making coffee, getting ready to start her day. She looked up as I walked in, took a look at my face, and reached for a bottle of aged whiskey.

She poured me a drink, not asking any questions until I had finished the first cup she had poured. Then, refilling my glass, she raised her eyebrows in silent question.

Not able to explain my fear or the gratitude I had felt at seeing the woman and later her son, I simply stood, walked around to her, and hugged her tightly. She hugged me back, patted me, and pushed me away.

"Are you going to be alright? This is a little déjà vu from Ryan last night, and he cried until he fell asleep." Her tone was joking, but she was serious as well. I was sure Ryan had had a hard time sleeping after seeing the woman and the little boy left behind. He, like me, had put his personal life into the tragedy and had to pay for it.

"It was a bad night, and if Ryan didn't tell you, I will simply say that I am glad you are alright."

242

She looked quizzical but had been around me enough to know that I would elaborate more…later.

She hugged me and said, "I'm fine, we all are. We had fun, and later, after you have slept and bathed, Jobe would like to tell you about how much candy he got." She smiled, and I had to smile in return thinking of how excited Jobe had been when I had left for work. "You have blood or something on your neck, and I think it's in your hair too. Go take a shower." She grabbed her coffee cup and ushered me to the stairs.

I did as she bade, soaking in the hot stream of water until it ran out. Then I climbed into my bed still wrapped in my terrycloth robe. I woke momentarily to bid Jobe a good day and promised to pick him up, as was our usual schedule. He kissed my cheek and bounded down the stairs, something I would normally have yelled at him for. Today I was already asleep, not even caring that he made the racket.

Ryan and I were haunted for a brief time, as the woman died as a result of her injuries. We had flashes of Halloween night and the efforts taken to save the woman. The hospital offered a counselor for everyone who had been involved to speak to. I simply went back to Laura.

I had been seeing her two times weekly. My conversations now mostly revolved around how happy Jobe made me. I told her about the living arrangement that had only gotten weirder since Halloween. Ryan had moved in, not able to sleep without Heather.

Laura would ask about my feelings for Jarrod, a subject I tried very hard not to think too much about. It had been weeks since I had mentioned Davlin, requiring some form of prompting, a special date or phone call, to get me to mention him. My latest rant was my physical need for sex.

Laura pointed out that women and men find ways to provide self-comfort without putting their morals at risk. I had found a way to meet my needs of compassion in Heather, security in Ryan, and friendship in Jarrod as well as my need to feel as though I were part of a family. It often helped to have Laura point things out to me to help me realize what I had right in front of me.

243

I no longer cried every time I saw a Hallmark commercial, although movies about soldiers were still beyond me. I was able to interact with people more like a human and less like a machine or a crazy person fresh out of the hospital. I hadn't even realized how much I was living until Laura pointed it out to me. I hadn't even realized that I had accepted my new reality without Davlin, one that involved Jarrod.

The holidays were eventful. Thanksgiving was a blast in that everyone in attendance had to bring a tradition to the table. Be it food or some other tradition, everyone who attended made the day worthy of the celebration.

Heather had invited her father and mother over from DC, so she and her mother made the turkey in their family's tradition. I did both mashed potatoes—red not white, peels in place—and candied yams drowning in marshmallows and brown sugar. Ryan asked his parents to come, Irish folk who brought an excellent bottle of whiskey for toasts, and his mother made dinner rolls in the shapes of clovers.

With all the women in the kitchen, Jarrod was shy to enter, but he had promised us green bean casserole and his secret gravy. He purged the kitchen for the gravy making and everyone agreed that it was worth the cloak-and-dagger bit.

Dr. Dewri and his wife and son arrived bringing a beautiful cornucopia filled with fruit and gourds, the largesse spilling out on the sideboard in the dining room. Jobe and Alex, the doctor's son, ran into the living room to challenge each other in a video game, leaving the adults to talk.

As dinnertime was arriving, and the smells wafting from the kitchen were becoming thick enough to cut with a knife, Rachel and Derick Tombs, a traveling nurse couple, arrived fresh from visiting a homeless shelter. Rachel apologized for not being able to stay long, but they were making rounds to collect coats and blankets for some of the homeless shelters in town.

Finding this to be a noble tradition to embrace, Jobe and I raided the closets, clearing out all but our current coats and

Heather's inherited fur as well as the old comforters we had. Jobe happily handed over his WALL-E blanket, having now moved on to Transformers.

Rachel and Derick left without eating but had achieved their collection goal. They moved on to the next house to spread kindness and hope around Boston.

Dinner rolled around, and everyone came to the dining room to sit and enjoy the feast. Groups of twos and threes came to the table, drinks in hand. Everyone had a place and sat for a prayer offered by Heather's father. Then, before we began filling our plates, Ryan asked for the floor.

Dressed in suit pants and a button-down shirt with a tie loosened at the top button, he was dashing as he stood. All eyes turned to him as he raised his glass.

"I would like to make a toast, I guess the first of many for the night. To friends and family, the only thing worth living for." He raised his glass to the people at the table, who all raised theirs in return.

We drank and expected to move on, but Ryan was still standing. He blushed, looking first at his father who gave him a smile and a nod, and then to Heather's father, who did the same.

"I, ah… I have been a lucky man this year. I met an amazing friend who inspires me with her strength and passion." He turned to me, sitting across the table from him. He smiled, a glaze coming to his eyes. "You have the kindest heart, Becks, and I can't tell you how I pray for your continued strength and eternal happiness. I love you, girl." This speech was met with a collective "ahh" from the people around the table.

I smiled at him and raised a glass to him.

"I've also been blessed with a brother! Jarrod, damn man, smarter, stronger, and sexier…everything I never wanted in the guy who walks my lady home at night." We all laughed at his joke. "Thank you, brother. You are the man I aspire to be."

Jarrod was sitting next to me. He blushed and looked down at his plate, then smiled at me.

245

In a whispered tone, I asked him, "Is he drunk already?"

"No, just building up."

Heather sat smiling at her boyfriend's confessions of friendship. She knew she had a good man. She was surprised when Ryan dropped to a knee, and in tears when he pulled out a ring for her.

She gasped, speechless...

"Heather, you are the best part of this year. With all the blessings I have been given, you have been the one I am most grateful for. And please know"—he opened his arms and Jobe, totally aware of what was happening, came in and sat on Ryan's knee—"that when I say you, I mean both of you. I can't live without you." He sat there looking at her in such a truthful way. "Heather, I ask with your father and your son's permission; will you marry me?"

The words were barely out of his mouth before she responded, hugging both Ryan and Jobe tightly. Jobe took the ring, an antique handed down in Ryan's family, and placed it on his mother's shaking finger. He smiled at her and gave her a kiss on the cheek, then directed them both, "You two kiss now! I'm not the one getting married!" They did to a chorus of whistles, claps, and glass clinking.

The proposal and declarations of love done, we passed the food around and began to gorge ourselves. Conversation was easy, even with the array of professions at the table. Steering away from war and soldiers in an unvoiced agreement, people instead became interested in the next big holiday to come up.

Heather's father made the mistake of asking Jobe what he wanted for Christmas. The result was a conversation-ending list of gluttony.

After dinner, dessert, drinks, and a few card games, food was stored for the night and a mountain of dishes had been built, so we drew straws to declare the losers of the night...the dish washers.

Ryan and I pulled the short straws. Aprons and rubber gloves in place, we began the arduous task of scraping and rinsing the dishes. We were working companionably when Heather snuck up behind her beau, grabbed his butt, and winked at him conspiratorially.

"Hell, go consummate your engagement. I think that's a real thing now," I urged. Removing his gloves, Ryan followed Heather up the back stairs as she giggled in anticipation.

Dr. Dewri and his wife came in to bid me good night. I walked them to the door. Alex and Jobe were still chattering in their high-pitched tones; the new fast friends hugged at Alex's departure. As I shut the door after seeing them to their car, Jobe chimed in, demanding a new form of entertainment for the night.

"Auntie Becks, I think I just might be tired enough to sit down for a cartoon or two." His voice and face held such honesty and surety that his plan was a good idea. I had to laugh at him.

"What about a bath and brushing your teeth?"

"Nope, just enough strength left to make it to the couch!" he advised me as he ran away from my outstretched hands. "I'll be fine just the way I am, Auntie."

With little left by way of a fight, I shrugged my shoulders. Jobe would survive without a bath and dirty teeth for the night. Returning to the kitchen, I found Jarrod at the sink, finishing with the pots and pans too large to fit in the dishwasher.

"Thank you." I said with honesty. "I was going to let them soak overnight."

"I know. That is disgusting." He smiled at me as he wiped his hands. "So what do you think about Ryan and Heather getting engaged?"

I paused a moment before I replied. Heather was my best friend, and I wanted her happy and safe. Ryan was a good man with a good heart, if also a dangerous job. Together, I knew they would be a beautiful couple with stunning children, a couple that turned heads.

"I'm happy for her," I finally replied as I stared into the dark and greasy water. "I guess I'm surprised that they are both…" I started, then couldn't finish. In that moment, I realized I was jealous of my friends.

Jarrod stood leaning against the counter, looking at me. He understood how I felt. We were both envious of the ease with which

247

Ryan and Heather had entered into their relationship. I knew he wanted what they had... I wanted it too.

Year by year, I felt my resolve in waiting for Davlin slip away, especially when I was so readily faced with a man who was wonderful. I no longer dreamed of Davlin holding me. I rarely remembered my dreams in my drug-induced sleep. I no longer wasted days staring at framed photos of our past, remembering the assumed details of the day captured in film. I made no effort to embrace the future, yet I no longer dwelled in my own nightmare...I was losing my fight for Davlin with myself.

Jarrod continued to look at me, his face impassive. "Becks, you know that you get sadder during the holidays...The anniversary is coming up."

"I know," I snapped at him, feeling immediately worse and regretful. "I'm sorry, Jarrod." I paused, trying to wrangle in my crazy that was threatening to boil up. "I ..." Looking at him and seeing the concern etched around his eyes, the depth of yearning deep in their core, I wanted to answer his need, to give in to the desire that roiled off his body, to apologize for each time I had to turn him away.

"It's almost four years," I stated quietly. I looked up at my friend who stood unmoving, but he had become more distant.

"I know, Becks. You keep announcing the countdown. I know exactly how long Davlin has been missing! You keep throwing him in my fucking face!" His voice raised with each sentence. No longer at a distance, he had been advancing on me while yelling until he was able to grab my shoulders and give me a shake to emphasize his point.

We stood inches apart, anger and pain, betrayal and lust flowing through Jarrod, his emotions colliding with my pain, fear, loneliness, and desire. I wanted to hit him and smack his face for yelling at me! I wanted to grab his hair and crush his face to mine, to bite his lips in our kisses, to rake his back with my nails! I wanted to hurt him and love him and have him hurt me and love me back!

A wash of emotions overcame me. I couldn't stop looking at him as he stood in front of me. He had expressed his devotion and

248

concern, if not outright love for me, often enough. Something was different tonight. I had had little to drink, so I knew I wasn't hallucinating. I was simply more aware of Jarrod now than I ever had been.

A simple movement of my face brought my lips to his. Chapped from winter's abuse, Jarrod's lips were like a stranger's lips. He tasted of the red wine we had drunk over dessert. He smelled of sawdust and wood varnish, scents that were his. His arms held me tight to his body, sharing his warmth, and I melted into his embrace.

Our kiss lasted for an eternity. Neither of us wanted it to end; neither of us wanted to open our eyes and feel guilt. The kiss lasted, as did the embrace. Jarrod began to lessen his crushing hold and began to allow his hands to explore my body. His hands crept to my waist, pulling free my blouse from my pants, and then re-ascended my torso, stopping at my breasts. Wanting the pleasure of skin on skin, I too unbuttoned his shirt, exposing his body to my bare midriff.

Jarrod moved from kissing my lips to my neck, causing my breathing to quicken and my panties to moisten. His hands moved away from my breasts to the buttons of my pants. Undoing the waist, his hand slipped between my legs and his fingers began to tease.

I felt like a dirty teenager again, leaning against the kitchen island and allowing my restraint to completely dissolve. I needed something! I needed physical love. I had the emotional contact of the people around me; I had realized that much. Now I needed the physical contact Jarrod could give me, the physical meeting that I wanted so badly for him to give, and to accept.

We were lost in our fog of desire, panting and petting like kids, that we didn't hear Ryan when he first addressed us. Attempting to get our attention with a throat-clearing didn't work, so he knocked over a stack of cookbooks at the end of the counter, startling Jarrod and I enough to break our embrace, his hand pulling out of my pants. Jarrod blushed, having been caught red-handed.

249

I pulled my shirt down over my open pants, as Jarrod did the same. We looked guilty of several sins and had been caught committing them all.

"Um, sorry for interrupting," Ryan said truthfully as he padded past us, aiming for the refrigerator. He had the decency to look bashful, but he was biting a grin at the corners of his mouth. Avoiding my glance altogether, he opened the fridge, grabbed a bottle of champagne, and made his return trip toward his bedroom where he was going to get the sex Jarrod and I were now going to be denied.

Stopping at the bottom of the stairs, he turned and addressed me, "Becks, everyone deserves to be happy. It's nice to see you blush." He winked and continued, "But it's nice to see you both smile. Good night." Ryan went up the stairs, turning the light off behind him and leaving Jarrod and me in darkness.

Awkward and feeling guilty, I buttoned my pants and began to straighten my clothes. Jarrod's shirt hung at an angle, buttons not matched to their holes. He was having a hard time controlling his face. A shit-eating grin broke through just as he began to laugh.

Unable to resist joining him, I too began to laugh at the insanity of the situation. Had Ryan not come through the kitchen, Jarrod and I would have been having sex at that moment, breaking our vows, complicating an already complicated relationship, and enjoying every moment. I stopped laughing and groaned, leaning over the island.

Coming to comfort me, Jarrod put his arm around my shoulder. "What's wrong, Becks?"

"I want sex!" I exclaimed. I had a bone-deep need! Every inch of my body wanted, needed to be satisfied by the male form. I wanted to lay skin-to-skin with a man and have him put his weight on me, crush me into the mattress, and use me. Hard! "UUUGHHH! Jarrod, it's not fair! I really, really, really want sex," I whined.

"Alright, let's go upstairs," he said with absolute certainty. "Let's go up to your bedroom, lock the door, get naked, lay in your bed, and see what happens."

"I feel bipolar around you, Jarrod. One minute I want to kick you out of my house for loving me, and the next I want to sit on your face and smother you between my thighs."

He burst out laughing. "Shit, with those options, I'm not sure if you feel the same way about me as I feel about you, Becks." He kept laughing as he poured us both a glass of wine. "I love you. I know I complicate your life, I know I can't have you…yet. But Becks, I'm not going anywhere yet, and there are ways I can make you feel…better, without us having sex."

Intrigued, I raised my eyebrows in question. "Ways, huh?"

Taking my glass away, he turned me toward the stairs and gently pushed me toward my bedroom.

Chapter 25

That night in November became the first of many when Jarrod and I spent the night giving pleasure in every sense of the word without the physical act of sex. His hands touched his body; my hands touched mine. He asked, I showed; I asked, he acted. It was live porn in my bed, or phone sex without the phone.

"Unbutton your shirt."

"Take off your pants, leave your panties on…"

"Just tease a little, don't give in yet."

The erotic and fantastic version of our relationship started in November and continued through the biting cold of December. On nights I didn't work, I would spend the night in Jarrod's arms either at his new bar or in my room. Heather and Ryan didn't say anything seeing Jarrod at the house in the morning. He was as much of a fixture at the house after Thanksgiving as Ryan was. But what went on behind the closed doors of my room was no one's business but mine and Jarrod's.

We were daring in our instructions and descriptive in our asking. At times I would feel Jarrod's hand on my own, slowing my pace or correcting my touch, guiding me. He would whisper in my ear as I closed my eyes and enjoyed his instructing my own actions to lead to my own pleasure.

Confused and wanton, I just followed his words, and Jarrod was amazingly clear in what he wanted me to do and in what he wanted to do to me. I could hear his breathing quicken as I began to orgasm, my body arching off the bed as I pleasured myself to completion.

Lying panting as I enjoyed the aftershocks of my completion, I looked at Jarrod. His eyes remained intent on my face.

I leaned up and kissed his lips, not thinking of what I was doing. I kissed him, and he returned the kiss. My hand went immediately to his ready cock, his hand wrapped around mine and together we stroked him to completion, never ending our kiss, never breaking our touch, never stopping our exploration of each other.

As his breath caught in his throat and he groaned, I pulled his face to mine to continue the kiss. I didn't want to stop kissing him. I loved everything about him—his patience, his friendship, his humor. Jarrod was a perfect man, a live perfect man who had helped me for almost three years, who had patiently waited for me to confess my feelings and allow myself to feel the way he felt. I wanted to spend every night with him and wake up in the mornings next to him. I did want those things….

I rolled myself under his body, forcing him on top of me. As I opened my legs to him, Jarrod pulled away from our kiss.

"What are you doing, Becks?" His face was expectant and his voice hopeful, but his eyes were questioning.

"I love you, Jarrod." Stated out loud, I had said the truth and I wanted him to act on my love for him. I pulled him back to my lips and kissed him again, long and deep.

His body was warm, his weight pleasantly anchoring me to reality. We remained joined, just kissing when he pulled away from me.

"I can't." He sat up and got out of the bed.

I lay stunned, staring at his buttocks as he pulled on his pants and his shirt. Having partially donned his clothes, he finally turned to face me. "I can't, Becks. I've asked you so many times to love me and to… " He breathed deeply, as though he couldn't believe what he was saying. "What changed tonight? What happened in the last months that we have been together has suddenly made this alright in your mind? Are you going to give up on Davlin and let me take care of you? Are you going to be mine? Are you lonely and hurt because Heather and Ryan are engaged? Because they get to move on? Can you tell me? What changed in your life that I am finally the man of your dreams? When did I become the man you love?"

I was stunned. I didn't know what the hell had just happened, but I suddenly felt like a whore. I pulled my blankets up over my body, covering my nakedness.

253

"What, what are you saying?" I stuttered, shocked and hurt. "You don't…I'm confused. I am so confused. Oh my God, I fucking feel crazy again! Get the hell out!" Screaming at him as I ended my rant, I sat up in the bed, wanting to throw something at his head! I was hurt and lost and confused.

"What do you want from me, Jarrod?" I quickly asked at his retreating back, as I climbed out of the bed and wrapped a blanket around my body. "What do you need me to do or say? I just said I love you, that I want you in my bed. What the hell else do I have to say or do?"

He turned quickly and grabbed me. Crushing me to his body, he held me in a bone-breaking embrace. I fought against his body, trying to push away. He twisted a hand into my hair, forcing my face toward his. He crushed his lips to mine, making them hurt as he ground my teeth into them.

Breaking away, I slapped his face, bringing him out of whatever crazed state his mind had gone to. For a moment I thought perhaps he was the crazy one, not me.

Hurt and ashamed, Jarrod stepped back. He stood staring at me. He looked hurt. He looked scared and older suddenly.

"Why couldn't you have said it before tonight?" he asked in a whisper.

"Said what? Jarrod, what the hell?" I was angry, hurt, offended, and more confused than I had been in ages. "What is wrong with you? I said I love you, I invited you into my bed! What more can I offer you?"

He stood silent for a long time, staring at the floor. I grabbed his arm and began walking him to the door.

"I'm done. You have to go, Jarrod. Get out, leave, don't come…."

"I'm going to die, Becks." I stopped and stood staring at him. He finally met my gaze.

"I have… My… I'm going to die," he repeated. Then, too tired to try anymore, he sat on the edge of my bed, pulling me toward him, so he could rest his head on my belly. I wrapped my arms around his shoulders and vaguely noted that again, I felt totally disjoined.

We didn't talk anymore about what Jarrod confessed that night. We both needed sleep, and we were both hurt. I had held him until my feet were blue and numb; then I had climbed in bed. Jarrod had joined me, and we fell asleep nested like spoons, both of us locked in our own thoughts and with questions unanswered.

The morning sun didn't stir us awake. Afternoon shadows had long since passed when we stirred awake and faced the day already defeated, our souls sore and aching from the night before. Every ounce of pleasure we had shared had evaporated in the aftermath of Jarrod's confession, and I felt overwhelmed with pain.

Stirred to life by my need to use the bathroom, I didn't want to break our embrace. I didn't want to walk away from Jarrod, suddenly fearful he wouldn't be there when I returned.

He knew I was awake. He held me tighter for a moment, then spoke, "I really have to pee."

I smiled and giggled at his sentiment as we both ran for the bathroom.

Returning to my room we lay back in the bed, lying so we faced each other, holding hands but not speaking.

I studied his face, memorizing the lines and scars, the freckles and the angle of his chin. I noticed how the tips of his eyelashes were red but the roots were dark like his hair. Unable to stop myself, I reached up and traced the line of his lips and felt the rasp of his beard one day in growth.

I didn't realize that I had started to cry until Jarrod reached up and brushed a tear away.

"I didn't want to tell you. I wanted to... Fuck, I don't know." He tried, inelegantly, to explain himself. "I don't want this again. That's what I fucking want!"

"What form? What type of cancer is it?"

"Lymphoma. Stage three." He was silent, as was I in response to his news.

255

Lymphoma, easily spread from node to node, as is the nature of the lymph system. Meant to be a return system of the fluids and wastes from the cellular bed, the lymph system parallels the vascular system, adding in the nodes, collections of white blood cells to fight off infection before dumping the lymph back into the blood. Cancer within the nodes spreads quickly, simply because of the layout of the lymph system. Stage three lymphoma…his cancer was spread above and below the diaphragm.

"What do you need me to do to help?" I held his hand, kissed his fingers, then returned my attention to him.

The corners of his mouth turned up, the slightest hint of a smile reaching his eyes. Returning my kiss, he leaned back and replied, "Nothing. I'm not going to do anything this time."

"What? Of course you are. You need to get treatment!" I was appalled at his lack of desire to fight. "You need to go see an oncologist, now! You have to fight, you have to get…get up!" I was already up and trying to pull Jarrod out of the bed.

"Becks! Stop. Stop it." He was calm and in much more control than I was. He took my hands that I had feebly been trying to move him with. Jarrod pulled me back into the bed so I rested against him as he rested against the headboard. He rubbed my arms and held me until I had partially calmed down.

"I already spoke with an oncologist." He breathed deeply, and I braced myself for bad news. "The cancer is at my mesentery. It's not going to get better this time." I closed my eyes and tried not to hear what he was saying to me.

I didn't want to hear bad news; I didn't want to face reality. I wanted to be someplace else, or to wake up from this nightmare that had started out as such a damn sexy dream. There was no way my karma was bad enough to give me two men in my life to love and lose.

I turned to wrap my arms around his waist and I buried my head and tried to block out the real world.

"Becks, are you going to talk to me?"

"No," I replied to his shirt. Coming up for air, I finally looked at his face. Jarrod seemed to have aged overnight. The eyes I had stared into the night before had lost some of their color; he had more wrinkles around his eyes, and his beard was peppered with gray.

"I can't lose you too." Tears streamed down my cheeks, and my nose began to run. "It's not fair. I can't lose you too." Shaking my head in denial, I buried it again. "I love you, and now you're going to leave me." I felt like an orphan again. I was being forced to repeatedly feel the loss of the people I loved, being forced to try to deal with death as though two loved ones weren't enough!

I sat up again. Taking in the room around me, I breathed deeply. "How long?"

Sheepishly, Jarrod replied by kissing me. "Three months maybe. I already feel pretty shitty." He took a deep breath, then slowly releasing it, he smiled. "Do you know how long I've been waiting for you to say it?"

"I'm an asshole. I don't know what you see in me."

"I've got something I want you to do for me."

"Oh, hell no!" Jumping out of the bed, I was against the wall before I knew how I got there. "You are not giving me your death wish to fulfill. Fuck that!"

Shaking his head, he stayed where he was, giving me time to get my crazy under control again.

"Done?" he asked, knowing full well I would be drinking by the end of the day.

"Maybe," I lied. I was mentally unable to tolerate any shocks in that moment. My brain would have exploded if so much as a knock on the door occurred.

"I want you to come someplace with me." He continued to sit looking completely harmless, so I came back toward the bed. Afraid of the where, I was still cautious and prepared to run if need be. My crazy was not very well reined in.

"I want you to come meet my parents with me."

257

I wasn't expecting that. Taken entirely off guard, I sat down on the bed, confused.

"Where are your parents?"

"Colorado. They have a ranch there."

"Umm. Okay." I was still confused and off guard. "That's it? You want me to go to Colorado with you?"

He laughed at my confusion and disbelief. "Yes, that simple. Come to Colorado, to a cattle ranch, see cows, pet cows if you want, say 'Hi' to my mom, hold my hand when I tell my pop."

"Ohh, I'm your moral support."

"Yes, you are my moral support. You are my person for when I go to tell my parents...when I go to tell them I'm going to die."

I nodded my head in agreement. Taking his hands, I kissed them, then leaned in and kissed his lips. We were still kissing when the door burst open to admit Heather, Jobe, and Ryan.

Jarrod and I sat in an apparent lovers' embrace, causing them to smile.

"Whoo hoo, hot stuff! Becks, it sounded like you two had a lovers' quarrel, and I had to come and make sure poor Jarrod was alright. Since you never came down... What?" Heather caught on to our mood quickly.

I looked at Jarrod, raised my eyebrows in question. "Should we tell them?"

He nodded assent.

"Ryan. Heather. We have something we need to tell you."

Chapter 26

Winter in Colorado can be beautiful, if you're equipped to deal with weather cold enough to numb your nipple off. I was slightly acclimated to Boston winters, which were one degree warmer than an arctic ice cap, but the wind chill gave Boston the edge. Colorado was bone numbingly cold. There are no words to describe the coldness that I was feeling!

Jarrod laughed as we got off the plane in Denver and I refused to exit the airport. Bundled in my new North Face parka, knitted wool hat pulled over my hair to my eyes, scarf covering my nose and mouth, and down-insulated mittens cradling my hands, I was still freezing! My eyeballs were icicles by the time I went from the door of the terminal to the door of the waiting car outside.

Having to blink ice out of my field of vision, I was less than thrilled to be in Colorado for the New Year. Not only was it cold, but Jarrod forbid me from mentioning the anniversary of Davlin being MIA. We both knew that when the day rolled around, I stayed in bed all day long, worrying Jarrod's mother. He explained the situation in whispered tones out in the hall, then quickly returned to me, wrapping me in his arms. I was allowed this one day to mourn.

After his confession in Boston, Jarrod and I had become inseparable. I talked him into seeing an oncologist at Boston General, who had told us what Jarrod had already known. His cancer was very advanced, and treatment would be extensive and have little effect. Hearing it myself from a doctor I deeply respected, I was forced to accept Jarrod's fate and his plan for his last months on earth.

Although his spirits remained high during Christmas in Boston, where we remained to be together as a "family" with Heather, Jobe, and Ryan, his body was beginning to have trouble coping with the invasive cancer that was continuing to spread throughout his body. Jarrod was wilting away before my eyes. I was seeing his strength sapped away with any activity that involved more than walking a flight of stairs.

Sex was no longer an issue between us with the return of his cancer. Jarrod had begun to take pain medications that caused impotence. With his libido gone, sleeping with Jarrod was like sleeping with Jobe. What wasn't gone was his mind. Jarrod and I spent our days in the den of his parents' ranch or at the kitchen table, surrounded by the scents of fresh baked bread and fried ham. He told me stories of his childhood, growing up in this house, surrounded by his family who had returned to spend time with him as he wished.

January passed day by day. Snow and rain fell outside the windows, but within the house Jarrod and I sat holding hands, talking about places he had been and people he had met. I was deeply jealous of his life.

He was a privileged boy growing up. His parents had been quite successful in their cattle ranching, and Jarrod had been given the freedom to actually pursue his dreams and fantasies. He had wanted to be a carpenter; he wanted to learn how to design and manufacture furniture and houses in the manner of trained artisans before him. His desire and his parents' pockets had allowed a younger Jarrod to travel to Germany, Austria, Italy, and China, where he learned the arts of wood crafting from skilled carpenters. For his home-building skills, he returned to the US and sought his degree in architecture from a small college in Nebraska.

It was after he had returned to Nebraska that Jarrod had a girlfriend who had found a lump on his testicle. It was that blow job that changed everything about Jarrod's life. He was diagnosed with testicular cancer and underwent immediate treatment that included sterilization since part of his treatment was the removal of both testes. Jarrod had never really thought about having kids, but he had never ruled it out either.

His individual sense of his manhood changed, he quit dating, and he began drinking. He got his first DUI in a small town called Allington, deep in corn country of Nebraska. Sobering in the local drunk tank, Jarrod had no "come to Jesus moment." He woke up to the sight of Magdalene Frayer vomiting into the garbage can beside a desk of a very irritated county sheriff.

"Damn it, Maggie. Can't you get your shit together for one damn night?" the officer was yelling at her.

Jarrod didn't think she looked drunk. To him, she looked sick. To him she looked like one of the people he had seen at the cancer treatment center he had refused to go in to.

Hey, officer," Jarrod had called. Being ignored, he called again, "Hey Po'Dunk! She's sick! Catch her before she falls!" Jarrod had yelled from the cell just as Magdalene passed out and hit the floor.

Her concussion and his DUI were the beginning of a beautiful friendship that crossed their age gap and socioeconomic differences. Magdalene sought out the young man who had been concerned about her. She found him where she had last seen him, sleeping off another D.U.I. She bailed him out and dragged him to her Al-Anon meeting. Jarrod sat next to her, deep in denial.

"I refused to talk about my drinking. I didn't think I had a problem. I just thought I had a right to be pissed off about losing my balls," he admitted to me. "Other than the surgery, I hadn't undergone any additional treatment that my oncologist had recommended. Your mom talked me into it."

He surprised me with his statement. From what he had told me, Jarrod and Mom met at the beginning of her fight with cancer as well. I was amazed that she had coped with it well enough to encourage an angry young man to seek treatment.

"She's why I settled into Allington, your mom. She and I went to AA meetings. I was more her support person than an actual alcoholic."

"Denial?" I teased.

He smiled and continued with his story, "Nah, Magdalene was always telling me how hard her life had been, but she still needed to fight, to make you proud of her. I figured if a woman who had been raped, beaten, watched her brother die... Well, if a woman like your mom could endure all the pain and sorrow her life had been

261

wrought with, I figured I could find one bright thing to look forward to in my pampered life. So I did my radiation. Magdalene came with me and held my hand."

I smiled thinking of my frail mom sitting next to Jarrod as he went through his therapy. But that wasn't right. My mom was small and frail in her appearance, but not in soul. Mom was the strongest person I had ever known. I was prouder of her this day, after hearing Jarrod talk about how they had met and become friends through the bars of a jail cell.

He continued to amaze me as days went by. Before he told me about his cancer, our conversations had always included Davlin. He had always been the elephant in the room that tapped our shoulders, never letting either of us forget his existence.

Now that we were in Colorado, other than the anniversary, I had not mentioned Davlin, and in truth, I had barely thought of him. I was focused on Jarrod. I wanted to know more of him, more of his past, his dreams, his trials and errors. Jarrod was happy to share his side of stories, and his family was more than willing to tell their side of the stories.

Jarrod was one of seven children. The middle of the lot, he was also one of two boys. His oldest sister Joan was taking his impending death very hard and had stayed only three days. Unable to see her brother wasted away from her previous visit a year before, she had kissed his forehead, shaking her head as she left the ranch with tears streaming from her eyes.

Evelyn, the next oldest sister, lived at the ranch with her parents and her daughter Josselyn. Joss had severe autism, and Evelyn's husband had left when he realized something was wrong with his child. Evelyn did what was best for her child and moved home to where the village could help raise her. Evelyn took on Jarrod's diagnosis much like her daughter's diagnosis; nothing to do but deal with it. She helped me get Jarrod out of bed each day. She cajoled him until he finished his Ensure shake. She gave him a hand when it was necessary. Not hovering, but readily available, Evelyn was ready to help her brother deal with his death.

Olive was the next daughter. A rogue, she traveled the country producing a web-based show about weapons and such. I had a hard time believing that there were that many people making homemade weapons! Jarrod took me to her website, and I was schooled in the art of home production of hand guns and other less-than-sensible home-defense options. Jarrod informed me that they had been in a constant fight since they were fifteen and fourteen, something about Jarrod shearing the buttocks of her FHA sheep just before showing.

His mom clarified that not only had Jarrod shaved the ass-end of the sheep, but he had apparently dyed the newly bared end red, using food coloring. The sheep ended up turning pink with washing, embarrassing Olive to the point that she would not forgive him.

In their adult years, Olive had passed through his life with varying frequencies. She had eventually forgiven him his youthful indiscretions, having paid him back with varying pranks in their teen years. She had gone to visit Jarrod when he was in Austria learning how to carve furniture pieces. She had stormed into his life, upsetting him by having an affair with one of the men Jarrod was learning from. He was asked to leave after the affair was made public.

Jarrod and Olive had a rough relationship, but with his illness, she had softened and begun to be a friend to her brother. His cancer had forced her to view her own mortality and her health. Whereas Jarrod had found testicular cancer, Olive had found ovarian cancer and been treated at the same time as her brother. Their remission had paralleled, and they had formed a different bond with their shared survival.

She had arrived at the ranch the day after we arrived and had been a shadow when allowed. She spent many hours with both of us, and as many as possible with Jarrod alone. Not knowing what they spoke about, I gave them the time they needed to say their goodbyes.

Jack was the only other boy in the family. He was nine months younger and the Irish twins were so alike in looks, I would have otherwise mistaken them as such had Jarrod not been so proud of

263

his nine-month head start. Jack and Jarrod were comical when in the same room together, continuing lifetime jokes that outsiders did not get the gist of. I enjoyed the rare glimpse of them quietly staring out the window. Rarer were the times when Jack would watch his brother sleep, waiting to see him breathe each breath.

Colleen and Cara were the youngest girls. Actual twins, they were blonde and beautiful. They were also following in the footsteps of their mother in becoming successful cattle women. Both shared land adjacent to their parents' ranch, expanding the family's grazing land for their herds. They had business minds and wonderful work ethics. They also had soft spots for their oldest brother. Each woman would stop by in the evenings after ensuring their cattle were accounted and cared for. Living close, they visited often for short amounts of time.

Joseph and Kay, Jarrod's parents, were amazing. Having essentially turned their business over to Colleen and Cara, they were able to spend time with Jarrod. Kay looked in on him hourly through the day, even if just from the door. Joseph silently made himself available to Jarrod. He would sit on the couch while Jarrod slept, waiting for his son to wake. Several times each day Joseph would pass by Jarrod, placing his hand on his shoulder to let his son know he was there.

With so many bodies in and out, visiting and watching, Jarrod was never alone. We rarely had times through the day when we were alone. Our conversations usually involved three or more people. Many were stories of Jarrod's youth. We spent our days through January and February reliving Jarrod's youth.

By March, his siblings had to be more present in their day-to-day lives back at their own homes. With the exception of Josselyn and the twins, who continued to stop by daily, Jarrod and I were alone with Joseph and Kay until the siblings were summoned to say their farewells.

Jarrod maintained his strength through the cold wet months of deep winter. Not venturing outside himself, he would send me on quests to the outbuildings on the grounds to visit various areas that

264

triggered his memories. I knew he sent me out so he could be sick or indulge in his pain meds without looking weak. I gave him what space he needed and relished the times he would let me be around him.

As March nights grew colder, I continued to spend every moment I could with him. One particular night as I lay next to him in his childhood bed, I dared to ask him, "Jarrod?"

"Hhmm?" He slowly opened his eyes and smiled at me. "What's wrong, Becks?"

"Are you scared?"

"No." The smile never left the corners of his mouth. Though he may have discussed his death and dying with his siblings or parents, Jarrod had never spoken of his feelings with me. We had spent our time creating memories and remembering better days, long since past. "I hurt, and I think I'm going to be okay when all this is over."

His eyes were duller tonight, his skin paler and thinner. He was always cold, and he had dropped half his weight to just over one hundred pounds. Jarrod could hardly eat without being sick, and he was in constant pain even with his medications. He hated to take them, but he could barely tolerate even a sweater if he did not have morphine in his system. Jarrod was fighting, he was suffering, and I hated to see him like this.

"What do you think dying will be like?" My voice sounded foreign in my ears, and I choked on the words as I spoke them.

"I think," he started, then leaned in to give me a kiss. His lips were dry and chapped from dehydration. They were also cold, and I could feel his teeth behind them. It was like kissing a stranger, like kissing Death. "I think it will be like going to sleep."

He closed his eyes, the odd smile still at the corners of his lips. Opening his eyes again, he looked past me to sometime long ago. "I always knew I'd die young. I knew I had to find my purpose early or my life would be wasted. I almost did, waste my life I mean." He was looking at me again, the past forgotten.

"You didn't waste your life, Jarrod. You've done so much more than I ever could have in a lifetime."

265

"You will. Becks, you don't get to lay around and wait anymore, waiting to die, waiting for Davlin, waiting for me… That was my purpose." The absolution and urgency in Jarrod's voice scared me a little. He took my hands, kissed them, and continued. "You have to promise me that you will do something great. Within one year of me dying, you have to stop crying and go someplace amazing, someplace with a beach and blue water. Go dive in and try to catch a damn fish or something." He was smiling and having fun planning my immediate future.

"Jarrod, I can't think about …"

"I'm thinking about it for you. I want you to have the best part of my life. Live for me, cause I'm going to quit this soon." He laughed at his own joke; then seeing the look on my face, he got serious again.

"I worry that when I'm gone, you're going to become the person you were when I met you, the lonely depressed shell that didn't think she had anything to live for."

He was on a roll, and his voice held a bit of his previous strength and conviction.

"If loving me has given you anything, it should be that you can… You can function, you can live, you can love after Davlin. You can do it all again after me." He smiled, a true smile that met his eyes; seeing it made my heart ache. "I need you to go on, to wear a beautiful dress in Heather's wedding, to dance with some tall dark handsome stranger, to get drunk on a beach, to take a cruise that I never got to. Becks, I want you to make a difference in someone else's life the way you did for me…keep living, keep moving…."

He trailed off, finally exhausted and having stated his wishes for my near future. His eyes had closed, and his breathing was relaxed. I continued to watch him for a while. Dozing off myself, I was awakened when Jarrod touched my face.

"Promise me," he whispered.

I shook my head in denial, not even able to think about how I would cope with Jarrod dying. But I saw his need for my consent.

He was making himself ready to die, and I couldn't be the one to stand in his way.

"I'll try". Tears had begun to fall as I considered my answer, and my response was the best I could do. I'd try? Try to be happy when the only men I had ever loved were gone from my life? To try to live a life of adventure and happiness? The thought of losing Jarrod, of accepting that Davlin was in fact dead, the enormity of the thought crushed me… How could I promise a dying man that I would go on? That I would be happy without him?

But that was it; Jarrod would be dead and I would be the one to mourn and live as I could. That was the truth of my future. My present actions could give him the comfort he needed. I could give him my false declaration and try to live as I might.

"I promise, Jarrod, I'll dance and wear my dress for Heather. I will find some beach to walk on. I'll try…try to be as amazing for someone else as you have been for me." My voice cracked, as did the dam of my emotions. I buried my face in the front of his pajamas and emptied my soul of any more hope.

Jarrod rubbed my back until I fell asleep sniffling in my sleep. I woke several hours later cold and frightened. Jarrod was not in bed. The space he had left was frigid with the night air. He had been vacant from his place for awhile.

I found him downstairs in front of the large fireplace in the main living room of the ranch. He was wrapped in an old blanket, sitting on the floor, staring at the fire as it licked and consumed a freshly added log. He didn't turn when I sat next to him on the hearth rug. He did lift his arm to allow me the grace of his blanket and shared warmth. I moved closer and wrapped my arms around him.

We sat in silence for awhile, watching the natural process of fire with fuel. I was beginning to doze off again when Jarrod spoke, "I never thought you would tell me you loved me."

I was surprised by his comment. "I guess I was too scared to really say it out loud. You kind of killed it though, when I did finally say it." I thought back to the night in my room, when Jarrod had told me he had cancer again.

He laughed at me, a snigger at my imposed hurt. "But you meant it. I got you to love someone other than Davlin."

"Yeah." I began to stew in the irony that is my life. Anger boiling up in my heart, I had yelled at Jarrod, his broken body that meant yet another loss to me and my heart. "Why did you let me say that?" Tears rolled down my cheeks, anticipatory grief suddenly overwhelming me.

"You need to know that you can move on after your seven years of waiting for Davlin. You have a purpose in life, and it wasn't only to be his wife." Jarrod held my hand. His voice held his power. His body was a weakened vessel at this point. "You need to move on again, Becks. Don't dwell on me and my death. I have cancer. I fought and lost, but I lived a hell of a life in my time… You haven't even tried to live. You don't want to move on without Davlin, but I'm asking it of you." Looking deep into my eyes, Jarrod willed me the best he could with his beautiful brown eyes. "Go live our life together. Think of the places I've told you about and go see them or plot a new course, but please move on and don't look back to this sadness."

I leaned in and kissed him again, once again feeling the frailness of his body, no longer able to be mad at Jarrod for his dying, no longer feeling a traitor to Davlin.

"I will…try. Jarrod, you may be the straw." Tears slipped down my cheeks as our foreheads rested against each other's. "You may be the end of me, but I promise to try."

"Not good enough, Becks. You are too much to let go. You have too much life, too much love, too much compassion. I forbid you to let go. Pick a direction and go. Go do something that you never dreamt of! Please, for me."

Unable to speak, hearing his fear for me in his voice, I nodded.

Jarrod grabbed my face, forcing me to look into his eyes. "Promise me you will."

"I promise," I answered, not sure if I would want to keep his promise.

Chapter 27

Jarrod lasted less than a week after our night in front of the fire. He had put his last effort into our conversation, needing to be carried up to his bedroom in the morning by his father and me. He smiled at me, accepted a kiss, and then fell asleep for the day. I sat beside him watching the rise and fall of his chest, ensuring his continued breathing, until his mother forced me downstairs to eat.

"Jarrod told me to keep an eye on your weight," Kay explained, placing a bowl of chili and a plate of warm cornbread in front of me. "He said to keep an eye on you and to have you check in with me sometimes." She smiled into her cup of coffee.

"Are you going to hold me to it?" I asked, tasting the chili.

"Yes. Jarrod cared enough to bring you here, now of all times. I'm going to honor my son's wishes."

We were silent for awhile. I ate the chili, suddenly ravenous with the first bite. I finished my coffee and pushed the dishes away.

"He already has his funeral planned," I started but got cut off by Kay.

"I know what my son has planned. Becks, what are you going to say at the funeral?"

Stunned, I felt as though a piece of cornbread was stuck in my throat. "I have to give a eulogy?"

Kay smiled and laughed a little. "He didn't tell you?"

I shook my head.

"Yes, darling, you get to be the one to let everyone know how amazing Jarrod is. Kind of an egotistical thing if you ask me, at least in Jarrod's case. We all know how wonderful he is. I'm not sure what you can tell us that we don't know." Kay stood, taking the dishes to the sink and said nothing else to me.

I returned to my seat beside Jarrod, watching him breathing, counting each breath. Considering it a gift.

The next morning, Jarrod awakened and asked for his family. He was ready to say goodbye. Tearfully, his mother made calls to the siblings, who arrived within hours. It didn't matter what they had been doing; they all placed their lives on hold when the call came.

Cara and Colleen were the first to respond to the call. Anxious that Jarrod had died in his sleep, they burst into the front hall, tears already streaming down their cheeks. Kay met them, calming their anxiety.

The girls ascended the stairs to Jarrod's room, where I was sitting vigil at his side. His strength was minimal. He slept between conversations. With the arrival of his youngest sisters, Jarrod brightened and sat up more in his bed to receive them.

I gave them their privacy as the girls wept and Jarrod bestowed what he would to them. Just out in the hall, I stood contemplating the eulogy yet again. I had avoided mentioning it to Jarrod as yet and dreaded asking him if he really wanted me to give it. I felt slightly unworthy and unprepared in retrospect to his family, who stopped everything for him. Their love was so evident when mine was a war hard won.

Cara popped her head out the door, asking me to come back in the room at Jarrod's request. I entered and saw his shoulders slightly slumped, but he smiled at me, a half smile, just enough to let me know he hurt emotionally, not physically.

"We were just talking about how the girls better be as hard on their girls' boyfriends as Jack and I were on them. When you have kids of course," He smiled at his twin sisters perched on the edge of his bed, each holding one of his hands.

"This ass answered the door with a shotgun when our prom dates showed up," Colleen clarified, laughing and crying at the same time. I gave a halfhearted laugh along with theirs. The scene was only too easy to envision, but the reality of the cessation of the memories was too heavy to laugh through.

"You had just had your surgery and were so mean then," Cara said.

"Yeah, I'm sorry about that, sis," Jarrod said abashedly.

271

The twins simply shook their heads, dismissing his behavior from long before. There was a gentle tap at the door, and Jack popped his head in, smiling.

"The boss has summoned me," he said in a joking tone.

Jarrod responded again with a wave of strength at the new arrival. "Yeah, we were just talking about you. Well, you and I and how mean we were to the twins' boyfriends."

"Well, you girls had such bad taste in boys. Who was there? The Dongoughly brothers? Redheaded assholes. The Kennedys? All of them were terrors." Jack and Jarrod continued to list the suitors and their negative attributes in an animated conversation. By the end of the list, the girls were red with embarrassment. Jack and Jarrod were laughing at their embarrassment, while Kay and Joseph stood in the doorway, drawn to the sound of laughter from their children.

I too sat back listening to the exchange, watching Jarrod light up with memories, and taking in the banter he had with his siblings. Evelyn and Josselyn showed up, having arrived from Denver where Josselyn was having behavioral modification therapy.

Evelyn also thought she was late until she heard the laughter from upstairs. I met her at the door, having come downstairs for coffee.

"Hey, Evelyn. Hi, Josselyn. How are you today?" The little girl simply continued to stare at the picture she carried with her at all times, a snapshot of the beach in Hawaii.

"The therapy isn't doing much yet," Evelyn said, failure evident in her voice.

"Well, give her some time. It works best when started early in life, and it isn't a fast fix. Is she having any improvement?"

"Um, I don't know. Is Jarrod alright? It sounds like a party up there." She was already going up the stairs, leaving Josselyn to stare at the beach.

"Oh, yeah. Jack is here." Explanation enough in that statement, Evelyn rolled her eyes and rushed up the stairs.

The day continued on with an air of hilarity maintained by Jack and Jarrod. Joan arrived in the evening, worry and fear on her face.

She was still, obviously, unable to deal with the impending death of her brother. She sat near her mother with a steady stream of tears rolling down her cheeks until Jarrod summoned her to his side.

Evelyn gave up her spot on the bed, taking a seat in one of the chairs that had been added to the room throughout the day. Joan sat on the bed carefully, as though Jarrod would break with the movement that jostled his body.

"It's alright, Joanie," he told his big sister. "I'm tired. I'm ready to go, so…just be all right with this and know that I won't hurt anymore."

With his words, Joan and the other girls allowed tears to fall. Unable to bear the scene in front of me, I got up from my spot at the head of his bed, feigning the need to use the restroom. Down in the front room, I met Olivia. She was sitting on the couch with Josselyn, staring at the picture of Hawaii.

"How long have you been here?" I asked her. She looked horrible. Her nose was red from cold and crying; her eyes were red and puffy. When I got closer, I realized she was drunk.

"Long enough to drink a bottle of Mom's wine," she replied, unable to focus her vision on me completely. She turned her head toward the stairs, hearing a peal of laughter as Jack lifted the mood of the room upstairs. "I can't go up there yet. He's waiting for me."

Realization hit me, and I took a seat beside her on the couch. We sat for a moment in silence, she staring at a beach thousands of miles away, me staring at a fire, unwilling to envision the pending future. Olivia suddenly grabbed my hand.

"If I don't go up…" she began.

"He's going. If you don't go up, you don't get to say goodbye and he doesn't get to say it to you." I was certain of everything I said. Jarrod had hours, no longer days, and I knew if Olivia didn't go up those stairs, she would rob Jarrod of a certain peace he deserved and she would regret missing the last moments they could have together. "Have a cup of coffee, get your shit together, and go up. You're the last one, and he deserves to say his goodbyes."

273

She swallowed hard, then stood up. "I can't, Becks." She moved toward the door, then stopped, hearing a step at the top of the stairs.

"That's some shit sister," Jack challenged from the top of the stairs. His words drew the rest of the family from Jarrod's room. "You're going to leave without seeing him, without saying goodbye? Are you really that scared of death?"

I hadn't yet seen Jack angry. At the top of the stairs, he appeared furious. His face was turning red with fury. His eyes bore into Olivia, and she was unable to look away from her brother. As he was yelling at her, Jack had descended the stairs until he was only inches away from her.

Smelling the alcohol, he grabbed her jacket. "Thinking of drinking and driving again, sister? You're a fucking idiot! " he spat in her face, pushing her toward the stairs where Joseph and Kay had come down. Joseph caught Olivia and herded her up the stairs.

Jack stood at the base of the steps, breathing hard as he tried to quell his anger. Unable to do it in the house, he turned and headed out onto the porch, slamming the door behind himself.

I followed him, not wanting to go up yet, wanting to give the family time to put their private affairs in order. Jack didn't stop on the porch but instead went to an outbuilding, a small cottage not far from the main ranch.

I followed him to the cottage, not wanting to stand on the porch freezing and not wanting him to have to be alone. I didn't want to be alone myself. I knocked before entering.

Jack had his back to me. He was gripping a chair at the table, which stood in one corner of the small house. I could see the tension in his body. His shoulders were drawn taut with fury as he tried to crush the chair with his hands.

"Jack," I whispered, before putting my hand on his shoulder. He turned to me and buried his face in my neck, crying. I held him as he shook, not allowing my own tears to fall. I was tired of crying; I was tired of misery and loss. I needed a small amount of happiness. I needed something good in my life.

Jack looked up at me, then leaned over and kissed me. I returned the kiss, wrapping my arms around him and pulling his head toward mine. The kiss gave me a strange sense of déjà vu. Jack was so like Jarrod. When we broke away from each other, Jack took a step back.

"I'm sorry, Becks," he said. I didn't believe him for a moment.

"It's what people do with death, right? Prove they are still alive," I replied lamely. "I'm going back inside." I turned away from him, sure that he no longer wanted to kill Olivia and ashamed of what I had just done. Again, I had to ask myself what the hell I was thinking. "Becks, you belong in a jungle far away from people," I told myself, walking up the steps of the house.

I went back up to Jarrod's bedroom. Olivia was lying beside him on the bed. He had his head rested on hers. Jarrod opened his eyes when I came in the room and smiled at me.

"Jack gets emotional when it comes to Olivia," he whispered in explanation.

"I noticed." I took my seat again by Jarrod, leaned over, and kissed him again, a chaste kiss, completely opposite of what Jack and I had had in the cottage minutes before.

"You alright?" Jarrod asked.

"Thinking." I searched his face for any emotion. All that was there was exhaustion. "Do you really want me to do your eulogy?"

Jarrod sniggered at my tone. "Yeah, I do. They know me," he nodded to the door and his sister who was sleeping off her alcohol. "But you know me in a different way. You and I have been confidantes, friends, lovers...well, kind of lovers. You are the only woman I have never had sex with but had this intense of a relationship with."

I laughed with him, thinking back to the many nights we had laid in a bed together. Where our hands would caress and fondle. Jarrod had long ago lost the ability to make love, though not to provide pleasure. He could make my body respond in ways I had feared I would never have again after Davlin left.

275

I spent a hundred nights in his arms, enjoying the strength that was Jarrod, talking and reminiscing, wishing for a future that was unobtainable together. Often, he would tell me about places he wanted to take me, places he hoped I would go some day. Most often though, we lay facing each other, not talking, bodies touching our lengths, sharing warmth. Our breathing pacing together, our hearts seemingly so. He would doze off, but I would stay awake memorizing his face.

I didn't want to lose Jarrod, but I knew it was inevitable. I wanted to be stingy and take the rest of his time as my own and had wanted to since we arrived here in Colorado. I wanted to go to the places that he spoke of, to meet the people of his past. I felt robbed of happiness in life, and in a way, I hated Jarrod for causing this. When could I find a little happiness?

Apparently, my thoughts passed over my face because Jarrod took my hand and squeezed it.

"I'm sorry I brought you here to watch me die."

Appalled at the accuracy of his mind reading, I shook my head in denial. "It's not that," I tried lamely.

"Yes, it is. You're mad at me, but can I play the dying guy card?" He gave me puppy eyes as best he could in his health. Making me smile, I kissed him, enjoying the knowledge that I could still do that.

"I was wondering what I was going to do after this…." I trailed off, feeling guilty for my continued life when he lay here dying.

"Help Heather plan a beautiful wedding. Go on a honeymoon of your own. I'd take you to someplace cold so I could make you lie naked next to me."

"It is cold here," I argued.

"And yet here I am lying with my sister and not my hot naked girlfriend." He waggled his eyebrows at me.

"You're not sick, you're horny!"

"Again, here I am lying with my drunk sister and not my girlfriend!" Chuckling, I swatted playfully at his ear.

Taking his cue, I got Olivia to her feet and escorted her down the hall to her readied room. Everyone except the twins had stayed at the house. They had gone to sleep after Olivia had been deposited with Jarrod. I returned to our room and shut the door.

He watched me with half-hooded eyes as I removed my sweater and boots.

"This is the world's worst striptease, Becks! Please, give me something to lust over," he jested.

I rolled my eyes; then, turning on the music from his MP3, I began to sway my hips as I unbuttoned my shirt and tossed it to the floor. Removing my pants, clad only in bra and panties, I was freezing.

"God you are beautiful, even pale blue and turning into an icicle. Come over here before you freeze to the floor." I rushed to the bed at his invitation, curling myself to his pajama-clad body. "You are beautiful, Becks." He kissed my head and held me as best his wasted form could.

I fell asleep to his heartbeat, the sound soothing to my soul.

I awoke the next morning cold again. Thinking Jarrod had gained a second breath and gone downstairs, I stretched, readying for the day, until my hand felt cold, hard flesh.

My eyes sprang open as I sat bolt upright, turning to the side of the bed where Jarrod had turned away from me. Though not yet dead, his breathing was in rasps, his pulse slow. I cried out and fell on him.

The door opened, and Kay and Joseph came in the room, followed closely by Jack and Olivia. Kay let out a cry and fell beside the bed, grabbing Jarrod's hands, willing him to open his eyes. Olivia pulled me off Jarrod, draping a robe over my naked shoulders, and pulled me to her. Our shared grief seemed more tolerable than trying to endure alone.

Joseph and Jack rolled Jarrod onto his back, propping pillows under his shoulders in an attempt to help his breathing. With blankets tucked around his body, Jarrod already looked dead. He hands were cold to the touch as his body tried to continue to pump

277

blood to the more vital organs. His breathing was labored, with long pauses between each breath. He didn't respond to our calls or kisses. We all sat waiting for the rise and fall of his chest to stop.

The other girls arrived to take part in our morbid vigil. No one spoke today. No one laughed at remembered pranks or conversations long-since ended. What a difference a day had made.

No longer was there laughter or lightened moods. No one had the heart today, nor did they have the strength to argue or bicker. We sat praying for Jarrod to open his eyes once more.

He never did.

By evening, the strain of waiting had made Kay sick, so Joseph and Joan took her to lie down. Joseph returned to be with his son when he died, just as he'd been there when he was born. With the evening came the arrival of Heather and Ryan as well as the hospice nurse.

Heather came to the room in her usual bright dress, her hair immaculate even after taking off a knit hat that would have made my hair stand on end. She took in the mood, then deciding on an action, she came to me, stood me up, and gave me my needed bone-crushing hug. Then turning me to Ryan's waiting arms, she went to Jarrod in the bed and knelt beside him.

Holding his hand, Heather said a prayer calling for an end to his pain and passage into Heaven. She asked for strength for the family and those who loved Jarrod and asked for the will to continue for those of us who needed it. Everyone present heard her prayer and echoed her "Amen."

Heather had an amazing ability to bring calm when it was most needed. It was this gift I loved most about her. She sat next to Jarrod, still holding his hand, and leaned forward to speak into his ear.

"I promise I'll take care of Becks, Jarrod. I won't let her slip or go hungry. I'll make her get up each day and live. I promise to take her places until she is ready to go on her own. I promise to continue to let her know she has someone, several someones, who need her in our lives, just like you needed her. Rest easy, brother." She kissed his cheek. "You can go to sleep now, Jarrod. You don't have to worry about her anymore."

I don't know when Jarrod and Heather had conversations about death and dying, but whenever it was, Heather had taken it to heart. She was the most important person in the room at that moment. When we all thought Jarrod had been waiting for Olivia the night before, tonight it became apparent that he had been waiting for Heather. She took on the task of being my care provider and relieved Jarrod of any burden he may have still felt.

He died within an hour of Heather and Ryan's arrival. As death and dying goes, his was peaceful and seemed painless. Jarrod had been asleep or unconscious through the day, and he just stopped breathing. His chest no longer rose, and his heart stopped minutes later.

I was the second-to-last person to leave his room that night, second only to Joseph, who obviously needed a moment with his son alone. Preparation for the death of a loved one is an illusion. There is no true way to wrap your brain around the emptiness your heart suddenly feels when they are gone. Each of us was forced to deal with the new reality that was life without Jarrod, and we were all ill-prepared for that life.

Joan was loud in her mourning, as was Kay. The twins pulled to each other, depending on the other for strength. Olivia went downstairs almost immediately and began to drink. Jack, angry at Olivia and her coping mechanism, stormed out of the house, slamming the door behind him. Evelyn stared into the fire, holding hands with her daughter, who stared at the beach in Hawaii.

I buried my head in my hands and wept, deciding that the reality of death was much worse than the anticipation or assumption of it. Up until the moment his heart stopped beating, I was able to have hope that Jarrod could get better. I knew he wouldn't and that this moment was inevitable, but I was still allowed to hope, just as I was still able to hope for Davlin's return.

Heather let me know she was there; then she too went downstairs to help with the preparation of food for the guests set to arrive for Jarrod's funeral. Ryan kissed the top of my head as he left the room. He had lost many friends and family in his life, so this was no new feeling. He had lost a great friend in Jarrod and was having a hard time keeping his face under control.

After everyone else except Joseph had left, I lifted my head. I looked at Jarrod, so changed since I had first met him. This was a man who had first stirred my heart after I lost my husband, a man who had befriended my mother and helped her through her darkest times when I was not able to.

He was my friend, and yes, my lover. This shell of a man was the person who made me feel comfort in a man's arms, a feeling I had thought lost to me. He was the person who made me want to look forward to more than just my next day. He had made me want to have a future and to accomplish things I had never dreamed of before Davlin.

I sat holding his hand, kissing it and not yet able to put it aside for the last time.

"I didn't get a chance to tell you what I came up with for your eulogy," I told Jarrod, knowing he wasn't there, but feeling better for being able to still speak to him. "I guess it is a rare person who gets to hear their actual eulogy.

"I'm going to get up in front of your family and say this: 'I can't speak for everyone in this room, explaining what made Jarrod important to each of you. I can't tell stories about him when he was a baby learning how to walk or tell you what his first words were. I need some of you to tell me those things.

'I can't laugh along remembering the jokes Jarrod and Jack played on their sisters, or even funnier, the jokes they played on their dates. Again, I have to depend on Jack to bring those times back to life.

'I don't know the pain or fear you felt as a family when Jarrod first discovered his cancer or the anger and frustration you must have felt when he refused treatment. I can only speak as a second party when I tell you what it took for my mother, Magdalene Frayer, to get him into a doctor and into his own future.

'I can't really speak of Jarrod's past, but I can tell you what we wanted together. We wanted to go to Hawaii and take Josselyn. He wanted to walk her on her beloved beach, to see if she would recognize it. We wanted to snorkel and take pictures of an underwater world neither of us had seen.

'From there we wanted to go to Ireland to see the green hills, to walk in dew-moistened heather, to see a homeland that was the origin of both our families. Then he wanted to move on to Austria to return to the workshop where he trained, learning his beautiful craft. Jarrod and I wanted to go and see the colors of the world, to taste the foods of different continents, to smell the scents of flowers unknown to us.

'We wanted to have a great adventure, to make our own memories, to live a life that we could be proud to tell about when we were old and gray. We were not content to settle for a house with a picket fence, a dog and cat, and our nine-to-five jobs. We did want those things, but first, first we wanted what we wanted.

'We can't have all those things now. Not together. So, I will have to go and do, go see, go smell and taste and touch. I have to make memories for the both of us. I promise to live a life that would make Jarrod proud, so when I come home to see all of you, and you tell me stories of Jarrod's past, I can share too.

'Go do the thing that you always dreamed of. Those are the words that Jarrod said to me, and they are the words I pass on to you. I won't say go live for Jarrod. We don't live for someone else. Go live a life that would make you proud and let him be your inspiration...' "

Chapter 28

Heather and I had planned her wedding for the second weekend of May. It was going to be quite an event with more than five hundred guests in attendance. A true 'society wedding'.

I was slated as her maid of honor, a job I had taken on wholeheartedly and one that had not allowed me much time for mourning Jarrod's death. Not only was I in charge of her bridal shower, which I stupidly thought was the extent of my job duties, but I also had to attend the dress hunt and fittings, the cake tasting, the meal selection, site selection, china selection.... The tasks went on and on! Heather once again proved to be more than capable of numbing my mind from sadness. It was difficult to be preoccupied with Jarrod's death when I was so busy dodging pink taffeta dresses and satin shoes.

There were daily tasks like confirming guest attendance, rearranging the seating charts, ensuring the other bridesmaids and groomsmen were on task with their fittings and colors... I felt like a sheep dog yapping at an unruly flock.

Not wanting to wait until the wedding night to get drunk and have a weekend tryst, several of the maids and men had met at a dinner hosted by Heather and Ryan. Three couples out of the nine in attendance had flamed up, had several weeks of great new-relationship sex, and had already cooled off. Apparently, tax attorneys and cops didn't go well together—great sex; horrible pillow talk!

I had already had to change the lineup of groomsmen and maids. I was tired of the immaturity displayed by the people involved in the wedding party. The best man was by far the worst! Ryan's best friend, Connor, was an officer in the State Police. As a State Police officer, Connor felt superior to Ryan, and they would often get into arguments about whose job was more important.

On the weekend leading up to the wedding, we had arranged for yet another dinner at the brownstone, to reiterate expectations over the next week. I had a checklist of items that needed to be completed: final fittings for both men and women, gift selection for the wedding party, and final room arrangements for the guests coming from out of town. Whereas Heather was relaxed, I was a mess.

With her air of authority, and a clear picture of how her wedding was going to be, Heather kept the wedding participants in order, including her husband-to-be and his best man. The pre-wedding-week dinner party was a success. I was able to get everyone appointment times for their fittings. I was able to get the girls to the side to discuss Heather's bachelorette party planned for Wednesday, and I made the guys aware of Heather's list of "shit to not do at your bachelor party." She had an actual list.

Relieved of some of my duties, I was able to focus on my plans for after the wedding. While Heather and her upcoming nuptials were time consuming, they didn't take up every minute of my day. In the evenings after Ryan and Heather had gone upstairs, long after Jobe had gone down for the night, I would lay out my great plan for the upcoming months.

I had renewed my never-used passport a month before. I had bought a sturdy internal-frame backpack, a good pair of boots, and a book titled Europe by Foot. Deciding on easing into my trip with a group tour, I signed up for a ten-day hiking tour of Ireland. From Ireland I would be going to the United Kingdom for another seven-day tour with a group. After that, my choices were endless. Europe was just a boat ride away; I had the opportunity to continue on with group tours or venture out on my own.

What I really wanted was solitude. I felt like I hadn't been alone in ages. I had moments of alone time, not days or weeks like I had had the first year Davlin had been missing. I was looking forward to being alone in my head again.

After Jarrod died, I had spent hours at a time looking out windows. My train ride back to Boston was a week after we had Jarrod cremated and had his ceremony. The view that sped past my window on the train went from the browns and whites of the

283

Midwest to the dull gray of urban Chicago, where snow is ruined by asphalt and tires. I floated through the busy train station to the next train that took me past Lake Erie over to the Eastern Seaboard. Boston was only slightly less gloomy than Chicago but was made brighter by Jobe and Heather.

I felt like I hadn't slept the entire trip. I had three days in a private sleeper car on the train, and I had only come out to use the restroom. Taking my meals privately and refusing to be sociable, I had kept my curtain to the train closed and stared out the window to the world that passed me by.

Back in Boston Jobe had hugged me, held my hand, and sat on my bed asking endless questions. He rooted through my bags, finding the small treats I had brought back for him. He sat and watched me as I sat looking out the window to the sleeted street below. Jobe could talk the bark off a tree, but he could also simply be when I needed him to. The day I got home, he climbed up on my lap, wrapped my arms around his chest, and sat with me until our combined stomach grumbling and the darkening of the sky made us both move out of the window seat.

Heather had much the same comforting effect on me, just with less snuggling. Down in the living room she had a fire going, and hot tea and hot meatball sandwiches with melted cheese and sauce ready. She didn't require ceremony that night. She gave me what I needed, handed me tissues when tears slid down my cheeks, and parked me between Ryan and Jobe, then sat next to her son. We watched the fire and listened to the sleet hit the windows. I was unbelievably content and relieved to be back in the house that had held good memories.

Heather and Ryan had given me enough space to remember what the silence of my head could be like, but they both kept close watch of me to make sure I didn't slip back into the deep darkness that I had lived in when Davlin went missing.

That was something that worried me about leaving and going on my trip. I would have no support. I would have no one to lean on if a memory became too heavy to bear or a fear became too real.

I had been on antidepressants on and off since Davlin was listed MIA. I had had to add a second medication after Jarrod died. Now weaned off one, I was working my way off the other. I had taken up journaling, capturing my thoughts on paper since I would have no doctor or therapist to speak to. I was trying to work my way to independence again. I felt like I was totally dependent on the people in my life. I looked at this trip as a way for me to test my strength and will.

Heather and Ryan knew about the first part of my trip. We would be traveling to the airport together, though that would be the extent of our shared trip. They were bound west to Hawaii for their honeymoon. Ryan had surprised Heather by planning an amazing trip with island hopping, scuba diving, whale watching, hiking, and plenty of time in their hotels and cabins. I was jealous of her honeymoon to come. I couldn't help but think back to the car ride back to Nebraska that had counted as our honeymoon after Davlin and I had eloped.

We had only a few hundred dollars between us, his graduation money from family and my life savings from odd yard jobs and snow shoveling. We had to pay two hundred in gas there and back, and one-fifty to the ordained (on the internet) minister who had married us. Our license had been eighty dollars, and a blood test had been another fifty. With a squat two hundred left for food and lodging, Davlin and I had been married in Vegas, spent the night watching bright lights on the strip, and strolled hand-in-hand past colorful waterfalls and replicas of the Wonders of the World. As the late night got later and the darkness deeper, we left Vegas.

We had to drive for three hours until we found a motel Davlin was willing to park his Jeep outside of. It was in the middle of nowhere. A motel, a gas station, and a diner. The sign out front of the group of buildings read, "Last Chance Stop, Next Gas 150 miles."

The man at the front desk glared 'critically at Davlin and warned us both not to mess up his room. Handing over the key to room number ten, he winked at Davlin. "Honeymoon Suite," he chuckled.

285

The last door in the building, the last light in the vast darkness around us, Davlin opened the door, picked me up piggy-back style, and carried me into our honeymoon suite.

The room was plain like any cheap motel room. I had to refrain from wondering when the bed had last been changed. There was an old box T.V. with aluminum foil attached to the antenna for added reception. The curtains were brown and orange to roughly match the horrendous bedspread. The smell of stale cigarettes wafted out of the wall air conditioner when Davlin turned it on, and there was a hum of florescent light bulbs when we turned on the bathroom light. It was heaven.

We didn't think about the bed too much. Davlin wasted no more time than what we had already done early in the evening in Vegas, consummating our marriage. He had my dress on the floor before I even felt his lips on my mouth. He was as eager for me as he had been early in the day at my mother's trailer. Quickly removing his shirt, he returned his lips to mine; then, laying me back on the bed, he removed my panties.

Pants just beyond his hips, Davlin thrust himself home, urgently kissing and thrusting at the same time. His force and depth and fierceness made me come quickly, but he didn't. I quivered, unable to participate in our coupling as my husband continued claiming me. He had stopped kissing my mouth and had moved to my neck. Further warm sensations moved over my chest and through my thighs.

I didn't think it possible and I had never experienced it before, but Davlin was making me orgasm again. My back arched, bringing my clitoris to him, increasing the stimulation. Again, my legs shook and my breath came short. Davlin was claiming me as his, and in doing so, I couldn't breathe or move. He went from viciously claiming to gently loving and enjoying. My back and legs ached by the time he orgasmed. He fell on me exhausted.

I had the pleasure of enjoying my husband over the next three days. We stayed at the cheap motel, lounging by the defunct pool that held only brown water and chipped paint. We ate two meals a day in the small cafe, learning both the staff members' names. We stayed up late into the night, talking about college and dreading going home when our funds ran dry.

By Tuesday, we had to burst our bubble of illusion and return home to Guernsey. Our departure was sorely greeted by Bob and Maria, the chef and waitress at the dinner. They gave us our breakfast of pancakes and eggs gratis and wished us well in life. Bob had told Davlin how he fell in love with Maria when they were in middle school, a romance that oddly enough echoed our own quite a bit. As we drove away watching the rotund Bob and the exhausted Maria in the rearview mirror, Davlin patted my leg. "We will never end up here. I promise."

"It wouldn't be the worst thing to happen if we ever did," I replied.

Shaking off the memory of his touch and his words, I came back to the reality that now faced me. I was beyond becoming a waitress in Nowhere, USA, but I was still unsure where I would end up. I was open for suggestion and ready for my adventure to hopefully find a direction that would suit me.

The days of pampering and smiling at luncheons and rehearsals, pictures in dresses and during preparations, parties for men only, and then the bachelorette party two days before the wedding went quickly. Hungover the day of the rehearsal in the church, I spent the morning pampering my head and the early afternoon pampering my stomach. By evening, I was recovered enough to put on a smile and a dress for Heather and Ryan.

At the church, the entire wedding party milled around the chapel until Dana, Heather's mother, took control of the activities. We practiced our timing walking down and up the aisle, the guys all the time making faces at us. I would be walking back up the aisle alone just after the newlyweds. After five trips up and down the aisle, the flower girls and ring and Bible bearers were getting fidgety. The girls were complaining about their shoes pinching, and the guys were getting drunk off the flasks hidden in their jackets. It was time to go to dinner.

287

The herd of people that made up the wedding party headed to a local country club where Dana had been given a temporary membership. We were escorted to a private dining room with a buffet of food and drinks waiting. Joined by the parents of the children in the wedding party, the remaining parents and grandparents of the bride and groom, and spouses of those in the wedding party, our number had swelled to upwards of fifty.

I was the only single person in attendance, and watching all the happy couples made me a little lonely. As the meal progressed, I had to excuse myself from the happiness around me. Feigning a need to use the powder room, I left the dining room and went out the nearest exit to the surrounding grounds.

I found myself on a patio overlooking the golf course. The beautifully manicured lawns held deep pools of shadows intermixed with lights from the pathways. I was contemplating going for a walk when I heard a throat clearing behind me. I turned, startled, to see Jack smiling from the door through which I had just escaped.

My heart skipped a couple of beats seeing Jack. Though not his actual twin, Jack's resemblance to Jarrod was amazing. My guilty feeling from our shared kiss just days before Jarrod passed still weighed heavily on me.

"What are you doing here?" I asked as I hugged him. I had to smile; he was handsome and a friend I hadn't seen in a while.

"I was invited to the wedding. Heather came and picked me up from the airport earlier today. She asked me if I would come tonight to keep you company." Still holding me but at arm's length, he searched my face for my thoughts, then asked, "Is it alright with you? Me being here?"

Smiling again, I replied, "Of course."

I hugged him again and then broke away. "Let's go get you some food then." Pulling the door, I realized belatedly that it was locked.

"Let's find a way back into this place and then get you some food." Embarrassed and slightly nervous being so close to Jack again, I took his offered arm as we walked the patio toward the front of the clubhouse.

"I make you nervous, huh?" he asked, not watching where he was going, but instead still trying to figure my thoughts out on his own. He was doing a great job of it.

"No," I lied. "Yes. I haven't known you outside of your parents' house, and I really want you to understand... The kiss, it was just stress and need. It...I don't want to say it didn't mean anything, because it did. It was what I needed; I think what you needed too... But we... We can't be more than friends. That is what I need right now." We had stopped walking and stood facing each other.

I could see his face clearly and could see a smile reaching from his lips to his eyes.

"Becks, you are amazing. And I know the kiss was a way for us to be alive during a time of loss. I got it. I even enjoyed it, which is fucking amazing!"

Confused, I asked, "Why is that amazing?"

"Because I'm gay."

I was stunned!

"But you kissed me," I responded stupidly.

"I've kissed girls before. I've had sex with women before. I even have feelings for you, but I have deeper feelings for my boyfriend. So a friend is as good as we are going to get." He was so innocent and trusting with his confession, I was relieved to have heard it but shocked by it too.

Suddenly I was happy. I started to giggle like a child. Not really knowing if I had lost my mind or cracked in some other way, Jack stepped back and looked for reinforcements.

"You alright, Becks?"

"Yes. God, thank you for being you! For being gay, and wonderful!" Still laughing, I had to let my hysteria pass before I was able to explain myself. "I have been nothing but a confused mess since Davlin went missing. How do you cope with having your heart taken away? I felt so guilty for so long over Jarrod. Then when I was willing to...to accept that I had actually fallen in love with someone

289

else, he left me too." Jack stood nodding his head in understanding. "I really wanted to run away from you after that kiss, but couldn't… Now, I just want to…kiss you again! 'Cause it would be…."

Jack took a couple steps back and started to laugh. Red faced with tears streaming down his cheeks, he finally caught his breath enough to reassure me,

"Jarrod said you were one of the most confusing women he had ever met. 'A contradiction to yourself,' he would say. I think you just don't know what you want in life." Still smiling but having successfully shut me up, he took my arm again and continued to escort me to a set of stairs that led down to the golf course. "Fancy a walk?"

"Sure, a contradiction of self, huh? What, I went against my own morals? Is that what Jarrod meant?" Hurt and angry, I was trying to not feel betrayed by my dead lover.

"No, not that you went against your morals," Jack reassured me, his tone serious. "He said that he thought you were definitely not a woman who should be alone. You need to love and to receive it in return. He explained to me one night that you had had a pretty abusive childhood, not really receiving praise or love until Davlin came along. How could Jarrod compete with the memory of a man who had been your hero all your life?" Jack cocked an eyebrow, then continued.

"Jarrod understood that you went to great lengths not to be around him. You tried not to have feelings for him. But he loved you, and he was sure you understood that. He said he felt protective of you, especially when Caleb was around. He didn't want you to go against your heart. He knew you needed to continue to love Davlin, but he really wanted your love too."

"I do love him," I whispered dreamily. "Jarrod had been a friend since the first time I had met him at The Metro, when he showed how caring he could be by being my mother's friend. I loved him from the time he spent the night in my apartment, after Eric had told us about Davlin's mission. My heart and head had been through so much turmoil up to that point that I didn't trust what I was feeling. But Jarrod always gave me what I needed. He would show up when I needed him, gave me space when it was best, a shoulder to cry on, and a motivational hand to push me even now after his death."

Jack continued walking, pulling me along. "Jarrod loved you, and he knew you loved him in a way too. But he knew it was different than what you had given Davlin. How could it not be? He asked me to look after you, to make sure you get happy again, eventually. I'm supposed to make sure you do something."

"What?"

"I don't know, but you have to do something for yourself. Jarrod said you were too good to sit around and waste your life away waiting for ghosts to make you happy. You aren't supposed to look back anymore. That is what he said. 'Make her look forward. Help her do it, Jack, in any way you can. Make sure she goes forward.' "

Standing on a fairway, far from the clubhouse, our walk had brought us to a moonlit stretch of grass, freshly watered. I took off my heels and started to walk on the wet grass, admiring my footprints as I looked back over my shoulder at Jack standing still watching me.

"So what are you going to do with yourself, Becks?" he asked, raising his voice at my retreating form.

"I don't know. But I have a plan. Is that enough?"

Chapter 29

I went to Ireland and it was beautiful! My group backpacking trip was amazing. I was used to being the lonely girl in the groups. I was the only person on the trip without a significant other or family member, but I still enjoyed myself.

The ten days of backpacking were time I spent enjoying sights never seen, hearing voices never heard, and meeting people I never would have known otherwise. Each day was spent walking paths and along roadways barely wide enough for cars and trucks. The ups and downs of the many hills made me regret not buying the recommended hiking sticks. Each day ended at a bed and breakfast or other small accommodation along the way. No tent camping or fireside dinners, I slept each night in a bed after a hot meal from a kitchen and a few drinks with my fellow hikers.

By the end of the trip, I had decided on my next step. I was continuing east to Scotland. I had a list of names and places from Jarrod, people who had taught him his craft or friends from his childhood. One of the names on the list was Argyll, a place on the islands that were part of Scotland proper. Jarrod had spent a summer there in his youth.

I arrived at the island by ferry and immediately wanted to place roots. The view before me was breathtaking, and I hadn't taken but a few steps. A tourist island, and tourist area as a whole, the collective islands counted on the bevy of visitors each season. I walked from the pier to an outfitter close to the water's edge. I purchased a personal tent, some food, and a book about the islands and areas of interest to see.

I left town and headed away from civilization, following a sheep path through a green pasture. Sure I was on someone's private property, I hurried along the path until I came to a narrow road. Choosing a new direction, I took a step, then another....

My life continued in this manner for several months and in several places. I started my journey in Ireland, taking in the sights and sounds that had given memories to Jarrod and his siblings when they were children.

I spent many nights in my tent, cold in the morning, but greeting each day with a renewed sense that the day was going to give me a new challenge that I would overcome.

With my self-imposed denial, I learned to live without luxuries like soft beds and reliable heat. I fished for my dinners at least once each week. I tried dinners that were alien to my plate and palate, I viewed sights never before imagined in my mind, and learned history of which I had been entirely ignorant.

By the time I left Scotland for the mainland of Europe, I had gained a new confidence that I had never known I lacked. I knew that I could...I could live without many things, in ways I had never believed, and without the people I had depended on so completely. I felt like a bird pushed out of my nest, now soaring above the land, not falling to the earth.

Backpacking from place to place, picking trails and destinations by chance and on the advice of the people I met along the way, I was afforded time to ponder my life with Davlin and Jarrod. I had time to relive conversations with my mother and my friends... Eventually, I didn't think of those things. I stopped dreaming about my past life and focused on my surroundings. I sought the knowledge of the placed I passed through. I learned the history. I celebrated in churches and streets among locals and tourists. I fell into my bed each night tired from my expenditure through the day. I had no energy to dream about the arms that had once held me. I had no time to miss the men now gone from my life.

Using the money Jarrod had left me in his will and the continued paycheck I received from the military, I was able to extend my trip from country to country. My passport sported the colorful stamps of many European countries. I saw Germany in the summer; lay on a hillside in Austria listening to the sounds of the wind and the birds. I passed through Amsterdam, Spain, and Portugal, train rides allowing for my rapid movement from country to country. My desire to continue on was now nearly an obsession. I

293

needed to continue to move, to see places I would have never otherwise seen, to hear foreign languages spoken and meet strangers and hear about their lives and dreams.

By the time August rolled around, I had been gone from Boston for three months. I received a message from Heather and Ryan. Heather was pleading with me to come home for the holidays to celebrate with family. Spending a rare night in a hotel, greedily enjoying the feel of Egyptian cotton sheets and down pillows, I called her to keep her up-to-date on my plans.

"Heather, I'm not ready to be back there yet. I'm still... I don't know, looking for something, I guess," I tried stupidly to explain myself.

"Becks, what are you looking for? Davlin? Some other man? God? What? I don't understand what you are doing there! You need to come home. I miss you. Jobe misses you." She was whining by the end of her rant. I kind of wanted to hang up the phone on her.

"Heather, I don't know what I'm looking for. Purpose, I guess. Certainly not a man! Lord knows I've met plenty over here."

"Any hot hook-ups? A strong European lover perhaps keeping you there with his charm?" She joked with me, forgiving me by her jest.

"Oh yeah, one in each country! Two in Italy."

"Speaking of, thank you for the shoes. Amazing, and the girls at the office wanted to kill me for them...." Our conversation continued on in friendly chatter. Heather was able to have her best friend finally spend quality time with her, even if it was over the phone.

During my treks, I could go days without speaking to another person. I would often listen to the conversations around me, even those in foreign languages. I avoided other people for fear of answering their questions about myself and why I was backpacking alone.

Heather truly did know why I was on this pilgrimage. Perhaps I was looking for meaning in life or some higher being that would explain my depth of loss and misery.

I had begun to write each night about my day, often by the scant light of my headlamp. I would describe where I was, the people I was around, and the senses I had experienced. After the physical assessment of the day was done, I would write the thoughts that had passed through my mind during the day. Memories I relived, many very personal, or simply thoughts about where I was and what I was doing, so later in life I wouldn't feel that this time was wasted.

It was after my conversation with Heather, while I was resting in Italy, that I decided I needed a change from my European travels. I wasn't yet ready to go home. I hadn't figured out why I was here yet, I needed something else still.

So it was that I found myself basking in the sun on a sidewalk at a restaurant, enjoying the sounds that engulfed me. I was content. I hadn't been this content in a long time…

I sat, enjoying the peace that had found me, when I let my mind drift back to Guernsey, to a day spent in the sun, a day with different sounds and smells. I was laying in the grass on a hill. Davlin lay beside me, his shirt was off, and I was playing with his nipple.

Attempting to ignore my exploits, he lay with his head resting on his arms, breathing slowly. I hadn't been able to see him for a week; his family had dragged him out of town, and I wanted to see all of him! Davlin, ever the patient one, just lay like a log on the grass.

Straddling him, I sat on his lap, gaining his full attention.

"Do you still love me?" We weren't yet married; our bodies had not yet fully matured nor had our relationship. But we knew each other and loved each other. I was feeling needy.

My comment got him to crack his eyes. He looked at me through his thick lashes.

"Becks, why would you ask me a question like that?"

"I just need to hear it," I theorized.

"Oh, well," he paused, thinking. "I don't think that love is the proper word."

295

I sat frozen by his words. My mouth hung open as I contemplated his kissing another girl or his parents finally wearing him down about our relationship.

"So," I looked down at my hands, unable to look at him, not sure why he was being so cold. I was no longer enjoying the sun or the sounds of the bugs in the field. I only wanted things between us to be alright again. "So, you don't love me?"

He took my hands and pulled me toward his chest, smiling as he rolled over on top of me.

"I mean that too many damn people say 'love.' I know what I feel is something that needs a bigger word. A stronger word. What you mean to me needs to be a song or a poem or carved in stone. Epic! Something so great, you can't describe this feeling the same way you would describe the way you feel about your car or a pair of shoes." His face was serious, his tone absolute. "That is what I feel for you." He kissed me then, a chaste kiss, and then leaned back again. "But if you need to hear it, I'll say it. I'll say it every day, think it every minute, feel it every breath of my life. I love you, Becks."

Speechless after his declaration, I could find no words to reply to him. We stayed crushed together on the long grass of the field staring at each other. I was never sure if it was the reality that Davlin was my first love that made everything so much more intense when we were together, and so much more miserable when we were apart, but I knew I didn't want to live without him. I knew I wouldn't be able to breathe or function without him. That my heart would be broken.

I never expected to be able to find love after he was gone. I felt desolate. I wanted nothing more than to die and go to wherever he was… But I lived. I loved and received love in return. I had had someone who had never known me in my youth, someone who helped me through the worst time of my life. I had found a friend who made me feel warm again, a bit cooler, but warm and loved. He made me smile; Jarrod made me laugh, and he made me want to live. And he too encouraged me to find some new form of happiness, some form of love and a reason to go on with life again.

I was looking. I was, at the very least, living. I was enjoying the places I went, the people I met, and the things I was doing. I was accomplishing a goal that had never been in my plans when I was younger. When Davlin and I were together, I had wanted nothing more than to have children and a house, to grow old together. With the dream of children out of the picture, we had decided to travel and enjoy our youth. We had even considered adoption as a possible option, but Davlin never expressed much interest after we were moved to Georgia and he was deployed.

When he went missing, I had to focus on something else. Jarrod had given me that. His success in business and his history of amazing travel were motivators for me. I had wanted to see the places he spoke of. I had wanted to see the Swiss Alps and swim in a lake in Austria. I had seen the beautiful fields of heather and breathed the crisp air of Ireland and Scotland, I had walked the streets of London, and now, thanks to Jarrod, I had tasted the wines of Italy.

Sitting at my table, the lunch crowd now gone, I had to make a choice. I could continue to tour Europe and Asia—there were infinite places to see, innumerable tastes to experience, unimaginable sights to see—I could, but I felt useless. It was time for me to find my own meaning and my own cause.

It was on a cobbled street, surrounded by the soft glow of the afternoon sun off the yellow stone homes of my current stop, that I decided to find someone who needed me. Someone who would accept my aid, take my hand, and allow me to help them as Heather and Jarrod had helped me.

During my tour of Europe, while my passport was being filled with colorful stamps from the countries and borders I crossed, the world continued to exist and change. The day I arrived in Vienna, a hot and sunny day in August, the day I took a tour of a castle and enjoyed the festival that was being hosted; a very different event was occurring five thousand miles away. My day was spent sipping wine, taking in the soaring beauty that surrounded me; elsewhere, a heavy rain triggered a landslide in the Gansu Provence of China. A river of mud and trees killed more than a thousand people.

As I moved further south in Italy, the relief workers in China tried to find survivors. They found none in the debris. The children and families of those killed in the landslide were left to try to rebuild a life after disaster. Days of misery turned into weeks, as Red Cross and other relief workers tried to treat the injured, clean up the site of the landslide, feed the people, and provide shelter. The tasks were daunting. The people affected by the disaster were in the thousands, and many were slipping through the cracks.

The day I decided to find a purpose again, the landslide had occurred little over a month before. Not ready to go back to the US and work in a traditional hospital, I instead pulled a name from my past and called in a favor. Stosh hadn't changed his phone number since I had last worked with him in Boston, and he still had contacts in Doctors Without Borders as well as other aid groups.

"Hell, Becks, I'm happy to hear from you!" He actually sounded genuine. "I've been working in Boston again. Why don't you swing by, and we can see if I can't get you in on one of the groups I'm organizing? I've got one going to Costa Rica, one headed for China, one…"

"Stosh, I'm not in Boston right now. I left the hospital a while ago, but my certifications are all up-to-date. I'm in Italy right now."

I heard him let out a breath. "Wow, Italy! I'm jealous. My job— I set up relief missions, have since the tsunami in '04—it keeps me super busy."

"Yeah, I get it. You're a big shot with a fucking super important job! Congrats, but I just need you to help me help someone…. Not in Boston."

He laughed at my fake disgust and tapped on his keyboard. "Well, you are lucky I didn't take your monkey comment personally all those years ago." He laughed at his own joke, then continued, "I can get you in with one of the groups, if you feel like going to China. I am assuming you want to volunteer, which means no paycheck.

But you will be able to leave when you want, no commitment, no guns and bullets."

"Wow, guns? No, I don't want to go to Somalia or anything. God Bless those who do, but no. I'll take a plain old Red Cross relief."

"Becks, there isn't anything plain about where you are going. The workers who have been onsite for the month since this happened are having their asses handed to them. That's why I'm organizing more people to get to the site."

"More what?"

"Everything! Meds, doctors, tents, food, water…everything. I'm working with groups from food kitchens to Merck and Johnson and Johnson. Shanxi is no joke. There are a couple thousand displaced people still! One month after the big landslide and the fucking hillside keeps sliding. It's monsoon season in China, and those poor bastards are hurting."

Stosh continued to paint a rather depressing picture of what I should expect in China. After giving my verbal commitment and arranging my arrival date with Stosh and buying an airline ticket, I sat back and let the feeling of contentment wash over me again. Still at my table, no longer washed in daytime sun, instead illuminated by the candle at my table and those at the tables around me, I felt eager for what may come. Two emotions I hadn't felt in ages— contentment with my life and anticipation for the future.

I felt alive again.

Chapter 29

January 2010, the seventh of the month was the date.

The date.

The fucking date I had never wanted to come around. It was a day to reconcile my feelings, the jumble of emotions I had inside.

Seven years!

I had spent seven years waiting for this date, and I kind of wanted it to be memorable for many reasons. I wanted to find relief from my guilt and pain. I wanted to be able to be happy that the waiting was over! I wanted to feel something other than the anxiety that sat on my chest making me wonder if I was having a heart attack.

I closed my eyes, willing time to go back, even if just one day. No, not one day, go back six months to when it was warm and sunny, not the dreary cold of winter in Nebraska. No.

I didn't want to wish my life away,

to go back...I would have to give up everything I had received in that time.

I rolled on my side, looked at the sleeping form that now shared the hotel bed with me. I don't know why I always got two queen-sized beds; he always ended up in bed with me.

From the day I had first seen his big brown eyes look at me from beneath his long lashes, I had loved him.

Joseph was my reason.

He was a three-year-old victim of the landslide when I had come across him at the Red Cross field hospital where I had volunteered when I arrived from Italy. Grateful to have a purpose and task, I delved into the insanity that was the field hospital. The sound of rain on the tent became music to my ears, though it made Joseph cringe when he heard it.

Joe had been a sole survivor brought in from a search group a week after the initial landslide. He had several broken bones, including a compound fracture of his right tibia, and had undergone surgery in a mobile hospital unit and then taken to a field tent for recovery.

He had been my patient. Each day I noticed the little boy opened up a bit more. By the time he had been in my care for a week, he would say my name and request simple things like water. I spoke no Mandarin, and I had assumed he spoke no English. As a near infant, I had thought him too young for traditional schooling. I was wrong.

It was evening, after a long day, one of many that had begun to blend into each other. I had given an impromptu rundown of the patients in the tent to the nurse who was arriving to care for them during the night, when Joe called my name. I went to his bedside, and he held out a worn copy of Curious George. I smiled at his expectant face.

I had been reading the mischievous tales of George to the children who were in my care. One by one the other kids had been returned to their families, but Joseph had no contact with his family. Pictures were posted. The Red Cross and local aid groups were trying to find someone he was related to, but he had been found in an area where there had been no other survivors found. His home and his family, his neighbors and surrounding people were all gone.

Joe and I were kindred spirits in that sense, he and I had both lost our people. I had a soft spot for him, and he seemed to accept me too. I sat on his bed as I had done the night before and leaned against his headboard. Able to move even with a cast in place, Joseph snuggled up to me, resting his head on my shoulder. I wrapped my arm around him and began to read about George's trip to the hospital.

As I read, the day began to catch up to me. I was yawning rudely with each sentence when Joseph looked at me.

"I'm sorry kiddo, I'm tired," I explained and smiled at him.

"Is okay. You sleep here, I look at George," he reasoned in perfect English.

Surprised and proud, I grabbed him in my arm. "Joey, you speak English?!"

301

He nodded his head and returned to Curious George. I smiled at his tact and watched him turn the pages of the book. He studied each picture and giggled quietly as George got into more mischief.

Not intending to fall asleep, I lay my head against the backboard, breathing in the scent of Joseph's hair. I fell asleep to the soft sounds of his breathing and the occasional rustle of pages being turned.

Adopting Joseph had been a nightmare! There were numerous trips to the embassy. I had to fly an adoption lawyer to China and provide letters attesting to my stability and background. I had to buy a house in Boston, so I bought the brownstone from Heather and Ryan, who had moved to a suburb. I had to arrange a stable job, though thanks to Jarrod and the success of the Metro in Allington and in Boston, I had a steady stream of income. There were hoops to jump through, procedures to follow, assessments to be made, and through it all, I never left Joseph.

After he was able to walk and run, he was discharged from the hospital, though he had no one to take him. He had stayed with me at the Red Cross camp, playing with the children who were around, but always in eyesight of me. He had begun to have nightmares that caused him to start sleeping with me in my cot. He was fearful of being left and of being taken away.

I spent every minute I could with him. When a semblance of normality had been returned to the area, the Red Cross moved to a new location. I couldn't leave. Instead, I opted to volunteer at the orphanage where Joseph was now living along with other refugee children. I stayed as close as I was able, but often I was forced out of the building.

Each day was a gamble on whether I would be allowed to spend time with him. There were weeks when the heavy wooden door of the building would be shut in my face. It was those days I walked the length of the fence to just watch him, to let him know I was still there. I would talk to him, let him know I was not going to leave him.

Other days, I was allowed to spend the hours of the day with him. I would play with him and the other kids, read to him, help him make his letters with pen and paper. He would sit on my lap, resting his head on my shoulder as I told him stories about Disneyland and the San Diego Zoo. Places I promised to take him.

Many mornings I would arrive as the children were leaving breakfast, and I would wait in the hall as ordered until all the children filed out to the courtyard or to their classes. When Joseph would pass by, I could see his eyes were red from crying and he had bags beneath them from his nightmares. These were the days that I held my son on my lap and softly sang him songs, gently rocking him to sleep.

I ached with despair! I had taken up residence in a small apartment-like room. The culture that surrounded me did not welcome me. I learned Mandarin by force of emersion into the culture and with the help of Rosetta Stone. I did this so I was able to communicate with the adoption board. Every bit of evidence that Joseph had no family left had been submitted! I didn't understand why the process of adoption had to be so long and drawn out, why they couldn't just give him to me!

He was mine!

I was forced to return to my miserable accommodation each night. The air and my loneliness weighed on me. I wanted nothing more than to be away from China, to be away from the oppressive heat, the monsoon rain, and the difficult tone of the language. Adam, the lawyer, had asked me many times on his various trips why I didn't just adopt one of the other children.

"Would you trade in one of your kids for another one just because they give you a hard time?" I asked.

He took a moment and abashedly replied, "Ah, no. Point taken. Becks, I do see that you and Joseph are well fitted, that you care for him, love him. And I do see that he loves you in return. I'm sorry I suggested you taking a different child."

Adam never brought it up again, and I never considered adopting anyone in place of Joseph.

303

Many nights I would lay listening to the world pass by: the sound of tires on the wet street, the dogs barking, an old woman yelling at some foolish children. How different were the places I had lived. Here in a Chinese village, an area that could be swallowed by the earth; Boston with its brick buildings and historical statues. Then there was Guernsey, the most alien and inhospitable of all. The locations, the surroundings, language, culture...everything infinitely different. But the sounds at night, the ones that lull you to sleep...those apparently didn't change from place to place.

It was almost a year after Joseph had been placed in the orphanage, a year we had to spend visiting always with the watchful eyes of the orphanage staff upon us, a year of tearful ends to each day. It had been a year of fighting the international adoption board, meeting their every demand with the help of Heather back home, and Adam in China.

It paid off. On August eighth I was approved to adopt Joseph. Adam Richter stood by as I signed the papers that would make Joseph mine, that would give me the freedom to take him to the United States. He smiled at me as I looked up from signing my name the last time, done with a flourish. There were tears in my eyes, and my nose was running. Adam offered me a tissue and then led me out the door to the courtyard where Joseph and the kids were playing.

Seeing me walk out the door, Joseph dropped the ball he had been playing with and ran toward me.

"Mama!"

He sprang into my arms, hugging me as tight as his baby arms could hold.

I kissed his forehead and buried my face in his hair. I held him to me, afraid of being separated from my life again. I carried him out the gate to the waiting car. I carried my son toward our new life together.

When we left the orphanage, we left China. Joseph and I had spent time talking about it, about leaving his home behind. His need for a mother and his desire to explore gave him drive and incredible bravery. We had to stop at the American Embassy en route to the airport. Adam had brought along a bag that Heather had sent. In a room provided while our traveling documents were authenticated, I changed Joseph from the blue dress pants and white button-down shirt worn at Catholic schools the world over into a Boston Red Sox shirt and a pair of Osh Kosh B'Gosh denim overalls. Heather had sent several pairs of shoes, unsure of his size. Most were close enough, and Joseph picked out his first pair of Air Jordan's. Rolling my eyes as I helped him tie his shoes, I knew this little man was going to be expensive.

A knock at our door let us know Adam was back, and we were ready to go. I picked up his uniform and threw it in the trash can.

"No more of that, baby. Its jeans and Jordan's for you now." I winked at him as I took his hand. He picked up a stuffed bear, also wearing a Red Sox shirt, and followed me home.

In my worst times, I remember his face, the beauty of his face when he first called me 'Mama.' My son lay sleeping beside me, a son I had dreamt of for so long. I could still lie watching him sleep, seeing the hints of smiles that touched his lips or the questioning raise of his eyebrows. Rarely, did he have the nightmares that woke him in terror. They were fewer and farther between…but Joseph knew terror, and he couldn't forget it. On the nights that my son would wake crying and screaming, I needed only to turn on his light to show him where he was, hold him in my arms so he knew who was with him, and sing to him so he remembered what a mother's love was.

Caring for Joseph came naturally and easily. With his age, I had missed out on the infancy and diaper stage, the breastfeeding and bonding of early motherhood, but we had other special traits to our relationship.

As he grew, and America became his home, Joey became like many American children, guided by his 'cousin' Jobe, Joe grasped culture with both hands and flourished. Our first Christmas in America was memorable for all his surprise. The New Year came and went, but I was so fixated on Joseph that I spent the day at an

305

indoor water park, not drunk and crying, grieving as I had the years before.

Heather, Ryan and Jobe were as excited as I was to have Joseph in our family. Anything Jobe did, Joseph had to do too; baseball, bike rides, water balloon fights. There was no end to the happiness that Joe found in each day, and shared with me.

Of all the trips, holidays, and celebrations he learned of his first year home, Halloween was Joe's favorite. The costumes and candy were too grand for him to ignore. My favorite holiday was the one I made up the day Joey officially became mine, my Mid-August Mother's Day, it took the place of my deeply depressing count-down day annually observed in January.

With Joe in my life, I couldn't grieve the way I had in the previous years. He depended on me, and I thrived having him. I loved and cherished that little boy more than I had ever felt capable.

Joseph was my friend, and I his. He could make me laugh or smile when he saw me drifting to the past, his childish innocence made me want to protect him from the sadness of his past.

He made me happier than I had been in all my life. Joseph filled in the piece of me that was missing. At times I would dream that he was still in China in the orphanage and wake with the weight of anxiety and fear again. But as I could calm his nightmares, his face calmed mine.

Chapter 30

"I'm wasting time," I said to myself. My voice sounded foreign and echoed oddly in this room. Knowing I had to get back up, that I had places to be today, I really wanted to procrastinate and just stay where I was. I wanted to go back to sleep until Joey woke up and then get up and eat Lucky Charms and watch SpongeBob SquarePants.

That sounded better than what I was going to have to do today. January 8, 2010. Seven years. Seven years since the man who had been my life went missing. Seven years of change and growth, of the reality of loss and death, the sin of hope. Seven years of floating and trekking, moving from one goalless place to the next. Seven years of aid and help…. So much change in seven years.

When he had left, Davlin and I were Us. We were pieces of each other's life, to the end that there was no beginning or secrets. We simply had been there for it all, had done it all together. We were seamless, not knowing where he ended and I began. We had grown old together! Disregarded that we started young, younger than most, but he had become a man, and I a woman, in each other's shadows. We had loved and lost together and fought to stay together. He had been a husband and a hero, and today was the day that I truly had to say goodbye and allow everyone else to say it too.

I quietly rose from the bed, went to the heating unit, and adjusted the temperature so the room would warm before Joseph got up. I smiled at his sleeping form as I went to the restroom to dress and do my hair.

Davlin's "funeral" was today.

But truly, it was a celebration of his life.

I looked at the face in the mirror, how it had changed. How the years had worn on me. No longer the young woman of twenty-five whom he had left behind, now at thirty-two, I was a world traveler, a widow, and a mother.

A widow…

307

A mother…

widow…

I never asked for any of the things that had been bestowed upon me. I never thought I would lose my mother to cancer, but I never thought I could love her the way she had allowed me to. I didn't mean to fall in love with Jarrod, but he loved me with such devotion, I had to return it. I loved another man! I could have never pictured myself living anywhere other than in small-town America, white picket fence and all…I had a brownstone in Boston.

I had only ever dreamed of traveling, perhaps on a honeymoon or vacation. I had backpacked Europe and lived in China as an aid worker for a year! And there was Joseph. My thought of motherhood had long since died away, until I saw that little boy. Joey was the answer to a prayer long ago prayed, and a desire in my heart that had needed fulfillment. None of these accomplishments, gifts, memories would have been possible had I never left Guernsey behind, had I never taken a step away from Davlin and our shared past.

I didn't ask for these things to happen to me,

    or to change me;

        but they did.

Eulogy:

Measure your life.

Take stock of what you have done with your life.

Have you saved a life? Have you loved with conviction? Borne a child? Been a parent? Did you fight, drink, sin, kill, forgive, lie, steal, cheat? Weigh your sins...

Choose the best! The best that you have ever been. The best you that you have ever been. Now know that the man that we honor today made you better. If you are here, you are here to honor him, and know that he made you a better person by being himself.

A son, husband, friend, brother, soldier, teacher...Dedicated, brave, honest.... There are words that come to mind when you picture his face, when you put him in context.

He made me the person you see today. But he made me what I am by leaving, by being brave enough to serve, brave enough to be his best. He made me the best I am, the best I will ever be by having given me so much of himself when he was mine.

Davlin made me a mother, not by our son we lost, but by planting the seed of maybe in my heart. I have traveled the world with him, always in my heart, always in my thoughts. I have taken steps on land we would have never seen had he not promised me "Someday." I am content in my life, because I know how he helped shape me.

I have no doubts about my life with Davlin. No regrets about our years together. Because I loved him, I know that my years to come will be better because of him.

And when the time comes that I must measure my life, I know the words that describe me are only possible because I had Davlin to be all those things for me.

The End

Post Scriptum

So a few things...

Davlin was always dead, his body just wasn't recovered along with his fellow soldiers besides Sargent Pallen. I'm sorry for the hard-core hold outs who really wanted him to come home. I love Davlin and his relationship with Becks but Seven Years is about Becks learning how to live and grow independent of Davlin. He was important to her early in life, and he continued to be a factor guiding her choices through the seven years, when Becks needed him, but she did learn to live without him and that was the point.

I personally don't hate Nebraska, that is just a way to start my story and for her purposes, Becks did hate where she grew up (which is a made-up place) with good reason. I think Nebraska is a beautiful state with a kick ass football team and wonderful people (Go Corn Huskers!).

I write what I know, so if you read more of my stories, you will find that many of my main characters are nurses. What can I say? It's a challenging and interesting career and you're never short of drama. None of the situations in my book are in reference to any of the people I have seen or cared for in my years of work, and all names are fictional, any and all similarities are coincidental.

The characters in this book are all fictional, the places are a mix of real and imagined, the historical events, Magdaline's tropical storm, Joseph's landslide, are real events. I have attempted to keep my timeline accurate, but my slacking in writing this and my research may be off and my dates may not make since to the true historian. Please don't grill me for this. Writing a book that spans seven years was a challenge! Keeping dates correct was daunting and my manuscript became a post-it note nightmare! I think the ultimate result was a story that was logical, realistic (if a bit tragic), and one that will give you reason to hug your loved one and be grateful for what time you have together.

I cannot thank you enough for your support and for reading my first novel Seven Years to Die. I hope to continue to write and entertain through story telling. If you enjoyed Seven Years, please take a moment to give a review at your selected retailer.

Thank you for your support!

Betsy Michener-Lachino

Next from Betsy's brain: Screen

It's a queer thing to ask a philosophical question as to your own existence. I had often wondered why I had the gifts I was born with, questioned whether they were indeed "gifts". I think the term curse would be more suited to what I have. The curse of knowledge with no ability to change what I know. I hear people in medicine use that term, the curse of knowledge, when they have a family member who is sick.

 Mine is truly a curse, screening, as I have come to call it. I don't know anyone else who has ever had this thing I have, nor have I told anyone. There is one person who knows about my affliction, my best friend Rene who found out by accident when she found me in the midst of one of my episodes.

 To Screen, or screening, is when I fall into someone's conscious. They are still there, still in control of their own body and actions, I am simply a passenger in their life. A fly on the wall per se, unfortunately I screen during the other person's darkest times. I have been privy to abuses, rapes, murders and any list of sins. I have "seen" a woman sell herself for drugs, been in the body of a heroin abuser as she injected for her high and spent a night frightened of the walls that melted away in her drugged state of mind, I have ridden along for a drive by shooting laughing at the people who scattered as my automatic rifle sprayed into a group of teenagers waiting to get into the movies.

 Those are the kinder, gentler crimes I have been an unknown witness to. It is one thing to know that mankind does evil things, like knowing that people in other parts of the world suffer from lack of food and water, it is another thing entirely to feel the elation and power an abuser feels as he pummels a victim with his fists. It is truly sickening to have understanding of the sick drive that compels the rapist to choose who he does and then be along for the act, unable to close your eyes and not see.

I am cursed.

 Nature is a bitch to women! As if monthly bleeding, bloating, cramping and hormone surges weren't enough to make women crazy, chocolate eating, stretchy pant wearing, emotional heaps of blubbery mess, I had the added blessing of experiencing my first Screen when I started my menses at age fourteen. In that particular occasion, screening meant passing out in my bedroom and waking two days later. At the time when I left myself, I passed into the body of a man.

As you can imagine I had no idea what was going on. I was looking at a person I had never seen before, a woman in her forties, blonde hair and pretty face; well it would have been pretty if it wasn't blotchy from her tears. She was pleading with me, crying and trying to get as far from me as she could. I tried to speak to her, to calm her down and tell her not to cry, but I was nothing. I had no voice, no body, and no choice in my actions. I was merely looking out of his body at his life while being the passenger in his brain.

There are no words to explain my confusion, my fear, my feeling of hopelessness and horror. I didn't know if I was hallucinating or having a vivid nightmare. My fear and horror only amplified when the body I was in beat that pretty blonde lady. The hands I saw did not simply hit her once or twice, no they pounded her flesh until it swelled and broke. With each landed punch I felt the body swell with exhilaration and excitement, ever encouraged to draw more blood, to inflict more damage. When the punches turned to kicks, he didn't seem to like that as much, his heart stopped pounding as hard as it had been, and his breath was easily caught. He was what I came to identify as a 'hitter'. Less aroused, a feeling that I was feeling along with him; something up to that point that was so alien to me at my young age, he grabbed her hair and pushed her face into the floor smacking her against the carpet. He drove her head into the floor, using her hair as a sort-of handle to control how hard she hit.

Her head made a dull thud as he pounded her repeatedly into the Berber carpet of the bedroom. I was trying so hard to shut my eyes, to not see the growing area of red that seeped into the carpet. I tried to turn away, to scream, to feel remorse for this woman. I so very much wanted to help her, to act as the driver of this nightmare train wreck, but the body I was riding in was enjoying the sight of the blood too much to turn away even for a moment.

It wasn't until the woman was obviously no longer aware of the pain he was inflicting, her body long since limp, and no fight left that he finally stopped. She was unrecognizable, both eyes swollen shut, nose broken and bleeding, her right cheek was shattered a large purple bruise ripping her skin as the swelling continued to increase. Her mouth was hanging open and I could see she had lost several teeth. Her hair was no longer blonde

313

but rather a pink at the ends that became a maroonish-black mass of hair where it reached the base of her skull.

Her breathing was ragged and labored, her clothing ripped and hanging from her body. I could see teeth marks on her breasts and bruises on her abdomen and back. The body, the man I was in, was taking stock of the damage he inflicted. He was methodical and almost gentle as he turned her head from one side to the other admiring his handy work. It was as he was turning her over I realized the hands were wearing gloves.

Strange that I would remember that after such a vivid and exhilarating experience, I remembered the gloves. The hands turned the woman over onto her back, brushed the hair away from her broken face, and leaned close once again. This time, instead of closely examining the blood seeping from her eyes or nose, not opening her mouth to revel in the quantity of shattered teeth, this time he kissed her swollen lips. A gentle action that felt so personal and real. I had to be in a dream! But why the hell was I dreaming of beating the shit out of some poor woman, then kissing her?

As the body stayed close and simply took in the damage of the woman before it, I tried to fight myself, to wake myself up. I tried to pinch myself, I had no hands. I tried to think about falling, I had no ability to control my thoughts. It was as though the only thing I could do was to live the current nightmare I was in. I had had bad dreams in the past, woken from falling off a cliff or from a car accident; I had always thought my dreams were so vivid and frightening, but never in the past had I been able to smell the metallic scent of blood, to take in the dents in the carpet from long sitting furniture that had been disturbed during the brutal beating, to feel the slight breeze from the spinning overhead fan. In the past I had never been stuck with no control, I had always known my body was my own, that my dream was from my life, that when the night was over that I would wake up in my own room...I had no way to be assured that I would wake in my own room, I was truly frightened that I had just killed a woman and that I would never wake from that nightmare.

After staring at the poor woman's face for what seemed like an eternity, the body finally got up off the floor, took the gloves off and put them in the pockets of a jacket that hung on a chair back. Walking into the bathroom that was just off the bedroom where I had just witnessed the brutality of man, I was face to face with the abuser.

Looking into the mirror at himself, proud as a peacock, was my high school principal; Mr. Smith. He was in his forties and known to be a hard ass when it came to discipline. He looked at himself, which meant I was looking out his eyes at his reflection, seeing some splattered blood on his face he leaned down to the sink and rinsed it off. I could feel the water hitting my skin, rinsing away the blood I hadn't realized had gotten on me. Standing back up, he grabbed a hand towel and dried our face. I smelled the damn fabric softener as he patted our face dry, I could feel the pull of the towel as it rasped ever-so-gently on the stubble of beard that dusted his chin and cheeks.

Staring at himself in the mirror, Mr. Smith began to smile then his smile melted to a heartfelt sob and tears began to flow. As he seemingly lost control of his emotions he began to practice his call to 911.

"Yes, my name is Abel Smith, I need an ambulance." Sniff, sob. "My wife is, Oh God! Please help she's...." Sniff, sob, fake moan. In his heart, I began to feel a sense of distain for the woman lying on the floor. It wasn't really me, but rather Mr. Smith. He really hated that he had to call for an ambulance. He was like a child that was angry at his toy for breaking and not at himself for breaking it.

Standing straight again, he dried the tears from our face then turned to leave the bathroom. I tried to take in as much about the face and the clothes and the surroundings as I could; but why? This is a dream! A vivid and insane dream about my principal. I just wanted to wake up, I didn't want to remember that he was wearing grey pants and a blue button-down shirt, or that his ring finger had the tell-tale tan line of a man who removed his wedding ring. I didn't want to see it, feel it, smell it or experience any more of this fucked up dream, but I still couldn't wake up or control what was going on around me.

Along for the ride, we returned to the bedroom where Mrs. Smith, as it were, lay breathing much more shallowly. Her color was pale and I could see she was dying.

"Call 911 you prick!" I wanted to scream, I tried again to gain control of the arms of this body, to infuse my morality to his obviously lacking brain. All I could do was sit and watch as he made us watch her breathing slow then stop. He reached for her wrist to feel a pulse, I felt none. I did, however, feel the coldness of flesh devoid of warmth from circulation, I noticed the lack of assistance a living body would offer with muscles that still responded to movement. This woman was dead, and I was sure that I had been a part of her death.

315

He stood and headed to the phone at the bedside, then stopped and changed direction remembering to put his jacket back on, the bloodied gloves in his pockets. I figured they were evidence he would probably hide. He returned to the bedside, took a deep breath and picked up the receiver. A feeling of guilt tried to infuse into his brain, a feeling he quickly pushed down, then a different feeling, remorse.

He stood looking at the body on the floor, his confused feelings fighting for acknowledgement in his brain. He didn't truly feel guilty about killing his wife, but he did feel a bit sorry that he had had to. He felt only a modicum of guilt for having enjoyed the act of beating her to death, and it was at that realization, that moment he relived the act of murder that he swelled again with satisfaction and desire. He was remembering the feeling of hitting her face, forcing me to remember it too. I wanted to feel sick, to cry for this woman, to run away from this situation and never think about it again, but I was so cruelly stuck in this nightmare of rage.

With wisps of power spinning round his thoughts, Mr. Smith finally dialed 911. He wailed and cried, falsely claiming to have come home to find his wife's dead body on the floor of their bedroom. He dropped the phone and threw himself upon the corpse, all the while thinking how he hated her, how he hated that this charade was part of the evening. He lay upon her body moving her as much as possible, all the while thinking of how he must disturb his crime scene. I could hear the sirens of police cars and an ambulance off in the distance.

Darkness......

I woke up two days later. I was in my bedroom, covered in blood. Seeing my bed clothes and blankets stained red made me scream. What the hell had I done? Who had I harmed? Did I hurt Mrs. Smith? Was that whole fucked up experience real?

Rushing out of my bedroom to the bathroom I found that my hands and face were not bloodied, but they wouldn't be! I vividly remembered the smell of fabric softener as my face was dried. But that hadn't been me! What the hell was going on?

I tried to peel my bloodied pajamas off and found that the source of blood on my pajamas and in my bed was me. I had been out for so long that I had bleed well beyond the volumetric capacity of my regular absorbency tampon, and soaked my panties and pajamas as well as my sheets. Disgusted, I pulled the rest of my clothes off and jumped in the shower.

Disoriented as I returned to my bedroom I didn't realize how long I had been out. My bedside clock read 8:05, I didn't know if that was p.m., a.m. Monday, Wednesday or Friday. The last thing I remembered that I was sure was not a dream or a hallucination was coming home from school Monday finding a note from my mom that she was going to be at David's house for the next couple days and if I needed anything to call her. David was her boyfriend who hated kids. She didn't mind leaving me alone for a couple days at a time, I was trustworthy and always where I was supposed to be. So what if I had a crisis of maturation on Monday, I could figure a tampon out without her! What I needed to ask her about was if I was going crazy or if I was just developing an overactive imagination.

I turned on the TV as I got dressed and changed my bed sheets. I didn't mind that mom left me alone, hell, I almost preferred it, but I didn't like being in a house that was so quiet. I didn't really pay attention to what was on TV, but I knew I could at least find out how long I had been passed out and what time of day it was.

Half listening to the news, completely exhausted and starving I put my bed together and slumped onto the fresh sheets. As I lay on my bed staring at the ceiling, recalling the "dream" I had just awakened from, I began to understand the content of the news.

"...brutally beaten to death Monday evening. Police have interviewed the victim's husband, the man who found the body..." The female reporter was saying as she stood in front of a two story colonial with an elegant lawn. The headline at the base of the television screen read 'Local Tragedy: Mannisport Wife Found Brutally Beaten in Home'. "Police are still collecting information but at this time there are no suspects..."

317

www.ingramcontent.com/pod-product-compliance
Lightning Source LLC
Chambersburg PA
CBHW071444170626
46811CB00007B/2477